I0694380

"*The Pirate's Curse* is a thoroughly enjoyable addition to the Veritas Code series....The author does a wonderful job of building on previous stories. Lauren and Rowan Pierce's family continues to grow, and each member plays a part in the adventure. The story has plenty of twists and turns, and the protagonists must take significant risks to come back together as a family. Great story from a great author, and highly recommended. I'm looking forward to the next."

— MARK EDWARD JONES, AUTHOR OF
*PECULIAR ACTIVITIES AND SHADOWED
SOULS*

"*The Lost Templar* is a fantastic return to the world of The Veritas Codex series. Kulakowski knocks it out of the park mixing history and the supernatural. No one does it better!"

— R.J. JOHNSON, AUTHOR OF *THE TWELVE
STONES AND MODERN MAGIC*

"In *The Lost Templar*, Kulakowski brilliantly weaves the past and present with historical facts in an exceptional narrative that drives the story forward with pounding intensity . . . This is a fast-paced suspenseful ride that keeps you gripping the edges of your tablet. Tension and family connections that tug at your heartstrings. Mind-blowing twists and turns. Lauren and Rowan are a dream team."

— JENNY SIMARD LABRANCHE, AUTHOR
OF *INNISFALLEN ACCURSED*

"The Veritas Codex is an amazing series that keeps the pages turning and your mind spinning. Suspenseful like Stuart Woods, yet thought-provoking like Dan Brown, Kulakowski has the incredible ability to weave together the threads of fact and fiction and sew them into an amazing literary tapestry that leaves you wanting more."

— BRANDON MARSH, HOST AND
EXECUTIVE PRODUCER, THE PARAUNITY
PODCAST

"The Veritas Codex series is a hearty paranormal narrative entree seasoned with suspense. It satisfied my craving for everything paranormal! Thank goodness there are more in the series—Betsey Kulakowski has whet my appetite and I am begging for more! "

— XANDER ZWEIG, CO-HOST OF THE
XANDER & STONE SCIENCE &
SUPERNATURAL PODCAST

"Realistic heroes and villains. International intrigue. More plot twists than a cup of nightcrawlers. Betsey has definitely raised the bar [in *The Jaguar Queen*]."

— J. DON WRIGHT, AUTHOR OF *BEHOLD!*

"Relatable characters and crisp pace…*The Veritas Codex* combines the intrigue and chemistry of *The X-Files* with the intensity of *The Da Vinci Code.*"

— JAZ PRIMO, AUTHOR OF *GWEN REAPER*

"Engaging characters and remarkable plot twists jump from these pages. They pulled me into a thrilling world I did not want to leave."

—JOHN WOOLEY, AUTHOR OF *SEVENTH SENSE*

"I enjoyed [*The Veritas Codex*]. The writing is well done. I really liked the characters. It kept me engaged to the point I was speed reading (to find out what was going to happen) and I had to slow myself down!"

—TERRI FOLKS

THE SULTAN'S STONE

THE SULTAN'S STONE

THE VERITAS CODEX
BOOK EIGHT

BETSEY KULAKOWSKI

Life is too short for enemies. This one is for all my friends and readers who have supported me. You are my soul.

"Never put too much trust in friends, learn how to use enemies . . . If you have no enemies, find a way to make them."

— ROBERT GREENE, THE 48 LAWS OF
POWER

PROLOGUE

"I don't think you understand what's at stake," the man with the gun said, pressing the dark weapon to Rowan's temple. It was so close to his eye that he couldn't focus on it—couldn't tell what kind it was or if the man's finger was on the trigger. The gunman's hand shook.

Rowan took a deep breath and lifted his hands, moving slowly. *Jeez. Not again.* His mind instantly went back to Sudan. "My wallet is in my right hip pocket. I have thirty dollars. Take it."

"You think this is about money?" The man pressed the barrel of the gun with a bruising force against the side of his head. His voice trembled as much as his hands.

"Let him go," the frightened clerk insisted. "Take the money from the till. You want beer? Cigarettes? Take it! Take whatever you want! Just . . . don't hurt anyone."

Rowan swallowed, thoughts of his wife and children flooding his mind. He closed his eyes, picturing Lauren's face as clearly as a full moon on a cloudless night, clinging to the image as he searched for a way to return to her with all his gray matter intact.

A quick trip to the hardware store for a new faucet sent

him out on a Sunday afternoon errand. A stop at the convenience store to pick up treats for the kids was just an afterthought. He was five minutes from home—until a gun was pulled on him at the checkout.

"I said it's not about money!" the thug screamed as Rowan came back to the present. The cashier opened her mouth as if to speak, but the man swung the gun toward her. Rowan's heart skipped a beat as the weapon and the assailant came into full view. Before he could process the danger, cold steel pressed against the side of his head again.

Rowan sized up his opponent based on the limited knowledge he had. The man wasn't tall, but his muscles bulged beneath a tight olive-green USMC T-shirt, radiating strength. He handled the gun like someone who knew what he was doing, despite his unsteady hands. He wasn't afraid to shoot. Something else had him on edge. Was this a flashback? Rowan had suffered plenty of them over the years, though they were never anything like this. He regretted not being able to save his professor, Tima, and he replayed her murder in his mind often. His therapist suggested that when these moments came, he might try to do something to change the outcome. Nothing worked. In every iteration and every scenario, Tima died, and nothing he did differently seemed to change the outcome. "You don't have to do this, Devil Dog," Rowan said, assuming he was a Marine based on the T-shirt and his ability with the gun. "Just tell me what you need."

"I know who you are," he said. "You're going to help me."

"Okay," Rowan said with some hesitation. His hands sank gradually. His shoulder hurt too badly to keep them up any longer than he had to. He and the boys spent the morning doing chores for Lauren while she sat down at the computer to pay the bills and do some work. His joints were starting to give out on him one by one. Years of hard travel and one too many broken bones were catching up with him. The small four-dollar bottle of ibuprofen on the counter next to the Icees were proof of that. "Just tell me how I can help."

"I need you to make it go away," he cried. As the man's hand shook even more, the gun came off Rowan's temple. The assailant crouched down. His hands—including the one with the gun—tried to cover his ears as he pinched his eyes shut. "It's watching me. It's always watching me. I can hear it in my head, tormenting me. It's following me home from work, and I can't make it stop. Make it stop!"

Rowan turned, instinctively reaching for the Marine. He wasn't sure why he didn't go for the gun. He should have gone for the gun. But he recognized the signs of PTSD. He knew the desperation, the danger it fueled. A glance passed between Rowan and the clerk, Miss Debi. She nodded and moved slowly. Rowan shifted his focus to the Marine, who suddenly rose. He stepped back and leveled the gun at his face. Rowan saw his finger move to the trigger and tense. "Stay back!"

Rowan lifted his hands again. "Okay. I'll help you. Just tell me . . . what's going on?"

"I'm not crazy!" the man snapped. "Don't look at me like you think I'm crazy."

"I didn't say that," Rowan said, trying to project a calm that belied the thrumming of terror in his chest. "You said you need help. I'll help you. I just need to know what's going on. What do you need?"

The assailant blinked rapidly, eyeing him down the barrel of the Glock 19M. "Shut up! You can't tell me what to do." His hands went back to his ears, and pain seemed to wash over him. Rowan held his gaze as he moved to take a step forward. "Stop!" The Marine snapped, pointing the gun at him again. "Both of you! Shut up!"

Rowan's eye darted to the clerk, who stood wide-eyed, frozen. Her look told him what he needed to know. Now, he just had to keep the gunman talking, keep him calm. "Just tell me what's going on," he said softly. "Where do you work? What followed you home?"

The man's eyes went wide. Rowan noticed the beads of sweat gathering on his brow as he fought to control his breathing, but he began panting. He seemed to open his mouth to speak, but nothing came out. He swallowed hard and tried to steady the gun with both hands. "I . . ." he finally managed. "It's . . . I . . . I don't know, but it's watching me!"

"Hey." Rowan kept his tone soft. "I've been where you are. I can help you, and I will. But it doesn't have to be like this. What's your name? Where'd you serve, man?"

"Lance Corporal Riggs, Benjamin F.—Marine . . . Expeditionary . . . Unit . . . Sudan."

Sudan. Dammit. Rowan's blood ran cold. He knew exactly what that meant. Things had spiraled out of control in the Middle East over the past four years. The Great Accord crumbled, and chaos reigned.

The region was a powder keg—multiple political and religious factions were clawing for political domination and control of the rich oil reserves, especially after the discovery of an untapped field in Sudan. U.S. foreign policy soured against the nation, and Rowan understood why this young man was struggling. After the risky operation to free him, Sudan turned its anger on the U.S. and its allies. Troops were targeted. Civilians were caught in the crossfire. No one was safe.

The world was teetering on the edge. Discord spread like wildfire, leaving borders trembling and violent uprisings erupting from the shadows. Terrorist cells like *Ruka D'yavola*—the Devil's Hand—unleashed brutality, raiding through Ukraine, Belarus, Latvia, and Estonia. The February 1st dirty bomb in Astana, Kazakhstan, was a devastating reminder of the spreading tensions across the globe. Hundreds of thousands died, and entire landmarks were reduced to rubble. Even the National Concert Hall collapsed, killing almost everyone inside. Two survivors were pulled from the rubble.

The initial blast took lives, but the real killer was the radiation—spreading, invisible, and choking the world. Rowan's heart raced. The war raged on the other side of the world, but the madness wasn't just in the Middle East anymore. It was everywhere. Even the convenience store in Englewood, Colorado.

"I know what you've been through, brother." Rowan tried to ease tensions, wishing his golden-tongued sister-in-law were here to negotiate a peace treaty one-on-one with the agitated Marine. "I've been there."

Riggs swallowed hard, blinking rapidly. His finger seemed to stroke the trigger with the lightest touch. It darted to the side of the weapon occasionally as if the man couldn't quite figure out where to rest his finger. Conflict chased fear across the dark, sweat-glazed face. The Marine's breath came in gasps. Rowan decided the young man seemed to be suffering from a physical health crisis as well as a mental one.

Rowan had been there. He recognized a man in the grips of flashbacks. He had them himself. "Who's your C.O.?"

The Marine hesitated a moment, pinching his eyes shut. His hand trembled even harder. "C-C-Captain L-L-Lorraine Y-Y-York," he said.

"Are you still active duty?"

The man seemed to blink from his nightmare. His lips pursed angrily, and Rowan knew his answer. "D-d-discharged . . . b-b-bad papers . . ." *Dishonorable discharge. Not good*, Rowan thought.

"Unfairly too, I'm sure." Rowan took a step back, more so, to shift his weight and keep blood flowing to his lower extremities. His toes were tingling. Rowan felt sweat building on his skin.

"No," Riggs swallowed hard. "I deserved it."

"You wanna talk about it?"

"Not really," the man snapped. His finger was now firmly on the trigger. "*You* are going to help me!"

"Yes, I am," Rowan assured him. "I just like to know who I'm working with."

"It's not who..." he said, swallowing hard. A bead of sweat rolled down the side of his nose and dripped off his chin onto his already-damp shirt. "I'm not the one you need to be afraid of."

"Well, you're the one with the gun to my face," Rowan said, unable to keep his naturally sarcastic nature at bay. "It's a little hard not to be afraid. Put your weapon down and we can talk. I will do whatever I can to help you."

"*It* followed me home from work," the man repeated, not lowering the gun. "*You* have to get rid of *it* . . . make *it* go away." The words were clipped, and each one individually punctuated. "I didn't do anything to it . . ." his voice rose uncomfortably. "I just want *it* to go away."

"What followed you home from work?" Rowan's brow narrowed.

"I don't know *what* it is, but *it's* . . . it's dark . . . it's evil . . . it w-w-won't leave me alone . . . *it* makes me want to do bad things ...I don't want to do *this* . . . but I have to get rid of it . . . *you* have to help me get rid of *it* . . ."

"Why me?"

"*It* . . . knows you . . ." he said, his voice trailing off like a frightened child's.

Rowan eyed him warily, his mind running at warp speed as he analyzed the man's words and behavior, putting together his own hypothesis. This Marine was having a mental break. If he'd been discharged with bad papers, this probably wasn't the first time he'd gone off the rails. It made him dangerous. There was no way this man knew him. He might know the television personality, but he wasn't that man anymore.

Still, a man needed anchors to keep him on the straight and narrow. Rowan had anchors in spades. He was a husband and a father, with a home, a dog . . . and even that darn cat. If this man had lost his career, his identity, chances were good he had lost other anchors, too. His mental health failed him. "Sure," Rowan said. "I'll help you. I just have to know what we're dealing with."

"Not what!" he shouted, shaking the gun harder at Rowan. Then, the man's head snapped around. A flash of red and blue lights appeared outside the windows, creating strobes of light on the dingy tile floor, sticky with spilled sodas and Icee drinks, muddy with dirt from hikers and workers' boots. The sound of sirens joined the chaos, as three cruisers converged on the convenience store. The Marine whipped around, pointing the gun at the store clerk. "You called the cops?"

She screeched and flinched in terror, backing up against the counter behind her. Rowan saw his chance. He went for the gun as he shouted, "Get down!" The clerk did, and good thing too as the gun went off, right next to Rowan's ear. A screaming whine overtook the ambient sound of the room. If the clerk screamed again, Rowan hadn't heard it.

In the same move that kept the bullet from striking him, Rowan caught the weapon just over the man's trembling finger and torqued it to the side, twisting the young man's wrist enough that the nerves pinged in the hand, causing his fingers to splay and open. The weapon fell into Rowan's right hand, while his left flicked ineffectively at the man's face, unable to make contact.

The Marine turned back, and leaned into Rowan, throwing his arms around the taller man's body, and taking him down. Rowan's back protested as he hit the tile floor with the Marine on top of him. Rowan wrestled with him, managing to get out from under the bulkier man. Once on top, the former Army medic pinned the Marine to the floor mat as Riggs screamed in voiceless agony.

Rowan hadn't expected him to be so strong. He found himself hurled back, hitting the counter with a thud so hard it knocked his breath out. It also knocked an Icee off the counter. It landed on his shoulder as the lid split from the cup, cracking like an egg. The cold liquid bit his skin through the fabric of his plaid shirt, but not as hard as the fist that caught him across the jaw.

Lightning crashed, and the whole world seemed to go dim. Clouds blocked the sun and darkened the day. Thunder rumbled, shaking the floor. At almost the same time, another flash of lightning struck nearby and blinded everyone with its brilliance. The Marine took advantage of the moment and lunged for the gun. Rowan, deaf and blind, could only sense the onslaught. He tossed the gun down the hallway, towards the emergency exit, as hard as he could. No longer armed, he fought with the last thing left to him—his fists.

It was a fight for life as they grappled in a roiling ball of flailing fists and kicking feet. Rowan came out on top, wrestling the Marine face-first into the floor, his knee in the middle of his back. He glanced up, looking for help. But the police officers remained outside the doors, taking a defensive position behind their cruisers where they had cover. Having just arrived, law enforcement officers had no idea who was the good guy and who was the bad guy, and Rowan knew it. His vision cleared as he held down the assailant, debating what to do next. The man bucked, startling him. He was thrown with a force so strong that he landed flat on his butt. The Marine rushed toward the exit, slamming the front door open causing the glass to shatter. On the other side, the Denver Police Department confronted him.

"Freeze! Don't move! Put your hands up!" The words were muffled in Rowan's ringing ears. Disco lights swirled in his eyes as he rolled onto his stomach, trying to get to his feet. The scene unfolded in slow motion. Rowan could see Riggs skid to a stop, his empty hands lifting for a moment.

But instead of following orders to put his hands up, the Marine drew a large bowie knife from a sheath at his hip— hidden beneath the T-shirt. Rowan hadn't seen that weapon and knew if the Marine had decided to use it, he'd be bleeding out now.

Riggs side-stepped out of Rowan's direct line of sight. He hesitated a moment, then let out a beastly roar. Rowan struggled to move toward the door as the man charged the first police car, with the knife raised like a mad berserker. He seemed to leap into the air as gunshots rang out and windows shattered. Blood splattered the spiderwebbed glass façade of the store. Rowan could no longer see what was going on outside, but he could see the shadow of the Marine as he fell . . . and didn't get up again.

1

Rowan's entrance into the emergency department was nothing short of a battle. His back had seized up on him, and every move was a struggle. A nurse helped him onto the exam table as his body was wracked with agonizing jolts of lightning that raced up and down his spine like street cars down the hills of San Francisco. His shoulder throbbed with an unrelenting fury as each movement was a fresh torment. He gripped his phone tightly, white-knuckled as he prayed Lauren would be able to decipher the frantic, cryptic message he'd tapped out in the ambulance with trembling fingers.

The curtain rustled. The screech of metal hooks against the track cut through his fogged brain like a dagger. The physician's assistant entered, her face a concerned mask as she donned a pair of surgical gloves. "Mister . . . Pierce?" Her voice was a warm gesture of comfort as he lay his phone on the table beside him. She took in the sight of him. His shirt was torn and bloodied. A cut above his brow oozed drying blood. His panicked eyes spoke of the horror she'd just been given a glimpse of by the police officer who walked him in. He caught her glancing at the red stain on his shoulder.

"It's not blood," Rowan rasped, his voice cracking under the strain of what was supposed to be a pleasant Sunday afternoon.

"Oh?"

"It's cherry Icee." His voice caught in his throat, and he winced.

Her gaze focused on him as she pursed her lips. "I think some of it is blood," she replied, her voice distant, as if coming through a deep cave. Rowan's pulse pounded in his ears—the ringing remained a constant reminder of the concussive force that had nearly shattered his eardrums. *Maybe it had.* He wasn't sure.

She reached for a gauze pack and began dabbing at the gash on his forehead. Her touch refreshed the pain, and the bleeding renewed. He could see the magnitude of his injuries reflected in her soft brown eyes. "Let's get you out of that shirt." Rowan knew there was no way the shirt was coming off in one piece. His muscles were now seizing in unison.

"Of course, today had to be the day I wore my favorite shirt," he muttered through clenched teeth as she retrieved scissors from a nearby bin. The metallic snips were a cruel reminder of the battle he fought and lost. There were no winners today. Even his favorite plaid shirt was a casualty of war. A shiver ran through him as the cool air met his exposed skin, gooseflesh rising in response. Every muscle ached in reflex as a groan escaped his throat.

"Someone did a number on you," she said, her voice softening as she examined the bruises and abrasions that marred his skin. She moved to stand in front of him, her touch careful as she dabbed at the cut over his eye again. "Looks like you were sucker punched, and you hit your head." His hand floated towards the offended spot on his chin but stopped short, as fire burned in his shoulder.

"Among other things," he said, his teeth chattering.

She probed the swollen eye that bore scars of a past injury from his ordeal in Sudan. "Any allergies, Mr. Pierce?"

"No," he said. "Unless you plan to come at me with poison ivy."

She chuckled. "No. Nothing like that. Just some lidocaine, most likely. Maybe something for pain, if you need it."

"How bad is it?" he asked.

"Maybe some stitches," she said. "But I want a few X-rays, too. You've quite the bump on your head. Does anything else hurt besides your shoulder?"

"Everything hurts," he said, splaying his palm over his chest, running it down to his stomach. He screwed up his face as she examined him.

"I'll order a CT then," she said. "To rule out anything serious." She draped the gown over his shoulders. Rowan's relief was palpable as the warmth of the gown shielded him from the cold sweat breaking out over his skin. "I'll get you pain medication and a warm blanket for the chill. I know it's cold in the ER. We have to keep it that way, but we'll make you comfortable until you're discharged. Is there someone we can call for you?"

"I texted my wife," Rowan managed to say, his voice hoarse.

"What's her name? I'll have the reception desk bring her back when she arrives."

"Lauren." He said it like a prayer.

The PA nodded, pulling the rattling curtain behind her as she left Rowan alone.

***

ROWAN SHIVERED, trying to still his racing thoughts, but a warm hand on his shoulder made him flinch. A groan escaped his throat. "Sorry," Lauren said, softly, moving around from behind him. He hadn't heard her come in, but that wasn't unusual for her. She could move through time and place as silent as a shadow when she needed to. "I got here as quickly as I could. Rowan, what happened?" She came around to stand in front of him.

"Jesus," he muttered. "You scared the daylights out of me. What took you so long?"

"It took me a moment to figure out this cryptic message you sent me," she said. "You're bleeding." He realized it wasn't sweat on his brow. She found a piece of gauze and held it over the wound for a few moments.

"It's been a few years since I had to fight someone off. I guess I'm out of practice." He felt the room spin.

"Dizzy?" Lauren always seemed to know.

"Nauseated, too."

"Let me help you." He felt disconnected from his body as she propped up the head of the bed and then supported his back as he moved. She lifted his shaking legs and settled him. "Deep breaths." She leaned in and spoke the words softly in his ear. Rowan realized he was panting.

The curtain grated open again, and a nurse entered with an IV kit and blankets, pausing when she saw he wasn't alone. "Ah, Mrs. Pierce, I presume." Lauren greeted her but stepped aside so she wasn't in the way. "How are we doing, Mr. Pierce? Dizzy?"

"Yeah," he said. "Just a little."

"I'll bring you something for the pain," she said. She laid the IV aside as she worked to cover him up. She lay a second warmed blanket over his chest. "Feels good, doesn't it?"

"Mmm, yes." He closed his eyes and took a deep breath, finally getting a bit more control over his respiration. "Thank you." His muscles began to relax, though it did little for the pain in his body. "Maybe if I could lay back a bit more."

"Sure," she said, helping adjust the gurney. She got the IV started and the delicious flood of medication followed. *Just in time.*

Since he and Lauren moved into his parent's home after his ordeal in the Middle East, he'd had a few PTSD-induced panic attacks. It'd taken months of therapy to get his mental state close to *normal*, and every day was a struggle. It was a battle he felt like he was winning—until today. Now, it was closing in on him, and he wasn't sure the coping mechanisms he'd learned would do him any good. He caught the metal bedrail the nurse raised and gripped it tightly. When he could get in another deep breath, he tapped a gentle rhythm on it, hearing his favorite song in his head. The guitar riff his finger simulated began to help, if just a little. It was a way to control his breathing, though when he thought about the tempo, it began to spin out of rhythm.

PTSD was a cruel, insidious affliction, striking at the most inopportune moments. The sharp, acrid scent of diesel fuel was enough to transport his memories to the boat, adrift in the Red Sea. He spiraled into darkness on several occasions. The whir of a chef's knife through a head of cabbage had done it once. He'd watched—paralyzed by fear and helplessness—as his friend and mentor, Tima, was beheaded right before his eyes. *He should have tried harder*, he thought. But the haunting knowledge that he couldn't have done anything to save her gnawed on him like maggots on a fetid wound.

"Take a deep breath," Lauren murmured, her hand moving to the center of his chest. Rowan was certain she could read his thoughts, feel his panic growing. "You're safe now. Just breathe. I'm right here."

LAUREN REMAINED aware of the room around her, but her efforts focused solely on her husband. "Has he had panic attacks before?" the nurse asked. Lauren nodded but spoke softly to Rowan, encouraging him to focus on his breath and visualize his safe place. She knew he would think of home and her. His eyes remained tightly closed, his teeth gritted against the pain in his body and the chaos in his mind.

His breathing slowly returned to normal. He seemed to melt at her gentle guidance. She'd learned this technique at Walter Reed during those first rough weeks after his liberation from the hands of a psychopath.

"Does he have a mental health provider?" the PA asked. Lauren leaned back but kept her hand on him.

"Dr. Helen McLeish. He sees her once a month. He has for a while."

"Military?"

"He was," Lauren said. "He took the brunt of a roadside IED in Desert Storm/Desert Shield back in the early 90s. Four years ago, he ran afoul of a terrorist while he was teaching in Egypt." That was the *official story*. "He still has good days and bad. Did he say what happened today?"

"Let's go get some coffee," the PA said. "I've ordered a CT scan, and we'll get some X-rays, just to rule out anything serious. We can talk while the team assesses his injuries."

Lauren nodded, patting his arm as she snaked her hand from his limp fingers. "If he freaks out, come get me," she said to the nurse.

"We gave him enough pain medication," the PA said. Only then did Lauren realize he'd slipped off and that her efforts might have had little to do with calming him. "He should sleep through the procedure."

"Good idea."

Lauren waited in the lobby for what seemed like hours. Daylight was fading, and long shadows of trees waved outside the window. The acrid coffee in her cup went cold as she sat numbly watching the news on the television screen above the reception desk. The audio was off, but Lauren couldn't focus on the closed captioning. Video from the store's security cameras captured the scene, and Lauren had a rather good idea that her husband had been the hero of the day. She recognized the clerk behind the checkout as the kids' favorite, Miss Debi. Debi snuck them pieces of candy and told them funny jokes and puns when they came to get a cold drink on a hot day.

When the PA returned, she sat down in the chair beside her and turned to lean in. "His results came back," she said. "No broken bones. No internal injuries. Mild concussion and muscle strain seem to be the worst of it. We're going to get him cleaned up and ready to discharge. You should get him to see his counselor as soon as possible. Follow up with his family doctor. His shoulder may need additional evaluation. We'll give him some muscle relaxers and something for pain, but he might need to see a specialist if that doesn't help his symptoms."

"I'll make sure he follows through," Lauren said. "He can be stubborn about that."

"Give us about twenty minutes or so. I'll let you know when you can come back."

***

ROWAN SAT AT THE TABLE, gazing down at the plate in front of him. Meatloaf, mashed potatoes, brown gravy, and fresh steamed green beans were some of his favorites. Normally, he'd dig in, but at the moment, he was frozen—unable to move.

"Would you rather have dinner in bed? You don't look comfortable." Lauren always seemed to know what he needed.

"No," he said, his voice sounding even worse in his ears. "I need a minute."

"Would you rather have a milkshake or something lighter?"

"At the moment, I just want to sit here." Lauren watched him for a moment, his breath hitched with every sharp inhale. It was more than the physical pain—every breath appeared to betray his body. At least his ribs were only bruised—this time. She remembered the recovery when he'd suffered broken ribs so many years ago on Mount Saint Helens.

"Of course." Lauren walked into the kitchen and came back with her plate. She sat down beside him and nibbled at her food. Still watching him from the corner of her eye, she saw him wince as he lifted his arm onto the table and picked up his fork. His shoulder had been injured when he was held hostage in Syria four years before. At the time, it hadn't been surgical. Twelve weeks of physical therapy had eased the impingement. Still, even as he pushed his food around on the plate, she could see the pain in his eyes.

"I texted Dr. McLeish," he said without preamble. "She's working me in at nine o'clock tomorrow."

"That's good." That confirmed her greatest fear. After the events in the Middle East, his mind hadn't been the same. He suffered from unrelenting insomnia and became short-tempered with her and the children. The group therapy at Walter Reed helped, so they sought the aid of a therapist in Denver who worked with soldiers and victims of trauma. Counseling sessions weekly finally became monthly as he perfected his coping mechanisms. It had been over a year since he'd had any kind of an outburst.

"What did you tell the kids?"

Even the children had been aware of his struggles. He rarely snapped at them, but she could tell when they were on edge around their father. He was supposed to be their protector, but there had been days when he couldn't even get out of bed. "I told them you had car trouble and needed me to come get you."

"All I could think about was your father," Rowan said abruptly.

"*My* father?" She looked at him, setting her fork down.

"He left to get something to fix the sink and never came home. I ran to the hardware store to get a new faucet. I almost didn't come home."

That thought did cartwheels in her brain, and it took a moment for her to regain her balance. She reached over and took his hand. "But you did," she assured him.

"I had to fight for you," he said. "I am not going to leave you. Ever."

"I know that."

Rowan nodded and picked up his fork. Now he could eat. Lauren, however, struggled with every bite. A knot in her throat grew at the thought of what might have happened.

"THEY'RE CALLING YOU A HERO," Lauren said later as he followed her into the kitchen with his partially empty plate. John Carter had followed his mother's instructions, and everyone had gone to bed. Lauren was left to wash the last of the dishes. She took Rowan's plate and scraped the remains of the uneaten food into the garbage disposal.

"I'm no hero," he said.

"You saved Miss Debi's life."

"A Marine died."

"You're not responsible for that. You know you did everything you could. He was having an . . . *episode?*"

"I had one, too," he said, snaking a hand around her waist. "You helped me through it."

"I always will," Lauren said. She turned and kissed his cheek.

He nodded and withdrew. "Right now, I just want to take a muscle relaxer and go to bed. I want to put this day behind me."

Lauren nodded. "I'll be right there, as soon as I finish the dishes."

WHEN LAUREN CAME into the bedroom, she found Rowan sitting on the edge of the bed in the T-shirt he'd worn home from the ER and his boxer shorts. His jeans lay in a heap on the floor in front of him. She suspected he couldn't bend over to pick them up. She obliged him and tossed them in his hamper.

"They cut off my favorite shirt." He sniffed as if that was the worst part of the day. She'd seen the remains of his bloodied plaid shirt in the trash in the ER. She didn't ask about it. She didn't need to.

"Shirts can be replaced," Lauren said. "Don't worry about it. Now, what do you need? How can I help?"

He tried to lift an arm towards the pill bottles on the dresser, but he was so stiff he couldn't quite manage. Lauren got the gist. She retrieved the prescription medications, pausing to inspect the labels. "Flexeril and . . . tramadol," she said. "You want both?"

"The muscle relaxer," he grunted. Lauren nodded, handing him a tablet.

Once he was comfortable—or as comfortable as he could be—she changed into her pajamas and went to brush her teeth and wash her face. She curled up beside him, expecting him to be asleep, but he opened his eyes.

"You know you'll be all right, don't you?" She ran a cool hand down his warm cheek.

"As long as I have you," he said, swallowing hard.

She scooted up against him, and he put his uninjured arm around her. "You'll always have me," she sighed. "I'm not going anywhere."

He took a deep breath and sighed. A long moment later,

he said, "Our anniversary is coming. We should do something special."

"Yes, we should," she said. "How about a hike up to Maroon Bells? Just you and me. We can watch the sunset over the Vermillion Peaks. I can make red beans and rice, and we can sit by the fire and watch the stars."

"I was thinking about something . . . more," he said.

"More?"

"How about a week in Mexico? Maybe . . . Cozumel? Without the kids. Just you and me."

"Cozumel?"

"We didn't even get to go to the beach the last time we were there," he said. "We've never really been . . . you know . . . *tourists*."

"It sounds nice, but . . ."

"What?" he asked.

"Fall is the peak production time for me," she said, lifting her head. "I've got assignments."

"Well, we don't have to go right away," he said. "It won't be autumn for much longer."

"I've got a hiatus between Thanksgiving and Christmas," Lauren said, realizing he was rubbing her back, his thumbnail running along the line between her shoulder blades. She lay her head back down and felt comfort in the moment.

"Think Bahati and Jean-René would keep the kids?"

"If not, I could call my mother," Lauren said.

"Think she could tear herself from your father?"

"He might come with her," she said, yawning.

"Mommy?" Lauren startled. Sarah, their youngest, stood at her father's bedside, holding her favorite stuffed animal under her arm. Rowan winced at the sudden movement.

"What are you doing out of bed?" Lauren caught her breath. It took another moment for her heart to stop racing. "Do you need something?"

"I don't," the sober little girl said. Sarah's little face

scrunched in a way only a child her age could manage, her full lips pushing out in a perfect pout. She still had the roundness of a baby, but behind the dark eyes was a promise of the girl she would soon be. Her eyes were wide—glistening—and seemed to shimmer with the storm of emotions she generally kept hidden. She crossed her arms over her chest as if to protect whatever fragile thing had upset the heart within.

"Then what are you doing up?" Rowan snapped, probably more forcefully than he'd meant to. "Did you have a bad dream?" He tried to soften his tone.

The corners of her brows furrowed in defiance like she might be trying to hold in her frustration, refusing to let it go, no matter how small or silly the reason was. But it was neither small nor silly. "Indy's walking circles in the yard," she said. Lauren watched Sarah talk to Indy like he was one of her siblings, and the dog paid attention to her in a way that made Lauren wonder if the dog understood the child. Sarah didn't talk to Shadow like that. The cat preferred the company of her older sister—when the cat wasn't following her mistress around. The cat seemed to have her own mystical powers too, which didn't surprise Lauren any, considering they'd rescued her from the Bermuda Triangle. The dog? Well, Indy's *magic* seemed to be chasing tennis balls and stealing snacks under the table.

The dog often ran circles in the yard, but Sarah's pout told Lauren this was different. She was intent on making sure her parents knew that something wasn't right in her world. The air around her seemed to thicken with that stubborn energy, and for the moment, the world paused.

Lauren glanced at Rowan, who'd endured enough trouble for one day. "I'll go check on him." She threw back the duvet and rolled from the warmth of Rowan's embrace. She tossed the covers back over him, so he didn't get chilled. "Come on. I'll tuck you in first."

"I'm big enough to tuck myself in." Sarah was only four—

almost five—but she was as independent as her older siblings. She didn't need much. She paused, her expression refusing to soften as she gazed at her father, and climbed up onto the bed, nearly losing her footing. She pressed her lips to her father's cheek and climbed down. "I'm glad you didn't get shot."

Rowan glanced at Lauren. Questions raced like a ticker tape behind his eyes. Lauren shrugged. "Me, too," he said.

"Thanks for saving Miss Debi from the monster."

As Lauren followed her daughter into the living room, she couldn't help but notice Shadow sitting at the top of the stairs, peering down from between the banisters, staring at something out the door. The dim light from the kitchen's nightlight caught in the cat's blue eyes. Lauren tried to follow the cat's gaze toward the back door, but she couldn't be sure what had the feline's rapt attention.

Sarah paused at the bottom of the stairs. Her face was ever-serious. "You should sage the house," she said, matter-of-factly.

Lauren cocked her head. "Oh?"

"Sage Daddy, too."

Lauren paused, glancing back at Sarah, but the little girl had already disappeared into her room, the cat following her. Shaking her head, Lauren made her way to the back door, gazing at the wind-tossed trees, unable to see the dog.

Sarah was taller and sharper than most kids her age, quieter too—sober and contemplative, unlike her rowdy brothers, or her older sister. She observed everything.

She loved the outdoors, often retreating to the playhouse Rowan built for her in the trees. Here, she and Indy would spend countless hours out of the chaos of family life, especially her older brothers. She had even less interest in her older sister. Kate was too absorbed in music and friends to be bothered with a younger sibling. Music blared from Kate's closed door—*Panic! At the Disco.*

At least she has decent taste in music, Lauren thought.

Kate shared her mother's taste in music, while John Carter took after his dad, favoring heavy metal and classic rock. The teenager was also an accomplished guitarist, just like his father. He'd been talking about starting a band with some of his friends from school after receiving a bass guitar last year for Christmas.

Jamie, five years younger than John Carter, was into classic literature and poetry. He especially liked Robert Frost and John Keats. With his russet hair and dimples, he had a charm that would surely win the girls over—just like his dad.

Sam, Kate's twin, was still figuring himself out. Quiet and more reserved, he did fine in school and sports, but never quite stood out. It was tough competing with three older brothers, each of whom excelled as they carved their own paths.

Yawning, Lauren slid the door open. More storms were expected to move in overnight, and Lauren suspected they were getting close. The wind had picked up, and the sycamore and oak trees that shaded their yard were tossing wildly. The muted light from the utility lamp at the back of the property seemed to flicker as the branches waved back and forth.

Slipping into her flip-flops, she stepped out onto the lawn. What had been a warm autumn day had given way to a much cooler evening. The air was thick and damp with impending rain. The wind tossed her hair across her face, and she fought to control it as she walked outside.

Clouds gathered in the moonlight. "Indy!" Lauren called, still not seeing the dog. With nearly half an acre of property, the backyard was one of the biggest in the neighborhood. Their yard butted up against a wooded area where a creek ran from the mountains, giving the boys plenty of room to wander.

Lauren respected her mother-in-law's work in keeping up the yard. The garden remained immaculate. Heavy-headed daisies bobbed in the night breeze. Coneflowers, lantana, hollyhocks, and roses in a spectrum of colors were illuminated by the blue-white utility lamp mounted on the telephone pole at the back of the yard and the cloud-dotted moon. The perfume of lavender and lilacs filled the damp air.

She found Indy at the far back corner of the lawn. He was, indeed, walking in circles, but his eyes were locked on the sky, or more properly, the top of the telephone pole. He saw her and whimpered but never stopped his nervous pacing.

"Indy? What is it, boy?" Lauren shielded her eyes from the light, trying to make out what had the dog so agitated. Hawks and owls weren't uncommon. She'd interrupted a falcon recently as it attacked a dove she was feeding in the yard. The peregrine—smaller than a hawk, but larger than most other birds that frequented her lawn—had become a nuisance and seemed to be intentionally harassing both the songbirds and Lauren. Tonight, though, she couldn't see anything. "Come on, Indy." She patted her leg. "Let's go to bed."

Indy stopped, hurried over to her, and sat at her feet. He whimpered as his gaze fixed on the pole. Lauren started for the house, but the dog returned to the spot where he'd been and began barking. Indy never barked unless there was a problem. Lauren looked to see if perhaps there might be a raccoon clinging to the pole, hidden in shadow.

When she was a little girl, she'd run wild in the forest around her family home near Tahlequah, Oklahoma. She remembered the old raccoon who had made a nest in a hollowed-out tree. She wouldn't put it past a raccoon or a squirrel to hollow out a telephone pole for such purposes, though most raccoons were too large to fit in a nest so small.

"Let's go," she said. The dog didn't move to follow her. "There's nothing out here. It's time for bed." Indy turned and dashed past her, glancing back when she stopped to pick a handful of fresh sage from her garden. She bundled it up as she walked back inside. It needed to dry before she could properly sage the house, but that didn't stop her from swatting the door jams with one of the springs as she passed.

Indy sat at the door, watching her spread the herbs out on newspaper to dry. She headed to the kitchen to wash her hands and noticed the dog hesitated. She thought he might be debating whether to go up to Sarah's room. Tonight, however, he followed her, pausing at the foot of the bed where Rowan snored vigorously. Indy sniffed at him and whimpered. "It'd be a lot quieter if you slept with one of the kids," she whispered to the dog. Indy curled up on the rug beside Rowan's side of the bed. "Suit yourself." She took her earplugs out of her drawer and fitted them into her ears before climbing into bed.

THE DARKNESS WATCHED. It was always watching—waiting. The insidious presence slithered just beyond the reach of the sodium light at the back of the property, its presence a suffocating weight that pressed against the edges of the yard. It knew the woman was the true prey, but for now, she was little more than an irritating distraction. She was the creature the Dark Lord most desired but could not possess. Her power—flickering, fragile—was like a candle's glow in the face of an oncoming storm. Yet the amber aura that surrounded her was the reminder of the protection provided to her by a higher power. While she might be the Dark Lord's ultimate prize, the Universe commanded *The Darkness* to feed elsewhere.

Ah, but the target was close. So close. The darkness could feel him, just beyond her defenses—a faint echo, weak but undeniable. He was hidden, shielded by her aura, a thread fraying at the edges. He was supposed to be her protector, her weapon, but she had become both. His presence was a silent trembling pulse—a temptation that drove *The Darkness* into a frenzy of anticipation.

Patience. It was a curse to most, but a weapon to *The Dark-*

ness. It learned many centuries ago that the most satisfying prey could not be rushed. It had to be drawn out, lured into the abyss. Away from the light. Away from hope.

Yet, no matter how clever, no matter how strong her defenses, the moment would come. The Darkness knew it. The moment of reckoning was coming. When it arrived, *The Darkness* would be ready.

The power it craved was already building, a seething torrent, waiting to breach the defenses of goodness. This man's soul would shatter like fragile glass. And in that instant, *The Darkness* would feast—a banquet of righteousness corrupted. Every cry of despair, every flicker of hope would be snuffed out. Then, it would take the soul within the house and offer it to its master, Enlil. The man was merely a stepping stone, a brief flicker in the dark before the true work began. For now, *The Darkness* watched. It was always watching —waiting.

2

Lauren woke to the flashing of lightning and an almost instantaneous crash of thunder. The bed shook, and with her sleep-addled mind, it was a struggle to make sense of what was happening. The house was dark, and other than Rowan's snoring and the din of heavy rain outside, it was quiet—if you could call it that. She found the remote on her bedside table and tried to turn on the television to check the weather, but the power was out. The phone on her dresser bleeped. She knew what that meant. Her weather app was programmed to provide an audible alert at this hour of the night.

She rose and carried it into the living room, leaving Rowan to sleep as she assessed the situation. Weather like this was nothing in her home state, but in Colorado, it wasn't normally this violent, and certainly not this late in the year. A swatch of red mixed with orange and yellows painted the map on the radar, and she pursed her lips as she zoomed in to see if there was a hook echo that might suggest tornadic weather. Indy came and sat beside her at the door. She glanced outside as lightning flashed again. The trees bowed under the high winds and leaves swirled against the patio door, where the wet fallen foliage stuck. Bands of weather lined up to the southwest, all aiming at Englewood.

"So much for filming today, Indy," Lauren muttered to the dog, dropping her phone on the table by her recliner. The dog whimpered, following her into the kitchen. Without electricity, the coffee maker was useless, but Lauren had skills. She had to manually light the gas burner, but soon a blue flame came to life, and a few minutes later, the kettle whistled. Lauren made a cup of spiced chai, dressing it with her favorite coconut creamer. She carried it to her chair and curled up, pulling a blanket over her knees.

She and Jean-René were supposed to leave early for Buena Vista that morning, but the two-hour drive in this weather would have been a waste of fuel. She typed out a text message. If he wasn't up already, it wouldn't be long before his alarm would go off. At least he'd know he could roll over and go back to sleep.

By the time her teacup was empty, the power came back on. She turned on the television and verified that nothing tornadic was imminent, but the rain was still coming and would not end any time soon. She rose and put on a pot of coffee before slipping back into the bedroom to put on her workout attire.

An hour on the Peloton was part of her daily routine when she didn't have to leave for work at 0-dark-thirty. It was good for her mental health, and the last year of daily workouts left her with a sculpted physique she'd never had, even in her early twenties—even before six children.

By the time she finished her ride, Jean-René had texted back to confirm he'd received her message and that he'd call her later. As she came upstairs, John Carter was coming down. "You're up early." Lauren stepped aside to let him pass. He liked to ride the Peloton, too.

"Storm woke me up," he said. "And I thought I could beat you to the Peloton."

"You have to get up a lot earlier if you want to get ahead of me, son." The playful banter made John Carter grin, sheepishly.

"I stayed up too late last night reading," he said. "Want me to take the kids to school today?"

"If you'll take them, I can pick them up."

"I thought you were going to work today," John Carter puzzled.

"In this weather? No way," she said. "Besides, I want to stay close to your dad at least for today, if not longer."

"Is he okay?"

"He will be," Lauren said.

"I heard Dad saved Miss Debi from a monster."

"Did Sarah tell you that?"

"She did."

"I don't know what gets into that girl's head," Lauren said, then told him as much as she thought he could handle.

"A Marine? Dad took down a Marine?"

"More or less," Lauren said. "Go get your workout in. I'll make breakfast."

"Blueberry pancakes?"

"If that's what you want."

THE KIDS WERE all gathered at the table with plates of golden flapjacks covered in butter and syrup when Rowan made his way stiffly into the kitchen. Lauren was at the counter, with the phone tucked between her shoulder and ear. "No, there's no way we can film. It's supposed to storm all day."

"Is that Jean-René?" Rowan asked, moving behind her to get a cup of coffee.

"Yes," she said. "He wants to know how you're feeling this morning."

"I can't answer that in front of the children," Rowan complained.

Lauren pursed her lips. "That bad?"

"Yeah." His voice was gruff. He moved stiffly as she flipped a stack of dark brown pancakes onto a plate and handed it to him. "That bad."

"All the more reason for me to work from home," Lauren said to him, then addressed Jean-René. "Tell Bahati I'll call her this afternoon."

Rowan groaned as he sat down at the table, his children watching him with cautious reserve. "What happened, Daddy?" Sam asked. "Did you fight a bear?"

"I feel like I fought a bear," he grunted. He told them as much as they needed to know, not mentioning which store he'd been in, or how scared their favorite 7-11 clerk had been. He didn't lie, but he didn't want them to be afraid every time they went to get an Icee or a candy bar.

Kate glanced up from her phone. "You shot him?"

"What?" Lauren and Rowan said in unison.

"The bad guy you stopped," she clarified, holding out her phone. "The news says he was shot dead."

"Did you shoot someone, Daddy?" Sam gasped.

"I didn't shoot anyone," Rowan said. "You know how I feel about guns." Since Sudan, Rowan had sold his guns—most were historical or had sentimental value—but now they made him feel agitated and his heart raced every time he saw one. Lauren hadn't been upset about that either. He knew she was worried that he might harm himself, but he'd never felt that despondent, not even on his darkest days.

"The police had to shoot him," Lauren said, taking over. "I'm sure they didn't want to, but they wouldn't have done it if they had any other choice."

"Were you scared?" John Carter tossed his long bangs from his eyes as he looked at his dad.

"Yeah," he said. "I was." Lauren noticed his fists on the table, shaking.

Sarah got up out of her chair and without a word came over and stood with her arms out to her father. Rowan forced a smile and scooted his chair back, letting her put her arms around his neck. With a grunt, he lifted her into his lap. She leaned against his chest, with her arms around his body. He leaned down and kissed her head. He ate his breakfast like this, while Sarah repeatedly ran her finger along the edge of the Starfleet insignia on his T-shirt, never saying anything. While he was still stiff and sore, Lauren could tell he felt better holding his little girl.

"Better hurry up, guys," Lauren said. "John Carter is going to drive you to school, so you don't have to take the bus. It's supposed to rain all day, so I will pick you up."

Sarah kissed her father's cheek. "I love you, Daddy," she said before she climbed down from his lap. She came through the kitchen as the other kids brought their plates to the cabinet across from their mother. Sarah wrapped her arms around her mommy's legs and looked up at her and said. "Take care of Daddy."

"I will, sweetheart," Lauren leaned down and kissed her head. "Have a good day at school."

"Yes, Mommy."

Lauren refilled Rowan's coffee before she brought her plate over and sat across from him. When the door closed, he winced as he reached for his pocket. Lauren studied him through the shadow of her hair as he took out his cell phone and read a message that had come through. He glanced up at her, catching her eyeing his phone. "Will you come with me this morning?"

"You're in no shape to drive," Lauren said. "You can't even turn your head."

"Even if I could, I'd want you there," he said.

"I wouldn't want to be anywhere else."

Before he could even put the phone down, it bleeped again. He typed back a quick response. "Dr. McLeish pushed me back to nine thirty."

DR. HELEN MCLEISH met him at the door when he came into the office. "Hey," she said, snaking a hand under his arm as she walked with him to the sitting area across from her desk. "Need some coffee?"

"I've had three cups already today," he said. "I'm fine."

"I'm glad you called. How are you holding up?"

"I'm a mess," he said.

"You had a panic attack?"

"Yeah," he said, sitting back on the sofa, resting his hands in his lap. "Not the worst one I've ever had, but . . . it rattled me."

She sat down beside him, with her hand on his arm. "After what happened yesterday, of course, you're rattled. How'd you manage?" she asked.

"Lauren," he said. "She's my true north when this kind of thing happens."

"What do you think it was about yesterday's events that set you off?"

"It should have been the fact that I was afraid for my life and the clerk's life," he said, but hesitated. "Maybe it was having a hostage's life in my hands . . . *again*." He'd failed Tima, and that guilt hadn't entirely left him. He continued to blame himself for her death, despite everything. "Maybe it was the Marine. He asked for my help. I promised I'd help him, but in the end . . ."

"What could you have done?" asked Dr. Mac.

"I don't know," Rowan hesitated. Dr. Mac allowed a long moment of silence for him to think about it. "He said something was watching him, that it followed him home from work."

"Something?"

"Well, you know what I used to do for a living, right?"

"Ghost hunter." She nodded. "Yeah."

"Among other things." He could have argued his case, that it was so much more than being a ghost hunter, but it wasn't worth trying to explain. He no longer cared what people called him, or what they thought of his former profession. He wasn't that guy anymore. "It could be something completely different, and this is just a coping mechanism for me to think like this, but . . . I have to think he meant a spirit."

"But you don't do that kind of work anymore."

"No," he said. "But that Marine came to *me*. I wonder if he'd been following me, trying to get his courage up."

"Following you? Or *stalking* you?"

Rowan shrugged. "Does it matter?" He paused, considering her words. "He thought I could help him."

"But you couldn't, Rowan. He had a mental disorder. You're not a doctor. Anything you could have done to alleviate his worries, his fears, would have been superficial."

Rowan looked up at her. "I could have brought him to see you."

A smile softened the lines on her face. "Well, there is that."

"You know I have time on my hands these days," he said. "The kids are back in school. There's only so many home repair projects a guy can do."

"Like fixing the kitchen sink."

"It did not escape my notice that Lauren's father left when she was a girl, saying he was going to get something to fix the sink. He never came home. I left home to get something to fix the sink. It would have destroyed her if I hadn't come home. I think that's what bothers me the most."

"I thought Lauren's father was in Oklahoma," Dr. Mac said. "That they were close."

"She has a good relationship with him now, but it wasn't always the case." He went on to tell her about Lauren's family—without getting into the magical details—and realized he was just doing it to avoid talking about how he was feeling. Dr. Mac gave him an expression that suggested she recognized that fact, too. Before she could ask, he changed the subject. "I'm about out of fixer-upper projects since I finished the basement renovation." Rowan swallowed hard, looking away from the counselor. "I just don't know what else to do with myself these days."

"I thought you were writing?"

"I can't seem to get traction on anything," he said. "Maybe I'm not meant to be a novelist."

"You don't believe that," she said. "We both know that. It's all you've talked about since you started coming to see me. Have you tried going to the coffee shop or the library to write? Setting a word-count goal for the day?"

"Writing at the coffee shop?" That suggestion puzzled him. "The library?" He'd started taking Sarah to the library after school while they waited to pick up her siblings. She was in half-day pre-K at a private school across town, so they had lots of time together in the afternoons. She liked to play the *Clifford the Big Red Dog* game on their computers and get new books for him to read to her. He usually sat and scrolled through TikTok or checked out Lauren's Instagram page to see pictures from her adventures and watch for any lurkers trying to hit on her—which happened all the time. He'd had his fair share of fan-girls back in the day. He wasn't accustomed to the guys fawning over Lauren. He didn't like it.

"You can't goof off or nod off if someone is watching you," Dr. Mac said. "It's a good way to keep yourself accountable. Besides, you can treat yourself to a coffee or pick up a new book as a reward when you've met your goals for the day."

He nodded. "Why didn't I think of that?"

"That's not what you want to talk about though, is it?" She always knew how to read him.

He shook his head *no*. "I just . . . I wish I could have helped him."

"To what end?"

A flash of inspiration swelled in his chest and spread across his face. "Maybe I *can* help him."

"What?"

"Maybe if I knew more about him . . . what he did, where he lived, what his life was like?"

"Rowan," she cut him off, her brow furrowing. "I'm not sure that's the healthiest way for you to process this trauma. You can't do anything to fix things for that man. He made his choices, and the consequences are his and his alone."

Rowan deflated. "Maybe you're right."

"Look." She stood and went over to her desk. "I'm going to write you a prescription—"

"I don't want medication." Panic washed through him. They'd medicated him at Walter Reed, and he hated how it made him feel. It'd taken the better part of a year before he was able to wean off of it, and he wasn't ready to slay that dragon again.

"This is just temporary." She scribbled the prescription on the pad and tore the page off, bringing it over to him. "It's an incredibly mild anti-depressant. It'll calm your racing thoughts and still allow you to function. It shouldn't make you drowsy or take away your ability to function." She held out the prescription. "Will you take this?"

He reached out for the paper. "They gave me muscle relaxers and pain meds at the ER. For my back and shoulder."

"Take this in the morning but take those at night. You don't want to mix them," she instructed. "No alcohol."

"I haven't had a drink in months," he said. He started having a glass of scotch every night after dinner shortly after they'd settled in Denver. It seemed innocent enough. His father often enjoyed scotch after a good meal or a long day on the golf course. It didn't make him an alcoholic. But for Rowan, it quickly escalated into a bottle a week. He knew he needed to stop. Scotch didn't calm him anyway, and he decided it wasn't worth it.

"Good for you." She put a hand on his wrist as she sat beside him. "Once you stop needing the medicine they gave you at the ER, you can try taking one in the morning and another before bed. I want to see you every week for the next month or so." Rowan nodded. "You have to call me if you find your thoughts going dark, or you have another panic attack. Okay? 24/7. You have my number."

Rowan agreed. "Thank you for working me in today."

"Of course," she said. "I'm here any time you need anything."

———

LAUREN GLANCED up from her magazine when he stepped into the lobby. She stood and picked up her purse. "Okay?" she asked, giving the doctor a smile and a nod.

"Yeah," he said. He stopped at the desk to check out and schedule his next appointment. Lauren glanced at the doctor. A silent message passed through her kind eyes, and Lauren knew she'd made the right choice in bringing him. It had been his idea, but she knew he needed her support more than anything. At Walter Reed, they'd cautioned her that this was a marathon, not a sprint. It would be a race they'd run for the rest of their lives. She was committed to running it with him.

She'd spoken with Dr. Mac a few times over the phone. Lauren had been given some insight in how to support him and what to do if problems arose while he was being treated at Walter Reed. But gaining insight from Dr. Mac had been helpful, too. Dr. Mac never discussed Rowan's treatment specifically, rather she spoke in general terms. Lauren understood why—regulations required Rowan's treatment to remain confidential. Dr. Mac was one of the best psychologists she'd ever encountered, and she felt confident that if something required her attention, she'd find a way to make sure Lauren knew.

"Ready?" Rowan caught her arm as he turned from the scheduling desk.

"Want to grab a bite to eat before we go home?"

"Sure."

3

Rowan spent the early hours of the morning lying on his back under the kitchen sink, wrenching a stubborn pipe into place. His shoulder twinged as he twisted, arms raised above his head. It had been a mistake to take a nap during the day, curled up with Lauren, both of them worn out from a sleepless night before.

He'd struggled with sleep after coming home from Walter Reed. PTSD did that. The flashbacks from Afghanistan had already started to blur with the horrors in Sudan, Syria, and Iraq. Those first nights home, he'd spent in the recliner, watching television to numb the memories that medication could not take away. Then, he'd sleep all day when Lauren and the children needed him most. Eventually, he resorted to an occasional glass of Scotch after dinner until it became a nightly tonic that provided no relief. One glass became two until Lauren pointed out he was going through a bottle a week. He weaned himself off, but it was still a struggle not to turn to the bottle.

Dr. Mac coached him through a new routine, one that promised a better rhythm. Now, Rowan found himself fighting to hold onto that routine—and losing the battle. He told himself this was temporary. A slip but not a fall. He threw himself into his chores to keep his thoughts from racing out of control. But the sink took less than an hour to fix, even with the stuck pipe and his aching shoulder.

Through the window, he saw Indy sitting in the corner of the garden, watching something out of Rowan's sight and he remembered Sarah's concern about the dog. Indy was a good-natured mix of shepherd, border collie, and who knew what else. It took a lot to agitate him. He hated squirrels digging in his yard and defended it as if the rodents were wolves. The dog would be wet and muddy when it was time for him to come in, and Rowan wasn't looking forward to washing him or cleaning up the prints left by muddy paws on the kitchen floor he'd already mopped.

As he stood watching the dog, his eyes drifted to the prescription he'd left on the counter. *Should he get it filled?* He thought about Dr. Mac's advice but hesitated. *Why was everyone against him helping the Marine?* It wouldn't hurt anything to look into the man's life, would it? The Marine was dead, after all.

He weighed his options. The pharmacy would take a few hours to fill the prescription. He could drop it off on his way to take Sarah to school and pick it up when she got out of school. They'd have time to go to the library before he needed to pick the older children up. Or, he could do something else. His gaze landed on the detective's business card lying next to a stack of bills that needed to be paid. Two days had passed. Surely they'd found something by now. But then again, with cuts to the city budget and recent furloughs, the police were spread thin. Maybe they could use some help. Rowan was a trained investigator. He wouldn't get in the way. *What harm could it do?*

"Mr. Pierce," Detective Bronowski stuck out his hand to greet him. "Didn't expect to see you so soon." The detective rode in the ambulance with him to the hospital, conducting his interview while Rowan was still in agony, and while the paramedics assessed his injuries.

"I wanted to ask some questions about . . ." He hesitated. "About the Marine involved in the incident."

"Benjamin Riggs," the detective said. "Unfortunately, because this is an active investigation I can't tell you much."

"Can you at least tell me where he worked?" Rowan asked.

"No." Bronowski crossed his arms as he sat on the corner of the desk. "I can't."

Rowan pursed his lips, chewing on the tuft of his beard at the bottom of his mouth. "I get it," he finally said with a nod. "I'm an investigator myself. I understand."

The detective's brow flinched. "PI?"

"Yeah, something like that," he said. *Paranormal investigator. Close enough.*

"I wish I could be of more help." The detective clasped his hands together, then threw them up with a shrug. "Hope you're feeling better."

"Eh," Rowan said. "Give me another day or two and ask me again."

"Will do," Bronowski stood, indicating the interview was over. Rowan rose and followed the detective to the door. "I'll call you."

"Thanks." Rowan glanced at his watch, and the movement sent a jolt of pain from his shoulder down his arm into his hand. His fingers tingled and he winced. The muscle relaxers helped his back but did little for his shoulder.

The MRI had shown a torn labrum from the assault at the convenience store, with inflammation aggravating the impingement he'd worked so hard to recover from through physical therapy. The ER doctor recommended following up with an orthopedic surgeon, but Rowan didn't want to think about that right now.

He walked to the car, trying to decide what to do for lunch, but his mind kept returning to the Marine. If there'd been a Marine base in Denver, he might have gone to talk to the man's commanding officer. But he didn't expect the CO would know much more than the police. Maybe if he could track her down, he could at least ask. What was the worst she could say? *No comment?*

At home, Rowan settled in for a sandwich, eating while waiting for his laptop to boot up. He chewed thoughtfully and brushed the crumbs off the keyboard before typing in the soldier's name. The number of results that appeared shocked him. The AP had picked up the story—along with the fact that the Travel Adventure Magazine's Man of the Decade had thwarted a robbery. *Unfreakingbelievable.*

His phone chirped in the pocket of his cargo pants pocket. He pulled it out and grinned as he hit the green button. "Hey, *mon ami*! What's up?"

"What's it like to be a hero?" Jean-René's voice came through the speaker.

"Whatever," Rowan guffawed. "Where are you?"

"Hiking up at Marmot Peak with your wife. Man! You should see the view!" Rowan glanced at the time. It was later than he'd realized. But he still had plenty of time before he had to pick up Sarah.

"Lauren told you about what happened?"

"Dude! It's all over the news," he said. "I'm surprised your phone isn't blowing up."

"I've got it set to block any calls that aren't from someone on my favorites list," he said.

"Smart," Jean-René chortled. "You'll have to teach me that trick."

"I know how to do it on an Apple," Rowan countered. "But the last I checked you were still on a lousy Android."

"Because it's a good phone," he came back.

"I'm pretty sure you didn't call just to get phone tips," Rowan said, anxious to get back to his search.

"I just called to check on you," he said. "Lauren said you got as good as you gave."

Rowan shook his head. Jean-René knew him all too well. "Well, I'm not thirty anymore." He swallowed hard.

"You didn't hurt your shoulder again, did you?"

"Again?" He shook his head, his opposite hand going to the sore shoulder. "Still."

"Better go see a doctor about that," Jean-René said. "If you weren't hurt, we could sure use you here."

"Why?"

"You'd like this trail. The aspens are gorgeous . . . you groove on that kind of thing."

"Is there an ancient treasure involved?"

"No," Jean-René said, with an implied question in his tone.

"Sasquatch? Yeti?"

"Not that I've seen," he answered.

"Ghosts? Monsters?"

"No and no."

"Then I'm out," Rowan said. "Call me when you find respectable work, friend. In the meantime, I've got a little side project here I'm working on."

"Does Lauren know?"

The question caught Rowan off guard. "Well, of course she does." He swallowed hard. She knew what had happened to him. He'd told her everything about Riggs and what he'd said. *She had to know he would need to figure out what was going on, right?*

"Lauren said to tell you we'll be late," Jean-René said. "She wants to capture the sunset over the valley."

"Of course she does. Call if you find Bigfoot." Rowan snorted in return.

"She said don't wait for her for dinner."

"Hadn't planned to," he said. "The kids asked if we can have pizza. Last I checked, pizza isn't her favorite."

"Who doesn't love pizza?"

"Let me know if you find Bigfoot. I'll save him a slice."

"Save me a slice," Jean-René said, just before Rowan hit the red button on his phone and set it aside.

Captain Lorraine York was harder to track down than Rowan expected. The first search result he clicked on took him to a list of officer promotions. Captain York was now Major York. There was a picture of a very tall Marine pinning oak leaves on the lapel of a very diminutive woman who appeared to be in her late forties or early fifties. She had salt-and-pepper hair, slicked back into a tight bun at the base of her neck. Her hat perched on her head like a cheap fascinator at a royal wedding. She wore her dress uniform with a skirt and patten leather pumps. They didn't add much to her height.

He moved on. It took a while longer to determine where he might be able to find her. He made a few phone calls and got the run-around, even though he thought he had her pinned down.

Then it hit him—Jean-René had given him the answer he needed. He pulled up the Denver Post online and quickly scrolled through the headlines. The story he was looking for appeared immediately.

Retired Cable Personality Stops Robbery at Denver Convenience Store

That was exactly what he expected to see.

A former Marine, suffering what experts are calling a PTSD-induced mental disorder, was subdued by Exploration Channel star Rowan Pierce at a local convenience store in what was initially believed to be an armed robbery. Police were forced to open fire when former Marine Lance Corporal Benjamin Riggs, 38, drew a weapon. Riggs was later pronounced dead at St. Joseph Hospital. Pierce suffered minor injuries in the altercation but was hailed a hero by Cashier Debi DelMonico. The clerk indicated Pierce kept the man talking before being able to subdue him and knock the gun from the Marine's hand before he attempted to flee and encountered the Denver Police Department outside. Pierce was taken to a local hospital where he was treated for minor injuries. Efforts to contact Mr. Pierce for comment have gone unanswered. The officers involved in the shooting are on administrative leave with pay, pending the outcome of an investigation. Riggs was discharged from the Marine Corps following an incident in Sudan where he suffered a similar mental episode and attacked his commanding officer.

Maybe that was it—maybe something followed him home from that incident? That had to be what he was talking about. Rowan scowled as he read the article again.

Rowan laid his phone on the table, gazing at it for a long moment as he chewed on the tuft of hair on the bottom of his lip.

Indy sat at the door, peering out into the yard. The dog had been patiently waiting for Rowan to finish his call. "Hey, buddy," Rowan greeted him as he opened the door. But instead of coming inside, Indy backed up, whining. He turned and ran off, disappearing beneath the arbor of spruce trees near the fence. Rowan shook his head and returned to his computer to get back to work.

How hard could it be to find out where this guy worked? Maybe his CO knew.

He sat there for several moments, staring at the screen, his mind circling the problem. His fingers hovered over the keys before he sighed and picked up his phone. He hit the speed dial for his father, leaning back in his chair as he rang.

The voice that answered was familiar, steady—like the man himself. "Charles Pierce."

"It's me, Dad," Rowan said, trying to hide his annoyance. The man couldn't figure out that the phone would tell someone who was calling, and he didn't have to answer like it was some big mystery. Instead, he tried to keep his tone light, though his heart rate quickened. Asking *the Colonel* for a favor wasn't something he was accustomed to. But what was the point of having the kind of pull his father had and not taking advantage of it? "How are you?"

"Ain't eatin' daisies by the roots." *So predictable.* That was his father's standard answer. "What's on your mind, son?" His father's voice held that clipped, no-nonsense edge that came from decades of military discipline. Conversations with *the Colonel* were rarely long.

"I need a favor, Dad," Rowan began, leaning forward slightly. "I'm trying to find Major Lorraine York—United States Marine Corps."

"Marine," he said, huffing. Rowan knew his father's mind like he knew his own. Any other branch of the Armed Forces couldn't measure up to the United States Air Force. "York, you say?"

"Yes, sir."

"Is she still in?"

"Yes, sir. I believe so," he said. "I need to talk to her. It's important to me." Rowan let the weight of his words hang in the air. His father would recognize his urgency. He was now confident that his parents hadn't received news of the recent events in Denver, and he didn't want to explain any of it to his father for fear that his mother might be listening. Martha Pierce could be a busybody, and he didn't want to become the gossip of their RV club.

"I see." The tone shifted, the wheels in his father's mind starting to turn. "Some reason you're not going through usual channels? No stroke with your connections?"

Rowan ran a weary hand over his face, bumping a sore spot beneath his eye. He bit his lip and that hurt even worse. "I need to speak with her directly, Dad. You know how it is— usual channels take forever, and this isn't something I can sit on. It's time-sensitive. It's sensitive. I wouldn't have asked, but . . . I didn't know where else to turn."

His father was quiet for a moment. He could almost picture *The Colonel* at this very kitchen table when Rowan had been a boy—his father folding his hands, considering his next move. "All right," Colonel Pierce finally said, his voice crisp. "The trout ain't biting. Might as well. I can do this for you. I'll get you a phone number if I can. Just make sure when you talk to her, it's worth her time."

Rowan felt a small sense of relief, though the weight of his request still pressed heavily on his chest. "Thanks, Dad. I owe you one."

"You can come down here to Antonito and help me wipe out the trout population," his father replied, a touch of warmth breaking through the iron-clad façade.

"I thought you said they weren't biting," Rowan said. He could be mischievous when the situation called for it. He'd missed that part of himself. It had been lost in the last four years.

"Well," he said. "They're waiting for *you*, son." Rowan realized the din in the background was the Conejos River. He knew right where his father was—hip-deep in the babbling river. The water would be ice cold, even this time of the year. *The Colonel* went quiet. A moment later, he spoke. "Just keep me updated. And be careful. If this involves digging into something, you'd better know what you're getting into."

"I will," Rowan said, getting up. "I'll be in touch soon. Thanks again, Dad."

"Rowan," his father stopped him before he hit the red button on his phone. "I love you, son."

"I love you, too, Dad. Hug Mom for me."

The line clicked as his father hung up. Rowan stood there for a moment, phone in hand, thinking about what was at stake. He hadn't expected the path to be easy, but it was clear now—he was about to be hip-deep into something a lot deeper than he had any business getting into. His father wouldn't fail him.

4

The fishing must have been as bad as his father suggested when they spoke. Less than an hour passed before he got a text from Charles that included nothing but a phone number. *Typical.* There was no explanation—nothing to tell him where he was calling or whom he might have to speak to before he reached Riggs's CO.

He hesitated a moment but knew he had to call, regardless of the outcome. He couldn't let his dad's efforts be in vain.

"Camp Lejeune Duty Desk," the voice on the other end answered. "Corporal Bellingham. How may I direct your call?" His tone was polite, professional—and efficient.

"This is Rowan Pierce," he said, too late to debate if he should have used his rank and branch. He'd been out too long for it to come naturally. "I'm calling to speak to Major York. Is she available?"

"One moment, sir," the man on the other end said. He sat on hold for several minutes, again.

When the phone clattered and someone came on the other end, Rowan was about to give up. "Major York," she introduced herself curtly.

"Uh, yes. My name is Rowan Pierce," he said. "I understand you had a soldier under your command by the name of Lance Corporal Benjamin Riggs. Is that correct?"

There was a long pause. He could hear her swallow hard. When she spoke, he could hear her words through gritted teeth and realized immediately this might not be the best course of action. "Look, I don't know who you think you are, but . . . that name isn't spoken in my presence. If this is some kind of a . . ."

"He's dead." The words slipped from his mouth before he had a moment to think about it. He sensed there might be some comfort in that knowledge, by the vitriol in her tone. "He was killed a few days ago."

"How?" She asked but didn't seem to soften.

"Shot," Rowan said. "By the Denver Police Department." Still, she said nothing. "I was with him . . . before it happened."

"How do you know him?" she demanded, no joy in her tone.

"He put a gun to my head," Rowan said. "I recognized a fellow soldier with PTSD."

The ten seconds of silence were deafening. "And where did you serve?"

"Army, field medic with the 23rd Med-Evac. Two tours in Afghanistan and Iraq in Desert Storm/Desert Shield." He intentionally didn't mention recent events in Sudan, Syria, and Iraq.

The silence hummed between them. "I'm calling because . . . I . . . well, I hoped you might be able to tell me . . . what happened to him." He intentionally didn't say the man's name.

"I'm not in a position to have this discussion at the moment," she clipped.

"I understand, ma'am," Rowan said. "I had just hoped to . . . I . . . I truly feel for wounded soldiers."

"Give me your number, Mr. Pierce," she said, her tone

softened. "When . . . if I can call . . . maybe because I am not saying I will call, but . . . if I can . . . when I come to that place . . . maybe . . . I'll call."

"Fair enough," Rowan said, giving her his number.

"Mr. Pierce," she hesitated. He could hear her pen tapping against the notepad as if she were considering her options. "Are you okay? He didn't . . . hurt you . . . did he?"

That brought a lightness to his chest. "I've been hit by bigger." That was his standard answer, and he realized his response lacked the compassion she was offering, even though she didn't feel ready to grant grace. "I wasn't seriously injured . . . a few bumps or bruises is all. I will say that it brought back some pretty painful memories though. Maybe that's why . . . that's why I'm trying so hard . . ."

"Too many soldiers came home with . . . issues." Rowan had already figured out she was having issues of her own. Of course, she would. If the reports were correct, she'd been assaulted by one of her men. It hadn't occurred to him that she was still dealing with it until he mentioned the Marine's name.

"Yes, ma'am," he said. "And the best thing we can do is help each other. I'm here if you want to talk . . . when you're ready. But, I understand. If you can't talk to me, I hope you have someone you can confide in."

"Good day, Mr. Pierce," she said curtly before the line went dead.

Rowan lay his phone on the table, gazing at it for a long moment as he chewed on the tuft of hair on the bottom of his lip. He'd found her, but that hadn't been the conversation he'd expected. There were a million questions he hoped to ask her. Questions he still needed answers to.

Wow. Rowan stood and paced behind his chair, not even sure what to do or why that call caught him so off guard. He hadn't expected the venom in her voice when she spoke about *that man.* The article said Riggs had attacked her. *Maybe there was more to it.*

LAUREN STOOD at the summit of Marmot Peak, struggling for breath in the thin mountain air. The sun, now a steady presence, pierced through the lingering clouds, casting radiant beams of light across the rocky terrain. It warmed her skin, filling her with a quiet satisfaction that only the mountains offered. At the start of their hike, the chill had wrapped around her like a heavy blanket, forcing her to zip up her fleece jacket and shove her hands into its pockets as the biting wind grabbed at her hair and nipped her cheeks. The cold had made her teeth chatter at the start of the climb, but now, the transformation was complete. The afternoon sun was brilliant. The puffs of gray clouds drifted lazily in the cool air.

As Lauren gazed around, the changing landscape seemed to shift with her mood, from the tumultuous wind and cold to the serenity of the present. To her right, East Buffalo Peak loomed, nearly 14,000 feet above sea level. The mountain was vast, its bald dome stripped of trees and vegetation, standing stoic on the horizon. And beyond it, Mount Harvard rose with a commanding presence—its jagged ridge cutting the sky, towering over the valley below. The way the sunlight played off the early fall snow on its peaks made the mountain appear as if God himself touched it.

Her eyes traced the slopes of the surrounding mountains, the dark green forests beneath them shifting into a patchwork of rocky outcrops and wild-flower-filled meadows. The landscape seemed endless, stretching off into the distance—a vast tapestry of nature's creation, as beautiful as a Bob Ross—no, a Fredric Remington painting.

The crisp mountain air filled her lungs, and she sighed thinking there was nothing better than a little thin air therapy.

The fatigue from the climb melted away and she could hear her heartbeat, steady and strong. This—*this* was the reason she loved this job.

With a contented sigh, Lauren let out a slow breath and turned to her companions. "This is the spot."

"I'll set up the tripod," Bahati said. She shrugged the pack containing the equipment off her shoulder.

"Just watch out for the critters." Jean-René chortled. The way he said the word *critters* caught Lauren's attention. She didn't usually notice accents, but coming from his mouth, the word sounded . . . *off*.

"What—" Lauren started to ask, but a flash of something caught in the corner of her eye and it startled her. When she realized what it was, the tension that suddenly built in her shoulders melted. The yellow-bellied marmot, one of the most common creatures in the high-altitude regions of the Rockies, had come out to sun themselves before a cold night moved in. Marmots weren't anything to worry about. They weren't vicious. Instead, they watched with a great deal of interest as Jean-René took the camera off his shoulder and mounted it on the tripod. Bahati dug out the microphone and brought it over, helping Lauren run the wires under her now unzipped jacket. She tucked the battery pack into her hip pocket and turned to the camera.

Jean-René gave her a visual countdown. Lauren took a few steps towards the camera, before stopping with her foot on a rock. "At 11,730 feet, Marmot Peak isn't the tallest mountain in Colorado, but here in the Mosquito Range—just north of Buena Vista—the views are breathtaking." She read the script scrolling on the screen of the iPad Bahati held up over Jean-René's shoulder. "And you never know when you might just make a friend," she ad-libbed as she glanced down at a portly marmot waddling over to her foot. It grabbed her shoelace and tried to abscond with it. Jean-René panned the camera down to capture the escapade.

"Hey, you!" Lauren jerked her foot back, inadvertently flipping the creature around. It made the oddest noise at her—not quite a hiss, but almost a bark—before it redoubled its efforts at swiping the shoelace. This time, the marmot braced for her counterattack and nearly upended her as it fought for the prize. "Cut!"

The light on the camera went off as Jean-René came out from behind it, charging at the beastie. It yelped before he even reached it and ran to the safety of its fellows. The barking yips began as a chorus as they all seemed prepared to defend their own.

"Let's get out of here!" Jean-René said. "Sheesh! They're everywhere." The horde seemed to move closer as if to surround them. He shouldered the camera, tripod and all, herding the women back down the path until they were out of sight.

Lauren didn't argue until they reached a clearing overlooking the valley midway down the mountain. She paused, checking to make sure they hadn't been followed. "We can get another take if you need one," she said to her camera operator.

"No," Jean-René said. "I'm fairly sure I got it. I can edit out the part where you almost fell."

"Thank you. I appreciate not being embarrassed on television," she said.

She paused, studying the sun as it started that slow crawl behind Mount Harvard. The sky was now flaxen, streaked in crimson. The few clouds—no longer happy white puffballs—hovered like angry dark wraiths that knew the hour of their doom was at hand. A flicker of lightning danced between them as they took their last stand, raging against the dying of the light. Transfixed, Lauren held her position. Jean-René moved behind her and she could sense Bahati moving closer as well. The sun broke into colorful rays—a combination of darkness and light—as it dipped behind the mountain, turning it almost black in the instant it turned its face from the world.

"It will be dark by the time we reach the car," Jean-René said. "Come on. It's been a long day. I'm hungry. We can stop for a Viking Burger before we drive home."

"Sounds good," Lauren said and fell in behind him.

HE HAD INTENDED to catch the end of the Avalanche's preseason game against the Dallas Stars, then turn it over to watch Jimmy Fallon's monologue on the Tonight Show. Surely Lauren would have been home by then. Rowan didn't make it through the second period of the game.

He'd stayed busy all day but hadn't come any closer to finding out where Riggs worked. He had to abandon his search when his fatherly duties called him back to the mundane. He picked up the children from school, got them home, and set to work preparing supper. He sat with the older ones who had homework, after finishing the dishes, before sending them off to their rooms to read for a while before their appointed bedtimes.

"You're not going to find me like that." The voice came to him in the dark. Rowan was startled and found himself standing outside the convenience store again. There was no gun to his head or at his chest. He calmed, gazing down at the toe of his sneaker. A crimson pool glistened in the moonlight as a soft breeze ran down the neck of his shirt and chilled him to the core. The hair on his arms rose and his head ached in response to the panic that began to grow in his core.

The Marine—his body riddled with bullets—lay in the spreading pool of blood, his eyes opened as he gazed blindly into the sky.

Rowan swallowed the lump in his throat as he pinched his eyes shut and steeled his courage. "You didn't give me much to work with," Rowan said. "You said something followed you home?"

Riggs blinked, and without any effort, rose from the blood, wiping his hands on his olive-green T-shirt. "Bad papers made it hard to find work," he said, nonplused. "No one in Denver would give me a chance. Everyone I knew turned their backs on me. I was alone. No one would help me."

"I am trying to help you."

"*You came back from the war like me . . . broken.*" Riggs moved around him, and Rowan stiffened as the man sized him up as if seeing him for the first time.

"It's true."

"*We walked in the same shoes. We both found ourselves in the land of Kings. Where the key to redemption is whitewashed beneath the gates to the heavens.*"

"Hey." A soft voice drew him from the scene. He tried to grab the Marine by the arm to avoid losing his connection to the ghost that haunted him, but warm lips pressed to his forehead, and he bolted upright, suddenly wide awake. Lauren yelped, cupping her hand over her nose. "Rowan?" Her question was muffled beneath her hands.

"Oh, my God! Lauren. Are you okay?"

She drew her hands away, and he was relieved to see she wasn't bleeding. "Fine," she said, sniffing. "I didn't mean to startle you. Are *you* okay?"

"I must have been dreaming," he said, collapsing back into the chair. She moved into his lap and gingerly wrapped her arms around him, melting into him as he held her. Her clothing was chilled, and he realized she must have just come in from the car. "I'm so sorry. What time is it?"

"After midnight," she said. "I thought you'd be in bed by now."

"Back . . . shoulder," he grunted. "Been hurting all afternoon. I think it's the weather."

"Did you take something?"

"I'm sure that's why I fell asleep here." He hadn't taken anything all day, but she didn't need to know that.

"Come on, I'll draw you a warm bath and then tuck you in."

She got up, then turned and offered a hand, helping him to his feet.

"I thought you'd be home hours ago."

"Flat tire," Lauren said. "One of the lug nuts was stuck. It took all three of us to get it loose. I tried to call, but you didn't answer."

"I put my phone on the charger." He pointed to the outlet by the kitchen counter where he kept his phone at night. "Sorry."

"It's okay. Come on."

He let her help him undress, wincing as he sank onto the bed, pulling her down with him. She yelped, but he bit his lip, wanting nothing more than to feel her close to him. "Forget the bath," he said. "I just want to hold you." He reached for the button at the top of her cleavage and popped it open, exploring deeper, following with his lips.

"Seriously?" She chortled in a deep voice, but she didn't pull away. "It's after midnight, and I have to be in the studio by eight tomorrow."

"This won't take long." He reached for her bra strap, peeling it down her shoulder.

"Rowan? What's gotten into you? I thought your shoulder hurt."

"I need you . . . close."

She surrendered to him and was kind enough to help him finish the job of stripping her naked before she crawled into bed beside him. He made love to her in a way he hadn't for some time. He was more attentive to her needs than usual. He was efficient in his efforts but made sure it was worth her time. When he did let her sleep, it was tucked into the curve of his naked body, warm, safe, and deliciously complete.

5

Lauren found him in the kitchen the following morning when she came up from her workout. He was making breakfast alone. Water ran in the sink, filling it so he could wash the larger dishes he'd already used in his prep. Lauren hadn't had a chance to inspect his handiwork since he'd fixed the faucet but was pleased to see her sink was no longer leaking. She turned the water off for him.

"*It is a truth universally acknowledged, that a married woman in possession of an aged home must be in want of a maintenance man,*" Rowan said, with a bemused tone in his voice.

"Excuse me?"

"What?" he chuckled. "I can't quote Emily Dickinson?"

"Jane Austen," Lauren corrected him. "And I am *not* in want of a maintenance man." She snaked her arms around his waist. "I have you."

"I am handy, aren't I?" he asked with a strongly implied tone of innuendo.

"Yes. You are," she said. "I'd like the chance to return the favor. Are you free tonight?"

"Will you be home late?"

"Do you want me to be late?"

"Absolutely not." He turned, laying down the spatula, taking her in his arms. "I want to send the kids to bed after dinner. If you want to have a glass of wine, I'll pour it for you myself. Then I'll light some candles, and we can take that bubble bath. After that, Dr. Pierce, you can repay the favor however you like."

"However I like? However, *you* like." She kissed him.

"In that case, a proper back rub to start," he said, his hands snaking down her sweaty back to cup her buttocks. "And then we'll see about a proper front rub."

Lauren's brow lifted. "What's gotten into you?"

"What? Is there some rule that says a guy can't enjoy the company of his wife once in a while? How long has it been anyway?"

Lauren cocked her head toward the shoulder she lifted. "It has been a while," she admitted. "We both work too hard."

"Well, you do," he said. "With the kids in school most of the day and everything done on my honey-do list, I've got time on my hands."

"In that case, I expect to see the first chapter of your novel when I get home," she said, then kissed him one more time. "I'll be back in a bit for breakfast. I need a shower."

FOLLOWING HIS THERAPIST'S SUGGESTION, Rowan sat in a booth at the back of the café with a caramel latte and a large apricot scone waiting for his attention. Both remained untouched as he gazed into the computer. He hadn't finished a chapter, but he'd jotted down some ideas for a thriller with a female protagonist—one a lot like his own wife.

He'd been cautious leaving the house, watching for paparazzi—even legitimate news sources who might follow him. He hoped no one would bother him in his favorite coffee shop. The waitresses and the owner knew him—knew who he was—and never made a big fuss about it when he came in. He'd never thought to bring his laptop with him. Still, he found it was too easy to get distracted. The wi-fi was as good as the coffee here, and he quickly found himself falling down a rabbit hole surfing the internet for ideas.

"I heard you were writing a book." A voice caught him off guard. He gazed up. A woman in jeans and a Patagonia jacket smiled as she slid into the booth across from him and stuck out her hand. "I'm Vega Sanchez. I've been looking forward to meeting you." Rowan hesitated to accept her hand. "I'm the new CEO of the Exploration Channel."

Rowan sat back closing his laptop, crossing his arms over his chest. She was in her mid-thirties, radiating an air of both authority and warmth. Her brown hair was asymmetrical—one side cropped close to her scalp, the other falling in a sleek bob. Bangles clinked on her wrists and multiple necklaces layered around her neck. Her ears were pierced with several studs and hoops, while a tiny diamond pierced the crease of her nose. Her alabaster skin contrasted with her kohl-lined eyes and dark brown eyeshadow that shimmered in the light.

"*New* CEO? What happened to Jacob?"

"The Board issued a vote of no confidence after earnings dropped for a third quarter in a row. They're holding him responsible for the trend that began four years ago—when you and Lauren quit," she said. "The Network isn't the same without its *Veritas* Power Couples. That includes the Toussaints."

"I know where this is going, Ms. Sanchez. We're not interested. I'm retired. Lauren, Bahati, and Jean-René are happy doing public television."

"I also heard about what happened at the convenience store," she said. "Your name is buzzing on every media outlet in the world, not just the country. There's been a campaign launched by the fans to bring you and Lauren back. The Network has yet to respond."

"The media lies. I got my ass kicked by a deranged Marine and ended up wearing a cherry Icee on my head. Ruined my favorite shirt."

"You saved lives, Rowan. You're practically Batman at this point—*a hero for the people*. The Network wants the *Veritas Codex* team, and we'll do anything to get you back. Name your price."

Rowan gazed at her for a long moment, studying her and sizing up her character. She was younger than him by at least twenty years. She had the arrogance of youth and the attitude that came from someone who wasn't accustomed to being told *no*. He also saw the strength and confidence behind her dark eyes—moxie. She'd have to have moxie to lead the Exploration Channel. What Jacob had wasn't moxie. It was ego.

"Be generous," she added when he didn't answer immediately.

Rowan took another moment to plan his response. His façade softened, though his resolve never wavered. He rested and elbow on the table and leaned forward. "My price? Ms. Sanchez? There isn't enough money on this godforsaken planet to get me to go back to the life I had when I worked for the Exploration Channel. I missed my children growing up. I lost my professor—" His gaze lowered to the mangled hand in his lap. The use of his ring finger was the least of his heartbreak. "So the answer isn't just *no*. It's *oh, hell no*."

"I thought you'd say that," she said, nonplused. She reached into the breast pocket inside her jacket and withdrew a document. She pushed the folded paper in front of him and sat back. Rowan glared at it, then finally reached out and took it, giving her a stern gaze before he unfolded it.

The newsprint had been torn from the Mexico City newspaper—there was no date. The headline read "Mayan Treasures Among Missing Relics from Khartoum Museum."

"What's this got to do with me?"

"Keep reading," she urged.

Rowan complied. Realization swept over him as he lay the paper down in front of him. "So that's the link? This Marine who attacked me was accused of stealing treasures while serving in Sudan?"

"Did you know he attacked his commanding officer when she confronted him over the missing artifacts?"

This was the first Rowan heard of missing artifacts. That might explain the man's behavior. He'd been caught with his hand in the proverbial cookie jar. He wasn't willing to be busted for his crimes. "You think he took these Mayan artifacts?"

"I can't help but think this is more than a coincidence," she said.

Lauren's words echoed in his ears—*I don't believe in coincidence.*

"I don't think his assault on your person was a coincidence, either," Vega added.

Rowan sat drumming his knuckles on the table next to the article. His mind was racing, but not because of her proposition, but rather because of the reasons behind why the Marine had attacked *him.*

I know who you are, Riggs said.

That meant he must have known Rowan and Lauren had been credited for finding the largest cache of Mayan treasure in modern history. They helped authorities put an end to a massive illegal market ring for such antiquities. But that was over fifteen years ago. *Why now? What did any of this have to do with him? Had any of their treasures ended up in a museum in Khartoum?*

"This could make a great episode to launch a new series," Vega brought him from his reverie. "Missing treasure was your specialty. Right?"

"You have me mistaken for the man I used to be. I used to be a monster hunter, a treasure seeker. I'm not that man anymore, ma'am."

She reached out and put her hand over his, and he glared at it. His gaze lifted and cut through her. She withdrew her hand. "Rowan. You could be all that again—and so much more—if you wanted."

"I thought I made my position on that quite clear."

Vega arched a brow and rose from the table. She pulled a card out of her pocket and tossed it on the table. "If you change your mind, that's my cell. Call me."

"You're wasting your time," Rowan said, staring at the black card with the shiny finish, her picture on the top corner above the Network's logo.

"If you won't listen to me, listen to your fans." She winked, then strolled out of the café without looking back.

He thought the comment odd, but the newspaper article she left in front of him on the table had his mind racing. He read it again, and then a third time. Several artifacts mentioned in the article—not all of them Mayan—caught his attention: *the Veil of the Mourning Virgin, Axe of K'awiil, Saladin's Ring*, the *Vessel of Chaac, the Bell of Palden Lhamo* . . . the *Amulet of Nohochacyum.*

Oh, boy. That wasn't good.

A note at the bottom of the article mentioned that the *Vessel of Chaac* had been found in Virginia and returned to the museum in Mexico. He'd never heard of the bell or the veil, but he would most certainly be interested in learning more about them. But, of all the items listed in the article, one stood out as being out of place. The *Ring of Saladin* was most certainly not a Mayan artifact. Nor was it a Christian relic.

There was an image of the signet ring. A central diadem—a striated sardonyx stone, inlaid in gold. The inlay consisted of two crossed lines with crescent moons in three of the four quadrants created by the lines and a golden eagle in the fourth.

Rowan had seen similar stones before. Sardonyx was a type of gemstone that combined layers of sard usually reddish brown—and onyx—a banded variety of agate. The vibrant colors in the Ring of Saladin ranged from deep red, brown and orange to cream, white and a top layer of black. The interplay between the rich tones, made for a beautifully haunting ring, especially with the symbol inlaid in gold.

It was a handsome ring, even after centuries had passed. He could just imagine what a beauty it must have been in the 1100s when the Sultan himself wore it.

Then, he thought of Tima, who idolized the historical figure. Rowan still blamed himself for her death. He wrestled with all the what-ifs. *What if I had acted sooner? What if I could have saved her?* The vivid images of her defiance in the face of her attackers stirred up a cocktail of painful emotions—grief, guilt, anger, and helplessness.

Still, he thought fondly of her and her lectures on Saladin. They had been the stuff of legends among her students. While Christian theologians and scholars from antiquity—even into the modern day—villainized him as a monster, Tima spoke of his generosity. *"Saladin was, primarily, a man who exemplified the balance between strength and honor. He was a warrior, yes —a conqueror—but he was also a man of deep conviction and human-ity."* Her voice echoed in his mind and grew into a ball of regret in the pit of his stomach.

Salah ad-Din Yusuf ibn Ayyub was a Sultan of Egypt and Syria. Born in 1137, he hailed from a Kurdish family and was an important figure in the 3rd Crusade. He spearheaded the Muslim military effort against the Crusader States in the Levant. He led forays against the Crusaders in Palestine and staved off rebellions in Egypt. In addition to Islam, Saladin knew the genealogies, biographies, and histories of the Arabs, as well as the bloodlines of all the Arabian horses in his herd.

Jihad and the suffering involved in it weighed heavily on his heart. He spoke of nothing else. Through his conquests, he amassed a great fortune. Many of his treasures existed through antiquity, and their legends followed. His double-headed eagle appeared on a staff Rowan had seen in the Cairo Museum of Ancient History. The same eagle appeared on the Coat of Arms for Egypt, Iraq, Palestine, and Yemen.

"As a Muslim, Saladin had more respect for a man willing to fight and die for his faith, than for a man worried about his wife and children," Tima repeated that line so often—opening all her lectures on the Crusades with the line—that it remained engrained in his memory.

His heart ached as he thought of her generosity, even in the face of certain death. She could have cowered before the foe when his own life was on the line, but instead, she remained defiant, knowing it would cost her own. She'd done it to give him a chance to get home to Lauren and his children.

Saladin gave respect and dignity to prisoners of war. Captives were treated humanely and often released without any ransom. Rowan gazed at his mangled finger. Despite several surgeries, it hadn't healed well, and the doctor had even considered just amputating it. Too bad his captors weren't so just.

"Oh, you haven't touched your scone," the waitress said in a deep southern drawl that suggested she wasn't from around here. *Tennessee, maybe?* "Is it okay? It isn't dry, is it? I just baked them this morning. It's a new recipe."

Rowan shook off his dark thoughts. "No," he said. "It's fine. I just got off on a tangent." He pointed at the laptop, trying to shake off the ghosts of his past and present.

"Well, I bet your coffee's gone cold, too. I'll make you another one."

"It's fine," Rowan started gathering his things, tucking his laptop into his backpack. "I've got to pick my daughter up from school."

"You want me to wrap up your scone? I'm happy to get you a coffee to go."

"Sure." Rowan pushed the plate towards her while he

fumbled through his backpack for his phone. It wasn't there. He picked up his jacket and patted around, finding it in the pocket. He glanced at it. He still had over thirty minutes before Sarah needed to be picked up.

He put the phone back and glanced at the card Vega Sanchez left on the table. He considered it a moment, then tucked the card in his shirt pocket. He had no intention of calling or emailing her. But whether he cared to admit it, she'd sparked something he couldn't quite explain.

The Mayan treasures were interesting and all, but if Riggs had absconded with the Ring of Saladin—if he still had it—it needed to be returned to Khartoum, along with any other treasures he might still have in his possession. Of course, the Mayan treasures were no less important, the ring made him think of Tima, and if he could see it returned, he would do it for her. She would have wanted him to return it to Egypt. It belonged to history and her ancestors.

"Granting your enemy mercy and recompensing their sins in their stead is the act of a chivalrous leader," Tima often said of Saladin. But his eye kept going to the photograph of the Mayan amulet of the destroyer god, Nohochacyum. It was said to play a role in the Mayan apocalypse, which had come and gone unless the experts were wrong. A new theory being touted by scientists—some legitimate, some charlatans—was that they'd counted the days wrong, and the apocalypse was still looming on the horizon. None of the sources he'd seen had agreed on the newly recalculated date. But knowing what he knew about forces in the universe, the less he wanted some nutjob to control an amulet that could trigger the end of days. If Riggs had it—along with the ring—maybe Rowan could get it back, too.

LAUREN LISTENED to everything that was said in the meeting, but her mind was a thousand miles away as her fingers toyed with the compass charm on her necklace. While the change in her husband wasn't unwelcomed, it seemed out of place, perhaps motivated by his recent near-death experience.

He hadn't been the same since his captivity in the Middle East. *Who would be?* He'd been beaten, tortured, and seen his friend maimed and murdered. Lauren had tried to create a calm and comfortable home life for him, giving into his every whim. He seemed happy—most of the time.

He was industrious and involved in his children's lives. He attended PTA meetings and helped with bake sales when she was busy. Sometimes, they went together—baked together. It wasn't as miserable as she'd thought it would be, and she looked forward to it now.

She'd had her time home with the kids when they were little, and she was grateful for that. Now, she was industrious and had work that gave her a purpose she'd missed. She was happy to be working again.

She didn't do it for the money. Working for PBS was a labor of love. She made half what she did as the Executive Producer of *The Veritas Codex*, but she was home every night and hadn't had anyone try to kill her in a while. She didn't have to fight off the devil or worry about falling through time. Though they both remained a constant possibility.

In the time she was given, she followed through on her vow to prepare for anything. Her physical fitness was proof of that. She'd lost every ounce of baby fat from having six children. She exercised almost every day, and meals at home were healthy and satisfying. She made space in her diet for the occasional treat, and she was thinner and leaner than she'd ever been, even before children. Her muscles were strong and her figure—according to Rowan—was "stunning."

She remained on guard for signs of Enlil and his minions. Papa Dauphine remained locked up in jail in New Orleans and wouldn't be bothering anyone for an exceptionally long time.

Over the years, she felt like her powers were dissipating. It should have been concerning, but she was content and refused to let it linger in her thoughts—until now. Rowan had been the target of the latest attack on their family before dark forces came for her and her children. He wasn't the strong warrior he'd once been, and she worried for him.

Still, she'd found allies in unexpected places, including Andrew Miller. The FBI agent now knew everything. He'd seen her work her magic, and he'd been right there to help, without question.

The fact that Enlil had been able to snare their strongest magic wielders in what Henry called a "time trap" had been concerning, too. She knew now it had taken everything her father and Michael could do to bring Henry and her mother home. Even the cat had been a victim of the attack. Most days, the Siamese napped in sunbeams by day and stalked the hallways at night, making her security sweeps between the children's rooms before finally joining Kate in her bed just before dawn.

John came home briefly to meet his newest granddaughter after that, but he couldn't stay in her time-place, Lauren knew that. But he'd made a few visits when he could. Her children knew their Grandpa John as well as they knew Grandpa Charles.

John had explained that each of the children had their gifts, but so far, Henry was the only one to stand out. Though she was beginning to suspect Sarah might have some magic. She wasn't sure what the whole thing with Indy the night before had been about, but Lauren had followed her daughter's advice. She used sage smoke to cleanse the house of evil spirits and said prayers of protection over the family. She'd even sent her thoughts to Henry, hoping her magic helped protect their oldest as they sent him out into the world.

"So?" Desmond nudged her. "What do you think?"

"Hm?" She snapped out of her thoughts. "I'm so sorry. Say that again?"

"I said it'd be great if we could do an episode on the Bigfoot Museum near Rifle," the exec said.

"My husband might be interested in that," Lauren said, knowing the PBS station had been keen to take advantage of his celebrity, too. "Do you want us to go look for Bigfoot there while we're at it?"

"Think he'd do it?"

Lauren shrugged. She was over her Bigfoot era. It had consumed a good portion of her career at the Exploration Channel. But she knew the truth now. She didn't need to go look for Bigfoot. She knew where to find him—or more properly *when*. "I could ask," she said. "But don't hold your breath."

6

Rowan sat at the kitchen counter with his laptop while Sarah sat beside him, nibbling on apple slices and pretzels. It was her favorite after-school snack. The older kids didn't get out until 3:00 and 3:30. They'd ride the bus if there were no after-school activities. Otherwise, John Carter might pick them up or he'd get a phone call. If that call hadn't come, he still had plenty of time before they'd walk down and meet the other kids at the bus stop.

"What's that?" Sarah asked, pointing at the computer screen.

"It's the *Axe of K'awiil,*" he said, absentmindedly. All his attention was on the Wikipedia article. He was the Mayan god of creation, of thunder and lightning. The statue showed him with a torch—or maybe it was a cigar—coming out of his forehead. *Who could be sure?* Rowan knew that signified the spark of life.

"Did Thor let him borrow his hammer?"

"That's an axe," Rowan corrected her. Then paused, looking down at her. She was the perfect likeness to her mother, though sober and not usually so chatty, but she was a Daddy's girl, and when it was just the two of them, she opened up more than when her older siblings were home. "How do you know about Thor's hammer?"

"John Carter told me about *meow-meow*," she said, popping a pretzel in her mouth.

Rowan puzzled for a moment as he tried to make sense of what she was saying. "Oh, you mean *Mjǫllnir*." He pronounced it properly for her.

"*Meow-meow*," she said. "Shadow needs a hammer, too."

"What's that cat gonna do with a hammer?"

"What's that dude gonna do with that axe?"

"He's a creator god," Rowan said. "He holds it up into the sky to call down lightning and uses the power to create new life."

"Shadow is a protector goddess. She needs a hammer to keep the monsters away."

Rowan looked at her for a few moments. She had the most vivid imagination of any child he'd ever known. "She's *just* a cat, honey."

"Uh, huh," Sarah scoffed. "And Indy's *just* a dog." She took her last apple slice in her small fist and climbed down, running to the back door where Indy stood waiting for her. She turned and gave her father a dark glare before she slid open the door, stepped out, and then slid the door shut, slamming it.

Rowan watched her hug the dog. She gave him the slice of apple, which he inhaled before the two disappeared into the stand of trees along the right side of the large backyard. Rowan turned back to his work, knowing Indy would keep an eye on her.

She was right. Indy wasn't *just* a dog. He was a good dog. The best dog. Rowan waited a long time to get one, and to find one already named *Indy* was nothing short of a miracle. He never barked, unless there was some cause for concern, and Rowan was convinced if anyone tried to harm Sarah, Indy would tear them to shreds. The two were inseparable.

Rowan jumped when a paw came to rest on his pant leg and claws pierced his flesh. He glanced down at the stretching Siamese who yawned as she flexed her paws and let go. "It's not dinner time for you, cat," he said, nudging her away with his foot. "Go . . . catch a mouse or something."

An internet search also turned up an entry on Kukulkan, which was probably the most well-known Mayan deity. Also known as Quetzalcoatl in Aztec lore, Kukulkan was a creator god. Rowan had stood at the top of the Temple of Kukulkan at Chichén Itzá and watched the sunrise on December 21, 2012—the day the world was supposed to end. But it didn't.

The Maya had many gods, and more than one was credited with creation—and destruction. Alom, Bitol, Cococh, Hunahpu-Gutch—one of thirteen gods who helped create humanity—the list went on.

Rowan paused at Nohochacyum. He was a creator *and* destroyer deity, the brother of the god Kisin, and the mortal enemy of the world serpent Hapikern. Myths said Nohochacyum would destroy Hapikern as well as all life on Earth.

"*Meow-meow,*" a tiny but deep voice drew him from his thoughts. He glanced down. Shadow sat with one of her toy mousies in her mouth. She dropped it and repeated her *mew* a bit more clearly.

Rowan shook his head and got up from the stool. Shadow followed him into the kitchen, sitting like the goddess Bastet herself, waiting for him to get her a treat. If Lauren didn't love that cat, he might have run it off by now. It was a bossy little thing. When he wanted to snuggle with Lauren, he often found the cat between them in the bed, purring against her mistress's chest, and blocking him from any affection that might be found from his wife.

"Happy now?" He tossed the treat in front of her. She snatched it up and disappeared upstairs.

Rowan returned to his work. In Mayan mythology, Nohochacyum was the god of death and ruler of Xibalba.

Rowan knew about Xibalba. It was as wicked as Dante's inferno. Often depicted as a dark and dangerous realm inhabited by malevolent gods and spirits, it was central to the mythological narrative of the *Popol Vuh*, the sacred text of the *Ki'ché Maya*. He got up and went over to the bookcase in the living room, scanning through Lauren's tomes of ancient texts. One included the complete *Popol Vuh*, translated into English.

This ancient text spoke of the Twelve Lords of Death. There was Hun-Kame—also known as One-Death, and Yukaub-Kame—Seven-Death. The remaining ten Lords of Death worked in pairs and were more like demons—Scab Stripper and Blood Gatherer who sickened people's blood. The Demon of Pus and Skull Scepter turned bodies into skeletons. The Demon of Filth and Demon of Woe hid in the dirty corners of people's homes to stab them to death. That wouldn't happen in Lauren's home. She insisted on keeping things tidy, perhaps for that very reason. The Wing and Pack-strap caused people to die coughing up blood.

It was in Xibalba—the underground Court of the Twelve Mayan Lords of Death, also known as the Place of Fear—that the Death Lords would entertain themselves by humiliating people before sending them off to one of Xibalba's deadly tests. Much like Dante's Inferno, it was an allegory that represented the journey of the soul toward the gods.

But Xibalba offered no opportunity for redemption from sins. The Lords of Xibalba were tricksters who relished in the torment of the sinful soul. There were many places and means of torture in Xibalba, and, even after death, the Lords delighted in mutilating the remains of their victims. The book had illustrations of the demons and Mayan glyphs representing the underworld. Skulls and unreal representations of monsters were mixed with photographs of underground caverns and cenotes in the Yucatan including one specifically named Xibalba.

Rowan shivered and shut the laptop. He'd had enough

dark lore for one day. He glanced at his watch. It was almost 3:45. No phone call had come, which meant the kids would be home on the bus today. He stepped out to the back porch. "Sarah, it's time to go meet your brothers and sister," he called.

Indy came bounding to the door, wiggling and swishing his fluffy tail.

"Can Indy come too?" she asked appearing from the garden.

"Sure," Rowan said. "I'll grab his leash."

Lauren stepped into the lobby of the studio to meet a surprise visitor. It had been a long time since she'd had a gold badge flashed in her face. "Detective Bronowski, Denver P.D.," he said. "Is there somewhere we can talk?"

The tone he used suggested he wasn't asking. "Sure," Lauren said. "Let's go to my office." She glanced at her watch.

"I'm not interrupting anything, am I?" His question came off as one of courtesy, but Lauren suspected he didn't care. He had a job to do, though how it involved her wasn't immediately evident.

"No," Lauren said. "Not today." She led him down the hallway to the elevator. "Does this have something to do with what happened to my husband?" The elevator doors opened, and they stepped inside. Alone, she hoped he'd give her a clue about why he was here.

"It does, Dr. Pierce," he admitted. He had a manilla envelope tucked under his arm. "I've got something I need you to look at. Your expertise may come in handy."

"My expertise?" she asked as the elevator stopped on the third floor. "As a travel show host? Do you need recommendations for a weekend getaway?"

He chuckled as she led him into her office and offered a

seat. He pushed the envelope towards her. She sat down across from him. "I understand ancient languages are your true gift," he said.

That piqued Lauren's curiosity. She reached for the envelope and opened it cautiously. Inside, a photo appeared and she recognized it immediately as an autopsy photo. She picked up the photograph—an 8x10 glossy—and gazed at it for a long moment. An ashy hand with scraped knuckles took up most of the frame.

"Do you recognize that mark?" the detective asked.

Lauren did. The mark seemed to be burned into the flesh, like a brand. The edges were still red and raw, so it couldn't be that old. Forensics wasn't her specialty, but over the years she'd learned to tell a few things about a wound.

The mark consisted of two crossed lines with crescent moons in three of the four quadrants created by the lines and a golden eagle in the fourth. "It's a sigil—more or less," Lauren said. "Middle Eastern. Ayyubid Dynasty, I think."

"A sigil?"

"It's a type of symbol used in ancient magic."

"Magic?" The Detective's tone told her he was not a believer.

"A symbolic representation of energy, word, or intention. According to lore, when it is activated it manifests energy into the world." Sigils weren't a language, per se, and this one was a combination of several symbols.

"Do you know what it means?"

"Unfortunately, I'm not an expert in sigils," she admitted. "But these symbols individually can represent several things. The *crescent* and the heraldic *eagle* are often seen as symbols from the Crusades."

"The Crusades? Like The ancient Crusades? Knights Templar crusades?"

"Well, the eagle would have been found on Saladin's coat of arms, rather than the Templars, but yes," Lauren said, a sense of concern building in her core as she thought about her encounter with Crusaders some years before. "I wish I could be more help."

"Is there someone you could refer me to, Dr. Pierce?"

"I'm afraid the one person I could recommend is dead," she said. Tima might have known what the symbol meant, especially if it had anything to do with the Crusades. In addition to Egyptian history, she had been an expert in the history of the Crusades in the Middle East. Lauren had attended several of her lectures on the subject as a guest, but that had been a long time ago. She'd had four children since then.

"Do you know of any customs that might result in my victim being scarred with that kind of symbol?"

"Have you seen what kids are doing to their bodies these days? My older daughter wants her nose pierced. She's not even a teenager yet."

"My son has tattoos all over his body, not to mention these big giant holes in his earlobes," the detective admitted. "I guess this is just another one of these fads."

He stood and reached for the picture. "I suppose . . ." Lauren started, but hesitated, putting her hand over his. "I could do some research. Maybe I can find something or someone who might be able to identify the sigil, and what it means."

The detective withdrew his hand. "This is a confidential document, Dr. Pierce. I can't let you keep it."

"I can sketch the symbol if you'll give me a moment," she said. "I don't need to keep the photo."

"I'll allow that," he said. "But this is a confidential matter."

"Of course," Lauren said. "Mum's the word." Lauren reached into her desk and took out a pad of paper and a pencil. "Do you have a motive yet for why this man attacked my husband?" she asked, as she drew the sigil, carefully recreating each detail, including the orientation of the mark on the man's hand.

"So far, no," he said. "It would appear he had a mental episode. I can't provide details. You understand."

"I'm accustomed to dealing with a soldier with PTSD," Lauren said. "My husband came home from the Middle East a changed man. It's not easy."

The detective seemed intrigued by that statement. "How so?"

Lauren spoke in generalities. "Episodes can strike at the most unexpected times. PTSD affects everyone differently, but the slightest memory or even smell might trigger an episode. Sometimes its recurrent intrusive memories, traumatic nightmares, or flashbacks. It can create distorted beliefs about oneself in the world, manifest as persistent shame or guilt. Sometimes a person with PTSD is just numb—they can't sleep, they get irritable, act recklessly, or even demonstrate hypervigilance."

Rowan had suffered all of these symptoms at one time or another. Lately, he was having a hard time concentrating. She'd tried to keep the list of honey-dos on the fridge full, but after finishing all the renovations and repairs—everything including the kitchen sink—there was nothing left on her list. Lauren couldn't think of anything to add.

Lauren laid her pencil down and pushed the photo to the detective. He studied her sketch, nodding approval. He took a business card from his badge case and handed it to her. "If you find anything, you can call or email. Whatever works best."

"I'll see what I can find," Lauren stood and stepped around from her desk. "If there's anything else I can help with, please let me know."

"Thanks, Dr. Pierce," he said, taking one of her cards from the holder on her desk. "I'll keep that in mind."

7

Lauren came home to find Rowan in the kitchen. John Carter was setting the table, and the twins were at the coffee table, doing homework. She could see Sarah out in the yard running around chasing Indy.

"Where's Jamie?" she asked, hanging her purse on the hook by the door.

"Over at Robbie's house," Rowan said over his shoulder. "He'll be home by seven, he said."

"He's going to miss a good dinner. Something smells delicious," Lauren said as she came over to the counter. "Taco night?"

"Sarah's choice," John Carter said.

"Can I pour you some wine, or would you rather have a margarita?" Rowan asked, wiping his hands on a towel.

"Is that an option?"

"Certainly is," he said, nodding to the pitcher of limeade he'd prepared as a mixer.

"I guess I better go change."

"Supper in five minutes," Rowan called to the kids in the living room. "Could you go call Sarah in?" he asked John Carter.

Lauren came back in a few moments later in a pair of yoga pants and a T-shirt, her hair pulled up in a haphazard knot. It wasn't the sexiest thing she could have worn to the table, but it was the most comfortable, and besides, the kids were home.

She was already thinking about the hot bubble bath and back rub she'd promised Rowan, though. Dinner and an evening with the children were prerequisites before any *extracurricular activities*. She didn't mind that though. She got to hear about everyone's day and enjoy a nice meal. Rowan was a good cook, and he'd taken over the chore with enthusiasm on days she worked.

Jamie came in just as they were clearing the table. He had the honor of finishing anything that was left over. While Lauren and Rowan worked together on dishes and cleaning up the kitchen, he sat at the counter and regaled them with news of his day. Lauren considered mentioning her encounter with the detective to her husband. But Rowan seemed to be doing well, and she debated whether he was strong enough to have that conversation or if it'd put him in a tailspin.

She noticed he hadn't had a margarita and was proud of him for it. He'd given up his nightly scotch and had been a teetotaler since she observed that it was becoming a habit. His psychologist had given him orders not to drink alcohol, too. She didn't want him self-medicating.

The evening passed slowly, and Lauren didn't mind. She curled up next to Rowan on the sofa with a book in hand, while he had the remote control for the television in his. An hour later, Lauren announced it was time for everyone to get ready for bed. Amidst general moans and groans they surrendered to the school night routine, heading upstairs to brush their teeth and put on their pajamas. Kate, however, hesitated.

"Mom, I'm not a little kid anymore. Can't I stay up just a little later?"

Kate and Sam were the same age, but that didn't stop her

from making the request no one else dared make, though she waited until her brother left the room. Even John Carter, who was the oldest since Henry had gone off to college, went to bed when instructed. Lauren knew he'd be up reading for several hours, but that wasn't an issue. He still got himself up in the morning and helped her get everyone else ready for school, so she allowed it. Kate, on the other hand, was the last to drag herself out of bed and took the longest to get ready. It was a constant battle to get her to school on time.

Rowan turned off the television. "Kate, you know the rules. On school nights, you're expected to get ready and go to bed at 8:30, just like everyone else. You can listen to music or read until 10:00, but bedtime is a mandatory requirement."

"But I'm not a baby," she protested. "Why can't I watch television with you guys?"

"Because we're not staying up watching television either," Lauren said. "Your dad and I both work long hours, and we need some downtime before we can sleep."

"I'll be quiet," she said. "Please?"

"I'm sorry, Kate, but the rules are the rules." Lauren saved the lecture on her morning routine for another day. She was too tired to fight, and she didn't have to justify her reasons.

Kate scowled, standing with her hands in fists. "Rules are stupid."

"Good night, Kate," Rowan said, indicating the conversation was over.

She muttered under her breath as she stormed to her room and disappeared behind the door she slammed. Lauren winced, knowing that slamming doors was one of Rowan's pet peeves.

"That girl," he sighed, pulling Lauren into his arms. "She's testing us."

"Well, she just got an F in my books. "

Rowan shook his head, reaching for Lauren's empty glass. He got up and carried it to the kitchen.

Lauren rose and followed him. "Did you ever test your parents when you were her age?"

"You've met my father, right?"

"The Colonel has never been anything but kind to me," Lauren said. "Was he a disciplinarian?"

"He didn't have to be," Rowan said. "If I got sideways with him, it was a five-mile run at 0500 followed by yard work, housework, and any other work he could find. He even took me down to the base in Colorado Springs at 0400 and made me do KP duty in the mess hall once."

"Ouch." Lauren winced, snuggling into him. "What'd you do to deserve that?"

"I talked back to my mother."

"*Doh*." Lauren imitated Homer Simpson, then laughed. "Doesn't sound like a good idea."

"It wasn't," Rowan said. "I peeled potatoes for over four hours." He held up his hand. "See this scar?" He indicated the pointer finger of his left hand. The scar was faint but visible. "The knife I was using got away from me, and I cut out a chunk of skin."

"You never told me that story." Lauren sighed, taking his finger and kissing it. "How's your hand today? Is the typing still painful?"

"It's a little sore, but not bad. I did more research than writing, truth be told." He held it out for her to inspect. The knuckle of his mangled finger was swollen, and the finger didn't bend like it should. "You know what would help?"

"A nice hot bath?"

"Uh, huh." He buried his face in her hair, kissing her neck. "Need another margarita?"

"That last one just wore off," she said. "But I think I'm good. I'll go draw your bath, Mr. Pierce."

"I'll check on the children and join you in a moment."

Lauren was neck-deep in bubbles when Rowan came in. He said nothing as he stripped, still moving with the cadence of a man in pain. A groan escaped his throat as he slid in behind her. She scooted forward to give him space, then leaned back as his arms enveloped her.

"Did you miss me?" He nuzzled her ear, sending shivers along her flesh.

"You were gone five minutes," she said, enjoying where his hands were.

"Well, that's too long," he said, "after you were gone all day too."

There was a long hesitation before she sat up and turned around. The tub was spacious and slick, and it allowed her to face him. "So, I had an interesting visitor today . . ." they said in unison, then both paused, and Lauren wondered if the detective had been to the house before he came to see her.

"You go first," he insisted.

"No," she said. "You first."

He didn't argue. "Ever heard of a woman named Vega Sanchez?"

"Should I have?"

"She's the new CEO of the Exploration Channel."

Lauren was gob smacked. She sat up, sloshing water and bubbles over the edge of the tub. She couldn't form a logical thought in her head. She didn't know what locked her up. *Was it the fact that the Exploration Channel had a new CEO or that she hadn't heard about it? Or the fact that the woman had the nerve to show up in Denver?*

She sputtered for words, struggling to form a cognitive thought and extrapolate it into speech. "Was . . . how . . . why?"

"Why do you think?"

"Maybe we should start with what happened to Jacob?"

"Maybe you should come back over here and let me hold

you while I tell you about it." He opened his arms, and she couldn't resist.

After Rowan's bombshell, Lauren didn't want to talk about her visitor anymore. She found a way to distract him and make him forget about everything else.

AFTER MAKING BREAKFAST, seeing Lauren off to work, and getting the kids to school, Rowan headed to the den to ride the Peloton before his therapy appointment. The workout was cathartic. Sweating to the beat and following the instructor's commands, his mind wandered.

He hadn't slept well. His lack of rest stemmed from what he *hadn't* told Lauren—the missing artifacts and their link to the Marine. The previous night, he'd woken up just after 2:00 and come downstairs, trying to access records from their discovery in the Yucatán years ago.

Lauren oversaw cataloging the objects from the cenote where the new Mayan calendar was found, but strangely, none of the records were on her computer or any of the flash drives in her desk. He hadn't found them yet, but surely she had them somewhere.

At some point, he'd have to bring it up with her, but for now, he wasn't ready. He feared she might see his growing obsession with Lance Corporal Benjamin Riggs—an obsession he knew was consuming him.

He did bring it up with Dr. McLeish at his therapy appointment. She listened with concern as he spoke about his intrusive thoughts. When she spoke, her advice was direct. "It's noble that you recognize your obsession but letting yourself fall down the rabbit hole troubles me."

"But what harm can it do? I feel responsible for some of those artifacts. Lauren and I discovered them. They wouldn't have ended up in that museum in Khartoum if we hadn't found them first."

Rowan sat across the coffee table from his therapist, each holding a cup of coffee. A basket of snacks sat on the coffee table. She offered him Oreos, but he declined. The silence stretched between them as Rowan took time to decompress, appreciating the hour with no rush.

This was a customary process, and it gave time for Rowan to study his mental health provider in detail. Dr. McLeish always dressed in bright colors—today her turtleneck was a deep plum with a floral scarf of purple, plum, and hot pink. Her mauve lipstick covered more of her coffee cup than her mouth. "So, how's the shoulder? Feeling better?"

Rowan gave her the standard answer. "It's fine." It was chit-chat, as far as he was concerned. Physically he was better. His back wasn't so sore, but his shoulder still twinged when he picked up something heavy or slept too hard on that side. Sleeping in the recliner provided some relief but made Lauren worry. If he slipped out after she went to sleep, he tried to be back in bed before she woke up. If he met her coming down to get on the Peloton for her early morning workout, he'd tell her he hadn't been up that long, but he suspected she knew it wasn't true.

The conversation eventually circled back to the Marine and the missing artifacts. Dr. McLeish considered him a long moment. He could see her tongue run across the bridge of her teeth beneath the lipstick-stained upper lip. She sniffed and leaned forward. "Give yourself a time limit. If you simply must look into it, give it a week. No more, no less. And tell Lauren. She needs to know that you're doing this under medical advice . . . and caution. When that time runs out, you're done. Hard stop. You will let it go. You must also stop if you find the obsession becoming so intense you're not sleeping, or it's becoming dangerous. Can you do that?"

That was a good question. Rowan swallowed hard and smiled. Then, he lied. "Absolutely."

8

By Friday, his obsession had gotten the better of him. The Public Library in Englewood had a decent collection of reference books on archaeology, but not as good as the library at Colorado State University in Fort Collins. As a graduate, he had access to the reference library.

He'd earned his bachelor's degree in fire and emergency services with an emphasis on emergency medicine. The military had already given him field training and experience as a medic, and within a week of graduating, he landed a job in Estes Park working for the ambulance service there. It was a scrub job if truth be told, but it paid the bills and kept him out of trouble.

He stood at the computer searching through the library's directory. Little did he know before making the drive to Fort Collins, that he could have done this from home. Still, if he found anything, he'd want to get the original articles and the best way to do that was in person.

It was surprising the things one could find in libraries. Cicero said if you had a garden and a library, you had everything you needed. Lauren had a beautiful garden, and here he was breathing in the perfume of knowledge and printer's ink. *Yes, he had everything.*

It didn't take long before the computer spit back a list of articles that were published in the Journal of Mesoamerican Mythology and Archaeology by none other than Professor Octavia Vanderhorst of the University of Colorado. *Why had he never heard of her before?*

"Can I help you find anything?" the librarian asked politely in passing.

"Uhm, yeah," he had a flash of inspiration. "Do you know if Dr. Octavia Vanderhorst still works here at the college? I'd like to pick her brain about some of her articles."

"I don't know, but I'd be happy to find out," she offered.

"In the meantime, can you direct me to the Journal of Mesoamerican Mythology and Archaeology?"

She glanced at the computer screen a moment then pointed up. "Second floor," she said. "Jena should be able to help you. She's at the reference desk."

"Thank you," Rowan said.

"I'll check on the professor and bring you any information I can find."

"Outstanding."

THREE JOURNALS IN, Rowan stopped and asked for some paper and a pen so he could jot down some notes. The professor's work on the Maya was brilliant. A quick Google search on his phone told him she was the college's preeminent expert on Mayan mythology. When the librarian found him, he had scribbled three full pages of notes, questions, and general information. He'd also sketched out an image of what he thought might be the glyph that represented the Mayan god of destruction.

"Mr. Pierce, Dr. Vanderhorst does still work here at the

college. I contacted her office and she's speaking at a conference in Estes Park today. Her secretary said her lecture is over at three, and she'd have time to talk with you if you'd like to give her a call." The librarian presented a piece of paper with a phone number and the doctor's name on it.

Rowan glanced at the slip as he considered the offer a moment. "Would it be rude of me to go see her in person?" He glanced at his watch. It was just after noon, and he had plenty of time to finish here and make the drive. It was a beautiful fall day, and the drive might do him some good.

"I wouldn't think so," she said. "Her meeting is at the Stanley, in their conference center."

"Thanks," Rowan said, tucking the slip of paper in his shirt pocket. She smiled and returned to her work, pausing to stop at the reference desk. Jena had indeed been helpful, and Rowan noticed her glancing over at him, trying to be inconspicuous. Then it hit him. He hadn't introduced himself to the librarian. He'd been recognized.

He smiled to himself as he picked up the next journal and thumbed through it, skimming the headlines. It fascinated him that Lauren could go out in public and rarely be recognized. He couldn't even go to the library without getting noticed. It wasn't like Lauren was unapproachable. She was polite to everyone—well, almost everyone. She'd gotten crosswise with several people who got in the way of her work. That was the kiss of death as far as Lauren was concerned. He paused to think about what Lauren would think of all this. He'd have to tell her eventually. Sooner was better for his backside. She'd be angry if he let this go on too long. Still, he wasn't ready to bring her in on it. But he was ready for some lunch.

He left with a list of reading materials and a login for the college's website. He could read them from home when he couldn't sleep, or while the kids were at school and Lauren was at work. The drive from Fort Collins was a short one, and the onion rings at the Burger Barn were still just as good as he remembered. He hadn't splurged on a giant cheeseburger, onion rings, and chocolate shake in an exceptionally long time, and when he pulled up in front of the Stanley, he dug through his glovebox for a mint or a pack of gum.

The event was being held in the Stanley Museum & Conference Center, a building separated from the main hotel. It had the same aesthetic as the grand manse where Steven King was inspired to write *The Shining*, and where Rowan had rescued Lauren from the base of the stairs where she'd fallen so many years ago.

The Conference Center had that new carpet smell as he stepped into the lobby where a crowd gathered around a buffet table or stood at pub tables chatting over glasses of iced tea and plates of light snacks. He scanned the room to find the registration desk and went over to it.

"Good afternoon, may I help you?" the young man behind the table asked.

"Hi, I'm looking for Dr. Octavia Vanderhorst," he said.

Before the young man—perhaps a student at the college— could answer, he heard a voice behind him. "I'm Dr. Vanderhorst." He turned and found a woman in a navy-blue suit with a white blouse. Her hair was more salt than pepper but cropped into a short bob that fell just below her strong chin. Her eyebrows were stunningly sculpted and framed an arch over her chocolate-brown eyes. She had a wide smile, but teeth that had been stained by years of coffee and—perhaps —red wine. "You must be Rowan Pierce. My office said you came by the college today. Are you doing your television series again? I must confess, I'm a huge fan." She had a heavy accent that was hard to wrap his brain around.

"No," he smiled, turning on the charm. "I'm actually . . . I'm doing some research for a book. I found your name in some of the scientific journals and thought you might have some insight."

"Which ones? When your research covers as many ancient cultures as mine, you tend to be published widely."

"This article was specifically on the Maya," Rowan said.

"I'm fascinated." She took his arm and led him from the crowd to an area where it wasn't quite so loud. "Do tell me about this book you're writing, and how I can help you."

"Well, I haven't figured out where to start, but I found out that one of the artifacts we discovered in Mexico has been stolen and it got my mind all awhirl. I thought I might tie that into the plot of my book." He decided to keep details to himself, for the time being. He didn't know this woman, and she didn't know him. He wasn't sure if she could help, or if she could be trusted with the truth. The idea had been a cover, concocted at the moment, but as he spoke it for the first time, he started to think it might be a viable plot line.

"The Amulet of Nohochacyum?"

"You've heard of it?" Rowan shouldn't have been surprised, but he was.

"I've written tomes on it," she said, beaming. "Thank you for finding it, by the way."

"Well, I guess I'm going to have to find it again, seeing as how it was stolen."

"Yes, from the Museum of History in Khartoum. I heard about that. What do you know of the myth behind it, Mr. Pierce?"

"Rowan, please." He shrugged. He didn't know much more about it than he'd found on the internet.

She crossed her arms and set her feet hip-width apart, much in the fashion Tima did when she was about to start a lengthy lecture. His heart turned to stone in his chest at the thought of his late professor. "It was called *Tz'i'ik K'wil*—the Amulet of the Last Breath," she began.

He shivered in the conference center lobby, not sure if it was the hard-working air conditioner or her words that chilled him. He found the more he listened to her, the easier it became to understand her thick Puerto Rican accent.

"In the ancient, shadowed halls of *Xibalba*, Nohochacyum forged a delicate yet ominous pendant—made from obsidian and inlaid with a blood-red jade. The stone was rumored to be imbued with the souls of the dead, forever bound by the Dark Lord's power."

"Whoa." Rowan gasped. The hairs on the back of his neck stood on end.

"Legend foretold that one day, the amulet would be taken from *Xibalba* by a chosen one—a mortal—a soul so daring or cursed that they would invoke the powers of death to reshape the world. If wielded by a mortal, the amulet would bring forth the end of days."

"The apocalypse?" Rowan asked in disbelief as he stood back shaking his head. "I think we've already proven that the Mayan apocalypse was just a misinterpretation of the existing archeology. Right?"

"We are all greatly relieved that 2012 has come and gone," she said. "And we're still here."

"Yes. Thank God."

"The Maya were believers in a cyclic universe, Rowan. Kingdoms rise and fall. The world has been remade more times than we know and will continue to evolve, crumble, and be reborn. We are all the very embodiment of the phoenix. This too . . . shall pass."

Rowan's phone buzzed in his pocket, but he ignored it, wanting to hear more. "Are you the chosen one, Rowan?" she asked.

"Me?"

"You found it," she pointed out. "The amulet, that is."

Rowan considered this for a moment. He was the Protector not the Shatterer. If anything, he was the Shattered.

No. It had to be Lauren. Dammit. Now he had to tell her.

"No." He shook his head, ignoring the call, even though

he wanted to look and see who was calling. If Lorraine York called and he missed it, he'd regret it, he was sure. "I think my wife gets credit for that one," he said but realized he'd been the one to take her to the cenote where the new calendar had been found. There were several other cenotes attached to that one, and treasures had come from all of them. Still, neither of them might have laid hands on that particular item.

"Perhaps your protagonist would like to play the role of *X'k'ib*—the chosen one—the Shatterer, who wields the Amulet of Nohochacyum."

"I hadn't thought of that," Rowan said, considering it.

"If you ask me, the Near East mythos is far more interesting. You know about Nergal, the Sumerian God of Death?"

She had Rowan's complete attention. "You know Sumerian mythos, too?"

"I may be known for my work on the Maya, but it's because of my theories that the great ancient cultures all had singular connections."

"Which ones?"

"Cultures from Mesoamerica, the Middle East, and the Orient, primarily." She took a sip of her drink and swallowed. "Have you noticed the similarities between the ziggurats of Babylon, Angkor Wat, and Chichén Itzá?"

"I've seen all of them," he said, trying not to let memories from Kish come rushing over him. That was where Tima died, and he didn't need to think about that right now. Instead, he thought of the ancient temple in Cambodia. He and Lauren had made memories there, and they were easier to think about at the moment.

"You have? Then you know about the connection?" Her eyes lifted toward the chandelier.

Rowan played coy, lowering his chin and arching his eyebrow. "We're not talking about the light fixtures, are we?"

"I mean, they're nice, but think higher."

"Yeah," Rowan said, grinning. "I know the connection,

but I didn't know you subscribed to the ancient astronaut theory."

"I prefer the term Paleocontact. It's less *woo-woo*, don't you think?" Rowan nodded his agreement. "I studied under Von Däniken when I was a young scholar."

His phone buzzed again. This was the third time, and he knew he needed to answer it. He pulled his phone out and realized what time it was, and that it was Lauren calling.

"I'm sorry, Dr. Vanderhorst. It's my wife."

"Of course. Give my regards to Dr. Pierce." She rose when he did.

"You know my wife?"

"Just by reputation," she said. She reached into her suit jacket and handed him a business card. "I'd love to meet her," she said. "I'll be here all weekend if you want to sit down over a drink and discuss paleocontact. Maybe we can flesh out some possible plotlines for your book. I'm happy to consult if I can be of any assistance."

"Thank you so much."

"You have my number. Call me."

Rowan thanked her and watched her walk over to her colleagues. He glanced down at his phone. He'd missed the call completely. He hit the button to redial and put the phone to his ear.

"Where are you?" she asked without preamble.

"I made a run up to Fort Collins to do some research at the college library." It wasn't a lie. He just didn't happen to be in Fort Collins at the moment.

"The school called when you didn't pick Sarah up."

"Oh jeez," he said, glancing at his watch. "I lost track of the time."

"It's okay," Lauren said. "I needed an excuse to take off early. The Colorado Apple Growers Association didn't mind switching to a virtual meeting. I just got done with them. Are you okay?"

"Fine," he said. "I got an idea for a story, and I needed to do some research. Well, I guess since I'm this close, I'll run over to Estes and get a cheeseburger."

"I'm making dinner. It seems like a good night for oxtail pho, and I haven't used the Instant Pot for a while," Lauren said. He could smell the spices just thinking about her pho. She'd learned to make it in Vietnam. In his opinion, hers was better than anything he had in Hanoi. "Will you be home in time?"

"Forget the cheeseburger. I'm on my way home," Rowan said, gazing out the window at the hotel. He hadn't been in here in a while, and he debated checking it out. He hadn't seen the new museum either. Maybe it was worth a few moments of his day. "Wait. There's an Apple Growers Association? What'd they want?"

"We're doing a story on the Apple Festival," she said. "I think I might have mentioned it."

"When is that?"

"In two weeks, over near Grand Mesa. Wanna go?"

"Maybe." He shrugged. "What's in it for me?"

"Concerts, apples . . . apple fritters . . . apple cider . . ."

"Hard cider?"

"Most likely," she said.

"I'll think about it. I'm going to do a little more research here if you have everything under control there."

"Finish what you started," she said, and he could hear the smile in her voice. "I got this."

"I'm sorry I dropped the ball," he said.

"I'm not the one you need to apologize to," she said. "Your daughter isn't very happy with you right now."

"I'll make it up to her," he said. "And you."

THE MUSEUM WAS a walk through the horror movies of his youth, featuring *The Shining*. Rowan knew the hotel had been the inspiration for Stephen King's novel, which was adapted into the movie. He didn't know how many other stories and movies had been inspired by the hotel or filmed at the hotel.

Estes Park, Colorado was the perfect place for a movie, Rowan decided. Maybe—if he ever did a book—part of it might be set there. He realized it was too soon to be thinking about a movie. Blank pages made for poor film credits.

"Ah, Mr. Pierce, we meet again." The now familiar voice made him stop as he started for the hotel. "We're about to go to the bar for a drink. Care to join us?" Dr. Octavia Vanderhorst led the charge of her cohorts toward the hotel.

"I wouldn't want to crash the party," he said sheepishly.

"But, Rowan, these are your colleagues," she said. "This is the annual meeting of the Colorado Archeological Society. I'm surprised you're not a member."

"I didn't realize there was such a thing," he said, startled when she hooked her arm in his. "Come join us. I'll introduce you to everyone."

A moment of truth arose a few moments later after he'd met her circle of friends, when the bartender came over to take his order. He was grateful that the attention had shifted elsewhere when the bartender asked if he wanted something to drink. "Seltzer and lime," he said.

The bartender gave him a nod. "Designated Driver, coming right up," he said in a low tone, with a wink and a smile.

"And make it a double." Rowan raised his tone. *This guy was going to get a generous tip.*

Rowan's eye moved past the bar as the barkeep moved on to the rest of the party. A large photograph along with a wreath on a tripod dominated the lobby by the fireplace. Something about it beckoned him. His curiosity always got the better of him, and this was no different.

"Excuse me," he said to Dr. Vanderhorst. Rowan made his way to the lobby and hesitated when he realized why he'd been drawn to the photograph.

Lance Corporal Benjamin Riggs—dressed in a well-tailored suit—smiled brightly at him. His attire was indicative of the management staff at the hotel. This was not the same panicked man who'd come at him with a gun less than a week ago. This man was strong, vibrant, and full of life. *How could he have changed so fast?*

"Excuse me, did you know our Benji?" a voice behind him asked. Rowan turned and the man looked up at him, taking a step back. "Oh. Mr. Pierce?" The words came out as a gasp, and Rowan realized he'd been recognized.

Rowan softened his expression and stuck out his hand. "Rowan Pierce," he said, confirming his identity.

"Did Dani call you?"

"Dani?" he asked. "No. No one called me. Why would someone call me?"

"Maybe we should sit down," the man said, gesturing to one of the nearby sofas.

"I'm here with friends," he said, glancing to the bar, debating what to do.

"My name is Jim King. I'm Executive Manager here. Benji worked for me." He paused and seemed to know what Rowan was thinking. Rowan took a seat. "No relation to the author, by the way."

"So, Lance Corporal Riggs worked here?"

"He was just Benji to us," Jim said. "I still can't believe what the police said he did. I'm so sorry for you. We're still just trying to wrap our minds around it all."

"I can assure you, it's all true. I'm trying to wrap my brain around it too."

The man blanched, his ruddy cheeks flaming at the same moment. "That wasn't the Benji Riggs we knew. He was helpful and he was kind."

"And you hired him?"

"He was a soldier down on his luck." Jim sat back, folding his hands in his lap. "I hired him as a bellman about a year ago. He was open about what happened to him in the military. My son came back from Sudan about the same time. Well, Billy wasn't much better off." Mr. King paused. "I couldn't turn him away. I thought we were lucky. He was such a hard worker."

"Do all bellmen wear suits as nice as yours?"

"He didn't stay a bellman long," Jim said. "He was promoted to desk clerk and just a few weeks ago, he made it to Reservation Manager. He excelled at everything."

Rowan shook his head. "What happened?"

"I'm still not sure," Jim said. "Not at all. He was reliable and friendly, and the guests loved him. The staff too. He started talking about you and your show after he saw your wife on television. He said he needed a day off because he was going to meet you. He had something he wanted to talk to you about, but he wouldn't tell me. He said it had something to do with his time in the military—and yours."

Rowan sat, staring at his boot, trying to reconcile his curiosity about the Marine against the anger and fear he'd faced in those harrowing moments. He never expected to find the bright young man in the picture based on what he knew of him. "When you asked if Dani had called me, what were you talking about?"

"After the incident, we cleaned out his locker . . . there was a box with your name written on it. There was also a note."

"A note? For me?"

"Yes," he said. "Benji was a big fan of your show. He always talked about hunting Bigfoot and aliens, too."

"Interesting," Rowan said. "No, I didn't hear from anyone. I just happened to be here to meet with a colleague." He glanced back at the bar as Octavia waved at him, indicating drinks had been served.

"Stop by the front desk. Dani will have it ready for you," Jim said. He stood and straightened his jacket. "I'm sorry we had to meet under these circumstances. Please don't think poorly of Benji. That wasn't the man we all knew and loved."

Rowan nodded and glanced at the picture again. "I won't be long," he said. "Thank you."

AFTER LEARNING about the Marine's connection to the hotel, he no longer felt like being sociable. He wanted to go home. Still, his curiosity got the better of him. He excused himself from the cocktail party and went to pay his tab.

"Mr. Pierce, your money is no good here," the bartender said. Rowan was taken aback but not surprised. He pulled out a five-dollar bill and tucked it into the tip jar with thanks and made his way to the lobby.

He paused as he passed the grand entryway. Something caught his eye, and he did a double take. A shadow moved on the sweeping staircase where he and Lauren had met. When he turned to inspect the top of the stairway, nothing was there. He shook his head and started on his way but paused.

For a moment he could see her lying at the base of the stairs—pain in her panicked eyes. She writhed on the marble floor, her leg caught in the banister, bent at an unnatural angle. He could hear her cries as the crews parted to let him and his partner through. His gaze lifted to the top of the first landing where a dark shadow caught in the corner of his eye. Lauren said someone—or *something*—had pushed her. *Was it a spirit? Had he just seen it? Or was he being overly sensitive?* He'd seen plenty of things he couldn't explain, but after the last week, he knew he was fragile. This flashback was further proof. He'd faced death—yet again—and had walked away. Perhaps *it* was following him now.

He didn't dare go up the stairs, fearing coming down the

same way Lauren had. He turned from the stairs and focused on the task at hand.

"Mr. Pierce," the young woman at the counter said. Her name tag read *Dani, Guest Services.* "Jim said you'd be by for this."

Rowan shook off the ghosts that haunted him. The cardboard box on the counter, roughly the size of a dictionary, was heavy for its size. Wrapped in thick, brown paper and sealed with heavy-duty tape, it had his name written in an unsteady hand. An envelope with the same shaky script was taped to it.

"Dani, did you know . . . Benji." He hesitated to call him by his rank, but it wasn't any easier to be informal.

"Yes," she said. "He and I were friends. He played cello at my wedding last spring."

"What do you think happened?"

Her blue eyes seemed to darken like shadows crossing the sun. Her expression wavered as she swallowed hard. "Benji had his demons," she said. "He never talked about his time in the military—not to me anyway. I know *something* happened. I read about what he did to you in the news the other day, but I still don't believe it."

"Military service can change a man." At the moment, it was the truest sentence Rowan could think of to say.

"He said he did what Uncle Sam asked him to do, but he never said much more than that."

Rowan took the envelope and studied it. It was thick, and he tried to make out the object within. The hotel's logo was embossed in gold at the top left corner, and a wax seal had been pressed into the back of it, despite the adhesive that sealed it shut. He shook his head. "There but for the grace of God go I," he muttered, tucking the box under his arm as he put the envelope in his jacket pocket. "Thank you."

9

Lightning flashed and the lights flickered overhead in the common room of the Orleans Parish Prison as the Cat 2 hurricane skimmed past the Big Easy. Confined in the dungeons, Dauphine had paid the guards to leave him to face his opponent without interference, and the battle was raging as fiercely as the storm. There was a *code noir* in this cesspool. Anything Papa wanted, Papa got. And Papa might return the favor if you were lucky.

Dauphine took in a breath, steeling himself. The miasma of ozone, sweat, iron, and despair rose in the air as another rumble of thunder reverberated in the cinder block walls and concrete floor.

In the center of the room, the inmate across from the priest hovered over a battered chessboard, his dark fingers thrumming as he studied the board but kept an eye on the opponent whose eyes gleamed with a dangerous intensity.

The hardened inmate had a face scarred by violence and etched by a prison tattoo artist. After much deliberation, he reached to make his next move. Dauphine's lips curled into an almost imperceptible smile. His opponent had fallen for the trap the voodoo priest had set six moves before. "Welcome to my web, said the spider to the fly." Papa Dauphine reached for his queen. His opponent had made a series of questionable moves earlier in the game. His biggest blunder was a sacrificial knight that turned to this devastating attack. "Checkmate."

Three pawns and a rook blocked the queen's attack as she took out the rook and left the white king unable to move in any direction. "What?" the man muttered, standing, studying the board, trying to figure out where he'd made his mistake. Dauphine knew he'd never seen it coming and would replay the loss in his mind long after lights out. He balled up a fist as his anger grew at the defeat. No one had ever beaten him before in this prison. But he'd never played Dauphine.

"Who knew kings could fall so fast, eh, *Frair-oh?*" Dauphine's accent was thick, heavy with the weight of his ancestors. These bars had tried to strip away his dignity, but no prison could cage his powers. This wasn't just a game. He was playing for his life, not just for his pride. He had a reputation to maintain—the priest had a way of bending not just the rules, but the very fabric of reality itself. His reputation as a great and terrible *bokor* was whispered in every corner of the prison, his name spoken with a mixture of fear and reverence —even by the guards. In New Orleans, voodoo was respected and revered. Anyone who wielded it was given a wide birth and the respect they deserved. That was how Dauphine liked it. It gave him power over this ragged lot, and it allowed him to comply with his master's orders to bide.

He would not *bide* when it came to chess. His eyes never left the board, but in his mind's eye, the avatars weren't just pieces—they were soldiers in a battle for control over a universe where he sought to unseat the Most High god itself. The knights and rooks, the pawns and queens were symbols of power and order, but to him, they were more than that. They were tokens of a war for domination, each piece a hapless fragment of the greater design. Every sacrifice on the board mirrored his opponent's fate—and his desire to overthrow the balance of good and evil—to cast aside the shackles of morality and claim the ultimate victory. It would magnify more than Enlil; it would give him the power to serve at the right hand of the Dark Lord on that great and terrible day he sensed was coming.

No. This was more than just a game. He was playing for control over the forces of fate, manipulating the moves with the same ease he commanded spirits from the other side. The game had become his ritual, the board a sacred altar where he sacrificed the very notion of balance.

"You t'ink you understand how de game is played, but you forget de most important t'ing." Dauphine's voice was soft, dark as the clouds building outside the bar-covered windows. "Dis is not jus' about de pieces, not just de moves. It's about control. Over life . . . over death."

"You cheated!" the man spat at him.

"Cheat?" Dauphine stood, his smile widening as his opponent's face drained of color, realizing the voodoo priest had not cheated. He'd been bested, no way to deny it. "You see, *Frair-oh*," he whispered, his voice dripping with venom, "in the end, evil conquers all."

His opponent's brow furrowed, and Dauphine could read him like an open book. He wanted to flip the board and challenge Dauphine to a battle of fists. The man was twice his size, and he might have the physical strength to best him, but as the evilest of all evils in this prison, such a mortal could not best him. The man seemed to recognize it as his eyes locked with Dauphine's. In that moment he saw the depth of ancient magic, a certainty that evil would always, always triumph.

Slowly, the opponent's trembling hand reached for his piece, tipping over the king. "*J'adoube*. You win, Papa . . . this time." He swept his meaty paw across the board, scattering all the pieces as he rose.

"I win every time, *frair-oh*. Every time." His laughter followed the man as he made his retreat. It echoed through the empty hallways of the prison, a sound so guttural, so filled with malice, that it seemed to draw the darkness around him.

The game was over. At that moment, it wasn't just the chessboard that had been conquered. The cosmos, once still, now quivered with the whispers of demons crowding the Gates of Hell, crying out for freedom. From the heart of the ancient world, where the gods and mortals walked the same path, Dauphine sensed their enthusiasm. The signs of their liberation enthused them.

In the dim, suffocating gloom beneath the earth's cracked skin, the bars that held them prisoner in the fiery pit glowed hot from the flames of Hephestus's furnace. There, the darkest beasts of the worst order fought their chains as their cries became a merging din of discordant music that only the most powerful *bokor* could hear. Dauphine knew their suffering. The air in his prison had the miasma of rot. It lacked the fetid decay of brimstone, but it stank, nonetheless.

This was one of the portents the Dark Lord had promised. When the demon's chains were broken, his chains would be next. He could taste his freedom already, and it was delicious. He inhaled the perfume of the Dark Lord's forge and lay back on his cot, behind bars he could not break, and prepared for the feast.

For nearly five years, he'd obeyed his Master's command to bide. He kept his faith that this day would come. Humanity never learned. The evil in men's hearts was predictable, malleable—and easy to coerce. Demons were just as easy to command, and when his minions were free of their bonds, he would know and his commands would be followed. They were weak of mind, lacking self-will. Easy to control. The world would soon be broken and bleeding, with nothing but the mirror of chaos to reflect their destruction—so they would know their own gods had abandoned them.

Yes, it was happening just as his Lord had promised. The cities would burn. Their towers would collapse. The streets would soon be flooded with the blood of the innocent. More importantly, he would use these demonic minions to take his revenge on the woman who sent him to this prison. She had minions of her own, but the power that trembled in the cosmic ether told him she was no match for the seeds of her destruction planted so many years ago. Before, he asked for justice, but now, he wanted nothing more than revenge.

And revenge he would have.

ROWAN FEIGNED sleep until the house was quiet and Lauren was lost to dreams beside him. He was in enough trouble for being late. Sarah gave him the stink-eye the entire time he sat at the kitchen table eating his reheated meal. On Friday night, the older kids dispersed to various functions and friends' homes. Jamie was at a Boy Scout lock-in at the video arcade. Kate was babysitting for the Petersons across the street. They had three-year-old twins, but Kate, being a twin herself, knew how to manage them.

Sam and Sarah were home, but Sam went upstairs early. Rowan knew he'd probably gone to play video games with Henry. Sam missed his older brother, who was busy at college, but Henry made time for all his siblings and came home on the weekends when he wasn't busy with his studies or his busy college life.

Sarah, admonished for her behavior toward her father, asked to take Indy and Shadow up to her room where she had everything set up for a tea party. It was a frequent event, and the pets always seemed interested in participating, though Shadow endured the dresses and hats with haughty indignation. Indy seemed to enjoy it. Maybe he just wanted the animal crackers Sarah served with the tea.

Rowan had smuggled the box into the house carefully hidden beneath his coat when he'd arrived home. He took it downstairs and hid it under his desk, where it beckoned him all evening. He wanted nothing more than to come downstairs and open it, but he'd allowed Lauren to distract him. The quiet house gave them a sense of privacy they rarely experienced and attending to her desires allowed his mind to rest, despite the urge to give in to the distraction before him now.

His small office was suffocatingly quiet. The slice of the sharp box knife followed by the rustling of brown paper hid the thrumming of his own heart that had become so constant he hardly noticed it.

The contents of the cardboard box surprised him as much as anything. It was a simple wooden box, aged by time and the caress of hands that had long since passed from this world. Rowan's own trembling hands skimmed across the smooth façade. In the dim light of his desk lamp, he felt the wrongness that clung to the artifact like a bad omen.

His breath hitched, and the familiar taste of fear filled his mouth. He hadn't asked for this. He didn't want it. He wanted peace. The pounding of his heart became audible in his ears, joined by something otherworldly. The smell of wet hay filled his nose, and the memory of faces chilled by death replayed in the back of his mind. A gun pressed to his temple. The ting of a lethally sharp blade echoed in his mind, and a sword cut the air, severing flesh and hair. Tima's head hit the sand and rolled to where his eyes met hers. The spark of life hovered a moment before it faded into the abyss.

Rowan leaped from his chair, breathing in ragged gasps. Still, the box called to him. He stood like Lot's wife before he managed to steel his courage. When he thought of the envelope in his jacket pocket, he fumbled through the pockets. Inside was a note and a brass skeleton key. He studied the object, admiring the filigree bow and artisan etching on the shaft. It caught the light and glinted brightly as he turned it in his hand. The box may have been ancient, but the key was as bright as a new penny. Rowan knew by instinct it would fit the ancient lock if he dared to open it.

He studied the note. Two words were scribbled in the same unsteady script and black ink as his name on the box and the envelope. The message was a simple one. *Forgive me.*

Forgive me? For what? Rowan wondered.

A cold draft brushed across his skin as if the room itself exhaled a warning. His hand hovered over the box for a long moment, the key in his right hand. He glanced down at his mangled finger—a reminder of his own torture—as he thought of Benjamin Riggs. *What torment had he suffered?* Something followed him home. *Was it his guilt for having stolen ancient treasures?*

Come on, Rowan. You're being ridiculous. Just open the damned thing. His rational mind told him there was no reason to fear what might be inside. If the Amulet of Nohochacyum rested inside this chest, he would be hailed a hero for having found it —again. He would return it to the museum where it belonged.

Just open it. He scolded himself for his cowardice.

His hands trembled as he slid the key in the slot. He turned it, and the delicate clasp clicked. In the silence of his office, the click sounded like a gunshot. He withdrew his hand and sat back. A shiver passed over him, and he chided himself again. He lifted the lid, wincing as it creaked. Inside, he found a slip of velvet embroidered in gold thread. He'd seen this symbol before. There were two crossed lines with crescent moons in three of the four quadrants created by the lines and a golden eagle in the fourth. The fabric was dark with age, moth-eaten, frayed at the edges. He fumbled with it and finally lifted it from the box.

It was not the amulet he expected. Instead, he found a medieval ring.

The relic was made of dark, tarnished metal, jagged and uneven as if forged in the very fires of Hephestus. Dark red rubies caught the light and throbbed like a beating heart, pulsing with malevolent energy he felt deep in his bones. At the center of the ring, a black sardonyx diadem had been adorned with an inlay of gold. It was the same symbol embroidered on the velvet covering.

His fingers twitched as if they had a mind of their own, drawn toward it—compelled to hold the ancient relic. An icy surge of terror shot through him, and the world tilted violently as his skin brushed cold metal and stone. His fingers ached to feel the gold encircle them. His heartbeat crescendoed to a deafening din, drowning out everything as a flood of memories—too many, too vivid—rushed into him like a torrent. He saw the memories of fellow soldiers he'd lost in battle, their eyes wide in the moments before they died. Their pleas—the last of their dying breaths—echoed in his ears. He couldn't save them any more than he could save Benjamin Riggs.

Rowan lifted the ring, gazing through the middle, like a tiny portal to a realm of torment, a dark void that thrived on fear and regret. Born from the ashes of the Holy Land, it was a thing of relentless power, a force that had no place in the hands of a soldier who had already seen too much bloodshed. It didn't need to be in Rowan's hands either, and he realized it. The ring pulsed in his hand, throbbing with ancient magic. It was a relic of the ages.

The words escaped his lips against his will. *One Ring to rule them all, One Ring to find them. One Ring to bring them all and in the darkness bind them.*

As the images of swinging swords and dying crusaders swirled around him, desert heat warmed his shoulders and the grit of sand filled his clenched teeth. Rowan stumbled backward, his chest tight, his breath shallow, his palms were slick with sweat. But he couldn't tear his hand from the ring, which pulled itself toward his finger. It was as if the thing had already become a part of him, as if its curse had sunk into his flesh—into his soul. The war had never ended; it was part of him—a permanent scar in his heart and on his flesh that would never fade.

He balled up his fist and all his remaining strength. He returned the ring to the box, slamming the lid shut, turning the key, and shoving it into the pocket of his bathrobe. He backed into his chair and collapsed into it. His voice cracked as he whispered into the empty room, his words barely audible, "What have I done?"

The sacred relics that lined the office around him seemed to cry out. The ring answered, not in words, but in cold laughter that seemed to echo in the very corners of his mind. The box had been opened. The demons of every past conflict since the dawn of mankind were unleashed. And they would never let him forget the perils of war.

10

"You're up early," Lauren said as she found Rowan at the dining room table, staring into his cup of coffee. He was startled as her hand came to his shoulder. "Sorry." She hadn't realized how sore his shoulder must be. Her touch hadn't been overly aggressive.

"No," he protested. "It's okay. I . . . I just didn't hear you come in."

His tone was harsh, which wasn't like him. Even before coffee, he was usually chipper in the morning.

"Are you okay?" she asked, filling her cup. She joined him at the table, inspecting him carefully. He was pale and haggard, with dark circles under his eyes. "Rough night?"

He swallowed hard, his eyes still locked on the steam rising from his cup. "You could say that."

"What's going on?"

"I didn't sleep well," he said tersely, then got up, sloshing coffee from his cup. A foul word escaped his lips as he shook the hot coffee from his hand. He walked to the kitchen and poured what was left down the drain and angrily snatched a paper towel off the roll. Returning to the table, he cleaned his mess, grumbling under his breath.

Lauren put a hand on his arm. "Wanna talk about it?"

"No." Rowan's answer was definitive.

Lauren recoiled. She wasn't sure what was going on, but he was upset. She didn't know if it was from his sore shoulder or if he'd had more troubling nightmares. He hadn't had a night like that for some time, but after everything that had happened in the past week, it wouldn't be a surprise. She wanted to ask him what had been so important that he'd missed picking up Sarah. It wasn't like him to shirk his duties at home. He said he was doing research for his novel, but she hesitated to ask. It was better to let it go.

"It's supposed to be a nice day," Lauren said. "I'm going to the farmer's market this morning, and I might work in the garden this afternoon. Care to join me?"

Rowan hesitated. "I don't think I will be good company today. Go on without me."

"I'll take Sam and Sarah with me," Lauren said. "Maybe you can get a nap."

"I'm not a five-year-old," he snapped. "I don't need a nap."

Lauren recoiled at the venom in his tone. She lifted her brows and pursed her lips as he all but sneered at her. "Are you sure?" She didn't normally goad him when he got like this, but it wasn't usually this bad.

"What's that supposed to mean?" He glowered at her. She could see his knuckles flex as he gripped the empty cup in his hand.

"It means I can see you are upset. If you won't talk about it, then I suggest you find some way of working out whatever it is that has you so . . . so frustrated." She stood, abandoning her cup, making her escape, and slamming the bedroom door behind her.

She wasn't about to give him a chance to lash out at her any more than he already had. She needed a shower before she headed out. Rowan's mood was a marked turn from the night before, when he'd demonstrated more romantic notions. He'd been tender and passionate when he took her to bed, and she couldn't imagine anything that would take him from Romeo to Sourpuss in under twelve hours. No, she needed more than a shower, but a shower would have to do.

Her hair had grown out since her last haircut four years ago. She cut it to honor Tima and mark the loss of a life so vibrant—a life cut short too soon. As she shampooed it, her thoughts went to Tima, as they often did. Rowan's professor had been like a mother to her before she and her mother had reconnected. Lauren hadn't seen her much in the ten years before her death, but it had always been a comfort to know she could message her any time and she'd answer back as soon as she could. They swapped recipes online and shared book recommendations and even scientific papers on subjects they shared an interest in.

Tima had been influential in helping Lauren get her second PhD, even though Lauren hadn't known it at the time. Before she died, Tima had written a letter of recommendation, addressed *To Whom It May Concern,* and left it in her desk drawer. Lauren often wondered if the woman had a magic of her own. She seemed to know things before they happened. Lauren had no intention of going back to get another degree when she lived in Egypt, though Tima often encouraged her. When she applied at Oxford, the letter found its way to the dean of the college. She probably didn't need the recommendation, but when she learned about it, she'd been grateful for Tima's assistance—once again.

"I'm sorry," Rowan said, slipping into the shower behind her. She turned as he pulled her into his arms. She'd been so lost in thought that she hadn't heard him come in. "I'm cranky this morning and for no reason. I shouldn't take it out on you."

"You wanna tell me what's going on?" she asked, leaning

into him. "Does it have anything to do with why you were late last night?"

"No," he said. "Not really."

Lauren suspected that wasn't entirely true, but she wasn't about to call him out on it yet. "You know I'm here to help you. But I won't allow you to wallow in whatever it is that's got you down. You need to act if something is bothering you. At least share it with me. I'm always in your corner."

"I know," he said. "I know. I had some weird dreams last night, and I'm out of sorts. I had a good day yesterday, and I can't wait to tell you about it."

"So, tell me about it," she said and turned to rinse the shampoo from her hair.

On the way to the farmer's market, Rowan told her about meeting Dr. Octavia Vanderhorst and how he'd read about a missing artifact from their collection that had been stolen from the museum in Khartoum. He intentionally didn't mention which one. "I thought she might be able to help me with some information on it."

"To what end?"

"A plot element for my book," he said. "I don't know if that's the way I'll end up taking it, but when I learned she had some inside knowledge on Mayan history and lore, I thought I might meet up with her."

"Dr. Octavia Vanderhorst is one of the preeminent experts on ancient cultures," Lauren said. "Not just the Maya."

"So she told me."

"She has a theory that many of the ancient cultures were influenced by a common culture."

"She calls it paleocontact," Rowan said, explaining it as Octavia had.

"She's hinted at that in various lectures I've watched on

YouTube." Lauren gazed off into the distance. "But I don't think I've ever seen anything in her published papers that would directly suggest she subscribes to the ancient astronaut theory, per se. I'd love to pick her brain on that sometime."

"I can set up a meeting," Rowan said as he pulled into a parking spot and put the car in park.

"You can?"

"She gave me her number," he said. "How about dinner Friday night?"

Lauren lowered her chin and held his gaze from under her eyelashes. "Are you sure she just wanted to talk about the ancient Maya?" Lauren had become accustomed to finding women's phone numbers in his pockets after public events. Sometimes she wondered if he left them there to make her jealous, but he insisted he left them in his pockets to ensure she saw them and saw the numbers were properly destroyed. He insisted he'd never stray, and she was confident in his assurances. Lauren did not doubt in this instance either. She had seen pictures of the esteemed Dr. Octavia Vanderhorst, and while she was a handsome woman, she wasn't Rowan's type. "I thought you had plans for our anniversary weekend?"

"I don't see why dinner with such a notable professor can't be included in the plans. It'd be nice to talk shop with a colleague who understands the less mainstream parts of our research. If you want to."

Lauren smiled, nodding. "I think I'd like that."

* * *

ROWAN GOT Lauren's folding cart from the back of the SUV and set it up so Sarah could sit in it until it was time to fill it with autumn fruits and vegetables, baked goods, and honey. Lauren was a creature of habit and tended to visit the same farmers' stands and local home bakers. She could bake bread as well as any of them, but with her schedule, her sourdough starters inevitably died. It wasn't worth the hassle when she could find fresh bread at the weekly market.

"So," Rowan said, and she sensed the hesitation in his voice. He had come up with some elaborate plot points for his novel involving the Maya. "What do you know about the Amulet of Nohochacyum?"

"I'd never heard of it until we discovered it in Mexico, when we found the cache of treasures along with the new Maya calendar. I know he's a creator and a destroyer god, so from what I've read the glyphs on each of the two sides represented birth and death."

"It's one of the missing artifacts." Rowan took a deep breath and put his hand in hers as they walked towards the tents that were set up in the middle of the park. Sam pulled the wagon as Sarah sat patiently in it.

"What do you mean it's missing?" Lauren demanded. "Missing in real life or is that the plot of your novel?"

"It was stolen from Khartoum," Rowan said. "In real life."

"I thought you were researching something for your book." Lauren stopped.

Rowan took her hand and pulled her close to him, so he didn't have to raise his voice to tell her the whole story. "The Marine from the convenience store? He was accused of stealing it from the History Museum while he was stationed in Khartoum. I think that may have been why he came looking for me."

Lauren stopped again. "He came looking for *you*? Specifically?"

"So it would seem," Rowan said. "I wanted to know more about the Amulet and what it might mean if someone got their hands on it. Knowing what we know, I have to think there's something to fear when myth suggests it's such a powerful artifact."

"Nohochacyum was a destroyer god," she muttered, realization washing over her. If Rowan was right, that could be a problem. They'd had four years of peace. Four years of safety. Four years as a family. If Enlil or one of his minions controlled something so powerful, it could be tragic. "So, what did Dr. Vanderhorst say?"

"She said that, 'ancient legends foretold the amulet would be removed by a chosen one—a mortal—a soul so daring or cursed that they would invoke the powers of death to reshape the world.'" He quoted her verbatim.

"That doesn't sound at all ominous."

Lauren turned from him, searching the crowd for Sam and Sarah, but her heart racing at the potential ramifications. Sam knew which booths to go to, so she wasn't worrying about losing him, but he had gotten out of sight. She wasn't sure what bothered her more.

"Maybe we should have talked about this at home." Lauren's voice quavered.

<hr>

AFTER LAUREN'S reaction to the missing amulet, Rowan most certainly did not want to tell her about the ring or his encounter with Benjamin Riggs' friends and colleagues at the Stanley Hotel. He had been so focused on the amulet he hadn't expected Saladin's ring to be in the box. He also didn't know if the level of threat it posed was anywhere close to the Amulet of Nohochacyum. After seeing it—feeling its dark power calling to him—he had his suspicions.

He hadn't expected the events that unfolded when he opened the box. The ring seemed to be drawn to him, and he to it. It hummed his name when he came close. Electricity lifted the hair on his arms and tingled down into his fingers when he thought of putting it on. *Was that what Riggs was talking about? What followed him home? What had happened to the Amulet? Why did he keep the ring?*

Now, out of the house, away from its influence, he made a

vow to never open the box again—never let it influence him in that manner. He could never put the ring on. He knew that. Images of Smigel and the Ring of Power from the Lord of the Rings books ran behind his eyes, and he knew that no good could come from that cursed ring. That Precious.

No. No. It most certainly was not precious. It was . . . *demonic.*

Rowan turned his thoughts to Saladin and the legend of the ring. *How could such a haunted diadem be affiliated with someone like Saladin?* To Tima, he had been a hero—a noble warrior king. He was respected by his people and even by his enemies.

He was known for his remarkable sense of chivalry, which was not always typical in the era of the Crusades. He often showed mercy to his defeated enemies. He treated them with respect and allowed them to ransom themselves. He refused to slaughter the innocent.

Saladin was also a charismatic and effective leader, uniting the Muslim world—joining the tribes, and their armies into a powerful unified force. His victory at the Battle of Hattin in 1187 resulted in the Muslims recapturing Jerusalem. It was one of his most celebrated military accomplishments. Tima raved about him like he was a teenage idol. To her, he was the rockstar of his era, and Rowan respected him for that. Tima's praise was hard to win, but once you earned her favor, she was loyal to the end.

The ring, however, was another thing. No, he needed to do some more research on this artifact before he got close to it again. He couldn't let it consume him. And he couldn't tell Lauren.

"Call Dr. Vanderhorst," Lauren said. "I want to meet with her. If this missing Amulet is as powerful as its reputation, then we need to know more about it. I also want to know more about how it ended up in Benjamin Riggs' hands, if it did. We have to find it."

"I've got some calls in to people who might be able to help us," Rowan said. "I didn't want to exclude you, but you've been busy, and I didn't want to burden you with it. You worry enough as it is."

"As I should," Lauren said. "It's kind of my *job* to worry about that stuff." She made sure the children were out of earshot but still lowered her tone. "I am the *Hand of Anu*, after all."

"And I'm the Protector." He leaned down and kissed her. "Forever and always."

"Who protects the Protector?" she asked, gazing into his deep green eyes. "I've been so worried about you lately. Why have you waited so long to tell me all this?"

"Because I didn't want you to worry. Besides, I think the worst of it is past me."

"What was this morning all about?" she asked, not in a challenging tone, but he knew her well enough to know it was.

"Me being an idiot," he said. "And I'm sorry for that. I don't know what got into me."

Lauren studied him for a moment. He sensed her eyes burning into his soul. She had that effect on him. "I want you to talk to Dr. McLeish about it. When's your next appointment?"

"Monday," he said. "And I will."

"Good." Lauren rounded the corner where Sam stood with the wagon handle in hand. Sarah got out and stood in front of a table loaded with apples, apricots, and pears. She reached for one of the ripe apricots. They were her favorite.

"Hi, Sarah," the farmer's wife, Estelle, greeted her. They knew everyone here. "Go ahead. Pick your apricot."

The dark-eyed child glanced back at her father. Her look was a silent request for permission. "Go ahead," Rowan said, winking at her, then turning his gaze to the woman behind the table. "Looks like some good apples, too."

"We've been picking them fresh all week." Estelle reached for a large paper bag and handed it to Lauren. It was a weekly ritual by now. "Help yourselves."

Rowan watched as Lauren and the kids filled the bag with apples, some red, and some green. He could already taste Lauren's apple cobbler.

"Nanhi's apple cobbler," Sarah said, taking a bite of the apricot. Juice ran down her chin as she retrieved the pit and found a nearby trashcan, disposing of it.

"Excuse me?" Lauren asked.

"Nanhi will make us a cobbler," she clarified, looking at her father.

Lauren glanced at Rowan, her brow furrowed.

"I guess your mom's coming to visit," Rowan said, shrugging.

"Did you talk to her?"

"No," Rowan said, reaching for the pears. He had his own bag to fill. "But if Sarah says she's coming to visit . . ."

11

Just shy of midnight, Rowan crept back down to his office and collected the wooden box, a crackle of electricity racing through his skin when he touched it. The ring inside called to him, but he was feeling particularly strong after his day with Lauren and the kids. He hadn't realized how much he needed that, and how much confiding in Lauren could ease his troubled mind. He still hadn't told her everything, but he'd told her enough that he'd made peace with what he had to do.

He tucked the box under his arm. Quietly, he went back upstairs and out to the garage, where he'd left the door to the attic open before he came to bed. Lauren hadn't noticed, or at least hadn't said anything, and he was thankful for that. The stairs creaked as he climbed into the abyss above. He found the cord to the single bulb that hung just over the door. *Snick.* The bare bulb cast a cold glow over the entrance to the void above the garage.

The chattering of the ring from the box grew louder. A voice found its way to his ear. *We walked in the same shoes. We both found ourselves in the land of Kings. Where the key to redemption is whitewashed beneath the gates to the heavens. You found me.*

Rowan froze and turned. A dark shadow hovered in the far back corner of the attic. "Riggs?"

"I knew it," the voice said. "I knew if anyone could find me, it would be you."

"What's all this got to do with me?" Rowan demanded, keeping his tone even, his volume low.

"You can hear it, can't you?" Riggs asked. "You can. I can see it in your face."

Rowan glanced down at the box. "What is this? Where did you get it?"

The shadow moved, and a hearty laugh filled the room. "You already know."

"Where are the other artifacts you stole?"

"I didn't work alone. I just took the ring. But the other artifacts? They've found their places in the world." Riggs moved close enough that the light picked up his shadowy features. "You don't have all the answers now, but . . . you will."

"What do you mean 'I will'? How do you know that?"

"You're a smart man, Mr. Pierce. Smart man . . . with a pretty wife . . . such sweet little children . . ." His voice trailed off. Rowan felt his anger rising. "You have no choice now. My mistake."

"You leave my wife and kids out of it," Rowan snapped. "This is between you and me."

"This is between heaven and hell," Riggs' chest inflated, and Rowan took a step back. "Angels and demons . . . God and Satan. This has everything to do with them, and you know it."

"No," Rowan insisted. "I won't do this." He balled up his courage and pressed past the dark shadow, feeling the room go cold as the fog seemed to dissolve in a cloud that followed him. He found his footlocker and opened it. Inside, he placed the Pandora's box beneath every physical reminder he had left of his time in the military—scars notwithstanding. He took a padlock from his pocket and placed it on the chest. He locked it, making certain it was secure. He put the key in the pocket of his jeans. Two keys rattled against his leg as he stood.

"That won't do any good," Riggs said. "They know where you are. They'll come for you, just like they came for me. *Demons dwell in the Land of Kings, Where the key to redemption is whitewashed beneath the gates to the heavens. Where the demons lie, answers await.*"

"Stop it!" Rowan shouted so loudly the dark shadow blocking the door to the attic disappeared. He rushed for the stairs and hurried down, closing the door behind him. He started for the door to the laundry room and froze when it opened.

Lauren stood there in her gossamer-thin cotton night-gown. The light from the kitchen cast a glow around her dark-ened silhouette. She looked like an angel with her hair loose around her head. "What's going on?"

Rowan rushed into her, wrapping his arms around her. "You shouldn't be up," he said, breathing the words into her hair.

"Rowan? What's the matter? What are you doing up? Why are you dressed?"

He pressed past her and turned, shaking his head. "I must have been dreaming . . ."

"What?"

"I thought there was something in the attic. Mom was always complaining about the squirrels in the attic. I thought I heard something up there, and I went to check. I didn't want to have to fight off a rabid squirrel in my underwear."

"Did you find anything?"

"Just cobwebs." He ran his hand over his face as he took an unsteady step over to the kitchen counter. He managed to get seated before he fell over. "That's what makes me think I was dreaming. Stupid squirrel dreams . . ."

Lauren tucked herself into him. He wrapped his arms

around her and held her, burying his face in her hair. She smelled of springtime—flowers and herbs, everything good and earthly. The stench of demonic presence escaped his senses, and he felt safe. It didn't escape his notice that he was supposed to protect her, but she protected him too. Thank God. Someone had to.

"How about I make us some tea?" Lauren asked, drawing away. "Does that sound good?"

"Yeah." He turned as she moved around the alcove into the kitchen. He leaned his arms on the counter, hanging his head as he gathered his wits. God, he didn't want to tell her about the ring or Riggs or the Stanley Hotel. She'd lose her mind if she knew what was bothering him.

He flinched when the tea kettle whistled. Lauren already had their cups sitting on the counter with tea bags in place. She poured the steaming liquid into first his cup, then hers. She set his cup up on the counter and added the glass jar of honey she'd picked up at the market the day before.

"You know," Lauren started, watching him as he dressed his cup with the amber liquid, "why don't I take a few days off? We could make it a long weekend for our anniversary."

"What about what Sarah said? About your mom?"

"Even better," Lauren said, smiling. Rowan could tell it was forced. "Mom can watch the kids, and we don't have to bother Bahati and Jean-René."

Rowan didn't answer. He stared into his cup, stirring the honey and watching it melt, shivering as it reminded him of the shadow he'd walked through—shadow, ghost, whatever.

"Rowan?"

He looked up. "I guess I can revise my plans." He nodded, but he wasn't sure he was in any kind of mood for a romantic weekend getaway.

"You know what, maybe that's not a great idea. Never mind. Forget I even mentioned it."

Rowan didn't argue.

THE NUMBER WAS ALREADY PULLED up on his telephone, but he hesitated to hit the dial button. He didn't think Lauren would be on board with his plan, but Dr. Vanderhorst had suggested it when they spoke, and she had no idea of their history with the Stanley Hotel.

He debated the idea even as he hit the button and the phone rang. "Thank you for calling the Stanley Hotel. This is Dani. How may I assist you?"

"Hi, Dani. Rowan Pierce. How are you today?"

"Mr. Pierce, it's a pleasure to hear from you."

"Look, I know this is last-minute, but my wife and I are driving up Friday night to have dinner with Dr. Vanderhorst and I wanted to see if you had a room available."

"Just for one night?"

"Sure," he said. He'd be hard-pressed to get Lauren to stay even one night, and he debated packing the camping gear for the remainder of the long weekend.

He could hear her fingernails on the keyboard as she pulled up the schedule. "You will not believe this, but our guest in 217 just canceled. It's open all weekend."

"The whole weekend?"

"This never happens. It must be kismet. Would you like me to book it for you?"

"Well, who am I to argue with kismet?" Rowan laughed, but his inner voice was protesting. "Yeah. Let's book it."

"There's a ghost tour Saturday night, and we're doing our Sunday champagne brunch this weekend."

"It's our anniversary. Why not?" Rowan knew it would take every trick in the book to keep him out of the doghouse with Lauren. "Can we get a couples massage in the spa, too?"

"I'll put in a request and see when there's an opening. Is it okay if I text you a time?"

"That's perfect," Rowan said and gave her his number.

"I have you booked for room 217, arriving Friday and checking out on Sunday," she said. "I'll be on duty when you check in. We look forward to seeing you."

Monday came too soon for Lauren's liking. She'd spent her Sunday working in the garden, watching as Rowan sat at the patio table with his laptop. He'd said he was doing more research on the missing Maya artifact, but he seemed a million miles away. She had been tempted to text Dr. McLeish and give her a heads up about his unusual behavior, but she had a full agenda, which included an on-air interview with the local NBC news affiliate for the four p.m. newscast. She didn't mind being on camera, but she had scripts to write for her show, and, with a live event just a few weeks away, she needed to get as much done now as possible so she could get Rowan out of town.

Beneath the hot studio lights, her makeup melted almost immediately. She hoped her face hadn't gone shiny, but she knew it would if she had to sit here much longer. Technical difficulties got her bumped to the end of the news schedule, but they left her sitting on a sofa beneath the lights on a secondary stage.

She was here to discuss the upcoming fall festival events being held around the Rocky Mountain State, and she was excited to do it. The Apple Festival was the biggest of these events, and the organizers had been clear on what they wanted her to say when promoting the event. There was also a music festival in Fort Collins, the second-largest hot air balloon festival in the US—after Albuquerque's—in Limon this weekend. Lauren had the list scribbled out on a slip of paper in her lap.

Finally, the reporter came over and sat down beside her. He gave her a nod and a smile so fake she could see the alabaster veneers on his front six teeth.

"And we're back from break in three, two, one . . . ." A voice came through the earpiece at the exact moment the news reporter settled in.

"Fall is a time for festivals and family fun," he began. "Today we're excited to have with us Dr. Lauren Grayson, host of *Colorful Colorado*." The reporter turned to her. She felt the cameras burning into her even more than the hot studio lights. "Dr. Grayson, there's an old saying that goes 'Colorado will show you what you are made of.' Before you tell us about the festivals that make Colorado, I understand your husband is made of the right stuff . . ."

Lauren's whole body quickened, and her hair stood up on her arms. *What the . . .?*

"What's it like being married to a hero?"

What the literal hell? She had to think on her toes.

"He's always been a hero to me," Lauren dodged. "Just hope he has the laundry done by the time I get home so we can check out the Hot Air Balloon Festival in Limon." The segue was flawless as she deked left and led right into her unscripted story. She never gave the reporter a chance to ask any other questions, and before her pulse could steady, she was done. She even remembered her verbatim pitch for the Apple Festival.

"And we'll be back with Audra and the weather. Will it be too rainy for those hot air balloons? You won't want to miss her forecast after these commercial messages."

As soon as the director called, "Cut!" Lauren was out of her seat, unhooking the mic and earpiece and freeing herself from the associated wiring.

She started to walk off but sensed the reporter standing behind her. She turned and looked down at him, surprised that he was so much shorter than she'd expected. She wasn't used to wearing heels. "You could have given me a bone there," he snarled. "Everyone wants to know what happened, but your husband won't return anyone's calls."

"If you ever pull anything like that with me ever again, I'll . . ." Lauren hesitated. She wasn't sure what she'd do, but she was quite certain it wouldn't be pleasant.

"Dr. Grayson." Suzanne, the station manager, caught her arm. "Please, allow me to apologize." She gently guided her off the dais and out of the bright lights, into the darkened wings of the studio. All but dragging Lauren, she stopped at a small refrigerator, reached in for a bottle of water, and handed it to her guest. "I am so sorry about that. I promise it won't happen again. We discussed that during the production meeting this morning, and Kent was completely out of line. I won't put up with that nonsense on my watch."

Lauren was too angry to say anything but was certain the heat rising from her cheeks and the fire in her eyes was sufficient to demonstrate the depths of her . . . displeasure. That was putting it mildly. The gentle but heartfelt apology continued to the green room where she'd left her purse. As a means to delay any angry words that might spill from her lips, she paused, opened the bottle of water, and promptly drained it. She felt her cheeks cool and, with it, her temper. "Please, don't let it happen again," she finally said, letting go of her anger.

Lauren's phone buzzed in her purse. She snatched it up and put the phone to her ear. "*Osiyo, dohijunihi,*" her mother said in greeting.

"I'm well. How is it with my mother?" Lauren had fallen

into the habit of using her native tongue when she needed to curse in front of the children. She suspected they were beginning to catch on. She could converse freely in Cherokee with her mother though.

"I am well," she said. "But I miss my daughter."

"Your daughter misses you, too," she said, formally. She shouldered her purse as she walked out of the television studio and into the bright autumn day. The air was crisp, but not frigid. A light breeze tossed a few loose leaves from the limbs of the trees around the station's property.

"Have I been gone too long?"

"Are you back in my time zone?" Lauren asked.

"I am at your brother's house," she said. "George sends his love."

Lauren got to the car and tossed her purse into the passenger seat, wriggling out of her blue blazer. "Give him mine as well. You are coming to visit?"

"How did you know?"

"Sarah knew," Lauren said. "But I figured she was just playing a trick on us. She's been a challenge lately."

"She is definitely your child." Lauren could hear the laughter in her mother's voice. "Southwest Airlines is having a sale. I found tickets for a ridiculously low price. Would I be imposing?"

Lauren was amused. Her father would not have needed a plane ticket. Her mother didn't have the same magic, which told Lauren her father wasn't with Diana. "You know you're always welcome." It had taken a long time for them to come to this point, but they'd found peace. "When will you be here?"

"Would Thursday be too soon?"

"No, it's perfect. Will you stay long?"

"Perhaps," Diana said. "I am compelled to remain in my own time zone for a while. I've missed my grandchildren."

"Rowan and I have been talking about a weekend getaway

for our anniversary, just the two of us. He finished the basement renovation, so your room is ready."

"I am always happy to care for my grandchildren. It will be nice to have some time with them again. I'm sure they've grown while I was gone."

"Rowan can pick you up at the airport. Text me your flight information, and I'll give him a heads up."

"*Gvgeyu so'i.*"

"I love you, too," Lauren said, and she meant it.

<hr>

ROWAN SAT at the table with the kids as each finished their homework. He had some homework of his own, but it was difficult to surf the web and find anything related to ancient treasures that wasn't a myth from one of the many video games the kids were playing these days. Or something completely fabricated and turned into anime. The web was full of it. Writers seemed fascinated with Mayan lore these days.

John Carter was working on calculus, which was at the limit of Rowan's ability. Still, he was able to coach him through it, and the boy found his way without much help. Kate grumbled and bellyached about the futility of her ancient world history lesson. "Why do I even need to know about ancient Mesopotamia? Those people are all dead anyway. If they were so smart, where'd they go?"

"Ah, sweetheart," Rowan said. "Mesopotamian history is essential to understanding how the ancient world influenced our modern culture." This was right up his alley. He didn't want to throw a giant info dump in her lap. But he could have talked about the Mesopotamians for hours. He didn't mention any of the alternative history he and her mother had learned over the years. "Mesopotamians were among the first civilizations to develop a legal code. Has your teacher told you about

The Code of Hammurabi? Its famous eye-for-an-eye edict was adapted from earlier Sumerian law. You know, your mother can read and write in ancient cuneiform." He didn't mention that Mesopotamia was in modern-day Iraq. He preferred not to think about his history there. It was comfortable enough, though, to talk about ancient Mesopotamia. That was a different place and time in Rowan's mind.

"Blah, blah, blah," Kate intoned, scrolling on her phone. She seemed more interested in what her friends were doing than what her father was saying. She started typing out a response to a message with her thumbs.

Rowan's brow lifted as his ire rose. "Kate," he said in a low tone, "you know the rules. No phones until homework is done."

She looked at him sharply, her expression flattening as she closed Instagram and tucked her phone back in her hip pocket.

"Hey, Dad?" Sam laid his pencil down.

"What, champ?"

"What's for dinner?" The boy's stomach growled audibly.

"What sounds good?"

"Do we have stuff for burgers?" John Carter asked.

"Yeah!" Sam and Jamie both agreed. "It's still nice outside. Can you cook them on the grill?"

"I don't have any hamburger meat thawed, but I do have pork chops."

"Gross." Kate didn't look up from her work, but Rowan could see the Elvis-like twitch in her lip as she tucked her auburn hair behind her ear.

"Pigs are friends, not food," Sarah said.

"Excuse me?" Rowan looked at her. "You weren't complaining the other day when I made bacon for breakfast."

"Pigs are smarter than dogs," Sarah said, matter-of-factly.

"Not smarter than Indy," Jamie defended the family dog. Indy appeared at his elbow, having heard his name. The boy reached down and petted him, getting a lick on the cheek for his efforts.

"Shadow's smarter than that dog," Kate sneered at her brother.

Rowan got up and took the pork chops from the fridge. "How about apricot-glazed pork chops with wild rice and steamed vegetables?"

"Sure, Dad," John Carter said. Kate was still grumbling. "If Kate doesn't want hers, I'll eat it."

"I'd rather eat worms," Kate snipped, closing her book and gathering her things. She stormed off to her room without further discussion.

"Daddy," Sarah said, closing her color book. "Can I go outside with Indy?"

"Sure," he said, setting to work on his preparations for dinner.

ROWAN WAS JUST PUTTING dinner on the table when Lauren came in. She said hello to everyone as she passed through the dining room on her way to their bedroom. "Mmm." She inspected the plate of pork chops in the middle of the table. "Apricot pork chops? My favorite."

"Go change," Rowan said. "It's almost ready. Wine?"

"God, I could use a glass," she said as she passed.

As soon as the door closed behind her, she kicked off her heels, then unbuttoned her skirt and slid out of it, glad to take off the tight pencil skirt. She moved to the dresser and found a pair of yoga pants and a T-shirt, then walked to the bathroom to pull her hair up off her neck, clipping it at the back of her skull. She took off her earrings and bracelets before she pulled on a pair of socks to keep her feet warm.

Rowan put a glass in front of her as she slid into her chair at the dinner table. With one last trip to the grill to bring in the platter of sweet corn he'd roasted in the husks, Rowan stopped and called Sarah in from the yard. "Dinner's ready! Come wash up."

Indy came bounding through the door, skidding on the hardwood floors, his nails clattering to gain traction. He came over to sniff Lauren's leg, then sat down beside her. He knew he wasn't allowed to beg at the dinner table, and this was the one spot he knew he'd be more likely to get a morsel after the meal was over.

Kate had her nose in her phone as she plopped down in the chair across from her mother, not even acknowledging Lauren's presence. Sarah finally came in from the yard, carrying her bright yellow sand pail against her body. She paused to close the door behind her. Then, she walked over to Kate and dumped out the contents of her bucket onto her sister's plate before she continued into the kitchen to wash her hands.

Kate looked up at Sarah, then turned and looked at her plate. Lauren's jaw dropped as they both realized at the same moment what it was. *Worms*. "Jesus Christ! Sarah!" Kate screeched, leaping from her chair. Her face turned so red her freckles disappeared as her face contorted in horror.

Rowan looked at Kate, then at Lauren, then back to Kate. "That is what you said you'd rather have for dinner," he said. The boys were all grinning.

"Gross! Mom!" Kate wore a look of righteous indignation on her face. "Are you going to let her get away with this?"

Lauren reached for the plate of pork chops as John Carter passed it. "Uh, what prompted this?" Lauren pointed her fork towards Kate's plate before stabbing a pork chop and handing the platter to Rowan.

Sarah climbed up and sat on her knees next to her dad. "She said she'd rather eat worms than pork chops."

"Well, you should be more careful of what you ask for."

Lauren looked at Kate. The girl's face screwed up as she glared at her mother then looked down at her plate.

Kate started for her room, spinning on her heel. "Sit," Lauren commanded. "You have not been excused from the table."

The worms were now squirming towards the edge of her plate. One of them made it to the table and started towards the butter dish. Rowan caught it and tossed it back onto Kate's plate. Lauren tried not to show any emotion as she got up, collected the girl's plate, carried it out to her herb garden, and returned the earthworms to their home. She took a moment to have a good laugh before she forced her composure back to something more stoic as she went back inside. She got a fresh plate, putting the dirty one in the sink to soak before she took the clean one to Kate. "Pork chop?" she asked.

"Yes, please."

"That's more like it," Rowan said.

With any luck, that would be the last time Kate refused to eat what was prepared for dinner. Rowan and Lauren had a good laugh about it while they were tidying up the kitchen after the kids had been excused to go to their rooms. There was some discussion about whether or not Sarah would be admonished, but in the end, neither of them had the heart. Kate needed the lesson and that was a better demonstration than either of her parents could have delivered.

Lauren poured herself a second glass of wine before she settled in on the sofa and picked up her book. "So, how was your day?" Rowan asked.

"It was fine," she said, tucking her bookmark in the back of the book. She curled her feet up underneath herself, laying the book on the arm of the sofa as she leaned against it. She reached over for her glass and took a long drag from it.

"Talk to your mom?"

"As a matter of fact, she called this afternoon."

"Oh," he said, picking up the remote. Clearly, he wasn't surprised either.

"She'll be here Thursday." Lauren turned the page. "What's your schedule? Can you pick her up?"

"What time?"

Lauren picked up her phone and found the answer. "Noon. Any more thoughts on getting out of town this weekend?"

"Everything is scheduled," he said. "Can you get off work early on Friday? Dinner reservations are made for six o'clock."

"That sounds lovely," Lauren said. "We can go up to Rocky Mountain National Park and do some hiking or maybe even a little horseback riding."

"Dr. Vanderhorst is excited to meet you."

"Sounds good," she said.

She picked up her book again, but he could see she wasn't really into it. She paused and looked at him. "How was your appointment with Dr. McLeish?"

"It went pretty well. She gave me some mental exercises to do this week, and one of them was to focus more on us. She thinks my outburst might be putting extra pressure on you."

"She's not wrong." Lauren sighed and lay her book in her lap. Her gaze moved to the back door, where the wind was picking up and the trees made waving shadows in the land-scape lighting.

"Lauren?" Rowan asked, after a moment of silence. "Everything okay?"

She looked up at him. "Hmm?"

"You sure chugged that wine down fast," he observed. "You seem . . . tense. Was it me? Did I do that?"

Lauren considered him for a moment. "Something happened at the television station today."

"What?" Rowan got up and came over, sitting beside her.

Lauren shifted to put her weight against him, warming in the crook of his arm quickly. She proceeded to tell him everything about the anchor's attempt to bait her into talking about his little incident. "I didn't give him the satisfaction, of course. The station manager all but laid rose petals at my feet to keep me from being angry."

"Aw, honey." He kissed her head and leaned into her as much as she leaned into him. "I'm sorry."

"Not your fault," she said. "The reporter was a jerk."

"Still," Rowan said. "Let me make it up to you."

"You're already taking me out of town for the weekend. What else do I need?"

"I suppose I could think of something." He leaned over and kissed her neck.

"Gross," Kate grumbled. She had her nose in her phone as she walked behind the sofa on her way to the kitchen. "Why don't you two get a room?" She snagged an apple from the refrigerator and returned to her cave, slamming the door behind her.

"I made reservations this morning!" Rowan called out after her.

Lauren got up and caught his hand, snagging her wine glass off the table. "We already have a room," she said, "with a big giant bathtub."

"I'll be right there, Dr. Pierce."

"I'll be waiting, Mr. Pierce."

ROWAN FOUND himself pacing behind the computer at three in the morning. He'd already jotted down several pages of notes and he was trying to make sense of it all. He found several legends deep in the annals of history about Saladin and his ring.

The Ring of Saladin, the legend told, was not crafted by humans but rather by a Jinn magician, a spirit of the desert and the shadows. The name of the ancient sorcerer had long been forgotten, but the pact made with The Dark Lord promised the creator unimaginable power—the ability to master the Jinn and demons of the dark realm, even when unleashed from the abyss.

In time, the ring passed from ruler to ruler, each one using it for their own dark purposes. Blood was spilled by those who wore the signet ring, washing it in generations of bloodshed. The great Saladin came to possess the ring during the Crusades when the sultan reached the height of his power. Exalted, he was a hero to his people, yet a monster to his enemies.

Possession of the Ring marked the turning point of his reign. Unbeknownst to even his closest advisors, the ring granted him access to an army of demons—hell-borne soldiers of the worst order. The demon horde turned the tide of many battles, leaving a swath of destruction and plowing through armies of holy warriors.

Still, Saladin was known as a merciful warlord. When his armies captured Jerusalem, he allowed the innocents to leave the city. He forbade his generals and soldiers from molesting women and children. He was a noble warrior who was honored by his enemies and respected by his people.

A ring that summoned a demon army? That was worse than anything JRR Tolkien ever imagined. No, sir. Rowan did not need a demon-summoning ring. He needed one that vanquished demons.

In the dim glow of the small lamp on his desk, a wooden crate sat against the wall. It was unremarkable at first glance. Its rough-hewn planks spoke of centuries past. Its surface was weathered by time and dust, bound with iron reinforcements that protected its contents from man's gaze. Yet, Rowan felt an undeniable presence within the still air, a sense of quiet, suffocating reverence that wrapped itself around him like a sacred embrace.

Protecting the Ark of the Covenant and the other Templar

relics stored within was his sacred missive. It was an oath he held dear. These precious objects of Christendom protested the presence of the box containing Saladin's ring when he opened it. Now, the *status quo* was restored. Still, the unspoken tranquility felt like the calm before the storm, when the weight of the world seemed to pause, if just for a moment.

His Templar brethren—sworn protectors of the Christian faith—risked their lives to take the Ark from Jerusalem during the final desperate days of the Crusades. Amidst the bloodshed and ruin, they infiltrated Solomen's Temple, entering The Holy of Holies. What they found hidden in the depths of the sacred bastion was not just a relic of incredible power but a sign of hope, a significant harbinger of divine will. The city walls crumbled as the last defenders scattered, broken.

They could not allow it to fall into the hands of the Muslim armies. They did not come to claim it as a trophy of war, but to see the ancient relic safely spirited away through hand-dug tunnels that reached beyond Saladin's armies. Under the cover of a star-filled sky, they took it to safety. Some legends said it ended up in Ethiopia, others said it was in Rome. The Bible itself said it was safe in heaven with God. The Templars who entrusted it to Rowan for safekeeping claimed to have an ancestral connection with its liberation from the Muslim-occupied Holy Land.

Now, when Rowan gazed upon the crate, he felt his strength waning. He felt unworthy to carry out his missive. Still, a gentle warmth washed over him, dissolving the weight of his recent sins and offering solace to his troubled mind. He knelt before the Ark, feeling a moment of peace that had been absent over the past few weeks.

The Ark was no more a shield for him to carry into battle than the Ring was a weapon for him to wield. His job was not to make war or to ensure peace. His mission was to protect and allow his wife to carry out her missive. She was the Hand of Anu. If there was a battle to fight, it was hers and hers alone. It didn't mean she went into battle unaided. He would be at her side.

His feet went numb before he felt worthy to rise. The epiphany of the quiet hours left him weary. He slogged up the stairs to his bed, pulled the covers over his shoulders, and settled into the warmth of their Tempurpedic mattress. Lauren sighed beside him and rolled over in her sleep. He pulled her into his arms and gave into the amity of his tranquil heart—and slept.

ROWAN WAS busy packing his backpack for their weekend away. It had been a while since he'd had to pack anything. He couldn't remember the last time he and Lauren had even gone on a date. He debated taking a suit and tie for dinner with the professor but decided on a more casual sports coat. He paired the gray tweed jacket with a navy-blue sweater and a button-down plaid shirt.

He turned when his phone on the dresser chirped. He didn't recognize the number but felt compelled to answer.

"Mr. Pierce?" He did recognize the voice. "Is this a good time to talk?"

Rowan glanced out the bedroom door and found Lauren and her mother talking in the living room. He casually pushed the door shut. He sat down on the edge of his bed. "Of course, Major York."

There was a pregnant pause before she continued. "What do you know about . . . him?"

Rowan took a deep breath himself. "I know he had bad papers," he said. "I know there was a confrontation. I read he assaulted you."

"Assaulted is a bit of an understatement, Mr. Pierce." She swallowed hard. "We were assigned to reconnoiter an impoverished area of Khartoum." Her voice seemed to falter for a moment.

"You don't have to . . ." Rowan started.

"No. You need to know. I read about what happened in the news—after you called—and what he did to you. What you did for him . . ." Her voice trailed off again. "You have a right to know the whole story." Rowan wasn't sure he had earned anything from her but allowed her to continue. "As you know, after The Great Accord crumbled in the region, the death toll was extremely high on all sides. The Sudanese Rebellion was strong, but US forces held the Capital. We were supporting the UN on an aid mission to deliver food and medical supplies to the Red Cresent and Red Cross unified command center that was set up in the history museum." The narrative began to play like a movie in the back of Rowan's mind. He'd been on similar missions when he served in Iraq and Afghanistan. "Riggs and his unit were in charge of unloading supplies while the command staff met with the NGOs' leadership. I got called from the meeting by one of my officers. She'd witnessed Riggs and his buddies poking around in the museum's inventory of historic items. I reprimanded the whole team and ordered them to return anything they might have *accidentally* picked up." She paused and took a deep breath. "I know that kind of thing happened, but . . . I wasn't going to allow it on my watch. I didn't want my unit accused of theft."

"But it happened anyway." Rowan could extrapolate from there.

"Weeks later, when a full inventory was completed, several artifacts were missing."

"A few Mayan pieces and a ring," Rowan said, so she didn't have to.

"How did you know?"

"It's been brought to my attention," he said. "What you probably do not know is that I am an archeologist and my wife is an anthropologist. We initially found some of those artifacts in a cenote in Mexico, nearly twenty years ago. So, I have a connection to your story. I think it may be why he came to see me." Rowan avoided saying his name out of respect for her. She demonstrated a great deal of courage telling him all this. He owed her that much. "But I suspect that's not all of your story."

"No," she said, her voice dropping an octave. "He was a cocky jerk, so of course, he was my first suspect. I called him in and questioned him. He seemed perfectly innocent—at first. He said he'd looked at the artifacts, but he hadn't taken any of them. When the word court-marshal was mentioned, that's when things took a turn for the worst. One minute, he seemed fine. He was just standing there at attention like a proper marine. I'd already had the MPs go through his belongings. When he continued to deny it, I reached into my desk drawer and lay one of the artifacts where he could see it."

"Let me guess. A ring?"

"How did you know?"

"What happened then?"

"He grew enraged, and, quite frankly, I'd never been more scared in my entire military career. He leapt over my desk and grabbed the ring, then drew a knife," she said, her breath becoming raspy. "Before I could react, he struck me across the side of the face." Another long pause followed. Rowan was about to tell her she didn't need to continue, but she did. "I've seen men in combat—trained men. I know the look they get when they feel like they are fighting for their lives. He had that berserker blood rage in his eye. I knew at that moment it was him or me. But I never saw the blade in his hand. I certainly never felt it when he came at me with it. That's what he hit me with, and it slashed my cheek clean through. Then he began stabbing me—over and over. I must have screamed, but I don't remember. I know the MPs tried to get him off me, and I tried to get to my side weapon. But he was so strong, and I've never seen anyone so vicious."

"My God," Rowan said. "You're lucky to be alive."

"It took five MPs to get him off me, and three of them were injured in the process," she said. "I spent nine days in the base hospital before I was sure I wasn't going to die. Someone told me I needed seven units of blood before they could get the bleeding under control. He stabbed me twenty-two times."

"So, he was court-marshaled after all," Rowan said. It wasn't a question.

"He accused me of stealing. Claimed I had no authority to go through his effects without cause, that it was an illegal search. Of course, they threw the book at him."

"Major, I am so sorry you had to go through that," he said. "I'm sorry I had to bring up so many bad memories. But I needed to understand what was going on with him before he died."

"You couldn't have known," she said. "The JAG team sealed the records, as much to protect my career as anything. Someone alleged I was culpable because I knew they'd been accused and didn't make sure all the objects were returned. I argued that I did what any reasonable commanding officer would do. But here's the thing—when they took him into custody, he didn't have the ring, and none of the other artifacts ever turned up."

"But you said he grabbed the ring off your desk," Rowan said, his mind racing.

"That man had a monster in him," she said, swallowing the words. "I don't know how he did it, but . . ."

"We all have a monster within us," Rowan said. "The only difference is the degree."

"Do you know? Did he have the ring? When he . . . died?"

Rowan thought about the box hidden in the attic. "I don't think so," he lied and regretted having to rely on the technicality. The ring was in a box in his attic, not on his person. It was unavoidable. He made his mind up at that moment—he would find all of the missing artifacts, and when he did, he would personally deliver them to the museum in Khartoum.

"Do you have any idea what's gotten into that dog?" Rowan asked as he drove the scenic peak-to-peak highway. There were faster ways to get to Estes Park, but they were in no hurry. A much-needed long weekend didn't come with an agenda, just a few important high points—including the meeting with Dr. Octavia Vanderhorst. Lauren was most excited to meet such an esteemed colleague.

"No idea," Lauren said. "Maybe squirrels are building a nest in the light pole. It's the only thing I can think of to explain why he's wigging out."

"I'm surprised Sarah didn't know what he was doing," Rowan said. "Or why."

"She'd be the one to know," Lauren said. Her gaze lifted to the distant peaks. Her mind was still agitated over the interview at the television station. She didn't know why it bothered her so much, or why it lingered in her mind. "I have to admit, I was kind of proud of her for the whole bucket of worms thing." They both chuckled.

"That'll be the last time Kate refuses to eat her dinner," Rowan said.

"Would your mother have grounded you?"

"My mother was a strict disciplinarian," Lauren said. Her mind flashed back to the woman her mother used to be—an angry, broken alcoholic. "But she's not like that any more."

"There's a difference between being a mother and being a grandmother," Rowan pointed out.

"A mother exercises discipline, a grandmother—wisdom," Lauren said. "I told my mother what she did. If I know her, she'll coach her and guide her better than she ever did me."

"I'm happy to see you and your mom's relationship's improved," he said. "There was a time when I thought it might come to fisticuffs."

"She's not the same person she was," Lauren noted.

Rowan reached over and took her hand. "Neither are you," he said. "Crazy how things work out, right?"

"It means a lot to me to have her home again," she said. "I hope she'll stay a while."

Rowan chuckled. "Oh? Do you want her to keep tabs on me or are you tired of my cooking already?"

Lauren scoffed. "You're a good cook," she said, a laugh in her voice. "Is it wrong that I miss my mommy?"

"No," Rowan drew her hand to his lips and kissed her knuckles. "There's nothing wrong with having your mom home. She can stay as long as she likes."

"Thanks. That means a lot to me." Lauren's gaze panned to the eastern horizon, and she was silent for a few minutes. "Where are we staying? Did you rent an Air B&B?"

"I called in a favor," he said. "My friend Dani had a room available."

"We're staying at someone's house?" Lauren turned to look at him, her brow furrowed behind her aviator sunglasses.

"No, it's nothing like that," he said. "Can't I surprise you once in a while?"

"You know I'm not a fan of surprises," she said.

"You'll like this one."

Lauren most certainly did not.

13

The grand, imposing structure of the Stanley Hotel stood out against the backdrop of the jagged Rocky Mountains. The white manse seemed to glow in the afternoon sun. Three flags waved in the breeze. The stars and stripes were flanked by the Colorado state flag on one side, and a white flag—with a gold S—on the other. The signature red rooftops stood out, adding a pop of color against the otherwise muted hues of the valley. The front lawn was neatly manicured and green despite the lateness of the season.

The front entrance was marked by a wide porch with white columns and massive wooden double doors beneath the arch. They invited guests into the hotel's historic halls. The beauty of the building filled Rowan with awe and joy. This was where they'd met, and it conjured up memories of the night his heart began to beat again after the perils of his own experiences in war.

Lauren sat unmoving in the car, her eyes fixed. Her memories were quite different, and he realized at that moment he probably should have prepared her for his surprise. He came around to her door and opened it, noticing she flinched as he took her hand. She moved to stand by the car, but her gaze remained affixed on something in the top corner of the building. His eyes moved to search for whatever it was that held her attention. A shadow of movement—as a curtain closed in one of the windows—was all he saw. "What?" he asked. "I thought you'd be excited."

She turned on him and railed. "The last time I stayed here I got carried out on a stretcher. Have you lost your ever-lovin' mind?"

Big mistake, bucko, he chided himself. "Think of it as a do-over," he said. "I'm here with you. I won't let anything happen to you. You know that right? Besides, I thought you would enjoy a relaxing weekend of being pampered. Besides dinner with Dr. Vanderhorst, I set us up for the tour, massages, and even room service. We can hike or shop or do nothing at all."

Lauren wasn't convinced. "When you said you wanted to recreate our first date, I didn't realize you wanted to start with me breaking my leg—again!" Panic and fear now resonated in her voice.

"Lauren, I won't let anyone push you down the stairs."

She clutched his hand tightly. "You weren't there. You don't know."

"I'm here now," he said. "I saw the results of your last visit, Lauren. Better than you did, I'll wager." He drew her into his arms, kissing her head and stroking her hair. "I won't let it happen again."

He saw the war raging within her, a battle between the scientist and the paranormal investigator. The scientist wanted to argue that ghosts were nothing but *hokum* and that her smarmy former co-host had pushed her down the stairs. That was Rowan's theory, so he completely understood. But the paranormal investigator might think otherwise. He knew she'd felt the chill of cold energy that struck her in the middle of the back and sent her tumbling ass-over-teakettle down the stairs, like a whirling dervish trying to do gymnastics and failing miserably. She shivered in his arms, despite the sun's warmth on her back.

"Fine." She finally capitulated, and he saw her defenses collapsing.

"Are you sure?" He let her go but kept a hand on her arm.

"I'm terrified." Her voice came out in a breathless whisper. "But you are my protector."

<hr>

LAUREN'S SENSE of foreboding grew as they entered the hotel lobby and made their way to the registration desk. A gentleman in a suit appeared from behind the counter and crossed the room with his hand extended to her husband. "Welcome back, Mr. Pierce," he said, then turned to Lauren. "You must be Dr. Pierce. Welcome to the Stanley Hotel. I'm Jim. We're excited to help you celebrate your anniversary. How many years has it been?"

Lauren's brain stopped working as soon as she saw the staircase. She heard the snap of her bones echoing in her head, and Bahati's scream piercing the din of her memory. "She's lost count," Rowan chuckled, drawing her from the madness swirling around her.

"Twenty . . . twenty-five?" Lauren muttered, looking to Rowan. She could tell by his reaction that he saw the panic setting in.

"Well, let's get you checked in so the celebration can begin," the manager said, taking Lauren's bag. He placed it on the bellman's cart next to Rowan's bag. The clerk behind the desk turned to the rack of old-fashioned skeleton keys that hung from hooks on a red velvet board. She turned back with two ornate golden keys with the number 217 etched on a brass tag. The head of the antique keys were etched in filigree and polished to a brilliant shine.

"Is that . . ." Lauren started.

"The Stephen King suite," Jim said. "Only the best for you and Mr. Pierce. We have your reservations for dinner tonight at six with Dr. Vanderhorst in the dining room. Bison short ribs are on the menu. I highly recommend them."

"Thank you, Jim," Rowan said, taking the keys. "We have just enough time to freshen up before dinner then." He stuck out his arm and offered it to Lauren. She took it, tucking herself against him. "Come on. We'll take the elevator."

THE STEPHEN KING SUITE, despite being room number 217, was located on the fourth floor of the historic hotel. The room had an old-world elegance blended with Victorian designs and a touch of modern luxury. The king-sized bed was adorned with rich, dark linens and a large, intricately carved headboard. It had a majestic, yet slightly eerie feel to it. Moody tones of dark green, red, and gold gave the space a warmth, but the haunted atmosphere was overt, and Lauren hesitated in the doorway.

Rowan moved to inspect the sitting area and then the bathroom. "You'll like the tub," he said, coming back into the main area. Lauren still stood, like one of Medusa's victims turned to stone. A knock at the door launched her almost out of her shoes, and a gasp escaped her throat before she could contain it.

The door opened and the bellman came in with their bags. He was followed by an attendant who carried a silver ewer, with a bottle of champagne nestled on ice. "Compliments of The Stanley Hotel," the attendant said. "Would you like me to open it for you now?"

Lauren moved uncomfortably into the room and took a seat. "Maybe later," she said, glancing at her watch. It wasn't five o'clock just yet. "I haven't eaten since breakfast. I'm not sure I should drink on an empty stomach."

"I've got it," Rowan said to the attendant. "Thank you." He tipped them both, then turned to the room. "I should have brought my laptop. I would love to do some writing in this room."

Lauren's stomach growled angrily. She clutched at her shirt front, not sure if it was hunger or nausea gripping her. Rowan, seeing her distress, came over and sat down beside her.

"Let's freshen up and I'll get some food in front of you as soon as I possibly can."

Now he was talking.

WHEN THEY STEPPED into The Cascades Restaurant and Lounge, Rowan had on his sports coat and jeans. Lauren wore a navy-blue dress with a full skirt and brown riding boots with a bit of a heel. She'd left her hair loose, and it fell in waves over her shoulders. Rowan's cologne was comforting, and he rarely wore it except on special occasions. She hadn't even thought to grab her perfume when she packed.

Dr. Vanderhorst had already been seated. She rose when they entered, beaming as Rowan made introductions. Lauren was almost giddy. Octavia Vanderhorst was a legend in her field and yet their paths had never crossed. Lauren thought about how much the woman reminded her of Tima—not so much in her appearance, but in her mannerisms and how she commanded not just the table but the room. She was captivating, eloquent, and well-spoken. Rowan had commented on her accent, but Lauren hardly noticed it. Lauren immediately felt like they were old friends, instantly captivated by her presence.

The waiter came to take their drink order. Rowan had ordered a Coke when they had their snack earlier, but this evening he ordered a drink called a Dunraven Manhattan, named for one of the earliest robber barons to take over the valley around Estes Park. Lauren knew the story from her research twenty-some years ago. Windham Thomas Wyndham-Quinn, the Earl of Dunraven believed he'd found paradise when he came to Estes Park from Denver. He'd been lured west by tales of riches in the "uninhabited" west. When he arrived in 1872, he found marvelous prospects for his favorite pastime—elk hunting. He returned the following year and began buying land. The man wanted it all and would stop at nothing to get it. The veteran of the Boer War in Africa had a dream of building a game preserve, which began to dissolve when more and more settlers began to arrive. He'd already manipulated the Homestead Act of 1862 to purchase over 15,000 acres of land, but with the influx of pioneers into the area, he eventually gave in and decided to build a hotel—the first in the area. He went on to help build roads, buy a sawmill, and haul in machinery. His illegal land grab outraged the locals. Realizing his private game reserve would not come to pass, he established a hunting lodge in what was now known as Dunraven Gladie, north of town. He also established a cattle ranch called the English Dairy, where he raised Swiss cattle. He abandoned his claims to most of his property in the mid-1880s, before being made the Undersecretary to the Colonies by Queen Victoria. He sold most of his lands in 1908 to F.O. Stanley—founder of the Stanley Motor Carriage Company—who was stricken with a life-threatening resurgence of tuberculosis. Like many lungers of his day, the curative air of the Rocky Mountains drew him to the area.

"I'll have the Stanley Old Fashioned," Dr. Vanderhorst said. "Double splash of the orange bitters."

"And for you?" The waitress turned to Lauren. Lauren had been so lost in thought she hadn't even read the menu. She scanned it. "How about the Lucky Lucy?"

"Excellent choice," the waiter said. "One of my favorites. How about an appetizer?"

"How about the charcuterie board?" Rowan suggested. Both ladies nodded. "Would it be possible to add some bleu cheese and grapes to that?" he asked the waiter. "Dr. Pierce's favorites."

"Of course," the waiter said, giving Lauren a wry grin. "I'll have that right out."

The small talk lasted a few minutes—until the drinks arrived—then the conversation morphed into tales of Dr. Vanderhorst's work seeking the Lost City of Taino in the Caribbean and the time she found pirate's treasure in a cave along the coast of Belize. "I know you'll understand this," she said, her hand on Lauren's wrist, establishing a level of familiarity rare amongst strangers but perfectly normal in the company of friends. "But there are some places that feel *different*. The hidden temple in the shadow of *El Yunque* is one of those places. It's like the land itself has memories and secrets it wishes to keep hidden. And the hidden cenotes. Oh, every time I visit, I feel as if I have entered *Xibalba*—the very depths of hell—and I will never escape."

Lauren's chest tightened. Even stories about caverns and tight places sparked her claustrophobia and invoked near panic. "But you did escape." She needed to hear the end of that story.

"Of course, Lauren." The woman laughed, rich and deep, but unrestrained and full of *joie de vivre*. "With a cache of Mayan gold that would have made Cortez envious."

"One of your many great discoveries," Lauren complimented.

"Better you than Cortez." Rowan laughed, raising his glass.

"Here's to you," Lauren said. The Spanish conquistadors had been a plague on the Mayan Empire, and some theorized they were the reason the empire crumbled and all but disappeared. Lauren, like many in her field, had other theories. Drought made the most sense.

Rowan shared some of their stories, with Lauren interjecting here and there. It was rare they had time like this with other learned scholars who shared their passion for adventure and their thirst for answers to the world's mysteries.

The stories lasted even after they ordered and their meal was served. The bison short ribs were indeed delicious, and Lauren was pleased that Rowan did not behave like a Neanderthal and gnaw the meat off the bones.

"I was telling Rowan he needs to join the Colorado Archeological Society," Dr. Vanderhorst said to Lauren. "You, too."

"It would be a tremendous honor," Rowan said. "As I mentioned, I didn't know such an organization existed."

"It's a chapter of the International Archeological Society. We need someone to take over the leadership role for the Colorado chapter since Dr. Ethan Harlow retired. Do you know him?"

"*Of* him," Lauren said. "But no, I've never met him."

"He was one of the professors at Colorado State for a while, wasn't he?"

"He was," Dr. Vanderhorst said, beaming. "Did you take classes with him?"

"No," Rowan said. "I was taking courses in the Fire Safety department. I studied under Dr. Rex."

"She's still teaching," Octavia said. "I've met her at faculty events. Lovely woman."

"I think a lot of her, too." Rowan smiled. "I have so many stories to tell. She liked to blow things up in the lab—grain dust, mostly."

"Oh, that's one I haven't heard," Lauren said, prompting Rowan into his next story.

THE DARKNESS WAS WAITING, watching, always watching. It knew its mission. It had been patient, lingering in the corners of the old hotel, feeding off the remnants of fear and whispered secrets. For years, it bided its time, unseen, unnoticed, as the world around it turned. But tonight—tonight, something was different. Tonight, there was something new—something ripe with the scent of tension and confusion. The air was thick, and it knew it.

They had arrived—the pair. The man, Rowan Pierce, the one whose mind danced with the specters of doubt, whose soul was cracked just enough for *The Darkness* to slip in unnoticed. And the woman, Lauren, with her endless curiosity, her hunger for truth. She would know the truth soon enough. Her shield had fallen ever so slightly and continued to dim as the cocktails swirled in her veins.

But Rowan was a toy for *The Darkness* to taunt—a yarn mouse for the cat's claw to swipe. The man was the tool *The Darkness* needed to get the Dark Lord what he truly desired. If *The Darkness* remained true to his Master's command, he would topple them like a house of cards, and in the end, the woman would fall to kneel at the Master's knee. *This is indeed the night the Master would be given all he desired.*

Patience. The Darkness curled, twisting in the dimly lit corners of the Cascades Restaurant, writhing with an unbearable hunger to feed. It cringed at the clinking of glasses, brittle chimes of forgotten bells. *Ask not for whom the bell tolls . . .* "It tolls for thee, Rowan Pierce," *The Darkness* whispered. The room was full of life, but *The Darkness* did not care for life, warmth, or human joy. It cared only for the fear, the chaos—the madness of despair and broken hearts. It thrived in sorrow and torment.

Soon enough, the moment would arrive.

It watched as the man leaned forward, his hand hovering over his barely touched cocktail. Its pulse quickened. *The Darkness* knew that this was the path to the man's undoing. *The Darkness* felt his growing unease, the fear creeping like icicles along his spine. The man did not understand the fear growing in his core. He couldn't see it, but he felt it, and that made it all the more delicious.

Even as they spoke in quiet tones with their guest, *The Darkness* found its rage and longing growing into one roiling ball of bloodlust. The need to manifest into form and show its face would elicit the fear upon which it would feed. *Yes. Yes.* That was what it needed. Just a taste. It moved in the shadows, tempted into the light. The woman turned to reach for the sweater on the back of her chair and her gaze locked on *The Darkness.* It retreated. Did she see it? Did she know?

The man stiffened and tilted his head, looking past his woman. He gazed into the abyss and there was recognition— comprehension. His heart was racing now. He was on the edge, teetering between disbelief and panic. *Yes! The Darkness* felt it, tasted the fear in the air. *Delicious!*

"What is it?" their companion asked.

The two looked at one another, then the man's gaze returned to the void. "I'm just suddenly very cold," the woman said. "Like . . ."

"Like all the heat has been sucked from the room?" The man finished her sentence in query.

The Darkness stretched its form, curling around the edges of the room, feeding on the unease, feeding on the cracks that would soon widen. It didn't matter if they left tomorrow or the next day. The seeds were planted. Their minds were open now—fragile. *The Darkness* had found its way in.

And so it waited, as it always did. Watching.

The Darkness was always watching, waiting.

———

LAUREN SLAMMED the door behind her, but Rowan burst in, undaunted. "Lauren, stop!" He caught her arm and pulled her into him. She pushed him away, but he held her fast. "Please, take a breath."

"You saw it, too!" It wasn't a question.

Rowan ran his hand over her hair as he let her go, and she escaped to the corner. "I saw something. Yes."

"Of all the places, Rowan." She paced, one hand on her brow, the other over her abdomen. She struggled to catch her breath. She was angry, but she wasn't sure who to direct her rage toward. "Why here?"

Rowan collapsed into one of the wing-backed chairs in the sitting area. "I'm sorry," he said. "I wanted to redefine your feelings about this place, I guess."

"I can't stay here." She rushed to her bag and started throwing her things back into it, willy-nilly. "I have to get out." Panic overtook her.

He rose and blocked her path. "Honey, what's with you? In all the years we've been together, I have never seen you run from a paranormal experience. Not once?"

Lauren locked eyes with him, and she was certain he heard her teeth grating. "I thought you were out of that business? I thought this was supposed to be a romantic weekend?" She began a tirade in a language she knew he wouldn't understand but made sure the emphasis and punctuation of her anger conveyed her dismay.

"Come on now," he interrupted. "That's not fair." The sharpness in his tone made her freeze, the words locked in her throat. "I'm sorry if this isn't the anniversary celebration you would have liked." He softened his tone as he so often did when he wanted to turn away her wrath. "I'll make it up to you."

"How?" she asked, suddenly no longer as angry as she wanted to be.

"Margaritas and tacos on the beach in Cozumel? Just you and me."

"When?"

"While you're on Christmas hiatus," he said. "And tonight? Just you and me, here. Alone."

Lauren stepped back. "You can't guarantee that," she said.

"Look," he said, softly, coming up behind her. He moved her hair aside and pressed his lips just behind her ear. "There's a full bottle of champagne, a soaking tub, and no children around. We can drink the whole bottle. Then neither of us will care if this place is haunted." She let her head fall aside, encouraging him to continue. He complied as his hand snaked around her waist. "I'll bet money," he said between kisses, "I can make you moan louder than any banshee in this place."

A wicked smile curled in the corner of her cheek. She knew what he was capable of. "Let's see about that."

LONG AFTER LAUREN WAS ASLEEP, Rowan slid out of bed and quietly dressed. At the bottom of his backpack, he had several new devices—tools of a trade he hadn't plied in over four years. He wasn't sure when he'd have a chance to use them, but he wasn't going to get to sleep any time soon. Now was as good as ever.

He'd fulfilled his promise to Lauren, and she'd sleep until dawn and probably wake up with a hangover. After the incident at dinner—an event they'd managed to keep out of the dialogue with Dr. Vanderhorst—he was more convinced than ever that whatever Riggs had been afraid of was still here.

At dinner, he hadn't gotten to the one thing he wanted to talk about, but he wasn't sure how to explain it to Lauren without it making waves over how he'd heard about it. She hadn't taken the news that the Exploration Channel was sniffing around very well, and she was already mad at him. *Why add fuel to the fire? No, this was his burden to bear. He'd promised Riggs he'd help him, and by God, he was going to help him.*

He slipped out quietly, finding the hallways empty. The fourth floor was often said to be one of the most haunted areas of the hotel. It was most famous for unexplained sounds and shadows. There were reports from guests who heard children's laughter, the pitter-patter of footsteps, and who saw shadow figures walking down the hall. Rowan walked down the corridor and switched on his device, turning the volume down so as not to disturb other guests.

Taking a baseline, he tested the monitors and picked up nothing. *Typical.* He debated going back down to the dining room, wondering if it would be open this time of day. He glanced at his watch. Three in the morning. *No, it was probably closed.*

"Okay, ghosts or whatever I saw in the dining room," he muttered under his breath, "are you here?"

The shadow form he'd seen sent a chill through him, and he suspected the energy needed to allow the spirit to form such a wicked black shadow must have sucked the heat from the room. Even Lauren—who tended to run hot—reached for her sweater.

He found a spot in the corner and sat on the floor. He set his equipment up in front of him. From here, he could keep an eye on both the EMF meter and the SLS camera screen. He also set up a spirit box, scanning through various radio frequencies and listening for any responses. Rowan had done his research on the hotel over the years. He knew its ghostly history and the types of spirits that might be present in the old building. In all his years of investigations, he couldn't remember encountering anything he'd classify as a shadow person, but that black mass in the restaurant certainly seemed to fit the description.

If Lauren were with him on this, she might hypothesize that shadow people could be linked to several physiological, neurological, and environmental factors. She'd go on about the link between stress and perception most likely. He was stressed, that was for certain. The last thing he wanted was a lesson on high levels of cortisol and its effects on the amygdala —the part of the brain responsible for processing emotions and how it might interpret the vague stimuli, like a shadow in the corner of the room, as a threat.

His science—the craft he was practicing now—relied on measuring disturbances in the earth's magnetic field. The current theory was that the electromagnetic field, natural or man-made, disrupted the way the brain processes visual information. Another related theory suggested spirits—demonic or benevolent—used the electromagnetic fields to manifest into the same plane of existence humans existed in. They made themselves visible or generated a sound.

Watching.

Rowan realized he'd dozed off, but the disembodied voice from the spirit box brought him to attention. "Am I watching you?"

Waiting.

"Yeah," he said, standing up and using the camera on his phone to scan the hallway. "I'm waiting for you to do something." For a moment he had a pang of regret that Jean-René wasn't with him, hidden behind a camera, recording the evidence for all to see.

A flicker of light caught his attention, and he glanced down at the EMF detector. The six lights created a scale to measure the electromagnetic frequencies around the device; two were green, one was yellow, one was orange, and one was red. The green lights flickered into the yellow phase and then spiked into red before all the lights went out. "Can you do that again?"

The EMF seemed to be dead. None of the lights illuminated. Rowan picked it up and ran it along his arm to spark some static and get the lights to flicker, but there was nothing. "Unfreakingbelievable. I just put batteries in this thing this morning."

Dead.

"Yeah, well. I'll be dead when Lauren sees the bill for all this garbage. First time out of the box, you'd expect this stuff to work." Rowan answered the spirit box while he fidgeted with the device, taking out the batteries, switching them, then putting the cover back on. Still nothing.

Soon.

Rowan froze. The spirit box was still working. He'd answered a spirit without even realizing it.

He was having a conversation with a spirit.

"Watching. Waiting. Dead. Soon," he muttered. "Who will be dead soon?" he asked, not sure he wanted to know the answer. He waited, but no answer came. Rowan picked up the spirit box, which looked more like a lighted hockey puck than a box and tucked it in his pocket. He grabbed the SLS camera and walked toward the room where Lauren slept, scanning the hallway slowly with it. The hair on the nape of his neck pricked, and he felt a chill gather behind him. He turned, just as a dark form moved at the end of the hall, disappearing at the top of the stairs.

"Are you the one that likes to push people down the stairs?" Rowan asked, raising his voice a bit as he moved back toward the spot where he'd been sitting. The EMF detector suddenly flickered to light—frenetically. The lights went from green to red and back again, over, and over. *Yeah. That's what I thought, you little twerp. We're about to have a little discussion on revenge.* He would demand satisfaction for what happened to his wife all those years ago, though he knew better than to provoke the spirits. "Come out where I can see you."

He glanced down at the screen on the SLS camera, which was set in the infrared mode. The images generated by the Structured Light Sensor—or SLS—camera often appeared as human-like stick figures with dots where the joints might be when a ghost was observed. He'd seen them dismembered or hovering over the floor before, but this time the figure was not human-shaped. The lines representing what might be perceived as arms and legs were too long for a human. The spine was short and there was no head. It hovered in the darkened corner and seemed to flicker as if it were dancing to some unheard dirge with an acid rock beat. The movements gave it an intangible quality.

"Holy sh—" Rowan looked from the camera to check the corner with his own eyes. A dark mass coalesced and thrummed like a gathering fog. *God, this better be recording*, he thought as his eye shifted to the screen. The number of limbs seemed to grow—lengthening and shortening as this thing, this monstrous form, jerked and contorted.

Dead.

Dead.

Waiting.

Watching.

Soon.

The spirit box in his shirt seemed to vibrate with the inhuman voice. Rowan took a step back, trying to catch his breath. Trying to still his racing heart.

Hunger.

Feed.

Now.

The mass grew until it no longer fit within the space in the corner of the hallway. It moved toward him with inhuman speed. Rowan ducked and dodged, backing up as it circled at the other end of the hall. Every muscle in his body tensed, ready to fight. There was no doubt. He was under attack. He felt like prey.

Dead.

Dead.

Now.

14

Lauren woke to a frantic pounding on the door. She flew out of bed and realized she was completely naked. She felt in the dark for clothing and found enough to make herself presentable. In her T-shirt and yoga pants, she flung the door open, clipping her toe and sending shooting pains up her foot. "What?" she snapped, angrier at herself than the interruption to her beauty sleep.

"Dr. Pierce." One of the staff stood at her door, looking distraught. "I'm sorry to disturb you, but your husband—"

"Rowan?" She froze, her heart catching in her throat, her throbbing toe forgotten.

"He's had some kind of a medical episode."

"What? Where is he?" She followed the man down the hall to the stairway. She hesitated, a rush of bad memories flooding her mind, but she put them aside as she kept a firm grip on the handrail.

When she reached her husband, hotel staff were already performing CPR, and the desk clerk raced to the bottom of the stairs with an AED.

"Rowan!" His name caught in her throat. She managed to leap over the last three steps and still maintain her footing as she shoved the man on the phone—presumably calling 911—aside. She grabbed Rowan by the collar of his shirt, the buttons ripped off to expose his chest. She checked for a pulse as the AED hit her knee. She reached for it and opened the case, hitting the power button. "Rowan? Come on now! Not here!" She found the razor and made short work of clearing a spot to attach the leads while the machine powered up.

"Yes, we have a man at the Stanley Hotel in cardiac arrest," the man on the phone said.

Analyzing. The AED announced. Lauren extended a hand to indicate to the man performing CPR that he should pause.

"Give me that," Lauren said to the man with the phone, as the AED did its thing. She relayed Rowan's condition to the 911 dispatcher.

No pulse detected. Shock advised. There was a brief pause. *Administering shock.*

"Clear!" Lauren ordered. She heard the machine activate.

Analyzing. Resume CPR.

Lauren dropped the phone and resumed compressions, counting aloud to a tempo she knew to be 140 beats per minute. She paused periodically to administer a breath—praying each time that he'd draw one on his own—before she resumed compressions.

"Not here, Rowan," she panted between breaths and compressions. "Not now. I'm . . . I'm not done with you." *One-one-thousand, two-one-thousand, three-one-thousand,* she counted in her head. *Breathe.*

Those around her offered to assist, and when the AED cycled a third time, she collapsed onto her knees, feeling the weight of her world crashing down on her. Her arms felt like the muscles had turned into Jell-O, but her core had turned to lead. It seemed like hours had passed. Her hearing faded, listening for the beat of his heart—everything moving in slow motion. Then, the paramedics crashed through the doors, the noise deafening as everything raced into full speed.

Lauren found herself lifted from the floor and moved over to the sitting area by the fire. Someone wrapped a blanket around her, and she realized how cold she was. One of the paramedics knelt at her knee, inspecting her. Lauren's attention was drawn to Rowan's plight, but she couldn't see past the paramedics who continued to work on him. The medic, a young man with copper hair and a freckled nose, patted her knee and held her face in his hands so she'd look at him. His mouth moved, but no words seemed to find her ear. His bright blue eyes held genuine concern as he focused on her.

It struck her at that moment that, if he were ten years younger, he was the perfect likeness to her son, Jamie. Maybe it was Jamie. Maybe she'd been kicked out of sync with time when Rowan's heart stopped beating. He'd had a cardiac episode once before and had come to her in her dreams. She looked for him anywhere but on the floor. Her eyes moved to the top of the stairs and scanned down. She realized he lay just feet from where she had landed when she'd been pushed down these same stairs.

A chill washed through her core as she rose, feeling as if she'd left her body behind. Her ghost walked over to where Rowan lay and gazed down at him. His face was placid, as if he were sleeping, his eyelids hanging loosely over his green lifeless eyes. His beard seemed to shine in the glow of the firelight, and the dimmed lights that hung above him. His body moved in response to the paramedic doing compressions. Another medic put a mask over his face to deliver breaths at the proper intervals.

The crowd of onlookers was limited to five staff members, and what she assumed were their guests. Everything else in the hotel had stopped. She walked around the gathered crowd, moving between people she didn't know. They stood like ghostly statues, more solid than she. Her feet didn't touch the floor, and for a moment she thought of herself as a mermaid moving between pillars of stone in the ruins of Atlantis.

Lauren glanced over and caught her translucent reflection in a mirror. She was certain her ghost would be forever doomed to roam the hotel in her green CSU T-shirt and her yoga pants. She glanced back at Rowan. The medics had cut away another of his favorite shirts and started an IV. The AED buzzed again, the red light flashing. At that moment, she felt no warmth, no connection. It was as if he was someone she used to know, someone she had loved and had left behind —a broken and empty shell. At that moment, her own heart shattered. She balled up her fists and reached deep inside, screaming in her agony—something she never had done. The empty scream made no sound but scraped the tissues of her throat, and the mirror behind her shattered into a million pieces. Shards of glass blew around her like tiny projectiles, passing through everyone else, but imbedding in her ethereal form.

A deep rumble echoed in the room around her—a laugh that wrapped itself around her and gripped her tightly. A dark shadow gathered at the top of the stairs. It was without form and void, a darkness on the landing. A flash of light built at its core and mixed with the darkness, swirling into a massive expanse. "And my Father said, let there be light," a voice found its way from the void. "My Father separated the darkness from the light. That was the first time He turned his back on me . . . but it would not be the last."

Lauren's breath caught in her throat. The scene took on a sickly puce aura that made her stomach churn—the odor of brimstone and death filled the air. Laughter erupted from the void as the swirling mass expanded. A black fog—like a demon's hungry minion—snaked down each step, moving toward Rowan's prostrate form. *No*, she wanted to scream. *Leave him alone!* But her body refused to cooperate.

The darkness remaining on the stairs throbbed. It was as if the very void between realms exhaled something ancient— malevolent. The air vibrated with a presence that had been bound—long lost to time—imprisoned in the depths of Hell itself. Then, emerging from that yawning emptiness—an abyss where light had no dominion—he came forth. His figure rose from the darkness as though being birthed by the void itself. Ash and embers flickered in the dying shadow as he stepped into the light. Its face—or what was supposed to be a face—broke into a fanged grin, too wide, too cruel, stretching the emptiness of his features. This monstrous creature—this horned *thing*—slithered its way down the steps, pausing at Rowan's feet, gazing down at the dark-shaded minion that now held the form of her beloved. Even the medics seemed to stop moving as the world around her faded away. Nothing stood between her and the epitome of evil unbound.

Yes. Lauren knew this creature.

Enlil. She realized the demon made flesh—no longer just a shadow but an ancient force born of the darkness itself, a fallen angel with powers that were far beyond her comprehension.

"Yes." His voice, deep and soulless—as only a demon's soul could be—seemed to take delight in her recognition. He moved slowly, his eyes drinking her in as if she was his creation. He licked his lips, his tongue catching on a fang as he inhaled like a pack-a-day smoker getting his first cigarette of the day. "In the beginning, there was nothing, and from nothing came the light. And the light gave birth to *The Darkness* and all who would defy the light."

Enlil. The Fallen One. The one who had once stood among the hosts of heaven at the right hand of Anu circled her, drinking her in. She sensed his lust—his hunger for her fear and her grief. He towered over her, and an air of supremacy circled her as he moved with a mocking grace. "You think you can stop this? No, child. Maybe you delayed the inevitable. Know thy enemy as you know thyself," he quoted. "Strike at the heart and the enemy will fall."

Rowan is my heart, and I am his, she heard her words being used against her.

"Now, it's too late," he said, gazing down at the lifeless form. The insurmountable weight of the moment was not lost on her, and she felt all her power fleeing its mortal coil. Rowan wasn't just her heart; he was the source of all her power. "You were always too late."

Enlil's mocking laughter echoed off the marble tiles and filled the space around her, making the chandeliers quake above, their light flickering as they swung wildly. Lauren looked down at the limp form at his feet and felt the very heavens fall around her. She had not expected her defeat to come at the price of love. It was too great a cost—one she could not bear. "No!" she cried, staggering to her feet. "Take me! If you must take a soul, take mine!"

The demon spun around like an excited child, his wicked face illuminated by the fires of hell itself. "You give yourself to me?" The anticipation practically dripped from his fangs. "How generous."

The echo of a paramedic's voice reached her in the void, and it was the last thing she heard before the darkness overtook her and everything fell away. "We've got a pulse!"

15

"Nanhi," Kate said as she took a seat at the counter across from her grandmother. Diana was making breakfast. She'd let the kids sleep in late, and they were hungry.

"Yes, sweetheart?" Diana looked up in time to see the rest of the kids gathering around.

"You know we have a big Halloween party every year, right?"

"It's the stuff of legends." Diana chuckled. She'd seen pictures from previous years. The whole neighborhood assembled in the cul-de-sac outside the Pierce home, and each family ran a station where games were played. Snacks and baked goods were available for sale, and the funds were used by the neighborhood beautification committee to plant bulbs and flowers in the median at the entry to the neighborhood. Diana knew where this was going. "And the rules are nothing store-bought, right?"

"That's not the only rule," John Carter said.

"That's rule number four," Kate said.

"Oh?"

"Rule number one is if you don't ask for help before

October first, you're responsible for your own costume," Jamie explained. "Mom says, with so many kids, she doesn't want to be sewing us costumes on October thirty-first and not have time to work on her own costume."

"Makes sense," Diana said, leaning on the counter. "What's rule number two?"

"You can't tell anyone what you're gonna be," Sam said. "The surprise is half the fun."

Kate didn't wait for her grandmother to ask about the next one. "Rule number three is that we can't spend more than twenty-five dollars each, and that includes all the accessories."

"Usually, we decide on the theme a month before Halloween," John Carter said. "We haven't had a chance to do that."

"Ah." Diana smiled, her attention back on the dough beneath the heel of her hand. "How do you do that?"

"We pick a theme, and everyone has to agree to it," Sam said. "If there's any argument, all the suggestions go in a basket, and we draw for it."

"Fair enough."

"Okay," Diana said, moving to the sink to wash her hands before turning to the complement of grandchildren. "So, tell me about some of the themes you've done in the past?"

"Last year was nursery rhymes," Kate said. "So lame."

"The year before that was *Star Wars*," Jamie said. "Sarah was Yoda." His laugh made his sister scowl. She didn't like that costume.

"We've done Greek myths, cartoon animals, even monsters," John Carter said. "Dad came as Bigfoot. Mom dressed up as the Creature from the Black Lagoon."

"What are your ideas for this year?" Diana asked, taking the notepad and pen from the desk by the phone.

"*Blue's Clues*!" Sarah got in the first vote.

"That's for babies," Kate scowled.

"It is not!"

"How about Micky Mouse?" Sam suggested.

"That's for babies, too." Kate was spicy today. "I want to be a superhero."

"What about letting everyone be their favorite movie hero?" Jamie suggested. "That way, we have a lot more choices than just Blue and Steve."

"That's a really good idea," John Carter said. "Sarah? You wanna be Violet or Jack-Jack from *The Incredibles*?"

"No!" Sarah snapped. "I'm gonna be a secret. You're not supposed to try and guess."

"So, we can dispense with the basket of ideas, and everyone can pick their movie hero?" Diana hoped that would work. She didn't want to interfere with tradition, but Halloween had always been Lauren's favorite holiday. Diana toiled over costumes each year. Rainbow Bright, Strawberry Shortcake, Xena: Warrior Princess, and even Lt. Uhura.

The kids looked at one another. "I can work with that," Sam said.

"We'll need to go to the thrift store," John Carter said.

"I thought you weren't allowed to wear anything store-bought," Diana said.

"We're not allowed to buy a costume at the Halloween store," Sarah clarified.

"But we can buy all the pieces at the thrift store, and sometimes, Mom lets us get makeup or accessories at Spirit Halloween," Kate added.

"Dad has a box of old clothes in the attic he lets us go through," Jamie said. "Some of our old costumes are in there, too."

Diana looked at Sarah. "Maybe one of Kate's costumes will fit you this year."

"Ew!" Sarah mimicked her older sister's usual comment. "Gross."

"You don't want to be My Little Pony?" Kate snarked.

"No way!" Sarah's face remained wrinkled. "I'd rather eat worms."

"Be careful what you ask for," Diana said, having heard about the worm incident from her daughter.

"That's rule number five," John Carter said. "No costume can be repeated. At least, not by the same person. The accessories can be reused, though."

"Well," Diana said, inspecting the kitchen. "The cinnamon rolls need a little while to rise. Why don't we take Indy for a walk while we wait?"

"Can we go to the park?" Sarah asked.

"I don't see why not," Diana said. "Go put your jacket on. It's a little chilly this morning."

"I've got guitar lessons," John Carter said. "I need to practice. Mind if I bail?"

"Me too," Kate said. "I have to call Lizzy. She missed school yesterday, and we have an assignment due on Monday. She asked me to make sure she got the assignment."

"That's very considerate of you," Diana said.

"Lizzy's my best friend," Kate said. "I can't let her flunk."

"Okay. John Carter, will you keep an eye on the dough?" Diana asked. John Carter was happy to oblige. "Boys?" She turned to Jamie and Sam. "Do you want to come, too?"

Sam jumped from his chair. "Let me grab my new kite!"

Diana's phone rang on the counter, and she realized she'd almost walked out without it. She grabbed it but didn't recognize the number. "Hello?"

"Is this Mrs. Grayson?"

"Yes, this is Diana Grayson."

"My name is Jennifer Smith," the woman on the other end said. "I'm a nurse in the ER at the Intermountain Health Saint Joseph Hospital. There's been an emergency. I need you to come down as soon as possible."

Diana sat with Jean-René and Bahati in the waiting room at the top-rated hospital in the region when it came to cardiology, and so far all she knew was that Rowan had suffered some kind of cardiac episode.

"Lauren must be beside herself," Bahati said, pacing the empty rows of chairs in the waiting room.

"Rowan's strong," Diana said, confidently. "I'm sure he'll be fine."

"Well, if he isn't, then Lauren is going to kill him—and then she's going to kill me," Jean-René said, as if his fate was already certain.

"Why *you?*" Diana asked, catching Bahati's hand and drawing her over to a chair, beckoning her to sit and wait patiently for news.

Bahati already knew the story, but Jean-René—Rowan's best friend and frequent accomplice—told Diana all about what happened in Haiti and about the voodoo priest who'd slipped Rowan a near-fatal Micky Finn. "I had to do CPR on him until help arrived," Jean-René explained. "And then they sent him home from the hospital that next morning without so much as a dose of nitroglycerin for the road."

Jean-René was about to explain the aftermath of that moment, but a man in scrubs and a white coat stepped out into the lobby and scanned the room, finding just the three of them. "Are you the Pierce family?" he asked, looking haggard.

Bahati squeaked and her knees gave out from under her. The doctor pulled up a chair as they all sat, awaiting the pronouncement of what did not appear to be good news. "Rowan suffered a cardiac arrest," he said, without preamble. "We're still running tests to determine the cause. Normally we'd be able to see arterial blockages or structural defects, like those caused by hypertrophic cardiomyopathy."

Something he said must have clicked in Bahati's brain. Her hand shot out and caught the doctor's, pulling it towards her. "You're . . . you're still running tests?"

"Yes, ma'am," he said.

"That means he's still alive." Tears spilled over her cheeks.

"Yes, ma'am," he said. "He's not out of the woods yet. We can't treat him until we know for certain what's going on."

"Lauren must be so relieved," Diana let out a breath she hadn't realized she was holding. "When can we see him?"

"Not yet," he said. "And I went down to the ER to examine her myself."

"Wait, what?" Diana gasped.

"She's exhibiting all the symptoms of a woman in shock. She's conscious now, and we'll monitor her for a few hours and decide what to do from there. If anything."

"When can we see her?" Bahati asked.

"Not yet," he said.

"Wow," Bahati grunted. "Is that all you can say? *Not yet?*"

Jean-René put a hand on her knee. "That's not a no," he said. "Don't blame the messenger if you don't like the message."

FEELING the trembling of evil in the cosmic ether, John was alerted to trouble in his family's time-place. He sensed his daughter's fear and the need for an ally.

John felt his way through the unraveled threads that separated one time from another. It was rare for him to focus so intently on a singular moment between time and space. He found his daughter asleep in her bed. No, not her bed. This wasn't her room at home. This was someplace different. Her hair fell over her face as she lay on her stomach with her arm over the bed. Her skin was bare, and the room chilled. He sensed the presence of spirits in this place. They were not ancient ghosts, but they were old by his daughter's standards.

The wind whistled outside the window, and John's skin prickled with the cold. He moved to draw the blankets up over

Lauren's bare skin, tucking her arms in as any father would for a child. He missed all the nights of tucking her in, kissing her head, and seeing her safely off to dreamland. He was not sure she was safe, but he was there to protect her now.

There was a knock at the door and John went to see who it was. A chambermaid bobbed her head. "Here to see about the lantern, sir." She held a lit candle in one hand. This was not a spirit of this era.

"Thank you," John said. "But not tonight. My daughter is sleeping." He turned to direct the woman's attention to the form in the bed. When he turned back, the woman still stood there, but her face was severely burned and her clothing scorched. Smoke rose from her hair, and she had a terrified look on her face. Her candle smoldered but had melted into a puddle in the brass holder.

"Want me to tidy up a bit?" The maid's scorched brows lifted. "Bring fresh towels?"

"You've put in some long hours," John said, his hand moving between them. His Jedi mind trick might not work on a spirit, but he was willing to try it. "You've earned your rest."

"I am tired, sir." She tilted her head, gazing longingly at the king-sized bed. "A little nap might serve me well."

"Yes, but not here," John said. "My daughter is expecting her husband back shortly."

"This must be him out in the hall," the maid said, looking over her shoulder, her expression grim. "He's playing with fire."

She turned and seemed to disappear in a puff of smoke. John had to wonder what had happened to her so suddenly that she'd been so gravely injured and yet continued to perform her duties. *Did she know she was gone? Had it been so sudden?*

John returned his attention to the moment at hand. He found his son-in-law at the other end of the hallway.

"Are you the one that likes to push people down the

stairs?" Rowan asked, raising his voice a bit as he moved back towards the spot where he'd been sitting. John moved closer to the EMF detector as it suddenly flickered to light—frenetically the lights went from green to red and back again, over and over. *Yeah. That's what I thought, you little twerp. We're about to have a little discussion on revenge.* Rowan's thoughts came to John's mind as easily as spoken words came to his ear. "Come out where I can see you."

"I am here," John said, testing the waters, not sure how perceptive Rowan might be.

"Holy sh—" Rowan looked from the camera to check the corner with his own eyes. John saw what caught his attention.

A dark mass coalesced and thrummed like a gathering fog. *God, this better be recording.* Again his thoughts came to John's mind. John studied the demonic presence that seemed to be taunting Rowan. It sprouted multiple limbs as it grew, lengthening and shortening as it jerked and contorted.

A voice came from a device in Rowan's shirt pocket, momentarily catching John off guard.

Dead.

Dead.

Waiting.

Watching.

Soon.

The voice hesitated, and Rowan glanced down in his shirt pocket, before taking a step back.

Hunger.

Feed.

Now.

That's when all hell seemed to break loose. The demon screamed with all the vibrato it summoned from the fiery depths of Hell. It seemed to muster a tremendous amount of energy as it raced past the startled man, tearing past Rowan with a force that made him stumble. He would have fallen had the wall not been there.

Whether he had time to regain his composure or not, Rowan charged after the shadow person. John followed. At the landing, just off the lobby, Rowan skidded to a stop and, though he couldn't see it, John saw the coalescence envelop him. It seemed to crush him. Rowan's hand went to his chest, grasping the front of his shirt. His color went bright red, then paled as he stumbled down the last few steps. He made it to the marble floor and collapsed.

"You're too late, old man," an ominous voice said from behind him. John didn't need to see what it was. He knew. He walked calmly down the stairs, standing beside his son as he turned to face the monster. "Enlil," he said curtly but did not bow to the Dark Lord. "It's been a long time."

"Brazen of you to think you'd have any more luck helping these pitiful humans," Enlil said. "Seeing as how much you were able to help your friends at Chichén Itzá so long ago."

"This is different," John said, keeping any emotion from his voice. No creature or power on Earth had the ability to save the Maya from near extinction. Drought, famine, war, and disease had been the fatal superfecta that killed most and scattered those that remained.

"How so?" Enlil queried. His tone held the haughtiness of a dozen centuries of conflict—too much for one who had been defeated so many times.

"While I cared for the Maya and served as their Protector, this is different."

"You had an army behind you then, and yet I still conquered you. I conquered you all."

"Perhaps," John said. "But these aren't just my friends you come for now. This is my family, and I will not allow you to harm them, even if I must move the heavens and the earth to protect them."

John realized the scene continued to play out around him. Lauren raced down the stairs and fell next to his knee, leaning over Rowan as hotel staff tended to him. John lifted a hand and directed it toward Lauren. "This is the flesh of my flesh."

The Fallen One's massive head tilted, like a curious Boston Terrier. "Flesh?" John saw he'd put the pieces together when he began to cackle manically. His laughter boomed through the hall as Lauren performed CPR on Rowan. "Flesh is weak."

"Human flesh, perhaps," John said, stepping aside as paramedics entered the lobby. "But my daughter and I are no mere mortals. We both carry a spark of the Divine."

"A spark is but a mouse." The demon chuckled. "Easily crushed beneath a cat's paw." Enlil raised a hand and inspected his monstrous claws. The nails clattered against one another as he rolled his fingers into his palm.

"But a spark can ignite an inferno," John said, suddenly aware of his daughter facing the demon—somehow in between his time-place and hers.

The demon saw his distraction. "Aw, but you overestimate yourself, Wizard." He turned to Lauren. Shifting into her time-place, John tried to move to her, but the demon blocked him.

Addressing her, the demon's voice resounded in the spaces between times. "In the beginning there was nothing, and from nothing came the light. And the light gave birth to *The Darkness* and all who would defy the light. You thought you had the power to stop this? No, child. You just delay the inevitable. Know thy enemy as you know thyself." John's head throbbed with the force of his words that crossed the barrier between them. "Strike at the heart and the enemy will fall."

Rowan is my heart, and I am his. Her thoughts found their way to her father. Her voice was comforting, but he sensed her fear nonetheless.

"Now, it's too late," Enlil said, gazing down at the lifeless form. "You were *always* too late."

Enlil's mocking laughter echoed off the marble tiles and

filled the void, making the chandeliers quake above, their light flickering as they swung wildly. John watched as Lauren looked down at the limp form at her feet. John felt the very heavens fall around her. She had not expected her defeat to come at the price of love. He knew all too well how that felt. Indeed, it was too great a cost. He'd been lost to his wife and family, and now Rowan faced the same fate unless they figured out a way to defeat Enlil.

"No!" she cried, staggering to her feet. "Take me! If you must take a soul, take mine!"

"No!" John demanded, moving between her and the devil. He was still outside their realm, but he reached for his daughter, grasping thin air. He rounded on the demon, who gazed directly at him—breaking the fourth window—as drool ran from his deformed chin, hungry for victory. "This is going to be beautiful, Wizard. Your daughter is mine."

"No!" John demanded. "She is not yours to take."

"She says otherwise."

The demon spun around like an excited child, his wicked face illuminated by the fires of hell itself. "You give yourself to me?" The anticipation practically dripped from his fangs. "How generous." He looked at John, licking his fang, and moved down the stairs, closing in on her. John moved to stop him. The demon lashed out with his dragon-like tail. John was hurled from his feet. His body launched across the lobby. He landed hard, skidding on the marble tile. There was a hollow *thwack* that echoed in John's ears as his skull hit the floor, and for a moment, everything went dark. When he pushed himself up to one elbow, dots danced in his eyes. His vision blurred. Regardless, he managed to get up. When he stood, Lauren and Enlil were gone.

"Lauren!" He turned, searching for her, stumbling toward the medics as they loaded Rowan onto a stretcher. He was still outside of their time-place. Then, he realized Lauren's physical body lay limp on the sofa by the fireplace. Another medic tended to her, shouting for his colleagues to help. "Lauren . . . no."

<hr>

JOHN ARRIVED at the hospital just after noon. Diana rushed to him and fell into him, weeping. He wrapped her in his arms and held her, his tears dampening her hair. When the ancient wizard felt the trembling of the firmaments, he immediately acted. His journey had been made without the proper preparations. He had not armed himself for the battle. It hadn't mattered. It was too late by the time he arrived.

The old wizard paid a high toll for his sudden journey from his own time to the present—repeatedly attempting to shift between temporal barriers to reach his daughter or save her husband.

Even if he had been able to aid Lauren in her battle with Enlil, he would not have been an effective ally. He might have been another sacrificial lamb for the Dark Lord to slaughter. He did what he could. He hoped it was enough.

There had been enough violence for one day. Now, his family needed him.

"My love," John said. He moved like a man on his final breath. His strength was gone.

"Grandpa!" Henry rounded the corner, skidding on the tile floor. He had the strength of youth, motivated by a fear that was unknown to most. "Nanhi. Is it true?" He lowered his tone. "Did Mom have to fight Enlil alone?"

Diana dug in her pocket for a tissue and turned away from her grandson to dry her eyes. John moved in between them, taking the boy's hands in his. "It's true," John said in a low tone. "I sensed the battle, but I could not reach your mother in time to intervene."

"Where is he? Where's Enlil?" Henry's face was red with

all the anger and grief the young man carried. "I will bind him myself."

"You'll do no such thing." Diana turned and protested. "We've suffered enough losses for one day."

Henry's features twisted as the tears poured from his reddening eyes. "What do we do?"

John pulled his grandson into his arms and held him. Diana put an arm around them both. "We pray."

Henry pulled away. "We pray?" His words were harsh. "We *pray*? To Enki? To Anu? Where were they when my parents were attacked? When my mother stood to face that monster—that *thing*—all alone? Where was Anu? Why should I pray to him? Why should I pray to any god?"

"It is not good to take your anger out on the gods," Diana said. "Any of them."

"The arrows of the Most High will be with thee, Henry," John added. "But do not tip them in the poison of your rage, lest the anger of Anu be upon you."

"Don't talk to me of arrows or poison! Anu turned his back on my mother."

"I argue he did not," Diana said, softly. "He gave her the strength she needed to save your father. Just pray she has the strength to save herself."

Henry was ready to lash out, but at his grandmother's words, he paused, trying to make sense of them. "Wait. What?" The muscles in his jaw flexed as his brows narrowed.

"Your mother is in the ER," Diana said. "We can't be sure what happened to her, but the doctors are taking good care of her."

"She's . . . alive?" Henry, not quite a man but no longer a boy, seemed to buckle. John caught his arm to steady him.

"She is," John said.

Diana handed him a tissue. "We should know something soon."

"Where's Dad?"

"They took him up for a cardiac CT," John said. "Jean-René and Bahati are waiting for him to come back down to the Cardiac ICU. They'll text your grandmother when he comes back."

"Mrs. Grayson?" A nurse came out from behind the nurse's station. "Your daughter is being discharged from the ER. They're processing her paperwork, so you can see her now."

Diana nodded and looked at John. He leaned down and kissed her head. She put a hand on his chest, then reached up and cupped Henry's face. "Your mom will be okay."

"Thank goodness," he said. "I'll come with you."

"No," Diana said. "I'll bring her here. You know she won't leave the hospital without your father."

"True that," Henry said.

John studied his grandson as his grandmother kissed his cheek. He had stubble on his chin, his jaw sharp and angular like his mother's. His brows had grown thick and arched like his father's. He had the distinct cheekbones of his Cherokee heritage but the exact duplicate of his father's Celtic nose. His blond hair—cropped close to his scalp on the side, but longer on top—had grown darker since the last time John had seen him, which had been some time.

"Come on," John said, patting Henry's hand. The old wizard summoned enough energy to distract the young man's thoughts. "Don't they feed you at college? You are hungry."

<hr>

LAUREN GLANCED down at the bandage around her arm as she walked out of the ER, a handful of paperwork, including her discharge papers and prescriptions for medications the doctors felt she needed. The needle inserted in the field to provide fluids and medication had left its mark—a purple bruise that spread beyond the edge of the gauze bandage. She was startled as her mother appeared around the corner.

"Lauren, thank God." Diana embraced her. Lauren allowed it but did not reciprocate. "Are you okay?" Diana held her at arm's length and looked her over. Her hair was disheveled, and she looked out of sorts.

"Fine," Lauren said. "What's going on?"

"Rowan's in the Cardiac ICU," she said, taking Lauren's hand and leading her to the elevator. "They're still running tests."

"Oh."

"Do you remember what happened?"

"No. Not really," Lauren answered as the elevator opened and they stepped in.

"You don't look very steady," Diana observed, putting an arm around her. "Are you sure you're okay?"

"They gave me something," she said, her voice trailing off. She didn't feel like herself, but she couldn't put her finger on it. "God, I need a drink."

Diana hesitated. "I'll get you some water."

They made their way to the cardiac care waiting room where her friends and family gathered, keeping vigil. Henry rushed her and nearly knocked her down. He smelled of French fries and cheeseburgers. Lauren pushed him off, the thought of food making her mouth water and her stomach churn.

"Lauren," John said. He embraced her but withdrew quickly, inspecting her. The others gathered around to await their turns. "Let's give Lauren some space," John said. "Here, daughter. Come sit." Lauren complied and sat, gazing blankly at the faces that gathered around her.

Jean-René pulled up a chair and took her hand. "Boss, you don't look so hot."

"I'm fine," she said, withdrawing her hand.

"What do you need? What can we do for you?"

"Just leave me be." Lauren crossed her arms over her chest as she sat back. She shivered and turned her gaze to the window beside her, staring off into the horizon.

THE FAMILY DID as she asked, but gathered in the far corner, watching her with concern. "What's wrong with my mother?" Henry asked his grandfather.

"They said she was in shock when they brought her in," Bahati said. "She looks like she's still in shock."

"If you loved someone as much as your mother loves your father," John said to his grandson, "and something happened to them, you'd be in shock, too." His eye caught Diana's. He knew she'd been through hell when he left. He still regretted that he had to leave. They both knew their time was limited when they met, but it didn't soften the blow when the time came. Rowan and Lauren had no such opportunity to prepare for what had happened.

"Perhaps I can do something for her," Diana said, rummaging through her purse for a small metal tin. "Henry, can you get some hot water? I'll make her some tea and then see what else can be done."

"Sure, Nanhi." Henry headed out to the coffee service in the hallway.

"She looks exhausted," Jean-René observed. "Like she's been through the wringer."

"The tea will help her sleep," Diana said, accepting the cup of hot water when Henry returned with it. "If nothing else."

16

Much to Diana's dismay, Lauren rejected her mother's tea. Instead, she curled up on one of the benches and fell asleep. Jean-René sweet-talked one of the nurses into getting her a blanket and a pillow. Even with the blanket, she curled up into a tight ball and shivered in her sleep. Her teeth chattered at first, but Diana realized she had her jaw clenched tightly. She lay a hand on Lauren's head, trying to use her magic to coax her into a more fitful sleep, but the trembling force echoed away and seemed to do little good. She drained her reserves before she gave up. Her powers were not as strong—nor well-trained—as John's.

John made a similar attempt. "She's too far for my magic to reach her."

"If you can't get to her, then I understand why my magic isn't doing much." Diana sighed, returning to the sitting area across the room.

"The medication they gave her downstairs is doing its job, then," John said. "Sleep is clearly what she needs."

"Henry?" Diana turned to Henry.

"Yes, Nanhi?"

"Be a dear and get a dollar from my purse and fetch me a soda from the machine downstairs, please." Normally, she didn't drink soft drinks, but she needed the quick energy that nothing but a dose of pure sugar provided.

Henry gazed at her a moment before he moved to pick up her purse. He brought it to her and laid it in her lap. "My mother would kill me if I went scrounging through a lady's purse, Nanhi. Besides, I don't think a dollar will be enough."

Diana patted his hand and found four one-dollar bills in her wallet. "Do you think this is enough?"

"Probably," he said. "I have some money if it's not."

Diana gazed at her grandson, proud of the man he was becoming. He had grown tall and handsome, like his father. Like his uncles. Like his grandfather. Henry disappeared, leaving the adults alone.

JOHN KNEW his wife like he knew his own mind. It wasn't about the soda. She had something to say that she didn't want Henry to hear. She was a wise woman. "Speak plainly." John moved to sit down across from her when he was out of earshot.

"I have done as much for Lauren as I can," Diana said. "I sense the darkness she faced. But I fear there is nothing more I can do for her."

"I sense the same," John confirmed. "She's been to the void and returned with a piece of her soul missing. Until she and Rowan are reunited, I suspect her mood will not improve."

Jean-René and Bahati looked at each other with concern painted on their tired faces. They'd come to trust the Grayson/Pierce family more than two people ever could. Friends of lesser conviction might have walked away years ago, but not the Toussaints. *Two saints.* It hit John. It wasn't an exact translation, but if you split their last name, it made perfect sense. *Yes, indeed, they must be saints.* His daughter had chosen her friends wisely. She was lucky to have friends who stood with her in the light—and defended her in the dark.

"If you can't help Lauren, what else can be done?" Bahati's voice faltered.

"I will ask the spirits of her ancestors to intervene," Diana said. "I just hope it's enough."

"What about Rowan?" Jean-René asked.

"When they will allow him visitors," Diana said, "I'll see what can be done for him. I am already so drained, I can hardly move. Such a healing session is rarely as draining."

"I don't know what Enlil could have done to her," John said, his voice unsteady. "The old gods lose power when they are forgotten. Enlil has done something to gain strength since Lauren and Michael faced him in Slovenia."

"Like what?" Jean-René asked.

"I'm not sure," John said. "He had several demons around him when I found Lauren facing him. One had Rowan, the other stalked Lauren like a jaguar in the jungle. I'm not even sure she was aware of it."

"Lauren said she was afraid he'd gain strength from the failing peace accords in the Middle East—that he must be feeding off discord," Bahati said. "But she always suspected there was another force out there working against her. She didn't talk about it to me very often, but now and then she'd say she felt a disturbance in the force, or whatever you call it."

"We have to do something," Jean-René said, his brow lifted. "What can I do to help? He is as much my brother as he is your son."

"The children will need you and Bahati now more than ever," Diana said. "Lauren will not leave him, and we have work to do—me here and John in whatever realm we can find answers."

"I'll take care of everything at home," Bahati said. "I can see the kids get to school, do their homework, and eat."

"Don't be afraid to let my brother cook," Henry said, as he came back in. He opened the soda for his grandmother and handed her the bottle. "John Carter has learned quite a bit from our mother. He's catching on quickly."

"I was hoping you'd help me with that," Bahati said, her cheeks growing red. She was a notoriously bad cook, and everyone knew it. It didn't keep her from trying, and Jean-René didn't mind. He hadn't missed a meal in the years they'd been married, and the beginning of a paunch was starting to hang over his belt.

"I can't stay," Henry said. "I have responsibilities elsewhere. Classes of my own to attend to."

"Oh, Henry," Diana said, disappointment heavy in her tone. "Not even for a little while?"

"No," he said. "But I can check in from time to time." He turned to his grandfather. "If you need me . . ."

"I have been a great and powerful wizard for centuries, dear boy." He patted Henry's cheek. A twinkle lit his dark eyes, and he smiled a devilish grin. "I've managed on my own this long. I think I can handle a little reconnaissance mission."

"If you can't though, call me. You shouldn't have to face Enlil alone either." The boy's eyes knitted with concern.

John nodded his promise and turned to Diana. "I'd best go see what can be done."

Diana could tell her grandson didn't want to leave, but he was right. His job was doing well in school and his parents would expect no less of him, no matter the circumstances.

"You know how to find me," Henry said and was gone.

"We'd better go and see to the children." Jean-René rose and offered his hand to his wife. "I'm sure Mrs. McIntosh can manage, but she will be worn out by the time we get there."

"Call me if you need anything yourself," Diana said.

"I'll be back Monday as soon as I get everyone off to school," Bahati said. "Unless you need me sooner."

"I'll let you know if anything changes here," Diana promised.

AROUND MIDNIGHT DIANA awoke to her name being called. She had been nodding off in her chair with a magazine in her lap, but she sprang up as soon as she heard her name. A glance at the clock confirmed the time. A nurse stood by her. "Yes?"

"Mr. Pierce is awake," the nurse said. "Would you like to see him?"

Diana's heart leapt into her throat. "Yes." She gathered her purse and fell in behind the young woman. The nurse led her down a long corridor to a small room. When the nurse stepped aside, Diana froze in her tracks.

Rowan sat up in bed, his hospital gown hanging off his shoulders, multiple leads hooked to his chest. Bruises marred the skin over his sternum. But there he sat, with a cup of applesauce and a spoon, looking like the cat that just ate the canary.

"Rowan?" Diana was not expecting that. She heard the surprise in her tone.

"Hi, Mom," he said, taking a bite and swallowing. "What'd I miss?" Diana stiffened. Rowan set the cup and spoon on the table and pushed it away. "Diana? What is it? You look like you've seen a ghost."

"I . . ." She dropped her purse, feeling her strength ebbing. Her lip began to tremble, and she fell into him, wrapping her arms around him, suddenly beset by tears. He reciprocated with a grunt. "I thought I had . . ." she muttered.

"Diana, it's okay," he said. "I'm fine. Don't cry." He

wrapped her in his arms, running his hand down her long hair.

"We didn't know if you were going to make it." She drew back and slapped his arm with the back of her hand. "How dare you scare us like that?!" She scowled and took a step back. "And then I come in here and find you eating apple-sauce like nothing happened?"

"I'm sorry," he said, his hand going to the spot on his shoulder where she'd stung him. "But . . . I'm hungry."

"Do you even know what happened?" Diana softened, realizing she was angry at him for no reason. It wasn't his fault, and she had no right.

"The nurse said something happened with my heart, but they can't find anything wrong with me. She said the doctor might let me go home tomorrow."

Diana froze. "*Unfreakingbelievable.*"

"Hey," he picked up the applesauce again. "That's my catchphrase."

Diana shook her head and all but fell into the chair by his bed, holding her head in her hands. She heaved a heavy sigh and began crying again. She couldn't stop it, no matter how hard she tried. "What? What is it?" Rowan's voice reached her in her grief. "Lauren? Where's my wife? What happened?"

"She's in the waiting room," Diana said. "I don't know what caused it, but she's drained—exhausted."

"Oh, my God," he said. "You scared me. I thought something happened to her."

"She's been asleep for hours, and that's after spending the day in the ER being monitored for shock."

The applesauce cup fell from his hand and the last of it ended up in his lap.

17

Rowan was beside himself with worry. He insisted on being taken to Lauren, and when the nurses refused to let him go, he waited until they weren't looking and then made his getaway. Grasping at the back of his hospital gown and leaning heavily on the IV pole on wheels, he hadn't made it far when Diana came around the corner.

"Just where do you think you're going?"

"I was coming to find Lauren," he said. "Take me to her." It wasn't a request.

Diana looked around for backup, but the nurses were busy attending to the twenty or thirty other patients on the floor. She found a wheelchair and rolled it over to him. "Get in."

"I don't need that," he protested.

"It wasn't a request." His mother-in-law stood more than a foot shorter than him. She didn't back down when he looked as if he might fight her over it. "Get in or it's back to bed. Those are your options."

Rowan obeyed. Diana might have been small in stature, but she was as strong as she was spirited. She had no trouble moving him down the hallway, around a corner, and into an open waiting area. An older man was nodding off in a chair in the corner.

Rowan's heart broke as Diana parked the wheelchair next to the bench where Lauren slept. Rowan leaned over her and brushed her hair aside, kissing her cheek. Lauren stirred in her sleep, groaning as she did. "Honey?" Rowan prompted her.

Lauren's eyes flew open. She sat bolt upright. Rowan winced, his hand going to his sore chest as he moved faster than he was prepared to. Lauren sat staring at him for a moment. "You're not dead."

"You could at least try and sound happy about it," he said, furrowing his brow.

Lauren balled up a fist, and for a moment, Rowan flinched, preparing to be hit—again. But Lauren relaxed and let her hand drop. "You scared me."

"I'm sorry," he said. He yearned to take her into his arms and hold her, but she sat back and stared at him through the mess of hair that hung over her face. She still didn't seem placated. "I shouldn't have taken you to the Stanley Hotel. I should have been more sensitive to your fears, and I was a complete jerk. I swear. We'll get on a plane for Mexico as soon as they let me out of this joint if that means you'll forgive me."

"I'm still angry," she said, though any anger didn't show in her countenance. The conflict between her words and her expression was confusing. It suggested her words weren't truthful. Perhaps she was beyond anger.

Rowan sat back in the wheelchair. He'd done some pretty boneheaded things in his life, but this might be one she would not forgive. That thought was more painful than cracked ribs or a bruised sternum. "What can I say? What can I do?"

Lauren's eyes averted down, but her shoulder lifted ever so slightly.

"Mr. Pierce!" A startled voice came from the entryway. Rowan was busted. "What are you doing out of bed?" The nurse crossed the room in two long strides. "You can't be in here. We have to keep you on the cardiac monitors." She pecked like a mother hen who'd lost one of her chicks.

Rowan surrendered as the nurse unlocked the wheels. His eyes locked on Lauren's. She stared blankly at him as if there was no love left in her.

He'd ruined everything. He hadn't learned anything new about Lance Corporal Riggs, and he'd pissed off the one woman who mattered more than anything to him. He'd nearly died, but at the moment, he thought it might have been better if he had. Lauren would have been mad at him, but now he would have to live with the memory of those loveless eyes peering out from behind her hair.

When the nurse got him back to bed, she reconnected the electrodes for the heart monitor to the patches on his chest. She patted his shoulder and said something about getting him some water, but Rowan was lost in worry. In the twenty-plus years since he and Lauren met, she'd never looked at him like that. It was as if she had no emotion for him—no joy, no hate. Nothing. She'd said she was angry, but her tone had been flat. *God. That couldn't be good, could it?* He decided it would have been better if she'd punched him. He had it coming, and he'd have felt better if she'd shown the kind of emotion she'd professed to have earned.

He heard feet shuffle in the door and turned. Diana stood in the entryway. "Are you okay?"

"No," he said, his tone as flat as Lauren's had been.

"She's not herself." Diana came in and sat on the edge of his bed, putting her hand on his knee. "You know that."

"I do," he said. "But I deserved that."

"Nobody deserved that," she said. "But this is not the time to worry about that. You've both been through a lot. John is working to see what can be done to help you, but I want to make you aware of what we think happened."

Diana told him everything John had conveyed to her

about his efforts to stop Enlil. "He managed at just the last minute to pull Lauren back from the abyss. She gave herself up to save you." Tears built in his eyes, and he felt heat rising in his face. "She wouldn't have done that if she didn't love you, so, if that's what you're thinking, you can put that thought out of your mind right now. She loves you more than her own life."

"She shouldn't have," Rowan said.

"You'd have done the same for her, and you know it."

"Yeah, but," he started, screwing up his face, trying to keep the tears at bay. "It was my job. I'm supposed to protect her. I didn't listen to her. She told me she didn't want to be there. I should have—"

"Rowan," Diana softened. "The burden of guilt is too heavy to bear, and it serves no one. You can't blame yourself. You didn't ask for any of this."

"But I did," Rowan said. "When I asked her to marry me —fourteen times."

The nurse appeared at the door. "Sorry for the late announcement, but we're moving you to another room," she said.

"Oh?" Rowan cocked a brow. "After all the trouble to get me back to bed?"

"Well, the doctor says if you're going to get up and go galivanting all over the hospital, you don't need to be in Cardiac ICU," she mused. "I'll admit, I agree with him. We're not accustomed to having patients go AWOL on us."

"Is the bed less lumpy in the new room?"

"Nope," she said. "We're taking you bed and all." An orderly came in behind her as she started disconnecting anything that needed to be unhooked, moving his IV to a hanger on the bed, and disconnecting the electrodes at the machine. "We're going down to room 327," the orderly told Diana. "Give us about thirty minutes to get him settled, and you can join us there."

It happened so fast that Rowan didn't have a chance to say anything as he was wheeled to an elevator at the back of the hallway, away from where he'd found Lauren.

He pouted the entire way. He hated everything about this place. He was sore, but he'd hurt just as badly, if not more, when he had his little *cardiac episode* in Haiti. No, this was worse. Jean-René had broken ribs—hairline fractures—while performing CPR. This time, his ribs and sternum were bruised but not broken. He didn't know which paramedic he needed to find and thank—or punch—but he intended to find out. He'd known everyone on the team when he lived in Estes Park and had worked on the EMS team himself. It had been so long that most of his friends had retired. They must have had a new team of rookies who didn't know that effective CPR often required broken ribs. Then again, he was alive, so it had worked. He should be thankful.

ROWAN WOKE up with the sunrise. The light was dazzling and blinded him for a moment. Diana was sitting in the chair by the window, her head bowed, her chin propped up on her fist. The room was quiet. Even the constant cadence of the heart monitor had been muted, and he felt a bit better, though when he tried to stretch, a pain shot through his chest and into his shoulder. *Grrr.* He choked back a growl. Diana didn't flinch. He found the control and raised the head of his bed, finding it easier to move. He glanced around the room and realized the bed by the door wasn't empty. He didn't have a roommate when they moved him in. He smiled, seeing it was Lauren. But his smile faded as he realized she was glaring at him from beneath her hair.

She seldom let her hair fall over her face like that. Typically, she pulled her hair up the minute she got home from work—if she hadn't worn it up in the first place. She preferred braids most often. Her expression reminded him how much trouble he was in. He lay his head back down and closed his eyes. He couldn't do this. He needed to find a way to make this right. He had to get back in her good graces somehow.

———

TWO DAYS PASSED before Rowan was discharged. The ride home had been uncomfortable in more than one aspect. His seatbelt rubbed on the sorest spots on his chest, while Lauren's blank stare out the window, saying nothing, hurt worse. Jean-René drove, with Bahati in the front seat with him. Diana had a seat in the third row. Rowan could feel her eyes burning in the back of his head while he tried to maintain his composure.

Lauren stumbled as she started for the front door. Rowan attempted to help, but she pulled away. She retreated to her room, closing the door. The children, allowed to stay home after not seeing their parents since Friday, knew Mom and Dad were sick, but the full extent of their conditions was a mystery, at least to most of them.

John Carter and Jamie had a bit more knowledge than the younger children, but both had been sworn to secrecy. Sarah turned to her grandmother and hooked a small thumb over her shoulder towards her parent's room. "Who was *that?*"

"Your mother isn't feeling well," Rowan said, making it to his recliner. John gave him a hand to get down. "She needs to sleep." She'd slept for hours on end, but she couldn't seem to manage to keep her eyes open. She hadn't eaten—at least not that Rowan had seen.

"Are you sick, too?" Kate came out of her room, her phone to her face. Typical.

"Something like that," Rowan said. Sarah stood in front of his chair, and he knew what she wanted. She usually liked to curl up in his lap and watch television or read together.

"You can come sit with me if you're very careful." He opened his arms in invitation.

"No, thanks," she said. "You're in trouble. I don't hang out with people who get in trouble." Her tone was sharp, and the look on her face was familiar.

"Sarah," Diana scolded. "That is no way to talk to your father."

Sarah turned on her heel and went to the back door. Without asking if she could, she opened and closed it behind her in the same move. Indy was already outside. The dog ran over and barked at the door. Rowan felt as if his dog was barking at him. *Rude. Everyone is mad at me.*

"Dad." John Carter came over and put a hand on his shoulder. "Do you need anything?"

"No," he said. He was gutted by the cold reception. "Maybe."

"What?" John Carter had turned to walk away but paused when Rowan changed his mind.

"Do we have iced tea?" Rowan asked.

"You know we do," Diana said, already in the kitchen. She took the pitcher from the refrigerator and prepared a glass. "I thought I might make spaghetti for dinner if that sounds good."

"If Mom and Dad are sick, aren't you supposed to make chicken soup?" Sam asked.

Rowan's brow lifted. "That sounds good."

"Chicken soup it is," Diana said, setting about to see if she had everything she needed or if she needed to send John Carter to the store.

"Did Bahati make anything good?" Rowan asked, knowing the answer.

"She tried." Kate plopped down on the sofa. "One of these days, she'll figure out cinnamon doesn't go in everything."

"I've been to South Africa," Rowan said. "It's a common

ingredient in most of the cooking from that region." That's when he first considered that maybe Bahati wasn't a bad cook. Maybe she was trying to fit American customs and dishes into her South African paradigm. Come to think of it, she did put cinnamon in everything, even savory dishes. Spaghetti at her house never tasted quite right. Now he realized why.

John Carter brought him the iced tea and set it on the table next to his chair. "Anything else?"

"There's some medication in my coat pocket," Rowan said, pointing to the jacket he'd forgotten to take to Estes Park. He wondered what had happened to their luggage. Surely someone would pack their bags up, and Jim would hold them until he could get back up there, right? Maybe Jean-René would get them. Rowan wasn't sure he'd ever go back there. He knew Lauren never would.

"This?" John Carter handed him the bottle.

"Yeah," he said. "Thanks, buddy."

"Shoulder hurts, doesn't it?" Jamie said. "I could tell when you came in."

"Yeah," Rowan said. "I guess I'm going to have to go to the orthopedic surgeon and get it looked at."

"Surgeon? Do you need an operation?" Sam glanced up from the blocks he was assembling into a spaceship of some kind.

"I hope not," Rowan said.

"Will you be able to coach my baseball team next summer?" his youngest son asked.

"I sure hope so," Rowan said.

"Can you still type with a lame flipper?" Kate's question caught him off guard. She was so laissez-faire with her tone.

"Type?"

"Yeah," Kate said. "You're gonna write a book, right? My English teacher, Mrs. Bell, says she'll edit it for you. My history teacher, Ms. LaBranche says she wants to read it.

Remember her? You autographed a picture for her at the open house last month."

"The one with the beehive hairdo?"

"No, that's Madame Harlington. She's my French teacher."

"Have you learned any French yet?"

"*Le cravat du Jean Paul est dans sa poche,*" she said, in broken French.

"What does that mean?"

"John Paul's necktie is in his pocket." She laughed. "We listened to these recordings on old plastic records. Honestly, I've learned more French from Uncle Jean-René and Mom."

"Be careful," Rowan said. "Jean-René will teach you all the bad words."

"He says I need to know them, so I'll know if someone is saying something inappropriate to me. He also taught me what to say back."

"Do me a favor, don't say anything Uncle Jean-René taught you at school. If I get called into the principal's office because of something he taught you, I'm going to haul him down with me."

"I can't believe I even have to take it in school. It's so stupid. You can't graduate without at least one semester of a foreign language. Madame Harlington isn't even French. She married a French dude and lived there for two years. How does that make her qualified to teach? And that was like twenty years ago."

Rowan shook his head, the medication kicking in. His head spun, and the room dimmed. He'd gotten a decent night's sleep, but Lauren's attitude toward him today was exhausting.

Diana came around the kitchen, picking up her purse. "It looks like I need a few things before I can make chicken soup for dinner. Who wants to go with me to the store?" The chorus of children's voices didn't include Kate's. "Kate, can you keep a listen out for your mom and dad and help them with anything they need while I'm gone?"

Kate glanced at her dad, yawning widely. She lifted her shoulder. "Sure," she said. "Can you get some apples and maybe some oranges if they look good?"

"Sure." Diana smiled. "Do you want to pick what I make tomorrow for dinner?"

Kate considered that for a moment. "I'll text you," she said. "I need a few minutes to think."

"If you think of anything else we need, let me know," Diana said. "Rowan, will you be all right?"

"I think I'll have a nap," he muttered, his eyes already closed.

Diana walked over to the door and called Sarah. "Do you want to go to the store?"

The little girl bounded through the door without answering, but Diana knew. She never wanted to be left out of an outing, especially to the grocery store.

18

Kate sat on the sofa, happily tapping away on her phone. Lizzy had posted a picture of her favorite football player on the JV team. According to her best friend, Antony Lanois was every teenage girl's dream, and he knew it. Kate didn't care much for him. She thought he was arrogant, cocky even. She'd seen him flirting with other girls on more than one occasion.

Kate didn't have a boyfriend, nor was she interested in any of these middle school boys. She was too smart for boys. Unlike Lizzy, Kate's grades were exceptional, despite her protests about the homework assignments. She still did them. It's not like any of them were hard.

Her classmates all knew she was acing all her classes. She'd earned a nickname—one she didn't hate—*Katherine the Great* or *Kate the Great*. She was great. *Why should she care what anyone else said about her?* She was smart. She was pretty. She was good at field hockey. She could draw and sing. She had a great fashion sense, and that wasn't just her opinion. Everyone said so.

She glanced up as the room went dark and realized storms were moving in. The door to her parent's room opened. Her mother stood there looking like a dark shadow, watching—

waiting. "Mom?" Kate set her phone down. "You okay?" Her mother said nothing but stood there a moment longer before she turned, went back into her room, and closed the door.

"Weird," she muttered to herself, picking up her phone, stretching out on the sofa, and returning to the latest updated on Antony Lanois. *Lan-wah*, she mouthed his name in the proper French pronunciation. She flipped over to TikTok, scrolling mindlessly through the BookTok videos, looking to see when the next *romantasy* novel from her favorite author would be out. She'd gotten into Arthurian legends lately, and anything to do with Lancelot and Guinevere was her favorite.

Indy ran to the door and started barking viciously. Kate presumed he wanted to come in before the skies opened up, but instead of coming in, the dog turned and ran out into the yard. "Stupid dog," she muttered under her breath, walking out onto the covered patio. The wind picked up, lifting the girl's thick auburn hair off her neck. Her hair was almost as long as her mother's—twice as long as Sarah's—half as long as her grandmother's. The air suddenly turned cold as clouds coalesced overhead. Indy's constant barking was carried on the wind, and she tiptoed quickly out across the damp grass. Rain fell in hesitant drops, not enough to soak things, but enough she wanted back inside. But that dang dog was acting like a fool, barking at nothing.

"Indy! Get in here!" She shouted over the wind, catching him by his collar when he ran back to her. "You're going to get all muddy, and then you'll have to get a *bath*."

Indy ducked, tucking his tail between his legs. He knew that word. He didn't like it. He followed instructions and came inside. He sat on the tile by the door but looked longingly at the backyard, whimpering. Kate sat back down. "Cut it out, knucklehead. The squirrels will still be there when the storm passes. And if you wake Dad up, he'll put you out in the garage."

If there were two words Indy didn't like, it was *bath* and

garage. The dog lay down but whimpered softly. The door to the bedroom opened again, and Lauren stood in the doorway.

"In or out, Mom," Kate said. It was Lauren's most frequently barked order when kids were running in and out from the backyard. Kate was being tart with her, but Lauren said nothing. She just stood there. Kate went back to her text message, laughing as Lizzy responded almost immediately. "Girl, you need to give up on that dude. He's a player," Kate muttered to herself.

When she glanced up, her mother was no longer in the doorway, but the door was closed. She checked the time. Nanhi should be home from the store with her brothers and sisters soon. There was one apple left in the fruit bowl on the counter, and her stomach was growling. Kate got up, typing on her phone as she walked across the living room. She stopped to kiss her daddy on the head as he snorted in his sleep. She could tell he wasn't feeling good. He slept in the recliner when his shoulder hurt. He needed to get it fixed, but as his mother often said, he was *being a big baby*.

Kate looked outside, but her mother's Subaru wasn't there. Nanhi usually drove it when she came to visit. Dad's SUV was still in Estes Park, as far as Kate knew. She didn't know how they were going to get it home, but Bahati assured her they'd figure something out and that the priority at the moment was making sure her Mom and Dad were feeling better.

A rumble of thunder echoed through the house, the entire structure shaking. A heartbeat later, the rain was coming down in sheets outside. Kate hoped Nanhi would get home soon. This was the kind of weather no one should be out in. Lightning flashed repeatedly, and thunder seemed to echo from all directions. Kate went to the back door, where Indy lay with his head on his paws. "See, aren't you glad you came inside?" *Knucklehead.* Rain mixed with heavier raindrops that tapped on the roof and the windows, as tiny ice pebbles began to bounce off the grass outside. It looked like popcorn.

In minutes, the grass was white as the hail began to accumulate. A flash of light blasted the sky around the backyard, and Kate nearly fell over with the force of it. The giant sycamore in the backyard exploded in a fury of sparks, dirt flying up, mixing with smoke as it filled the air. Rowan rose from his chair, startled and gasping for breath. A huge crash shook the house again. Indy started crying and went running for his hiding place under the stairs. Shadow, lying on the landing at the top of the stairs overlooking the living room, opened her eyes and yawned, nonplused.

"What the—" Kate's dad started, but then the lights went out and the hum of the refrigerator stopped.

"I'll grab the flashlights," Kate said, panic in her voice. Her dad was still dazed. She came back from the hall closet where they kept their emergency supplies. It was daytime, but the storm made it seem like night. The high-powered flashlights cut through the darkness.

"Where is everyone?"

"Nanhi and the rest of the kids have gone to the store," Kate said. "Mom's still in your room. Is she okay? She's acting weird."

"I know she's furious with me," Rowan said, hesitating. "Lauren?" Rowan started towards the room.

"I don't think it's that," Kate said. "She came out of her room and just looked at me, then went back inside. Twice."

Rowan paused at the doorway, knocking. When he tried the handle, the door was locked. "Lauren!" He called out and the tone in his voice told his daughter something was wrong. "Lauren?" Not waiting for an answer, he charged the door with his shoulder. He let out a loud howl of pain as the door gave, splintering near the lock as it flew open.

Kate raced to follow him. Inside her parents' bedroom—a place the kids weren't allowed to enter unless invited—the ceiling and part of the wall were caved in, the shattered sycamore tree lay in the house, and embers of flotsam hung in the damp air but were quickly extinguished by the rain that poured in. The tree lay across the bed, splitting it in half, flattening it. The sheets and mattress were soaked.

"Oh, Daddy!" Kate cried out, afraid to look for her mother.

Rowan turned and caught her by the shoulders. "Go call 911." She had her phone in her hands, but she moved involuntarily into the living room while Rowan returned to his desperate search.

Kate watched from outside the doorway, the phone pressed to her ear, as he frantically struggled to move debris from his path, climbing over branches, pieces of broken furniture, and bits of the damaged house—all the while being pelted by hail that grew to the size of baseballs. Wind blew through the rip in the fabric of their home, tossing Kate's hair back. The window in the kitchen shattered, the sound resonating through the storm. Kate leapt, startled as the 911 operator answered the phone. But the din had grown so loud that Kate could no longer hear her father's voice as he dug frantically, looking for his wife, nor could she hear the operator.

"Send help!" Kate shouted into the phone, hoping someone on the other side could hear it. She remembered to give the address. "A tree fell on our house. Daddy can't find my mom. Hurry!" She hung up and paced the room, frantic for something to do. There had to be something she could do to help.

"She's not in there," her dad shouted, staggering from their room. "I don't think she's here."

DIANA and the kids arrived home a scant thirty minutes after the storm had passed. By then, EMS was already on site. Despite the parting clouds, the house was dark—the power was out. "What happened?" John Carter asked, bursting through the front door "Why are the fire and police departments here?" He found his dad and his sister sitting at the kitchen table, looking distressed. The paramedic wrapped an elastic bandage over an ice pack on his dad's shoulder. Scratches covered his dad's arms and hands. His sister's hair was wet, and she had leaves tangled in her copper locks.

Kate sprang from her chair and rushed to her older brother, throwing her arms around him. "We thought the storm got you, too," she gasped. "Is everyone okay?"

"We're fine," John Carter said, setting aside the bag of groceries she nearly crushed. "Where's Mom?" He glanced up as the team of cops and firefighters came from his parents' room. He noticed the look on his father's face. He'd seen it before. It was a look of impending hope held back by uncertainty and fear. "Where's my mother?" he demanded.

Diana put a hand on his shoulder. "Take a breath, John Carter." She pushed past him. "What happened?" she asked Rowan.

"Lightning hit the sycamore. It fell on our house. The damage is bad."

The fire chief came back through the bedroom door. "Unfortunately—or maybe fortunately—there's no sign of anyone in the debris. It looks like your wife wasn't in her room. Are you sure she didn't leave before the storm hit?"

"Where's Mom?" Jamie asked. Sam came up behind him and repeated the question.

"She came out of her room just before the storm hit. Maybe she went out the side garage door. I didn't realize she hadn't gone back to bed," Kate said, covering for her mother. She didn't know it for certain, but her mother supposedly could just pop out of her place in time and space all by herself. Not even Nanhi could do that, and Kate couldn't remember seeing her do it, but Henry told her all about when she'd done it before.

"Where would she go?" one of the police officers who'd aided the search asked.

"My daughter hasn't been herself lately," Diana said, softly. "She just got released from the hospital."

"Oh." The police officer seemed to swallow the question he meant to ask. "Would she go to a friend's house?"

"Maybe Aunt Bahati knows where she is," Sarah said. "Can we call her and Uncle Jean-René?"

"I'll call her and find out," Diana said, then turned to John Carter. "Why don't you take your brothers and sisters upstairs, and I'll order pizza for dinner."

"I can do it," John Carter said. "I have the app on my phone."

Diana waited until the children disappeared up the stairs and were out of earshot. "I'm very concerned for my daughter," she said to the chief. "It isn't like her to just up and walk away from the house. Lauren Grayson-Pierce is one of the most responsible women you will ever meet."

"Wait, did you say Lauren Grayson? Isn't she the Bigfoot Lady?" One of the firefighters laughed. "Hasn't she been missing like half a dozen times?"

No one expected Rowan to come up from his chair swinging, least of all the firefighter, who caught a fist square in the jaw and went down—out like a light when he hit the floor.

"Rowan!" Diana gasped as the police officers jumped into action, grabbing him.

He let out a pained cry as they wrenched his arms behind his back and bent him over the table, pinning him. Diana put a hand on the police officer and tried to do one of John's mind tricks. "He's just upset about his wife," she said, softly. "He'd never do that under normal situations."

The firefighter was hauled to his feet by his brethren, and

despite being unsteady, a hand to his jaw, he pushed them away. "I'm okay," he said. "Let him go. I had that coming."

"You can press charges, Williams," the police officer holding Rowan down said. "It's illegal to assault a first responder in the conduct of his or her duties."

"I said let him go," the firefighter—Lt. Williams—said. Rowan was released, and he stood, slowly. His opposite arm went to his injured shoulder. Rowan glared at the man, still angry at him, but he exercised restraint.

"I heard what you tried to do for that Marine a week or so ago," the firefighter said. "I'm sorry if I offended you. You're a hero, if you ask me."

Rowan hesitated. The firefighter stuck out his hand. Rowan looked at it for a moment. "I'm sorry I hit you," he said, taking the outstretched hand, wincing. "I have to find my wife."

"Well, someone needs to get a tarp over that roof or the whole bedroom will flood," the fire chief said. "We have more weather moving in later tonight."

"I have some in my SUV," one of the police officers said.

"I'll put it up," Williams offered.

"There's an anchor point on the peak of the roof, just a few feet away from the air vent," Rowan said.

"Sit down, son." Diana pulled out a chair and coaxed him down into it. Just as he was about to say something, his eye was drawn to the front door. Lauren stood in the entryway. She was drenched, her clothes hanging off her thin frame. Her hair hung in dripping cords around her face, and she looked like a walking corpse. Her face was pale. She had dark circles around her eyes.

"Oh, thank God!" Rowan rushed to her, pulling her into his arms. He had a moment of déjà vu, recalling the day she'd disappeared in San Diego in a storm and ended up in the San Diego Zoo. He took a step back when he realized two police officers were holding onto his soaking-wet wife. She was shivering but didn't look up at him. Someone had thrown a blanket over her shoulders. She trembled violently. "Lauren?"

"We got the missing persons BOLO on the radio," one of the police officers said. "We picked her up at the park down the street. Looks like she took a hailstone to the head." He looked to the firefighters. "Any of you paramedics?"

"I am," Rowan said. "Or I used to be."

"I've got her," one of the firefighters said.

"I'll let you know if I need help," Rowan said, pushing past him.

The rest of the team seemed to sense the need to make themselves scarce. Rowan led Lauren over to the table and instructed her to sit down. Diana went to the kitchen, drew a glass of water, and brought it to the table. She set it at Lauren's elbow, but her daughter didn't reach for it. "What do you need?" Diana asked.

"Flashlight." Rowan pointed to the one Kate left on the counter. Diana brought it over and switched it on. Rowan took it and began his inspection of his wife. She had a bright red goose egg on her forehead, and he found two others hidden beneath her hair. "Can you get Lauren a towel?"

Diana complied, bringing him a towel from the laundry room. She left them alone, sensing he needed some space with her.

***

Rowan dried Lauren, who bowed her head and didn't meet his eye. He worked gingerly but rubbed her arms vigorously to warm her. Their closet had been damaged in the storm, and the tree had crushed their dresser, too. Finding dry clothes might be a bit of a challenge for both of them. "I know I messed up," he said, softly. "I said I was sorry, and I meant it. I don't know what else you want me to say or do, but I hope . . . I hope that somehow you can forgive me." Lauren didn't answer. He continued. "You should know, the sycamore tree is now in our bedroom. I figured I'd be sleeping in the recliner, since you're mad at me, but I guess the joke's on you. You get to sleep on the sofa." He tried to make light of the situation. That was how he coped with her silence.

She lifted her head and looked at him, her eyes empty of emotion. "I don't mind," she said softly. It startled him, and he wasn't sure if he heard her at first.

"Think you can stand to be in the same room with me?"

Lauren's shoulder lifted. He brushed back her hair and lifted her chin with his thumb. "I love you, and nothing will ever change that. You know that, right?"

She blinked and nodded but said nothing. The firefighter decided it was time to step in. Rowan stood and let him. "I don't think she's got more than a mild concussion," Rowan said, turning away, using his thumbs to press the tears back into his eyes so they didn't spill down his cheeks. It wasn't like her to be so distant, so cold. It occurred to him that this might be a tipping point—a point of no return.

19

Diana and Rowan kept a watchful eye over Lauren in the days that followed. When she didn't get up for work on Monday morning, Rowan called Jean-René and asked him to let the station know she needed some time off. "We've got a meeting with the insurance adjuster later this week, and Diana's going through the remains of our bedroom to see what can be salvaged. We have some clothes and some pictures we've been able to save so far."

"What can we do to help?" Jean-René asked.

"At this point, nothing," he said. "We can't do anything until the adjuster comes."

"How are you feeling?"

"I've been better," Rowan said earnestly.

"And Lauren?"

"Still not herself," he said, taking the phone outside. He stood in the driveway with the lawnmower flipped on its side. John Carter had mowed the lawn the night before. Rowan was doing routine maintenance to prepare it for winter. The snow blower was next on his agenda.

Temperatures had dropped since the storm earlier that week, making it feel like autumn with hints of winter. It was

October, and the maple tree in the front yard was vibrant red. Sunlight filtered through the aspens on the hills, while orange sycamore leaves were scattered on the back lawn where the boys had raked them. The insurance company had advised waiting to trim the damaged tree until they could assess it, with removal costs likely covered in the settlement—though Rowan, with his injured shoulder, wasn't in any shape to handle a chainsaw.

"Any news from John?"

"No," Rowan said, glancing back at the house. He felt a thrumming that made the hair on the back of his neck stand on end. The feeling spread down his arms and legs. The tingling grew into a humming. Rowan moved to sit down on the stool by the lawn mower and felt the world tilt as he did. He managed to get himself down without going completely over. Whispers surrounded him—disembodied whispers speaking his name. The din grew into a vibrating growl. "Jean-René, I'm going to have to call you back." He hit the red button on his phone and let it fall from his fingers to the ground beneath his hand. The voices grew in quantity, proximity, and volume.

Rowan strained to make sense of the words. He should have been more afraid, knowing what he knew. He was on edge, but he no longer feared for himself. Maybe he should have, but he didn't. "What do you want?" he muttered. "Where are you?"

"Is that how you treat someone who helps you?" Riggs' voice came to him through the din.

"You asked for help," Rowan said. "I feel like I've done my part."

"You did. And now, I'm here to help you." The voice was so close it was as if Riggs still had him in a death grip, a gun pressed to his head. "You know what you have to do."

"No," Rowan said. "I don't."

"I've given you the last thing you needed," he said.

"The last thing?" Rowan questioned.

"The demons are no longer tormenting me. Thanks to you, I'm free."

"Lucky you," Rowan complained.

"You saved me, but they're not done with you," the voice said. "Or your wife."

"Leave my family out of this," Rowan stood, turning, finding no one there. He lifted his gaze, and he realized he was looking at the attic where he'd stashed Saladin's Ring.

"Enlil will not be easy to defeat." The voice was still behind him. "You'll have to fight fire with fire. The enemy of my enemy is my friend, Rowan. If you don't have any enemies, you will need to find some. I've given you the key."

"What are you talking about?" Rowan turned, trying to find the ghost that continued to haunt him, but he wasn't visibly there.

"Arm yourself, brother." The man's voice moved to the other ear. "Call upon your enemies. Peace comes at a price. Are you prepared?"

"For what?" Rowan turned again, feeling a presence behind him, but nothing was there. "For what?" he demanded.

When an answer finally came, it was a distant whisper. "You'll know when the time comes."

***

"Nanhi," Sarah said, climbing up in her grandmother's lap at the dinner table while John Carter and Jamie oversaw the dishes. "I think I know what I want to be for Halloween."

Rowan glanced up from his slice of Key Lime pie. "Halloween? We have to pick a theme first."

"I hope I didn't step on any toes, but I let the kids pick the theme already." Diana cut a slice for Lauren. She'd eaten—finally—and had been ravenous even. Lauren didn't hesitate.

She tore into it with reckless abandon, something no one was accustomed to.

"We decided to be heroes this year," Jamie said.

"Marvel? Or DC?" Rowan asked.

"Any kind of television or movie hero you want," John Carter said.

"We have options then," Lauren said, her voice still heavy and deep. She shoved a bite of pie into her mouth and chewed, still averting her gaze from Rowan.

"Nanhi," Sarah said. "Will you help me?"

"Of course, sweetheart," she said.

"And promise not to tell anyone?"

"I won't tell a soul." Diana used her finger to draw a cross on her chest, sealing the oath.

Sarah leaned in and whispered in her grandmother's ear. Diana leaned back, a surprised expression on her face. "Are you sure?"

"Yes, Nanhi," she said.

Diana turned to Lauren. "What about you, Lauren? Do you need help with your costume?"

Lauren sat using her fork to draw a design with the whipped cream on her plate. Rowan noticed the design formed two crossed lines with crescent moons in three of the four quadrants created by the lines and a blob—presumably her attempt to draw a golden eagle—was in the fourth.

"Lauren?" Rowan reached over and caught her hand. "What is that?" he pointed to her plate with the back of his fork.

She lifted her shoulder and shrugged. Sarah climbed up so she could lean her elbows on the table. "Looks like something from Indiana Jones," she observed, swiping her finger across the top of Lauren's pie, and sticking it in her mouth. "Are you gonna eat the rest of your dessert?"

"You already had your dessert." Diana came over and

swatted her behind affectionately. "Go play with Shadow upstairs."

"I wanna help wash the dishes," Sarah said. Diana handed Sarah an empty dessert plate and shooed her off to the kitchen.

"Rowan?" Diana asked. "What about you?"

"Huh?" His attention was still on the design.

"Do you need help with a costume?"

"I'll have to figure out what I want to be," he said. "But I think I can manage something."

"Let me know if you need help," Diana said.

Diana returned to the kitchen and Lauren stuck her fork in her mouth, licking off the whipped cream, still considering the design. "Have you seen this mark before?" he asked her.

"Yeah," she said. "A detective showed it to me."

"I've seen that mark before," he said. He didn't mention where.

"It's a sigil," she said, flatly. "Tenth century. Muslim."

"That's what I was thinking too," he said. "What do you know about Saladin?"

"Lauren," Diana said, coming over to sit down beside her with a cup of coffee. "Why don't you and Rowan take my room downstairs? I can sleep on the trundle in Sarah's room."

"Diana, you don't have to give up your room," Rowan contested.

"Nanhi, you can sleep in my room." The little girl beamed. "Then the monsters can't get me. They're scared of you."

Everyone in the room—Lauren notwithstanding—froze. Sarah never talked about monsters under her bed or voiced any fear of such fantastical things. She wasn't one to give in to such childish things. "Honey." Rowan stretched out his hand, summoning her over. Sarah climbed up onto his lap, leaning gently against his chest. "Have you seen monsters in your room?" After his encounter in the driveway earlier, he was feeling jumpy himself.

"No," she said. "Indy and Shadow keep them away most of the time."

"Most of the time?"

"Well," she shrugged, "they did. But I don't know how long they can keep them away now that they're in the house."

"In the house?" Rowan's flesh prickled.

"The monsters are getting stronger," she said. "I heard them. Their voices grow louder, and I can't make them stop."

Diana came over and knelt at Rowan's feet, taking the little girl's hand. "What did you hear?"

"Whispers," Sarah said, lowering her tone. She looked around as if checking to make sure she wasn't about to say something that might be overheard. "First, it was just in the yard. But now, I can hear them everywhere. They broke into our house, and now they're everywhere."

"What are they saying, sweetheart?" Rowan asked, concern weighing his brow down.

Her small shoulders lifted. "I dunno. It's just voices. I can't tell what they're saying. It's like when Momma talks funny."

"Like when she's mad?" Diana smiled, trying to comfort her granddaughter, but Rowan could tell she was concerned.

"No, like when she's talking to the monsters."

"Wait. What?" Rowan asked.

Sarah peered up at him with her big brown eyes. "She's been talking to them in her sleep—since you both got sick."

"How did you know that, honey?" Diana asked.

"I like to walk when I'm asleep. I've been watching out for Mommy."

Rowan's brow lifted as his gaze met his mother-in-law's. Rowan suspected Sarah would have some kind of power someday, but so far Henry was the soul wielder of magic. His skills increased with each passing year. Kate occasionally made observations that might be considered premonitions, but this was something new.

"Do you put on your shoes?" Diana's question caught Rowan off guard.

"Don't need 'em," Sarah said. "I leave my feet behind."

Diana seemed to have confirmed a suspicion. Rowan did, too. "Do you hear them now?"

"Not like you do, Daddy," she said.

Diana's brow lifted this time. "What's that all about?"

"I'm not sure," he lied, and he suspected she knew he wasn't being truthful.

"Do you know what's going on with your Mommy?" Diana asked.

"She only has half a soul," she said. "The devil got the other half."

LONG AFTER LAUREN and the kids went to bed, Rowan sat staring into his coffee cup, watching the dregs of a long day going cold. Diana's cup was empty, but she made no move to refill it. "I don't know what's going on with her," Rowan finally spoke. "She's just a little girl."

"She's not just *any* little girl, Rowan. You know that. We know the children all have potential."

"Doesn't mean I'm going to like it. I can't . . . ." His voice trailed off, as he wrapped his hand around his cup. "I can't reach her." He glanced at Lauren asleep on the sofa. "Lauren should be handling this. I can't understand what's going on with my wife. She's so distant, and I have to think it's my fault."

Diana didn't respond right away. She rubbed her temples as if trying to push away the dread building in her mind. "You're right, you know. Lauren hasn't been herself since she woke up in the hospital."

"It's all my fault," Rowan said. "I shouldn't have taken her to the Stanley. I knew what happened to her there. I knew she was afraid to go back. I should have left when she protested. I talked her into staying. I didn't understand the presence there that had hurt her, that she was afraid of."

"She's a strong woman, but she isn't the only one who hasn't been the same. She told me what you were doing."

"Huh?"

"The credit card charges? The purchases on Amazon? You couldn't let it go, could you? You miss being a ghost hunter. I saw the business card from the new CEO at the Exploration Channel. You want back in."

"Back in?" Her sudden attack came out of left field, and he had no idea what had gotten into her.

"Now that Lauren has something to do, you can't let it go."

"No," he said. "That's not it." He felt the trembling of anger in her tone, but that wasn't something he was accustomed to in his mother-in-law. Diana wasn't one to judge. She never spoke in anger. She'd lived with them before and never once interfered in their relationship or the running of the household.

"Of course I'm angry," she said. "This is my daughter we're talking about. Did John tell you what happened? When he went back to see the events through the shadows of time?"

Her words hit Rowan like a punch. He flinched, feeling the color drain from his face. "No." He gasped, shaking his head in denial. His hands balled into fists, and he sensed a rage building in his core. It was a monster taking over his mind, and he fought it, trying to listen as he endured the onslaught as Diana told him everything, just as John had conveyed it to her.

She spoke with vitriol in her tone. She lay the blame on thick like a heavy coat over his shoulders. "She gave her soul for yours, at least the part that was hers to give. She gave you half her soul when she married you. It's yours. It's always been yours, and now, she's paying the price for it."

"No. I can't believe it. I refuse to believe you. She'd never surrender to Enlil."

"Deny it all you wish, but Lauren had no choice. It was your life or her soul."

He stood fixed behind the table, running his hand down his face. "No. There must be a way. We have to fix this. I have to fix this. I am her protector. I can't lose her."

"You already have. I'm afraid she is too far gone to get back."

Rowan froze at her words—the finality of them. The cold truth struck like a shard of ice through his heart. It was a feeling he was familiar with. He'd felt this same feeling that night at the Stanley Hotel when Enlil's demons came for him. A deep pain shot through his arm, and his fingers went numb. He couldn't breathe for a moment. "No." He shook his head again as if to clear it. As if there was something he could do to save his wife from whatever dark spell had taken hold of her. "No!"

"Mommy's not Mommy anymore," Sarah interrupted. "But that doesn't mean you get to be mad at each other." The little girl's voice seemed to come from nowhere. She stood at the top of the stairs in her purple nightgown. Her visage wasn't quite solid. She had a spectral appearance that made Rowan's heart freeze even more. "That's the monsters making you angry. You too, Nanhi. That's the monsters."

"What are you doing out of bed? This is no place for children. Go to your room." It wasn't like Diana to snap at Rowan, but she certainly never lashed out at the children. It *was* the monsters doing it. It had to be. Rowan was certain of it.

"Honey," Rowan started, but couldn't find the words. He turned away, not willing to see her like that. Like a ghost. Not wanting to admit she could sleepwalk—astral project. He was not willing to admit his little girl, the very ilk of her mother, could have such power. *No. Not his baby girl.* "No, Sarah. There are things in this world that you are too little to comprehend. Dangerous things. Things that you need to let your Mommy and Daddy and the grown-ups who love you handle."

Sarah's shade floated down the stairs and stood in front of her Daddy before he realized she'd even moved. He dropped to his knees, afraid to touch her, his hands too heavy to hold. "Daddy," her voice was so small. "Henry has been teaching me. He wasn't supposed to, but he did. I asked him to. But I never do anything I'm not supposed to. I can't let the monsters win, Daddy. You know we can't let the monsters win."

"You have to leave this to the adults," Diana snapped, moving in behind her father.

"I know," she said. "But we have to save Mommy first."

Rowan suddenly felt weak. He slumped to the floor, burying his face in his hands. The weight of all this was too much. His wife—his true north—had slipped away from him, and he felt powerless to stop it.

"No," he whispered hoarsely as if saying anything aloud would somehow give the monsters the power to defeat them all. But deep down, he knew the truth. He knew it, and it scared him more than anything. Because if Sarah was right— if the monster was the Devil, if it was Enlil, and he had taken Lauren's soul—then there might be no way to save her. Rowan was just a man. He wasn't magical. He didn't have powers to astral project or the gift of the Ancient All-Language. He couldn't time travel or teleport. He couldn't use the force to control men's minds. He was just a man. He couldn't save her from a god, certainly not one as powerful as Enlil. And that thought—that cold, hard reality—chilled him to his very core.

Rowan's eyes darted from Sarah's face to the shadow that gathered like a quickening storm. "The monsters are here, Daddy. Do you see them?"

Rowan studied the corners of the living room, peering beneath the stairs, trying to find demons among the voids. The room grew warm, though Rowan hadn't turned on the furnace yet. The heat was suddenly oppressive, and his cheeks flamed. He felt the warmth rise from his ears. Nausea passed through him as the darkness seemed to close in.

Diana's breath caught in her throat. "Sarah, stop this!"

"I'm not doing it," she said. "It's the darkness. It's coming for us. We need help." The child's shade disappeared. Shadow, her hackles raised, her pupils dilated, came down with her tail held high, looking like an image of Bastet herself. The goddess was angered, and she hissed at the unseen specters that had moved in. As she did, it was as if the air itself split open, the temperature dropped, and the oppressive weight of the room seemed to vanish in an instant.

A bolt of lightning split the room in two, blinding them for a moment. The house shook as the thunder rumbled through every splinter and nail. When the fog lifted, Tsul'Kalu—the ancient wizard—appeared. In his form of the massive beast, he stood with his head just inches from the fan that hung from the vaulted ceilings. He held his hands open, apart from one another, coaxing a ball of pure magic that lit the room and chased the now shrieking demons from the corners. Rowan thought of a panicked squirrel, caught in traffic, damned to run right, damned to run left as they tried to escape.

"*Tso ta yo se ya.*" The deep tones of his voice were comforting, and the words—in English—found their way to Rowan's mind. *I am asking for Him,* and Rowan knew he meant The Great Spirit. He was calling on God. "*Hi ya giga iga giga-ge-iga.*" *Let us live in peace.*

Indy barked, and the familiar of Bastet spoke words in a language more ancient than that of the *Tsa la gi.* A powerful wave of light forced the darkness to recoil as a powerful burst of light radiated from the orb in Tsul'Kalu's hands, and the shadows screamed in agony, evaporating as if they were made of smoke. The floor beneath their feet groaned, crackling through the air as the evil was purged.

Rowan came to his senses and realized the room had returned to normal. Shadow sat on the fireplace, stretching and yawning, her long fangs showing as she licked her lips and mewed. Indy circled and lay down beside her on the rug in front of the hearth. Sarah was no longer present in her astral form, and John turned to him and grasped his arm. "It is well, my son." It was a formal greeting that required a formal response.

Rowan returned the gesture. "It is well now, Father. You have been missed."

"By the laws of the old world," John said, "the darkness cannot survive where the light and truth of love are present. But be warned—the evil that has taken your wife has been held back. It has not been vanquished."

Rowan's heart sank. "How do we save her then?"

John's eyes caught the light, and Rowan could see an ancient flame behind them. "There is a battle yet to be fought. What has taken my daughter is a form of corruption, but it is not invincible. If we are to win, we must be willing to fight. It will take more than magic to free her soul. The power to save her lies within you, and when the time comes, you will know what you are meant to do."

That made no sense to the mortal, non-magic wielder. "I don't have magic. I don't have any gifts from the Most High. How can I save her? How can I fight Enlil without her?"

"It will take the two most powerful weapons in the universe," John said, with a knowing smile. "Love and conviction."

Rowan swallowed hard, glancing at Diana. Movement at the top of the stairs caught his attention. Sarah stood in her nightgown with her stuffed baboon tucked under her chin. Sarah, who seemed to understand the gravity of the situation far better than her father did, saw her grandfather and squealed, running down the stairs.

She stopped just inches from her grandfather, sensing this was not a being she could approach so nonchalantly. She greeted him formally. *"Osiyo, Ga nv no wa."* *Hello, Grandfather.* Rowan had never heard her use the Cherokee language, but like her mother, she spoke it with mastery.

"O si yo, my granddaughter. It is well?"

"I don't know," Sarah admitted with the innocence of a child. "Will Mommy be okay?"

Rowan swallowed hard, glancing at Diana, then at Sarah. John's words echoed in his mind—love, conviction—the very things he feared he might lose in the fight for his wife's soul.

The wizard turned, his magical robes swirling around him like a shadow of their own. "I will be watching, waiting. The battle comes when the veil between this world and the next grows thin. You must be ready. We are but a few, but if the gods are willing, their Champion may come to our aid, for the Dark One will return."

And just as suddenly as he had appeared, John was gone. The magic faded, leaving the room an eerie but peaceful quiet. Shadow rolled over onto her back, purring loudly as if nothing were out of sorts and the last few minutes had never existed.

Rowan stood frozen for a moment, his mind racing, his heart still heavy with fear and uncertainty. The room felt lighter now; the oppressive weight of darkness lifted, if only for a time. "Wait, where did John go? We need him."

"He has expended all the energy he could," Diana said. "He'll come back if he can."

Rowan considered this turn of events. "We need to be ready."

Diana nodded. Her eyes were tired but resolute. "We will be. For Lauren. For Sarah."

"For my family. Our family." Rowan knew then that the battle for his wife's soul had just begun.

20

Lauren had a headache when she woke up. She felt like she'd been hit by a snowplow and then run over by a Mack truck. She stood, unsteady, her knees unable to hold her as she sank back down onto her mother's bed. *What was she doing in the basement? Why wasn't she in her room?*

Redoubling her efforts, she rose and staggered a few feet to the doorway, pausing to steady herself. It took a bit longer to get down the hall and up the stairs. The house was quiet, the light outside gray and overcast. Fog gathered around the windows. *Coffee. She needed coffee.*

She stood in the darkened kitchen, little more than a shadow. There was no coffee. The carafe wasn't even warm. That wasn't typical. Rowan tended to limit his coffee consumption to two cups in the morning, maybe a coffee in the afternoon if they went out. Her mother, though, could drink coffee 24/7. Lauren might have a cup in the morning, maybe one with dessert, but that was it.

A man she didn't recognize came out of her bedroom, with Rowan on his heels. They didn't seem to even notice her as the man paused by the kitchen table to make notes on his tablet. "I'll get this over to your insurance agent this afternoon. I have one more stop to make in Longmont, but I have everything I need. You should go ahead and reach out to some contractors to start gathering estimates. I have formulas to calculate what your insurance will pay, but that doesn't mean that's what the contractors will want. There could be significant variations, so getting several estimates is a best practice."

"I'll start making some phone calls," Rowan said, escorting the man to the front door. If he saw Lauren, he didn't acknowledge her.

Rowan returned and took one of the stools at the counter, pulling over his laptop and flipping it open. He typed in something, then sat back and scrolled. He wasn't writing. He must have been looking for something.

"Why is there no coffee?" she asked, her voice sounding hollow even in her own ears.

"It's three o'clock in the afternoon," Rowan said, unflinching.

"What day is it?" she asked.

Now, Rowan paused and looked at her, closing his laptop. "Does it matter?"

Lauren hesitated, considering. "I feel like I'm supposed to be somewhere."

"Not today," he said. "Your mother is picking the kids up from school, and then they are working on Halloween costumes."

"Why is it so dark?" Lauren asked.

"Storms have been coming at us like freight trains. One after the other."

Lauren shivered. "I can't believe I slept so late."

"You've been exhausted," Rowan said. "Do you want me to make some coffee? Do you want something to eat?"

Lauren abandoned the kitchen and came to the counter, pulling up the stool next to him. She slumped over against him, her head resting on his shoulder. She sighed heavily.

"Is that a no?"

"Maybe later." She sighed again.

Rowan went back to his computer and scrolled through a few more search engine results. It wasn't exactly easy to do with her leaning on his sore shoulder. He finally pulled her into him, putting an arm around her. "Let's go sit on the sofa so you can get comfortable."

Lauren didn't protest. "What are you doing?" she asked, once they were settled on the sofa and she snuggled up against him.

"Looking for a contractor," he said.

"Why?"

"To fix our bedroom," he said. "There's a giant tree in it."

"Oh," she said, yawning.

Rowan took out his cell phone and dialed a number. There was a pause before someone answered. "Hi," he said. "I need to get an estimate on repairing some storm damage."

LAUREN NAPPED while Rowan made several calls. He hadn't realized how many other homes and businesses had suffered because every contractor he called was either too busy or charged a fee to come out and give an estimate, which seemed ridiculous.

By the time Diana returned home from picking up the kids from school and running whatever errands they had rooked her into, he'd only found two that could be out in the next few days. One had agreed to work him into their schedule when he fed them the sob story that his wife had been sick, and he needed to get her back in bed before her condition took a turn for the worse. He didn't go into more detail, but the nice lady at Edifico Construction bought his sob story hook, line, and sinker.

"Hi, Daddy." Sarah came running towards him, and he

suspected she'd throw herself into his arms if he didn't put up a hand to caution her. She slowly climbed up onto his lap. He settled back in his recliner and hugged her affectionately. Her skin was cold, and her cheeks were tinged with pink. "Are you feeling better?"

"A bit," he said. "How was school?"

"I taught the teacher a new word today."

"Uh, oh." He looked to Diana as if she might know more. "What did you teach her?"

"Rapacious," Sarah said. "Mommy taught it to me before her soul was taken."

Rowan's brow lifted, and his gaze shot towards Diana. She threw up her hands as she stood in the kitchen, starting on dinner preparations. "First I've heard of it."

"Did Mommy tell you what it means?"

"She did." Sarah lay back with her head on Rowan's good shoulder and fondled a button on his shirt. "It means excessively grasping or covetous."

"And when did you need to use such a grown-up word?" Diana asked.

"I told Billy Flint if he ate all the M&M's in the teacher's candy jar I was going to punch him in the nose. When she got mad at me, I said, 'I'm not the one who's being so rapacious.'" Sarah sighed. "Then she got mad at me because she had to go get the dictionary off the shelf to look it up."

"Sarah, we can't threaten to punch other kids at school," Rowan scolded gently.

"It's not my fault she has a limited vocabulary," Sarah complained. "Am I in trouble?"

Diana glanced up, meeting Rowan's gaze, a wicked smirk on her face. She reminded him of Lauren when they had to discipline Kate in second grade. She'd been playing King of the Mountain with some boys on the playground, and when she got to the top of the dirt pile they were playing on— detritus from a recent construction project on the school cafeteria—and announced she was the HBIC of everything, one of the boys told her teacher.

Lauren took the phone call from the principal. He could hardly stop laughing long enough to tell Lauren that her daughter was in the lobby and was being sent home with a yellow card. That meant she could return the following day, but she'd lost her playground privileges for the rest of the week.

"No," Rowan said. He was a big teddy bear when it came to his baby girl. "But you cannot hit other kids at school. *That* would get you in trouble."

"I would have, too." Sarah folded her arms and sat brooding.

"I'll make a deal with you," Rowan said.

"What's that?" Sarah asked.

"You promise not to hit anyone, and I'll get you a big bag of M&Ms to take to your teacher so you can apologize."

"Apologize? For what? I didn't punch him, and it's not my fault she went to a po-dunk public college."

"Sarah," he scolded again. "That's not nice. There's nothing wrong with public colleges."

"Have you ever heard of Smith's Cedar County Teacher's College?"

"Where is that?" Rowan asked.

Sarah shrugged. "Arkansas, I think. Miss Amara said she grew up in the Ozarks. They had a pet raccoon in her sixth-grade science class. Her mom made them eat fried mush and molasses for breakfast and fried baloney for dinner. She said she didn't used to wear shoes to school."

"Maybe her family couldn't afford shoes," Diana offered from the kitchen.

"Look," Rowan said, getting back to the subject at hand. "Calling your teacher uneducated isn't fair. Punching kids is wrong. You should always try to find the positive and be nice even when you don't want to. Can you do that?"

"Do I still get the M&Ms?"

"If you promise me you'll be nice and won't hit anyone."

The little girl let out an exasperated groan as she crawled out of her dad's lap, elbowing him in his sore ribs as she did. "Fine."

21

After dinner, Rowan went down to his office. He'd wanted to sit down at his laptop to do research, but everything seemed to stand in his way. He hadn't heard the weird voices from the attic all day, but he wasn't sure they were gone. He needed to know more about the ring and where it had come from.

He began with a search for more on Saladin's Ring. The first thing that came up was Saladin's Ring from Mystics: The Quest for Eternity. The boys liked the card game, and they spent a good portion of their allowances building their decks and playing in tournaments at the local card shop. Henry had gotten a Black Sardonyx card, and that had put an end to the fun. The card summoned a legion of undead soldiers and was one of the most potent and rare in the entire game. No one could beat him after he added that to his deck.

The image on the card showed three golden rings, each the same, and Rowan was reminded of Fatima's lecture on "The Parable of the Three Rings." Tima raved about the logic and fairness behind Saladin's wise tale.

Rowan remembered her lectures well. "Due to his generous actions and the financial burdens of war, Saladin's treasury was nearly empty. In urgent need of funds, he wanted to seek the funds from Melchizedek, a wealthy Jewish man who lived in Alexandria," she said. "However, Melchizedek was known for his stinginess and would never willingly give up the sum of money the Sultan needed to fund the defense of Egypt. Saladin, not wanting to take the money by force, plotted to embarrass the Jew. To save face, the man would give him the money he needed."

She continued. "Saladin invited Melchizedek to his palace and praised him. *People say you are wise. Which of the three major religions is truly the correct one—Judaism, Christianity, or Islam?* Realizing the Sultan was baiting him into an argument, Melchizedek replied, *that is an excellent question, my lord. Allow me to answer with a story*."

Melchizedek went on to tell the story of a wealthy man who had a ring that was his most precious possession. He selected the favorite of his three sons to bestow the ring upon as his inheritance. That son became his heir, and so this became a family tradition, the ring passing from one generation to another. Eventually, the ring came into the hands of a man who had three sons. Each was equally virtuous and deserving. Not wanting to favor one son over the other, he sought a craftsman to replicate the ring, ensuring the copies were exact replicas of the original. It was, however, impossible to determine which of the three rings was the original, so their claims as heirs went unresolved. Melchizedek concluded, "The same is true of the three great religions. Each group believes they are the heirs of God's truth, but like the rings, their claims remain unanswered." Recognizing that Melchizedek had avoided the trap, Saladin directly asked him for a loan, which he later repaid in full, and their friendship endured all their lives.

Tears brought him from his thoughts as his vision blurred. He missed Tima and her wise counsel. She would know what to do. She would know all the answers to his questions about

Saladin's ring. In all their years as friends, he'd never spoken to her about their bizarre experiences or Lauren's call to serve as the Hand of Anu. If anyone understood, he suspected she might have been open to their plight. *Why had he never told her?*

He glanced over and saw the key lying on his desk. It was the one that opened the box containing Saladin's ring. He pushed the tears off his face with the back of his knuckle and picked up the key.

A hum of mystic power resonated through his hand as he turned it between his fingers and studied it. The key. *Demons dwell in the Land of Kings, where the key to redemption is whitewashed beneath the gates to the heavens. Where the demons lie, answers await.* Riggs' words came back to him in a flood. This time, however, he paused to write them down on a notepad beside his computer. He wrote it a second time, this time in the form of a poem.

Demons dwell in the Land of Kings
Where the key to redemption
Is whitewashed beneath the Gates of Heaven.

The key. The key to redemption. He circled the word *key*. "Are you the key to redemption?" he said aloud, holding up the crown of the brass object, studying it.

The enemy of my enemy is my friend. Riggs had said that, too. It wasn't the first time someone had said that to him, either.

Memories of Henry Sinclair and the cave in Oklahoma came back to him. Lauren had been in crisis, wounded and in the early stages of labor, back in an ancient time. King Henry and the Knights Templar who accompanied him carried a chest of wonders too holy for many to look upon.

He'd been knighted, for lack of a better word, by Prince Henry himself. He'd taken a vow to defend the cross, to take arms against the enemies of God—or *the gods*—depending on how someone wanted to look at it. He'd pressed his lips to the sword that now hung on the wall in front of him. The can lights made it shine as Rowan's gaze fell on it. He'd made an oath. In return, Prince Henry named him Sir Rowan, Protector of the Holy of Holies, Bearer of the Secret, Protector of the Sacred Heart of the Rose, Knight of the Cross, and Brother of Prince Henry Sinclair.

"If any harm should befall these relics, may this sword defend them or take thy life," Prince Henry had said.

Lauren had earned titles, too, though it wasn't customary to knight a woman. The King named her Sister of the Sacred Heart of the Rose, Most High Keeper of the Sacred Relics, and Mother of New Jerusalem. At the time, Rowan hadn't thought anything about it, mostly because he was just trying to get his family back to their time place before Lauren died or delivered, but Henry gave her one last missive. In addition to protecting the relics entrusted in their care, he'd mandated they return them to the Holy Sepulcher when the time was right.

When was that? How would they know? Was the ring of Saladin yet another relic they were entrusted with? Where would it need to be returned to? He glanced at his watch. It was too late to call Octavia, but maybe she'd have some insight.

ROWAN DIDN'T HURRY HOME IMMEDIATELY after dropping off the kids. Diana was home with Lauren and promised to meet one of the contractors coming by if they came before he got home. Octavia wasn't teaching that morning and agreed to meet him for coffee—his treat.

She'd heard about what happened that night at the Stanley Hotel and she hugged him fiercely, despite the pain it elicited, making him flinch. "I was so relieved to hear your voice this morning. Is Lauren okay?"

"She's still a little shaken up," he said. "But she's resting at home."

Their cups were half empty when Rowan finally got to the question he really wanted to ask. "What do you know about Saladin and a magic ring?"

"Magic ring?" Her sculpted brow lifted. "He was a sultan of Egypt and Syria, a wealthy man. He had many rings. There is a story that he gave one of these rings to *Le Coeur Léon*. Do you know who I'm speaking of?"

"Richard the Lionheart. King of England."

"Yes," she said.

"Why would Saladin give Richard a ring? They were mortal enemies."

"It was a complicated relationship." She sat back and folded her hands. She didn't have any jewelry on this morning, nor did she have on makeup. Her hair was combed but not styled as it had been when he met her. On her day off, she wouldn't need such trappings, Rowan decided. Still, she was a handsome woman. "While they were enemies, there was a deep mutual respect between the two. They each recognized the other's courage and leadership. They were skilled strategists who understood the value of honor and personal integrity in battle."

Rowan considered this, taking a sip of his coffee. "How would they know that about the other?"

"Oh, well, they met often for the purposes of diplomacy. Saladin admired Richard's fighting abilities and chivalric conduct. Richard respected Saladin's commitment to his faith and his ability to join the Muslim tribes into a unified force."

"My professor, Dr. Badr, always spoke highly of Saladin. She said that his leadership skills were unmatched in that era."

Octavia considered him for a minute. "I heard about what happened to Dr. Badr in the news. I'm deeply sorry for your loss. She was an amazing woman." There was another pause as she set her cup aside and dropped her eyes. "You may or may not know this. She and I had several professional disagreements. We argued every time we had the opportunity to debate a historical fact."

"You knew Tima?"

"Fatima was a stubborn old woman," she said sharply, then softened. "But so am I. I suppose our relationship was very much like Saladin and Richard's. We respected each other, but we battled over professional real estate."

"Why did I never hear anything about this?"

"Over the last thirty years, we'd negotiated an informal truce. I stuck to the Mesoamerican cultures, and she stuck to the Near Eastern cultures."

"That's odd," Rowan said. "I wrote at least a dozen papers comparing and contrasting those two cultures while I was in her program."

"Chances are good, she fact-checked you against my work."

"She never even mentioned you."

An exasperated huff escaped her throat. "Not surprising. Typical Gemini."

"Huh?"

"Fatima was a Gemini, June thirteenth, if memory serves me. Geminis never forgive and they never forget. Worst, when they are done, they are done. No turning back."

"Lauren's a Gemini," Rowan muttered, realizing what that might mean for their relationship.

"They have extraordinarily long fuses, but when they blow, best stand back and wait for the dust to settle. Saladin was a Pisces. He was mutable, adaptable, and creative. Geminis are also considered mutable, like Sagittarius. That's my sign. In astrology, it means we are go-with-the-flow kind of people who can adapt."

"I didn't realize you subscribed to the stars determining our fate," Rowan said.

She laughed and lifted a shoulder. "We come from the

stars, and to the stars we will return. Of course, the stars have a say in the way of things. Richard was a Libra."

"I'm a Libra," Rowan said.

"Then you, like Richard, believe in balance and justice. He was a charming and diplomatic creature, as I suspect are you."

Rowan blushed, lifting a hand. "Well, you know . . ."

She laughed, sitting back and taking up her cup again. "Libra and Gemini are considered good matches. There's a duality to both. Geminis have a duality that can make them unpredictable. They can be playful and inhibited one moment, then all business the next. Libras are hopeless romantics and can usually work out any kind of misunderstanding. But that isn't why you asked me here. Is it? You want to know about a ring. Describe it."

Rowan told her everything about the ring, without saying it was in his possession. "And the Marine that attacked me had the same mark on his hand as the sigil on the ring. He said something followed him home and he wanted me to help him, but he was killed before I got any more information." Rowan sketched the sigil on a paper napkin and sat tapping it with his pen.

"Oh, Rowan, I had no idea." Her hand went to his forearm.

"Lauren's upset with me because we would never have been at the Stanley if I hadn't been trying to find out what happened to Lance Corporal Riggs."

Octavia's eye sparkled. "Venus is your ruler. You are a people pleaser, sometimes at the expense of your own needs. But you're a diplomat and a charmer, and I'm sure you'll find a way to win back her heart. You may have to let her be mad for a while, but I could tell watching the two of you together, it won't last. She adores you."

That made Rowan feel somewhat better. Octavia didn't provide as much information about Saladin's ring, but just sharing a fraction of the worries on his mind had lifted his spirits. The revelation about Octavia and Fatima's rivalry had come as a shock, but knowing Tima as he did, it didn't surprise him any.

ROWAN CONTINUED to sleep in the recliner, unable to curl up on his side because of his aching shoulder. Late that night, he woke in a dream and found himself climbing up the stairs to the attic, the ring calling to him. He retrieved the wooden box from the trunk, pausing to study the key before he inserted it into the lock. Compelled, however, he could not resist. The key turned with a subtle click, and the lid seemed to spring open on its own. No longer present were the eerie whispers of demons and the overwhelming discord.

The ring came to his hand as easily as breath to his lungs. It no longer demanded his attention but seemed content with it as he stood holding the ring up to the light. The rubies glistened like lights on a disco ball, casting their reflection on the walls of the confined space. Then he tucked the ring into his pocket, closed the box, and put it back in the chest. He hurried back downstairs, flicking on the lamp in the living room by his chair.

Shadow appeared on her nightly tour of the house and paused by his feet. The Siamese had never been his favorite pet. He was a dog guy, and he tolerated the feline because Lauren loved it so much. That didn't stop him from feeding her canned cat food, even though Lauren tended to provide just kibble. He was usually the one picking up the toy mousies from the middle of the walkway, convinced Shadow was leaving them in his path on purpose.

"What do you want, cat?" He never addressed her by name.

"*What has it got in its pocketses, Master?*" The voice of

Gollum, from the *Lord of the Rings* movie, seemed to come from the cat, as she looked up at him with her large blue eyes.

Rowan hesitated, furrowing his brow and doing a double take. The cat blinked slowly as if awaiting an answer. "Trouble," Rowan answered, taking the ring out, and inspecting it. The cat hissed and took a step back. "It's just a ring, you stupid cat." Shadow hissed again, this time at Rowan rather than the ring. She flicked her tail at him as she turned away and went to find her mistress sleeping downstairs.

I pray we meet again on the field of battle outside Jerusalem on that beautiful Day of Glory, Sinclair had said. Deep in his gut, Rowan wondered if that day would be soon. Somewhere deep inside, Rowan had prayed that day would never come. He'd seen what Enlil could do, or at least a sampling of it. He also knew what Lauren could do, but in her weakened state, they were sitting ducks, and Rowan knew it.

I've given you the last thing you need, Riggs had said. Rowan held the ring under the lamplight. It looked like jewelry he'd seen at the museums in Cairo. It was tarnished, and the jewels clouded with age, but still caught the light as he turned it in his hand. He didn't even try to put it on, but it slipped onto the tip of his finger, and the world went dark. The familiar sense of displacement settled over him when he came found himself standing outside a magnificent brocade tent.

A man in traditional robes stood at the tent flap and signaled him to follow. Rowan, disoriented and unable to form a singular thought, obeyed.

He was led into the main room of the vast tent, which was dimly lit, the flickering torchlight casting long shadows across the brocade walls. Rowan stood at the edge of a low, wooden table, the weight of the ring heavy on his finger. "It seems time has brought us to this moment." A voice caught his attention. Rowan turned as a man in the robes of a Kurdish noble from the 12th century entered the room. "Please, join me at my table. Are you well then?"

"I'm . . ." Rowan hesitated, turning to the table. It was set out with a feast, more than enough for two men, no matter how hungry either might be. "I'm at a bit of a loss. Where are we? Have we met?"

The man hesitated. "My most noble enemy, have you been so ill that you do not remember me? I sent fruits and ice when you were in your fever bed. Yet, you forget me?"

"I'm not sure I understand," Rowan said, puzzled. "Let me start over." He stuck out his hand. "Rowan Pierce. It's a pleasure to meet you. *Asalaamu Alaikum.*" *Peace be with you.*

The man seemed taken aback, studying him through narrowed eyes. Then he noticed the ring on Rowan's left hand, a faint smile finding his dark eyes. "You are not *Le Coeur Léon.*"

"Richard the Lionhearted?" Rowan gasped. "No. I'm not. I do believe him to be one of my ancestors, though."

"You bear his blood? Of course." The man studied him more overtly. "You are the very image of him, if I may say. I am Salah ad-Din Yusuf ibn Ayyub." He accepted Rowan's hand, placing his opposite hand on his chest as he bowed slightly. "*Alaikum Asalaamu.*"

Rowan glanced at the ring, realizing he stood in the presence of Saladin the Great. "It's my honor."

"Sit," Saladin commanded. "I gave this ring to Richard the Lionheart, you know."

Rowan's gaze shifted from the ring to Saladin. "You gave it to him?"

Saladin nodded, his eyes distant, as if lost in a memory. "Yes. Richard is a formidable king—a warrior, yes, but also a man of honor. I admired him. There was respect between us, even when we stood on opposite sides of the battlefield. When we fought, there was no hatred between us. Instead, there was a recognition of strength and purpose."

Saladin reached for a jug and poured a cup for each of them. He handed a cup to Rowan. Saladin paused, looking at

Rowan with an almost sorrowful smile. "I gave him this ring as a token of that respect . . . and perhaps, as a reminder of something more."

Rowan frowned, unsure of where Saladin's words were leading. "A reminder?"

The Sultan's eyes grew darker as if he'd just peeled back a layer of his past. "A reminder that there is more to fight for than land. More than glory. There are ideals—things that transcend any empire, any kingdom. And it is not just power that drives men—it is the need to protect that which is sacred." He leaned forward, his gaze locking onto Rowan's, the weight of his words settling like blowing sand. "This ring is a symbol of that."

Rowan felt the warmth of the metal against his hand, but there was something else there, too. Something older. Something ancient. "I see you have many questions. *Le Coeur Léon* has the same look when he is troubled. There is something more you must know."

"So many questions," Rowan blurted out before he could stop himself.

Saladin took his hand, inspecting the ring, as if he hadn't seen it in a thousand years. "My Grand Vizier, a man of great knowledge and mysticism, placed a curse upon this ring. He did so to protect it. You see, only those of royal blood, the blood of the Lion's Heart, may wear it without falling into madness."

Rowan's jaw dropped. "It's cursed?"

Saladin nodded, reaching for the plate of grapes and offering it to Rowan. He took a few and held them absent-mindedly. "Yes. The ring had to be protected because of the power its wearer may wield."

"Power?"

"There is a price for the power to wield such a weapon."

"Isn't there always?" He thought of Gollum again. Once a simple Hobbit from the Shire, the ring of power had twisted the man into a pitiful creature, consumed by the desire to own the ring. All the while, the ring owned him.

"You see, there are demons bound to it," Saladin said, reaching for a date. He put it in his mouth and used his teeth to peel fruit from the pit. He chewed thoughtfully for a moment. Rowan sat forward, puzzled by the hesitation, anxious to hear more.

"Of course there is," Rowan muttered, putting a grape in his mouth.

"They are yours to command, of course," Saladin said.

"So the curse is on me as well," Rowan muttered, his voice barely above a whisper.

Saladin smiled a faint but knowing smile, one filled with the wisdom of the ages. "It is not a curse you need fear, Rowan. Not if you are who I believe you to be. You are of Richard's bloodline. The curse will not claim you. It will not drive you to madness as it did to others. It is a burden, but not one that will destroy you, if . . ." he hesitated.

"If?"

"If you use it wisely," Saladin said. "You have heard the call of God, have you not?"

"I have," Rowan said.

"Your God has given you a missive, and if you are like your ilk, you will obey the call of your God."

"As you obey the call of Allah." Rowan thought of the parable of the ring. "I've been thinking about a story my professor told me, about a man with three sons and just one ring."

Saladin's brow lifted, and his lips beneath his heavy beard twitched. "And what do you think of this tale?"

"I think we all serve the same God," Rowan said. "You call your god Allah; Jewish people call their god Yahweh. Christians simply call their deity God. In ancient times, the Sumerians called their god Anu. All are the holiest of holy. They are the same."

Saladin seemed to roll the concept around in his mind for a moment, chewing the date as he thought. "These are wise words," he said. "Your mission is to protect ancient relics and ensure they do not fall into the hands of those who might use them for evil. For if there is a God who is good and just, by whichever name we choose, then there is evil in the world who would seek to destroy that which is good. Do you agree?"

"I know this to be true," Rowan said.

"The fate of the world depends upon it, Rowan. You must ensure these relics are protected and returned to Jerusalem before that great and terrible day. It is not a task you may turn from. The ring is only the beginning."

Rowan swallowed, a sense of something deep stirring within him. The ring—this cursed but powerful object—was now tied to his fate. But it was more than that. The mission Saladin spoke of was one of profound significance. It was a mission that would require him to be stronger than he ever thought he could be. He would have to take the Ark of the Covenant, the fragment of the One True Cross, and the Spear of Destiny from the safety of his home and return them to the Holy Land.

"How will I know when . . . how . . . ." he started, panic flooding his mind as he tried to figure out his orders.

Saladin's eyes softened; his voice filled with quiet determination. "The ring will guide you, Rowan. But it is your strength, your heart, that will carry you forward. This is your calling."

Rowan felt a surge of emotion wash through him. Fear. Excitement. Confusion. But there was something deeper. Something that whispered through his veins, urging him to accept the challenge.

"My wife . . . she's been called by the Most High, too."

"Women are sacred." Saladin placed his hand on Rowan's arm. "You are called to protect all that is sacred."

"That's what I'm trying to do," he said, fear now the most

prevalent as he worried he might not be strong enough to protect her from a battle that now seemed almost inevitable.

"Take the ring, Rowan. Let it be your guide. Your destiny is already written in the blood of kings."

Rowan woke with a start, his mind racing and his shoulder throbbing. He realized his hand clutched something, and he opened it. The light from the yard made the stones in the ancient ring sparkle as he found it in his hand, impaled by the skeleton key that kept it safely locked away for centuries. He separated the two and studied each of them.

Tima always said keys were a symbol of hidden knowledge, power, and control, as well as freedom—opportunity. In Christianity, the keys of St. Peter symbolize the authority to guide others in faith. He needed more than faith to face what he sensed must be coming. The ring was a symbol of power and authority, commitment, and fidelity. *Semper Fidelis. Semper Fi.* The cry of the Marine Corps.

In the quiet hours between midnight and the coming dawn, Rowan made up his mind to face the demon head-on. He could only protect Lauren by defeating the ultimate evil—with or without her. He rose from the recliner, resolute. He had work to do.

22

As the days passed, Lauren's demeanor changed little, though she seemed more capable each day. Functional? Well, that might be a stretch. He took her to see Dr. Mac, hoping she might be able to get Lauren to open up. When the appointment was over, Dr. Mac drew him aside and shook her head. "This might be a case for a physician," she said. "If she suffered from some kind of a stroke or shock, I don't know that I can do much for her. She's not delusional, she's not psychotic. Maybe a little depressed, but I wouldn't dare treat her without more of a medical history. I'd need her records from the hospital."

"Can you get them?" he asked, stroking the tuft of hair beneath his chin as he watched Lauren over Dr. Mac's shoulder. She stood at one of the coffee tables, studying the magazines without any particular interest in any of them.

"I can request them, but it'll take a few days, and even then, I'm not sure what I can do."

"I'll see about getting her into a doctor," Rowan said. "But I'm concerned about her mental state more than her physical. She thought I died, and it's upset her."

"I'd expect grief, anxiety, and maybe even a bit of anger,

but it's like . . . she doesn't feel anything." Dr. Mac turned, watching her. "I'll get the records. You get her medical attention. We'll confer when I know more."

"Thank you," Rowan said, putting a hand on his therapist's shoulder.

"How are you doing, Rowan?" She caught him off guard with her question.

"Me?"

"You nearly died," she said. "No rebound depression? Anxiety? How are you sleeping?"

"A tree fell through my house, so I'm back to sleeping in the recliner. How would you be sleeping if it were you?"

"A few hours here and there?"

"Sounds familiar," he said. "But I'll sleep better when Lauren's feeling better."

Dr. Mac nodded. "Take care of yourself. That's the best thing you can do for Lauren."

"Honey? Are you ready to go?" he addressed his wife.

"Yeah," she said, still skimming through a magazine.

"Are you still having your big Halloween party?" asked Dr. Mac.

"The kids would be heartbroken if we canceled."

"Lauren? What are you going to be for Halloween?"

"I'm not sure," she said, glancing back. "I'll come up with something."

"I think her mom has something in mind," Rowan said.

"What about you?" Dr. Mac said, smiling at him.

"I've got an ace up my sleeve, but it's a big secret."

"You'd better have pics when you come back for your next appointment."

"Oh, I will," he said. "It's an epic event. The neighbors will be blown away."

LAUREN SAT on the back patio, gazing out over the devastation wrought by the storm and the fallen tree. Normally, the fall garden was her greatest joy. The rainbow of leaves and flowers, pumpkins, and other fall vegetables gave her a purpose. She'd busily bring in the harvest and prepare the asparagus beds for a long winter's nap. But today, she didn't have it in her. If left to her, there would be no pickled vegetables, canned corn or green beans, or canned pumpkin for Thanksgiving and Christmas pies.

She knew she wasn't feeling like her usual self, but she couldn't explain why. She also knew everyone was worried about her. Rowan had even taken her to see his counselor. He'd tried to play it off as a casual visit, but Lauren wasn't stupid. She recognized their attempts to get her involved in family events. Her mother was trying to get her to eat, but nothing tasted right. Even the Key Lime pie—her favorite as a child—hadn't been all that tempting. Diana was making all her favorite things, but it was a waste.

Her friends came by to see her, and even Bahati tried to coax her into getting a pedicure with her. Lauren's feet were in bad shape after a summer of running around in hiking boots or completely barefoot around the house. Diana dragged her to the farmers market and did not take no for an answer when it came time to mix up cookie dough and prepare dough for fry bread, which Diana insisted would be a favorite at the fall festival.

She felt like she was moving a step behind everyone else. Her mother handed her the bowl from the cabinet, but her reaction time was delayed and before she could react, it hit her toe on its way to the tile where it broke into a dozen pieces. Lauren wanted to cry, but there were no tears. The bowl had been a wedding present from Jacob, and while he was a jerk, she loved the hand-crafted mixing bowl that was part of a set. She also wanted to be mad, but she didn't even have enough energy for that much emotion.

And it was a damned shame that the bedroom was practically destroyed. The heart of their home, the sanctuary she and Rowan retreated to when the world became too much, had been breached. Nowhere was safe if the bed where they made love wasn't safe. Even Rowan's touch left her feeling empty. She wanted to feel something, anything, but the look in his eyes showed her he was struggling with all of this, but it didn't elicit any empathy. She couldn't feel love. She couldn't feel anger. She couldn't feel joy or sadness. She felt nothing for the children that gathered around them at the table, and she knew that should have made her feel a profound sense of loss, but to Lauren's chagrin, she felt nothing.

<hr>

"Good morning, Dr. Pierce. What brings you in today?" the nurse asked her as she came into the exam room to take her vitals and update her chart.

"Lauren hasn't been herself lately," Rowan said and explained what had happened and what he'd observed in his wife. The doctor came in while he was explaining everything, leaving the poor nurse frantically typing on the computer.

The doctor didn't interrupt, but leaned against the counter, folding his arms and listening intently. "I don't know how else to describe it, but . . . it's like she's lost her soul."

"Heaven forbid." The doctor tried to lighten the mood, but the joke fell flat. "Dr. Pierce, how do you feel about all this?"

Lauren lifted a shoulder. "Whatever."

The doctor nodded, considering her for a moment. "Let's let Jacie finish getting her vitals and I'll come back and visit with you, Lauren." He motioned Rowan to follow and led him down the hall to his office. "So, what have you done to help Lauren get through this crisis? Your health episode has affected her profoundly."

"We've tried everything," Rowan said. "I even took her to see my counselor, but she was concerned there might be something physical that hadn't been diagnosed. She wants to see Lauren back once she's had a medical workup."

He turned to the computer and pulled up the network linked to the hospital's medical records. He studied the doctor's notes from her visit to the ER for a moment. "Shock is a physical response to an emotional trauma. Has she been cooperative? Has she done anything to help herself?"

"Not at all," Rowan said. "She just eats because we make her. She'd sleep all day and all night if we let her. She sits and stares out into space when there's nothing else for her to do. She will do what you tell her, but you can tell there is no joy in it."

"We'll screen her for any possible condition the hospital might have missed, but my initial theory is she's suffering from a major depressive disorder or a dissociative disorder. Of course, it could include anhedonia, the inability to feel pleasure, dissociative depersonalization, or a feeling of being detached from oneself."

"Doc, I'm an archeologist and you just threw a whole lot of psychology in my face. I don't know if I care what the diagnosis is. What I want to know is, can you help her? How do I get my wife back? I need her. Our children need her."

"Look, once we know what we're dealing with, then we'll be able to talk about options. Typically, counseling and medication as well as lifestyle and holistic approaches can help a patient get through all of it. What I do know is that mental states like these are rarely permanent. It may take time, but you've got her on the right track. Why don't you have a seat in the lobby and let me work through my assessment? I'll draw some blood to see if there's a change in her hormone levels. I'll check for foreign pathogens and vitamin levels and rule out infection or other possible conditions that could be contributing to her mental state."

"And you can provide all her medical records to my psychiatrist?"

"She has to authorize it," he said. "Unless you have legal power of attorney."

Rowan shook his head. They'd never had to worry about living wills or power of attorney, do not resuscitate orders, or any legal documentation that people of a certain age had to think about. They were those people now, and it hit him like a stone.

23

Sarah was playing in the backyard with Indy, sitting on the grass, scratching his belly. She was happy to be allowed back in the yard, now that the construction crews cleared the debris and fallen tree. The wood from the tree had been cut and stacked along the back fence. The debris had been hauled to the Dumpster that sat in the driveway. Everyone had been worried about the roll-off being removed before the Halloween party tonight. It didn't look like that was going to happen. The workers went to lunch at noon and didn't come back. Sarah didn't mind, though. She rolled over and lay her head on the dog's side and got a wet kiss in payment for the belly rubs. She lay watching the fluffy white clouds floating overhead and listening to the birds. She liked birds. She was particularly fond of magpies and bluebirds that frequented her mother's bird feeders. Cardinals, too. They liked the sunflower seeds growing in the garden. The heavy heads had bent over, and Sarah wondered when her mother was going to harvest them.

Last Halloween, they'd put the seeds inside pumpkins the day after Halloween for all the birds and critters that came to visit the yard. Today, one particularly large raven was sitting on the fencepost, eyeing one of the seed heads. The bird seemed to notice he was being watched and eyed the little girl, looking skeptical. Sarah watched back, no longer paying much attention to the dog. Indy nuzzled her hand, trying to get her attention. When that didn't work, he got up and went to look for his ball, displacing Sarah. Without a canine pillow, she got up, brushing the leaf litter off the seat of her baggy overalls that had once been Kate's.

Unlike other ravens she'd seen, with shiny blue-black beaks, this bird's beak was faded and mottled, giving the impression he had wrinkles, like her Grandpa John. She stared at the bird, trying not to blink. The bird stared back. The game continued for nearly a minute before Sarah couldn't stare anymore. She blinked. The raven blinked back. She tilted her head, and the bird mirrored her, tilting its head.

"Why is a raven like a writing desk?" she asked, quoting from one of her older brother's favorite books, *Alice Through the Looking Glass*.

Because that which is nevar backward is always forwards, she thought she heard the bird answer. *And a raven is nevar backward, and a writing desk is always for words.*

Sarah blinked, rubbing her eyes. "I must be dreaming."

Then you must be sleeping.

Sarah pinched herself on the arm. "Ouch. Nope. Not dreaming." She took a step closer to the raven. "I didn't know ravens could talk."

"I'm told I speak quite well for a raven," the bird answered. "And, of course, I should be rather well-spoken. I've had plenty of practice."

"So, you're in the habit of speaking frequently?"

"It's not that I must speak often." The bird hopped down to the grass and walked around her, its tail swishing left and right. "It's just that I'm quite old."

Sarah sat down, cross-legged, leaning her elbow on her

knee, resting her head on her chest. She studied him as she formed a question. "How old is old to a raven?" she asked.

"To an ordinary raven, ten years is old."

"I will be five in May," Sarah said. "Ten isn't that old."

"But I am a great and powerful wizard," the raven said. "I have lived one hundred lifetimes for a raven—more, if truth be told."

"You're a wizard?" she asked, but she wasn't surprised. "My brother is a wizard. My mom and my Grandpa John, too. I didn't know ravens could be wizards, raven."

"Please, good child," the raven bristled, fluffing its feathers as the bird shook off. Once his feathers lay back, he bowed like a courtly gentleman. "I do have a name."

"And?"

"And, what?"

"Are you going to tell me your name, or do I have to guess?"

The bird seemed to consider this for a moment as he walked back and forth, his tail feathers swishing. "Guess, if you can."

Sarah considered him for a long moment. "Well, you are quite a polite bird. I would think a raven with such manners— one who is a wizard—should have a magical name." She tapped on her chin with her finger. "Merlin?"

"No, but that is a good name."

"Harry Potter is a wizard, but I don't think you look like a Harry. Nor do you look like Albus Dumbledore. Perhaps Severus Snape?"

"I am often confused with a Slytherin," the bird said, with a squawk that sounded like a guffaw. "But Slytherin is not a house to trifle with. I much prefer the Griffin to the Serpent."

"Of course you would," Sarah agreed. "I'm all out of guesses."

"You must ask me for my name if I am to tell you."

"Wait, it's not Beetlejuice, is it?"

The bird shook its head. "No."

"My Nanhi says it's poor manners to ask a man his name."

"But I am a raven," the bird pointed out.

Sarah considered him for a moment. She sat up and nodded her head. "My name is Sarah Connor Pierce, and I am pleased to make your acquaintance, raven. If I may be so bold, may I ask your name, sir?"

The bird nodded, seemingly impressed with her comportment. The bird spread his wings and bowed graciously. "Miss Pierce," he said, "I am Suleiman the Wise, Grand Corvus of the Long Haired Tribe and Wizard of the Thirteenth Order of Apollo."

"Are you an agent of Apollo?" Sarah asked.

"And what does a child know of Apollo and his messengers?"

"I know that ravens are considered messengers from Apollo," she said. "But . . . they are also seen as tricksters. Are you a trickster, Suleiman?"

The bird turned its back on her and looked over its wing at her coyly. "Now, why would you think that? I am far too old for games, Miss Pierce. Nor am I here with a message. I simply happened to be flying about and recognized a kindred spirit."

Sarah laid on her stomach, resting her chin on her hands, her elbows on the grass. She kicked her feet up and eyed the bird. "Some myths, like those of my daddy's family, say ravens are the spirits of the dead, returned to watch over the living."

The bird strutted as it walked back over to her and leaned down to put itself at eye level with the child. "I, my dear, am no ghost. Please be so kind as to remember it."

"What do you want, Mr. Sulu Man?" Sarah asked, rolling over onto her back, spreading out light like a starfish, gazing up at the puffy clouds against a dark blue sky. "Why don't you fly off with your friends?"

"It looks like you're having a party," the bird said. "I suspect there will be food, and I am rather hungry."

"There are seeds in the bird feeder," she said. "But you can't eat my mom's sunflowers. She hasn't picked them yet."

The bird hopped up on top of the barn-shaped bird feeder. "Ah, so there is." He leaned down to inspect the mix of sunflower seeds, millet, and other grains. "Hmph. I had hoped for a caramel apple."

"I like caramel apples," Sarah said dreamily. "I bet Mrs. Keaton makes caramel apples. Last year, she made one that was as big as my head."

"Oh, do tell?" The bird hopped back down and came over, settling in beside her.

"She used this apple called a Honey Crisp," she said. "And it was this big." She held up her hands to demonstrate the softball-sized apple. "Then she dipped it in caramel, at least two or three layers. I think it must have had six layers of chocolate, and she rolled it in mini M&M's and Oreo crumbs and then drizzled it with more chocolate and caramel. My daddy had to cut it up for me, and it took me four days to eat all of it. So good."

"I do like apples," Suleiman said, hopping up on her chest, peering down at her, turning its head to look at her with one dark eye. "Can I come to the party with you?"

"Can you pretend to be a parrot?" Sarah asked. "I'm going to be a pirate, and I have a fake parrot, but if you can sit on my shoulder, you can be my parrot."

"I have never been a parrot before," Suleiman said. "But for a bite of such an apple, I suppose I can try."

Sarah started to sit up, but the bird was heavy and had her pinned down. "I don't know. You might be too big to sit on my shoulder," she said. "You might just have to follow me around."

"So long as you share your apple with me, good child, I shall follow you anywhere."

Sarah insisted he prove it by following her as she marched around the backyard, singing at the top of her lungs. To her surprise, the raven joined in.

"Sarah!" John Carter called from the door. "Nanhi says you have to come in and get a sandwich before you can put your costume on."

Sarah came in, singing, with the raven toddling behind her, squawking. John Carter took a step back as they marched in. The bird didn't seem the least bit shy.

Diana stood at the kitchen counter, watching the parade. The bird hopped up on the stool beside his new friend, who reached for a plate to make herself a sandwich. "What is this?"

"Nanhi, this is my new friend, Suleiman," Sarah said. "Suleiman, this is my *A-gi-li-shi*."

The bird bowed and cawed. Blinking, it leaned its head against Sarah's arm.

"Why are you here?" Diana looked at the bird, dubiously.

"He's my friend," Sarah said. "He can talk. Tell my Nanhi you can talk."

The raven said nothing, watching Sarah make her sandwich with a hungry look in his eye. "Come on, bird. You are making me look bad."

"Ravens exist for themselves. They are not here for us," Diana scowled, crossing her arms.

"I'm not a liar." Sarah scowled, moving her plate away from the bird, blocking him from taking a bite. "Tell her, Suleiman. Show her you can talk."

John Carter came over to stand beside his grandmother, inspecting the bird. "What's wrong with his face?" he asked, popping a pickle slice into his mouth.

Sarah scowled as she put her arm around the large raven. "Don't listen to him, Suleiman." Sarah rested her cheek on his head, and the bird seemed to snuggle into her, tucking himself into her hair, gazing out at John Carter with a smug expression. "When you're over one hundred years old, I bet your face doesn't look half as good."

Diana had a sour expression on her face as she watched the exchange between the children. "The raven is a trickster," she said. "A portent of death or ill-luck."

"Don't listen to her, Suleiman." Sarah broke off a piece of bread and offered it to the bird, who took it without nipping her finger. "You're not bad luck. You are my spirit animal." She looked up at her grandmother. "I don't have a spirit animal, do I?"

Diana considered this for a moment. "Our people don't choose their spirit animals. They choose us."

"Do you have a spirit animal?"

"I do," Diana said. "But it is considered poor manners to ask."

"I'm sorry, Nanhi." Sarah considered the bird a moment. "He chose me."

"Well," Diana said as she eyed the bird, who stared back at her. "Eat, and then you can get ready for the festival. Kate is helping your mom finish getting ready."

"Yes, Nanhi." Sarah finished making a sandwich for herself, holding out a potato chip for the bird. "Do we have any apples?"

"Sure," her grandmother said, turning to the refrigerator and taking one out. "Would you like me to cut it up for you?"

She turned to the raven, who cawed at her. "Yes, please," Sarah said. "Suleiman likes apples."

Sarah shared both her apple and her sandwich with her new friend. When they finished, the raven cawed and bowed to Diana before hopping down off the stool, following Sarah to the stairs. It hopped up a few steps behind the child before taking to wing, meeting her at the top of the stairs, much to the child's delight.

LAUREN STOOD in front of the mirror in the bathroom, gazing at the image of a woman she didn't recognize. Kate had curled her hair and tied back a few strands in braids to give her a more regal appearance. She wore a top of leather pieced together to form a snake-like armor that stopped just beneath her breasts. Her abdomen was bare except for the henna tattoos Kate had spent the last hour carefully drawing on her stomach. It gave the illusion of a solid six-pack, though Lauren could have managed without it.

Her skirt was little more than a loincloth of leather and tiny metal coin-like disks. There were similar braces and knee-high boots that were a little tight, but tolerable. A metal cuff wrapped around her bicep on her left arm. Metal epaulettes cut into her armpits. The breastplate came up to her neck.

"Dad's going to lose his freaking mind," Kate said, touching up the tattoo on her cheek and forehead.

"Is this normal?" Lauren looked down at her stomach, feeling exposed.

"Nothing this family does is normal," the pre-teen said. "But you were born to play Deja Thoris. If you'd been an actress in Hollywood, you'd have been a sure winner for the role."

"Deja Thoris."

"You're the Princess of Mars, Mom."

"I'm a princess?" The way Lauren said it amused the teenager. It was as if she believed it and was actually kind of happy about it.

"Yeah," Kate said. "You are the Princess of Helium, daughter of Tardos Mors, the Jedak of Helium. You are the most beautiful and intelligent woman on Barsoom. You are a warrior princess."

"Oh," Lauren said. "Cool."

"Nanhi is a genius when it comes to making costumes," Kate said, wrapping her mother's hands in the scraps of linen her grandmother had dyed with tea bags to make them look old and dirty. Sarah had a picture of the actress who played the character in the Disney movie on her phone as a reference, but she was struggling to get the look right. "Good thing Nanhi made the bottoms different. Her butt's kinda hanging out."

Lauren turned and tried to eye her backside, her hands going to her hip, finding sufficient material to cover her tush. "I hope it's not cold tonight," Lauren said.

"You'd make me wear a sweater if it were me," Kate said. "Still, it'd be a shame to cover all this up. All the other moms are gonna be so jealous. I hope I can wear this costume when I get older."

"I feel like the whore of Babylon," Lauren muttered.

"What's that, Mom?" Kate stood back, looking her over.

"Nothing." Lauren shook her head, leaning into the mirror. The woman looking back at her had heavy eyeliner and artificial lashes. Kate had painted her eyes a bit more than the character in the picture.

"Here," Kate said. "Lipstick is it, and then I think I'm done. I've got to get my costume on."

"Can I go lie down until it's time?"

"Yeah," she said. "Just don't mess up your hair or your makeup. The henna should be dry, and it won't stain the bedding."

"Okay," Lauren said, pursing her lips so Kate could put the lipstick on for her.

"I'll come get you in a bit." Kate put away her makeup and left.

Lauren stood in front of the mirror a while longer. It wasn't the costume. Nor was it the make-up or the tattoos. She didn't know this woman. She was rail thin but muscular. Her stomach was flat, her navel painted with henna. Lauren's hand lingered on her abdomen a moment before running up her body, learning who this soulless new Lauren Pierce was. She knew what everyone was saying about her. She didn't know what it meant, but it had the family on edge. Her mother watched her like a hawk. Rowan doted on her, and the kids walked on eggshells around her.

This wasn't a good idea, but what could she do?

JAMIE AND SAM CAME DOWNSTAIRS, dressed and ready for the festivities. Jamie had made his own Iron Man costume from old football pads, cardboard boxes, and a motor cross helmet, all spray-painted and hand detailed.

Sam had a red leather jacket, a gray T-shirt, and black jeans. He'd found a plastic Honda logo that had fallen off someone's car that he'd made into a belt buckle. John Carter had taken two balsawood phasers they'd made for their Star Trek costumes and turned them into blasters. They'd found an old Walkman cassette player with headphones in the attic. With a new label that read *80's Mix Tape* on it, Sam was the perfect Peter Quill. He even had a fake beard.

When Kate emerged from her room, she had painted herself green and wore a long dark wig that she'd dyed the tips of with fruit punch Kool-aide. Her black leather vest and pants were snug. She had a matching blaster on the belt that was slung low on her hips, black fingerless gloves, and boots.

"Gamora!" Jamie cheered when she paused and posed.

Sam rushed over to his twin sister and inspected her. "Dang, sis! Nice job on the make-up."

"Don't touch me." She put up a hand. "I'm not sure if it's going to rub off or not." Then, she paused to inspect Jamie's costume. "That's the worst Iron Man costume I've ever seen," she snorted.

Jamie looked affronted. "What? I thought I did a rather good job! I'd like to see you do better."

"I'm just yanking your chain, dork."

"I told you. You should have dressed up as Groot."

"Bah!" Jamie waved her off. "Like I wanna be a tree."

John Carter appeared at the top of the stairs wearing his father's military flight suit. With the Ray-Ban sunglasses and his hair pulled back, he looked more like Maverick from Top Gun than his father. The stuffed goose under his arm sealed the deal.

"John Carter? I thought you were going to be Tony Stark," Kate said.

"I found Dad's flight suit in the attic," he shrugged. "Besides, Jamie is Iron Man."

"What's up with the duck?" Kate asked.

"That's Goose. He's my wingman."

He chomped on a piece of gum. "Is everyone ready to go to the party? Where's Sarah?"

"I'm here," a small voice came from the top step. Standing at the top of the stairs was a small version of Jack Sparrow, with an exceptionally large raven beside her, wearing a tiny eyepatch with a string around its head covering one eye. A gold earring dangled from the cord. "Yo, ho."

"Wait," Kate narrowed her eyes at the little girl. "What is that bird doing in the house?"

"This is my new friend, Suleiman," she said. "I couldn't get a parrot, but I did find a raven." The bird stepped up and bowed to the rest of the children, hopping down a few steps. "He's a very smart raven."

"So it would seem," she said. "Where'd you find him?"

"Out in the yard," Sarah said. "He can talk."

"Oh yeah?" Sam sneered. "He's probably got mange."

The bird recoiled, ruffling its feathers. It cawed loudly at the insult, eyeing Sarah's older brother with malintent. "He doesn't have mange! You have mange!" Sarah snapped at him. "You better be nice to him. He's a wizard, and he'll put a curse on you."

The bird squawked, almost in offense.

"Enough, both of you," Diana, dressed as Lady Olenna

Tyrell from *Game of Thrones*, said. "It's time to get ready for the pumpkin carving and apple bobbing. I have to get everything ready to make frybread and set up the tables for the bake sale. Kids, come help."

"Wait, Nanhi," Kate hesitated. "I thought we were supposed to dress up like a hero. Have you ever seen *Game of Thrones*?"

"Lady Tyrell is a hero," Diana said.

"She's a villain," Sarah said, shaking her head. "Everybody knows that."

"Well, first off, even villains are the heroes in their own stories," Diana said. "Who do you think was the worst baddie in *Game of Thrones*?"

"The Night King!" John Carter said confidently.

"No, the White Walkers!" Jamie said.

"Please," Kate scoffed. "Everyone knows the worst character on *Game of Thrones* was King Joffery."

"Right, and who killed the villain? Lady Tyrell. I rest my case."

24

Diana met Bahati and Jean-René as they came up the driveway. Bahati looked like she'd just come from a street fight. She wore a black tank top and olive pants and had a decorative katana—officially licensed by AMC television—on a strap over her shoulder. Jean-René gave it to her for her birthday. As a fan of the show *The Walking Dead*, she was hardcore into Michonne, who looked more like her than any other character on television. She carried a long walking stick, to complete the costume. And like Michonne, her braids were held back by a bandana.

Behind her, Jean-René followed, looking like a corpse, freshly risen from the grave, a manacle around his neck, connected to a chain that Bahati had looped loosely into her belt. They each carried trays of baked goods, while Jean-René dragged a wagon containing other snacks and sundries.

"What is this?" Diana asked, taking a step back.

"You've seen *The Walking Dead*, haven't you, Diana?" Bahati said. "I'm Michonne."

"And who . . . what is your husband?" Diana furrowed her brow. "A zombie?"

"They're called *walkers*, Nanhi," Jamie said. Jean-René,

ever the character, grunted and made horrible noises from the back of his throat, taking a swipe at Jamie, just as Sarah ran out into the yard with the raven in flight behind her.

She paused and screamed, taking two steps back before falling on her rump, startled by the monster. Jean-René broke character and started to help her up, but she screamed again. "It's me, *ma petite*. It's just me." He froze, letting her see that he wasn't really a zombie. "I'm sorry. I wasn't trying to scare you."

Jamie came over and helped her up, but the raven landed and stayed close to her, leaning against her leg as she recovered from the shock. "Let me take those." Jamie moved to take the load from the cameraman, leaving his hands free to open his arms for Sarah. The little girl hesitated but finally capitulated and stepped into him. He kissed her head and straightened her wig. She sniffed back tears as he let her go. "You are going to help me with the pumpkin-carving contest, *savez*?"

"*Oui*." Sarah sniffed.

Kate came out with a roll of butcher paper and a box of trash bags, pausing to laugh at Jean-René and Bahati's costumes. "That's perfect," she chuckled as Bahati approached.

"What's a hero without a sidekick?" Bahati glanced back at Jean-René as he was being introduced to the raven. "Where'd the bird come from?"

"I don't even know," Kate said. "As soon as we set up the table for the bake sale, you can put those out. If you want, you can put them in the kitchen for now."

"Where's your mom?"

"Probably still asleep downstairs," Kate said. "She's still out of it. But her costume is cool."

"I'll drop these off and go down and check on her," Bahati said. "Where's your dad? I thought the tables would be set up by now."

"He put them all in the garage," Kate said. "We'll have to

set up in the grass this year because of the Dumpster. Nanhi wants the fryer at the end of the driveway so she can make fry bread."

"Jean-René? Could you find Rowan and get the boys to help you set up?" She turned back, unhooking the chain from her belt. "I'm going to check on Lauren."

"Dad's upstairs getting ready," Sam said. "Jamie, John Carter, and I can put the tables up if you want us to."

"I'll help," Jean-René offered.

Bahati left the chore to the boys and went inside, setting her load down before she paused, noticing the caution tape across Lauren & Rowan's bedroom door. She shook her head and turned for the stairs that led down to the basement.

Diana walked with Bahati back into the house. "Any change?"

"Not really," Diana said.

"I'd hoped she'd be back on her feet faster than this."

"She's functional, but as they say, the lights are on—"

"But no one's home," Bahati finished her sentence.

"As I said, she hasn't been herself lately. She dropped a glass Sarah handed her yesterday and she snapped at the little girl so bad that she went running upstairs crying." Diana shook her head. "She didn't even go up to check on her later."

"Oh, no," Bahati said. "She can be stern, but I've never seen her snap at any of them."

"I'll admit, I've snapped at Rowan lately, too," Diana said. "It's been hard on all of us. I feel bad, and I have to think Lauren's mood rubbed off on me."

"I'm sure he understands. I hope she's up to tonight's festivities. She's never missed a Halloween party in all the years we've been doing this," Bahati said.

"I'm here." Lauren appeared in the doorway. Her voice was heavy, and she didn't look steady, but Kate was right. Her costume was cool. No, it was *hot*. *Total smoke show*. Bahati recognized it immediately. She bowed. "Deja Thoris, Princess of Helium," she said formally.

Lauren crossed her arms in front of her, looking uncomfortable. "The whole neighborhood is going to see me like this."

"Lucky them," Diana said. "Just be glad I didn't make it exactly the way it was on the movie poster."

"Is it cold?" she asked.

"No," Bahati said. "It hit eighty-four this afternoon. You'll be warm, at least until sunset."

"Great," Lauren said, flatly.

"Come on," Bahati caught her arm and pulled her towards the door. "You can help me get everything set up for the bake sale."

THE NEIGHBORHOOD FALL Festival was an extravagant affair. Every family who chose to participate was expected to set up a booth with activities and treats. The funds collected from the bake sale were donated to the neighborhood association to help with beautification and security projects, like the new streetlights and the neighborhood sign at the gate.

The cul-de-sac in front of the Pierce home was the final stop, where the families that surrounded the circle drive cooperated to set up games, a dunk tank, and contests, like bobbing for apples and pumpkin carving. Dr. McIntosh hosted a pet adoption booth in cooperation with the local ASPCA and several non-profit organizations and pet rescues. Mr. Peterson, the high school principal, was the hapless victim in the dunk tank. He always raised the most money, which was split between the neighborhood association and the animal rescues.

Diana had spent the last week baking. She'd been able to get Lauren to help with it, though she'd had to remind her of all the steps to making cheesecake bites or apple pumpkin gingerbread men. She failed miserably at decorating. The first cookie Lauren tried to decorate came out looking more like Jean-René's zombie than a gingerbread man.

While the women and girls covered the plastic folding tables with paper and decorated them with construction paper pumpkins and bats Kate, Sam, and Sarah had made, Diana finished packaging up the last of the treats, so they were ready to go out on the table. There were so many that they couldn't put out more than half of the inventory. They would have to restock as the evening passed.

The next step was to get the frybread from the fridge so it could finish its last rising, which wouldn't take long. She'd cook it up in batches as the evening progressed and serve it with butter and cinnamon sugar or honey. Some people opted for both. She went back into the house and took the dough out to rest on the counter for its final proofing.

From the kitchen, Diana watched the neighbors across the street out the front window. The cul-de-sac was beginning to fill with kids in costumes, parents with their wagons and strollers, and even some with their ice chests. Everyone got comfortable for the evening festivities. Diana noticed the other women looking at Lauren, silently judging her costume. In truth, every one of those women was most likely jealous of her figure, especially after giving birth to six children. She could have been a fitness model if her brain hadn't been so full of big ideas and questions about the universe.

Lauren worked hard to stay in shape, and she deserved the right to wear whatever she wanted. She was never one to worry about what other people thought. When the women started talking between themselves, Diana had about all she could take of it. She didn't need to hear what they were saying —she could tell by their posture and the expressions on their faces that it wasn't nice. She finished packing her last bag of chocolate chip cookies, washed her hands, and went outside.

"Nanhi?" John Carter met her at the door. "Where are you going?"

"This isn't any of your concern," Diana said, leaving the perplexed young man in her wake. Diana got a few steps, then stopped, turning back. She motioned him to her, and he moved quickly. "Though, if you could keep your mother occupied, I would appreciate it. I'm not trying to make a scene, and I certainly don't want to embarrass her in front of the whole neighborhood."

"Nanhi?" The boy stood perplexed and then must have seen where his grandmother's gaze went. "Oh."

The women, most of whom were from down the street, were not ones that Diana encountered daily. She knew all the ladies from the cul-de-sac and thought highly of each of them. These women, on the other hand, didn't know Diana or her daughter. Their kids were running wild, picking flowers from the neighborhood gardens, or generally being tiny menaces in their own right. The soccer moms in the Lululemon workout attire stood staring over their iced mocha lattes. All four of them had varying versions of the Karen haircut: tips frosted, faces too tan, and their makeup too over-the-top.

They didn't see Diana coming, they were so focused on Lauren. One of them made a snide comment about the costume, while another gasped about the lack of modesty, just within earshot of the old woman. "Is there a problem?" Diana's voice was calm but measured. She spoke with an edge of authority, challenging.

One of them recoiled, staring down at Diana over her long, slightly hawkish nose. "Well, I mean, look at her." The woman lifted a hand towards Lauren. "This is a family-friendly event, and she's walking around like *that?*"

"You know, we can put up with a lot in this neighborhood," one of the women behind her said. "But she doesn't seem to understand there are limits."

"What? Are you jealous that a woman almost twice your age can pull off a costume like that?" Diana looked the ringleader up and down. She wore skin-tight leggings that came just above her navel, a sports bra, and a light jacket over it. Her cleavage all but spilled out over the top of her bra, and a roll of belly fat hung over her waistband. "I'm sure everyone in the neighborhood comes to you for fashion advice," Diana said. "When *we* want it, we'll ask."

The collective gasp that rose from the gaggle made Diana smile inside, though she couldn't let it show. "And it wouldn't hurt you to get a non-fat latte and walk a few more laps around the park. Maybe by next Halloween, you could pull off an outfit like that. Maybe."

The soccer moms were stunned into silence. The ringleader balled up, drawing her chin back, extenuating the extra flab around her neck. "Why, the nerve!"

"You can't talk to her like that," one of her backers added.

Diana didn't even blink. "I absolutely can. It's called freedom of speech. Look it up." The women's faces reddened, but Diana wasn't done. "Next time you want to judge someone, why don't you take a look in the mirror first? If you're jealous, that means you need to change something about *yourself*."

"What the hell?"

"Maybe someone is standing on a curb across the street from your house talking about what a Karen you are." Diana hated that term, but at the moment it was fitting. "Did you ever think about that?"

For a second, she expected them to come at her *en mass*, but they didn't. Instead, their eyes widened and they took a step back, gathering their children and hurrying along on their way to find something better to do.

Diana turned to walk away but froze when she ran face first into a red cross emblazoned on a white background in the center of a tall, wide chest. Her eyes lifted and were met by the green eyes of her son-in-law, dressed in full Templar regalia, including chainmail, a metal helm, and a tabard. He had a sword in a sheath on his hip, and his beard had been oiled and combed into a point. The corners of his mustache had been waxed and turned up, the copper hairs of his face catching the afternoon sunlight. He smiled impishly at her, then glanced at the complaint of Karens who glared back but hurried along their way.

"Go with God," Rowan called after them, then turned back down to his mother-in-law. "Trouble?"

"Nothing I couldn't handle." She took a step back so she could inspect him. "Nice costume. But this looks storebought."

"I might have fudged the rules a little bit, but I didn't buy it. I borrowed the helmet, boots, and chainmail from a movie producer I happen to know from my days at the Exploration Channel. I have to return it next week."

Diana's hand ran along the red cross and the gold filigree embroidered into a rose. "This is from your office, isn't it? The sword, too?"

"Yes," he said. "I thought for a minute I might need to draw it."

"Mean ol' biddies were talking smack about my daughter," Diana said. "I have no patience for that."

"Do you have the patience to help me gird my tabard?" he asked. "I can't move in all this chainmail, and I need to belt up the fabric, so I don't trip over it."

Diana obliged and helped him get the wide leather belt around his waist, then secure it. "There you go," she said.

"Now come on, it's about an hour until sunset. We need to get the pumpkin carving contest going."

Rowan hadn't seen Lauren until that moment. Diana noticed the expression on his face as he paused and sucked in a breath. She remembered when John looked at her like that. He still gave her adoring glances, but they were different now.

She had never been built like Lauren, but she'd done okay back in her prime.

In that moment, she decided her long white hair and crone-like wrinkles had been hard-earned and were something to be proud of. She'd raised six of the largest men in the Cherokee tribe and a daughter who was both beautiful and brilliant. Her magic had been expended in that effort, leaving just enough to heal when called upon. She no longer needed the magic to draw her husband back to her. He would come to her when he could or summon her to him.

"I made her costume just for you," Diana said.

Rowan swallowed hard, visibly salivating. "Thank you." He swallowed again, then seemed to take a moment to gather his courage and talk to her like a nervous young suitor.

The Darkness waited, watched—always watching. It was the holiest of all High Holidays for the Master, and *The Darkness* was growing weary of waiting. But if all the stars aligned, this could be the night Enlil made his move. The protection of the house had been broken, and it allowed *The Darkness* to enter. But tonight, the entire family was outside of the protection it might have provided had the voodoo priest not whistled up a wind from behind bars and brought down the tree.

The energy of the Sultan's Ring throbbed around the man's aura, but it couldn't sense the ring's exact whereabouts. *The Darkness* didn't think it was on the man's finger, but it was close . . . *perhaps his pocket?* *The Darkness* moved closer, feeling the warm throb of the ring. *Yes, yes,* it was in the man's pocket. *Now how to get him to put it on?* That was the question.

But the man was weak, as the force had already proven in previous attacks. *The Darkness* moved in over him and whispered in his left ear. *Where is the ring?* *The Darkness* had learned it could plant ideas in the man's head, as long as the woman wasn't close by. *The Darkness* could manipulate weaker individuals, but the woman was strong—too strong.

It needed the man. It needed the ring. The two had to come together if *The Darkness* was going to wield the power of the ring. It needed the trinity of energies—flesh, gemstone, and dark energy.

The man had no idea of the power contained within the ring. The Sultan's Ring contained no ordinary gemstone. It was an ancient diadem, a pure *sardonyx* stone. Such stones were formed hydrothermally in hollows or voids in rocks, deep in the hottest regions of hell.

This type of silicate stone was an ancient one, known since biblical times, found in the Middle East, particularly Sardis in modern-day Turkey. The number of myths and legends to explain the energies and magic these stones held were countless. In the Exodus and the Revelations according to John in the Christian bible, sard was one of the precious stones chosen by Aaron to adorn his breastplate. But it also had a dark energy—particularly this stone, which was said to be wielded atop Lucifer's staff. It was shattered in the battle between the Archangel Michael and the forces of good. Its original owner may not have known the source of the gemstone, but Saladin—the Vizir of the Fatimid Caliphate—wielded the power without mercy. Having already conquered Damascus in 1174 and Aleppo in 1183, the power of the ring was demonstrated in full at the Battle of Hattin in 1187.

Yes, the coming battle would be equally glorious. The Dark Lord needed to know the time was at hand. *The Darkness* found the vibrations of the cosmic ether that would carry a message to the Hand of the Dark One. It was time.

25

Papa Dauphine sat in his cell. The day had been hot, and the cinderblock walls absorbed the heat, leaving the cell sultry and damp. Sweat dripped down his chest and collected in the dark curls, making them glisten in the fading light that cut through the glass blocks at the top of his cell.

Like Prometheus, who was punished for giving mankind fire, Dauphine suffered endlessly in this cesspool of humanity. It was an unjust punishment for a crime he did not commit. He felt wrongly shackled by an unjust society.

He rose and picked up the small bag of candy the inmates had been given earlier in the day from his cellmate's bunk. He took three of the wrapped pieces of peanut butter taffy to his makeshift altar. Speaking, he called to the Loa to attend him. He had a few other items he retrieved from their hiding spot in the void behind the wall beneath his cot. He'd been carving with a plastic knife for months. Aging masonry block and cheap mortar made it feasible, though it had been difficult. Tonight, the air felt ripe with possibilities—the veil was thin— and he would purify himself and pray to his ancestors for more than justice.

He prayed for a release from this prison. He'd bided his time, as the Dark Lord had commanded, but the compulsion to escape grew greater with each passing day, and the confines of the stone walls had held him for what seemed like an eternity. There was another thought on his mind beyond escape. Retribution. Like Prometheus before him, he would reclaim what was rightfully his. With the Dark Lord's help, he would break free of his chains.

He lay three coins on the altar beside a candle alongside the single match he'd been able to obtain by nefarious means. The bottle of cane syrup he'd stolen from the kitchens, and he'd saved the corn cob from one of the evening meals nearly a month ago. The drum he'd made from a cardboard oatmeal container, with a piece of rubber he'd cut from a tire in the prison's automotive shop where he'd spent the summer on work detail.

He had taken a twist of sage from the prison gardens and done his best to dry it. He used the smoke to purify himself. He waved it over him like water. "Darken my soul, o' ancestors."

The smoke curled into the corners of the room, mixing with the miasma of dark spirits that gathered. His fingers twitched with the silent incantation he repeated seven times. "Hear my prayers." The air grew thicker, charged with an unnatural energy.

He began to chant as he tapped on the makeshift drum, keeping the noise to a minimum so as not to alarm the guards. Papa Dauphine whispered an incantation in the language of his ancestors. "Papa Legba. *Louvri baryè pou lwa yo.*" His voice echoed through the halls of the prison as he called upon Papa Legba, the greatest of the Loa spirits. "Open the gates for Iwa!"

At first, there was nothing—just the usual sounds of the settling prison. Then, the shadows began to move, melding with the purifying smoke. They writhed in the corners of the small cell, stretching, expanding, until they covered the masonry walls like a living cloak.

From the shadows, the smoke congealed, and a dark shape materialized. The tall form was wrapped in dark robes, its eyes glowing green with ancient powers. The Dark Lord had come.

"The time has come," a voice came from the deep form, rumbling as if spoken from deep beneath the earth. "You have been faithful and kept your promise to me. Now I keep my promise to you. Go forth and wreak chaos upon the Hand of the All-Father. Bring me her corpse . . . and the remainder of her soul."

Dauphine's lips curled into a smile. The promise of vengeance flashed in his eyes. "What's in it f' me?" The voodoo priest wanted his fair share for all his suffering.

"What do you ask of me?"

"I wan' her head on a spear." Dauphine's lips curled back. "Her heart on a plate. I take her eyes an' show her de sufferin' of her world without a champion t' protect it. I'll take her ears so she can hear de screams of her chil'ren as de hounds of hell rip dey flesh from dey bones. I take her lights and her whiny pipes so her screams can be heard all de way to the ninth level of hell." He had served the Dark Lord for years, offering his soul and his power in exchange for this moment—the moment of liberation.

"So mote it be." The Dark One lifted his hand, beckoning the priest to stand. Dauphine rose to his feet. The priest knew just what to do as the Dark Lord melted into the abyss. He took the twist of sage and dropped it on the thin mattress that covered his bunk. The bedding immediately caught, and smoke boiled from the cell. The bars seemed to melt into nothingness as Dauphine walked through the flames, the smoke wrapping itself around him as he passed along the corridor. Outside the prison, the wind began to howl, finding every crack in the aging edifice. The breeze fed the flames, which consumed everything that might burn and even things that couldn't.

The prison shook, and with a deafening crash, the doors that might have held a mortal man were thrown open as if the very hinges had been torn apart by an invisible hand. The bars melted behind him as the flames even consumed the legs of his prison garb. A guard tried to block his path, raising a weapon, aiming it at his face. Dauphine laughed, raised a hand, and the gun crumpled, crushed by the force given him by the Dark One. The guard screamed, but it was too late. Dauphine stood at the entrance, a dark shadow wrapped in flames, yet unscorched. It crowned him in the power of the Dark Lord. His laugh, low and wicked, echoed on the wind.

"Freedom," he whispered, savoring the taste of it on his tongue, knowing that the world beyond would soon learn the true meaning of terror.

As the dark clouds gathered, the moon's light flickered in and out. But Papa Dauphine stepped out into the New Orleans night a free man—an agent of the Dark Lord Enlil, unstoppable. He was Prometheus, unbound.

IT WAS dark as Rowan walked the length of two tables, his hand on the pommel of his sword, his brow furrowed. He said nothing as he considered the task before him. Thirty-six jack-o'-lanterns had been entered into the contest. Five of them by his children. Those assembled in the cul-de-sac had voted, and the top six remained. It was Rowan's duty to make the final selection.

His eye lifted to his youngest, who sat feeding pumpkin seeds to the raven who'd followed her everywhere this evening. Her jack-o'-lantern had been eliminated by the popular vote, but his older daughter's remained. To maintain an unbiased position, he made sure he didn't know whose jack-o'-lantern was whose. He'd been absent during the carving, occupied by helping with the dunk tank. He asked the competitors to place their pumpkins on the table and return to their seats before he came around the Dumpster to make his decision.

It wasn't hard to pick out Kate's. He knew her style like he knew his own handwriting. She had skill with a paintbrush—maybe even colored pencils. Pumpkins were a different medium. Though he could recognize Shadow the Cat in the design, one of the teeth had broken off, and the mouth wasn't quite even.

"So hard t' choose," a voice said from behind him. He turned to stone recognizing the voice just in those four little words.

"Not here, Dauphine," Rowan said beneath his breath. "Not tonight."

"But dis be d'night when de veil is t'in." Rowan could hear the smile curling on the voodoo priest's cheek. "De Dark One says I ken take my vengeance. Dis seem like a good place as any."

Rowan turned, facing the voodoo priest who stood dressed like something out of a Disney movie. He had on a green striped vest, embroidered velvet and silk pants, and knee-high boots. His chest was bare but for the necklace of bones—presumably chicken bones—his dreads lifting in the breeze that made the candles in the jack-o'-lanterns flicker.

A din rose in the air, drawing Rowan's attention to the street where an army of the Walking Dead moved to block the road and seemed held back by an unseen force as if waiting to be summoned to take on the living.

"I brung a few of de dead ta' he'p me," he said, moving to block Rowan, who scanned the crowd for Lauren. He didn't want her to help him. He was more interested in getting her and the children inside, where they would be safe. How did this nutjob get out of prison? What was he doing here? "You picked de fight, Mistah Pierce." Vial breath blew into Rowan's face as he spoke the words. "Dis gon' be de last time you cross me," he said. "I made m' *offerndas* to de loa, and de Dark Lord, he find me worthy. Where dat women of yours?" He licked his lips, scanning the crowd. Rowan's eye found her in the crowd, but he couldn't let Dauphine see her. He let his eyes go toward the house.

Papa Dauphine took the bait. "Ah ha." He laughed wickedly. "Keepin' her fo' ya'self."

Dauphine started for the house. Rowan moved to block him, seeing the movement in the crowd he'd hoped to avoid. Lauren stood, gathering her skirts. He could read the expression on her face. It was the most emotion he'd seen in her since Enlil took half of her soul. That was the woman he knew and loved, but it was also the warrior he'd hoped to keep from the fray. Why couldn't she be a timid housewife, driving carpool and attending PTA meetings? Her biggest worry should be what to fix for dinner. This was not the life he'd wanted for her, but he knew her too well. This was the life she chose. She didn't want to fight any more than he did, but a call to action from a god could not be ignored, and she was halfway across the cul-de-sac before he could wave her off.

The front door of the house blew open before Dauphine ever got near it. Jean-René appeared in his peripheral vision. Rowan stopped and threw out a hand. "Get the kids out of here!" Rowan shouted. "Take Bahati and get away!"

The priest entered his home uninvited and unwelcome. Rowan was torn between protecting the children and defending his sanctuary. Lauren paused to gather the children and send them to the other side of the Dumpster. Sarah protested. Lauren must have said something to convince her. Diana gathered the children and started moving everyone away.

A shriek erupted in the crowd as the zombie horde moved in. *Screw Dauphine*, Rowan decided. He turned and drew his sword. The *ting* of metal exiting the scabbard melded with the shrieks of onlookers. The crowds scattered, and the screams rose to a piercing din when the undead army moved in. Rowan raced out and put himself between his friends and neighbors and the hellish horde.

They were slow creatures. It gave him a moment to steel himself and the crowds to back away. When the first hell-born thing reached him, he brought the blade down with all his might. The tang of metal cutting through rotted flesh and brittle bones sounded exactly like the sound effects on television. The heft of the two-handed sword was almost more than he could handle, and sparks erupted when it hit the concrete at the end of its arc. He struggled to lift it again and again, hacking down the army that seemed to keep coming. He realized he wasn't alone in the fight. Jean-René had the wooden walking stick, and Bahati was struggling with the katana.

He lost Lauren in the crowd. Rowan stood at the center of the chaos, dressed in the imposing armor of a Crusader, the heavy weight of it adding a surprising sense of strength as he hacked at the brittle beings. "Where's Lauren?" he shouted over the din.

"She was headed for the house," Jean-René called back.

No. Rowan sliced four of the demons in half and broke from the skirmish, leaving it in Jean-René and Bahati's capable hands.

Rowan burst into the house, which was eerily quiet. Their cozy home had always been welcoming—warm and safe, scented with whatever Diana happened to be baking. Now, it felt suffocatingly cold. The shadows seemed to stretch unnaturally, warping the wall as if space bent to the will of the dark forces gathering in the room.

His eye went immediately to Lauren, standing there looking like every teenage boy's dream, dressed as Deja Thoris. She held the smaller short sword she'd brought back from Slovenia in her hands. Rowan wanted to scream, to command her to run, but he knew better. There was no escape from Papa Dauphine now. Rowan knew in his gut that the voodoo priest had been drawn by the pull of the half-soul she still carried and would stop at nothing to claim it for the Dark Lord, Enlil.

"So, the Boss Man sent you to do his dirty work?" Rowan raised his sword and moved to stand by Lauren. Dauphine leaned casually on the hearth as if this was nothing for him.

"I do as he command." His thick *patois* made Rowan's lunch rise in his craw. The acid burned in the back of his nose, but he would not allow his foe to see him blanch. "But it bring me joy t' see dis day. De victories of de Dark Lord are victories for Dauphine, no?"

"No," Rowan stated flatly. "Not today."

"Ah, but ya' knew dis day was gonna come," Dauphine said, his voice as smooth as rancid butter. He turned to Lauren, addressing his next comments to her. "Ya fight hard, and ya bested me in court, didn' ya? But in de end, I gonna take what de Dark Lord commands. De last fragment of ya soul belongs to Enlil."

Rowan moved to block her as Dauphine seemed to draw up, his hands forming a circle. A miasma of green smoke built between his fingers, crackling with lightning. Rowan clenched his fists around his sword. He felt the weight of the magic in the air, thick and oppressive.

"You won't have it today." Rowan lifted the sword higher.

Dauphine chuckled softly, the sound like dry leaves scraping against stone. "Ah, such defiance. Is a pity, ya know. De Dark One could have given you more powah den you ever knowed. How does it feel, Rowan, ta has no magic? T' be de only one without a spark of de Devine?" His gaze moved to Lauren. "Y' know dat ya soul longs ta join wiff de piece de Dark One took. Y' hungah fo' it. Y' long for de pieces to be joined, for y' soul t' be joined."

Rowan noticed her sword lower, and her eyes glaze over. "Come on, girl. Give it t'me, and I'll be gone. Ya canna win. I am unassailable." His voice seemed to coax her forward, but she didn't take a step.

"Over my dead body." Rowan growled, no longer waiting for Dauphine to make the first move. He lifted the heavy sword and brought it down swiftly.

"Dat can be arranged." Dauphine dodged the blow. The ball of green power struck Rowan in the chest as his blade came down. It threw him back, and the sword flew from his hand. He was born aloft. The heavy armor was of no advantage as he was cast through the picture window of the dining room.

Crashing glass showered down around him, bouncing off the chainmail and armor but slicing the unprotected flesh around his face and eyes. Blood blurred his vision. He heard Lauren's breath catch as a scream was cut off. Gazing into the night sky, unable to move, certain his shoulder had been ripped from its socket by the heavy sword, he cried out to the universe for help. It seemed answered by a dark face that appeared above him. The raven hopped up onto his forehead and gazed down, cocking its head sideways, eyeing him curiously.

Rowan swatted the bird away with his uninjured hand and forced his body to obey as he rolled over onto the opposite side. He threw off the helm, getting to his hands and knees. "Get out of here, bird!" he roared, angry and frustrated.

"Jeeze, I thought maybe I could help." The bird morphed into a more familiar form. "Come on, Dad."

"Henry?" Rowan stood face-to-face with his oldest son, who was now equally tall as his father.

Cheers rose from behind the Dumpster where the children were shielded by their grandmother. "Best costume ever!"

LAUREN CLENCHED HER FISTS, her knuckles white, her breath coming in short gasps. His magic was strong, but hers could be, too. Her sword began to glow with her holy light; it pulsed and throbbed as she tried to build a force that could overtake him, but the crackle of it sparked in her hand and failed to grow. She felt like an engine that had flooded, unable to build the force needed. She had always known this day would come, and she refused to be a victim of this low-life.

"Come on, now," he said, waving her toward him with one hand, an orb of green energy building in the other. "Dis is not a fight y' can win."

"I've defeated Enlil before. That was like *Mission Impossible*. Defeating you will be difficult, but difficult is a walk in the park for me." In her current state, she knew she was vulnerable. Lauren stalled for time, quoting movie lines while trying to pull herself together. "'My name is Inigo Montoya. You killed my father. Prepare to die.'"

She made a quick lunge at him with the sword, but he backed away and spun, throwing the ball of power at her. She dodged, and it glanced off her arm, searing her flesh as it passed. She screamed and dropped her sword out of reflex. She got to her feet and snatched it up.

Dauphine cackled maniacally. "Dis is de way of tings," he purred. "Ya ain't strong 'nuff t' fight me. "An' once I take wha's left a y' soul, ya'll be not'ing more dan a shell. An empty vessel. *Une poupée*." He moved closer. "*Ma poupée*."

"I am no one's puppet, and I will die before I let you have anything of me," Lauren stated flatly.

"Die all you wan', *ma belle*." The light of her building energy flashed off his gold tooth. "I gonna take y' soul either way." Dauphine's eyes glimmered with dark delight. His hands, long and skeletal, rose slowly, dark energy swirling around his fingertips like an ancient storm. Shadows writhed, thickening. The room was closing in on her. She felt the pull of his magic on her soul, threatening to rip it from the seams of her life. "You ain't strong enough t' fight me. Dis how it ends."

Lauren's heart raced, but she held her ground. The last remaining fragment of her very essence was all she had left. She couldn't give it to him even if she wanted. A sacred oath secured it to her being. "Anu, give me strength." She reached deep within, allowing whatever rage and courage remained within her to rise to the surface. The energy built and rose to her arm, warming the muscles and burning in the bones as it intensified.

In an instant, the heavy air seemed to snap. A surge of putrid energy shot from his hands, aimed straight at her heart. She flung her arm out, instinctively using the power in her body to draw a shield, but the force of Dauphine's spell battered against it, pushing her back.

She resisted, using the entire force of her body and whatever magic she could conjure. But his power was strong, and her shield began to fracture. The dark magic oozed between the cracks, trying to get in. The demonic claws reached for her, swiping and scratching just inches from her face. She sensed her soul being pulled away. The magic gnawed at the edges of her soul, trying to break her apart from the inside.

Even as the pressure mounted, something inside her flared —a memory, a spark of defiance, a flicker of the woman she had become—perhaps had always been. She was not just a vessel of magic; she was its conductor. She had a promise from the Most High. She would never be alone.

Something soft brushed against her leg. She glanced down and found Shadow at her feet, her eyes glowing brightly as she provided energy of her own to Lauren's defense. The Siamese let out a caterwaul, as only a Siamese could, and Lauren knew it was time.

With a desperate cry, Lauren bundled up her strength and threw everything she had into a desperate salvo, striking Dauphine in the chest with the force of the heavens behind her. Pain shot through her arm, blinding her for a moment. The voodoo priest had not expected such strength from her and found himself cast out the same window Rowan had shattered.

Lauren rushed to the damaged portal and found Dauphine flat on his back, a furrow cut into the lawn nearly twelve feet long, tables overturned, and pumpkins shattered around him. She stifled a smile as she glanced over at her husband and son, who stood holding on to one another, clearly gobsmacked. She glanced back at Shadow. "Good kitty." The Siamese stretched and licked her shoulder like it was nothing.

Lauren went to the door. "Henry, you're here?" she asked.

"Looks like you don't need me," Henry said. "Seems like you've got this handled on your own."

"We could use a little help over here!" Jean-René's voice rose above the clash of the undead, which seemed to keep coming. The Toussaints fought back-to-back and were surrounded.

"I got this." Rowan picked up the sword, but a jolt of pain shot from his shoulder into his fingertips, twinging nerves that forced his hand to release.

"These are nothing more than chaos monsters," Henry said. "They're primordial creatures, here to distract us and overthrow the balance of power."

"Knock 'em on their booties, Henry!" Sarah called.

Henry moved closer to the fray—standing over Dauphine's prostrate form—drawing the attention of the undead soldiers, some of whom broke off. He had magic of his own, and it built between his hands in a blue glow that spread around him as he folded in on himself. The energy around him throbbed and darkened into a shadow that consumed the young man. When the hell-borne corpses were within reach of him, he stood abruptly, the magic radiating from him like a wave, knocking over the tangle of bones barely covered in flesh. They tumbled like shells cast into the sea by a tsunami, rolling over one another, until the entire horde was a single roiling ball of arms and legs, cloying hands, and flailing feet. They tumbled from the cul-de-sac, washed down the street and over the park into the pond where they sank like a singular stone.

Sarah ran out from behind the Dumpster and wrapped her arms around Henry's legs. "You did it, Henry! You slayed the zombies!"

Lauren rushed to Rowan, inspecting him for injuries. "Tell me you're not hurt."

"Not any more than I was before," he groaned. "I need out of this armor."

Diana and the rest of the children appeared timidly from behind the protection of the Dumpster. The family gathered in the yard, studying the aftermath of the battle. The neighbors had scattered.

"Where's Dauphine?" Lauren suddenly realized he wasn't there anymore.

"Does it matter now?" Diana came over and caught her arm. "You faced him, and you won."

The battle against Papa Dauphine felt like a hollow conflict. Nothing had been accomplished in defeating him. "Dauphine was no trouble. But there's something Enlil took from me. And I need it back. Keep the children safe."

She turned and walked into the middle of the now vacant cul-de-sac. Folding chairs had been toppled and crushed, tossed aside, leaving a void in the street. She turned, inspecting the battlefield. "Enlil!" Her voice rose high above the houses, but she hoped it reached the very depths of hell. "Stop sending your hired henchmen to do your job. This is between you and me!"

26

The ground trembled beneath her feet, threatening to topple her. The air crackled with unnatural energy, and the smell of ozone filled her nostrils. Lightning split the night sky and faded off in a rumble of thunder. The true power behind the dark forces had remained silent—until now. Enlil.

The ancient god of storms and chaos, the one who orchestrated the whole cursed sequence of events, was the last one Lauren had to defeat. Unlike Dauphine, who manipulated people for his own gain, Enlil's power was on a cosmic scale. He wasn't just another dark sorcerer. He was a god, and gods did not die easily.

Rowan, freed of the chainmail hauberk and breastplate, pulled the tabard back on. She knew he saw it as a sign of his promise to Prince Henry Sinclair. He picked up his sword and moved behind her, ready to defend her against whatever came at them. Rowan took the ring from his pocket and held it up, considering if now was the time to risk using the relic. Lauren furrowed her brow, puzzling over the new addition to his attire. "What's this?" she asked.

"What Benjamin Riggs died for," Rowan said, holding out his hand for her inspection. "Saladin's Ring."

"Wait. What?"

"There isn't time to explain," Rowan said. "But I promise I will when this is over."

She gave him a confident nod, then turned her face to the wind that began to blow with force. Her hair billowed around her as she held the sacred sword she'd earned in an ancient cathedral in middle Europe before Jamie was born. Thunder rumbled across the sky, and a crack of lightning hit an oak tree down the street, shattering it into a million sparking bits of jetsam. The ground shook again.

"Enlil!" Lauren's voice grew hoarse with the effort of her summons. "Are you afraid of me?"

The ground lurched again, and a monstrous roar of laughter filled the air. "Why so brazen, my half-souled child?" Enlil's deep voice reverberated through her core. "Are you so ready to die?"

The wind buffeted them, but the demon remained unseen. Clouds swirled above, and lightning danced around them. Lauren widened her stance, her sword raised, prepared for him to appear anywhere but in front of her. "Give me my soul back!"

A dark shadow rose from the earth to her left, then the demon's eyes opened, and their red glow was the one thing that assured her of his presence in the dark. As he materialized, a sphere pulsing with a red glow throbbed in an orb worn on a chain around his thick neck. "What, this?" His wicked paw reached up and cupped it. His claws wrapped around it as if to keep it protected from her.

"If you think you can take it, you're welcome to try. But you'll have to defeat me, and I cannot be destroyed." His voice was deep, full of contempt. It echoed through the battlefield. "You think you can stop the storm of ages? I am the storm. I am *The Darkness* and the Wind. I will tear you apart and rip the last fragment of your soul from your very core!"

The air cooled. Enlil's storm raged around them, the wind picking up debris, the earth beneath them cracking. Lightning danced from his hands, striking the ground with sufficient force to take her feet out from under her. She landed hard but rolled to the side and scrambled to her feet, escaping the growing void created by the splitting earth.

"It's time," Rowan said, slipping the ring to the first digit on his war-mangled finger. It was the only way that it seemed to fit. "How do you turn this thing on?" He fumbled with it.

The stones in the signet ring began to glow. Rowan could feel the heat building in the gold band, warming his skin. The heat moved into the back of his hand and burned like unholy fire. Smoke rose from the sigil as it burned into his flesh and marred his skin, just as it had Benjamin Riggs'. The pain dissipated quickly. Rowan shook his hand, holding it out, inspecting the wound. It seemed to fade into a scar within seconds.

Ghostly armies of the Great Sultan rose like ghosts from the depths of time. Each one was the embodiment of an ancient war and a time gone by. They were cloaked in magic and their hollow eye sockets burned with the fire of battle. They were bound to the will of the ring, and their loyalty would be tested against Enlil's storm.

But Enlil just smirked. "I come at you with demons, and you bring shadows? Do you think the ghosts of your fallen enemies can defeat me? Do you think they will protect you? They are nothing against me." Enlil's form, now fully made flesh, towered above them. His great horned head, too heavy for his neck, lashed side to side. With a wave of his hand, the winds howled louder and the storm intensified.

"*Labbayak Ya Allah!*" Rowan shouted. Lauren knew these words. *Here I am, O God! I am at your service.* He struggled to raise his hand enough for the ghostly forces to see the ring, and then he lifted his sword. *"Allahu Akbar!"* he cried, giving the signal to attack. *God is the greatest.*

Lauren didn't know how Rowan knew these words, but she knew both phrases were deeply connected to the Islamic faith and would have carried tremendous weight in the context of Saladin's leadership. If Saladin's ring had summoned the forces that charged past her, Lauren knew this rallying cry would send them into battle with a fervor.

She raised her sword and let out a battle cry of her own. *"Tsu sqv ani sdi gi ga ge sdi!"* *Stand strong and fight!* *"Tsu sqv ani sdi giga ges sdi tsu ni yi ga!"* *Stand strong, fight, and we will prevail!* Her voice broke as she led the charge.

As he had in Slovenia, Enlil summoned the darkest of his evil hosts. He summoned incubi, succubae, djinn, and hellhounds. Chimera and rakshasas came at the armies of Saladin but were driven back. A volley of arrows arced over the conflagration of unholy foot soldiers from the archers that formed lines at the back of the cul-de-sac. They stuck in Enlil's scaly flesh, looking like porcupine quills. The demon roared, ripping them out and tossing them back at his attackers. He summoned more creatures from the void. Dark, lurking shadows hovered above, joined by storm titans, wraiths, and harpies. *The Darkness* was unleashed after waiting and watching. Now it moved in to attack, commanding the aerial forces that struck from above.

"We need more forces!" Lauren shouted over the din. The armies of Saladin fell back against the new onslaught, regrouping and charging back into the fury. The archers, unaccustomed to flying opponents, adapted easily and began working to take down the wraiths and harpies. That wasn't much defense from the wraiths, but they could at least torment them.

Lauren looked over and saw Henry move in, changing form into the raven, taking wing. He hovered above, and his caws echoed, piercing the sky. The wraiths focused in on him and converged around him. They never saw the reinforcements he'd called. A large unkindness of ravens joined in the battle, tormenting the hell-bound aerial armies. Their voices joined to create a conflicting cacophony that confused the demons and emboldened the armies under Rowan's command.

Lauren fought her way through the melee, hacking and slashing through the crowd. Two of Saladin's guards flanked and protected her while two more did the same for Rowan. The echo of blade against blade—or in some cases, blade against claw—was deafening. The *thwack* of bowstrings behind the charge punctuated the soundtrack of the rising battle. *Where were the children? Anu, protect the children!* Her muscles burned as she cut a path through the battle, edging her way closer to Enlil. She had to get to Enlil. She had to take back her soul.

As the battle raged below, the fury intensified above. Swarms of flies, the spawn of Beelzebub, moved in on Henry and his feathered friends, tormenting them as they tormented the minions of Enlil. They burrowed into his feathers and weighed him down, sending him into a spiral toward the ground.

Just feet from the ground, he morphed into the form of a wolf, landing hard and rolling. The flies that hadn't been crushed dispersed around him. He ran over to where his brothers and sisters watched, along with their grandmother, and took his human form. "Henry, where are Mom and Dad?" John Carter asked.

"They're with Saladin's army," Henry said.

"We have to help them!" Sarah cried. "Enlil will crush Mommy's soul if she tries to take it."

"You stay here with Nanhi," Henry said. "Where's Uncle

Jean-René and Aunt Bahati?" He turned and scanned the battleground, finding them emerging from the chaos. Bahati had a cut on her forehead, and Jean-René limped, leaning on his wife. Blood streamed down the leg of his costume. This time it was real blood, and Henry knew it.

"We're here. We could handle a few zombies, but there are so many of those things!" Bahati panted.

"I'll go get the first aid kit," Diana said.

"You know how to do stitches?" Jean-René called after her.

She paused at the door. "I've sewn up more than a few torn britches."

"John Carter, if you were ever going to find your power, now would sure be a good time for it," Henry said to his younger brother, who was almost as tall as he was.

"God, I wish I knew," John Carter said. "I want to help. I do."

"You want me to tell you?" Henry asked. "I'm not supposed to, but I've seen your potential."

"How?"

"In the future," Henry said. "I've known you there, er, *then*. Just as I know you here—*now*."

Diana returned with the first aid kit as well as blankets, towels, and her sewing kit. "We'll set up triage over here behind the dumpster, safe from the fighting."

Henry and John Carter conferred while the others helped their grandmother and friends. Henry stood watching Enlil, who stood with his arms folded, overseeing the battle, tossing out lightning bolts once in a while. The demon had a wicked smirk on his grotesque face. He seemed to be watching their mother as she was pushed back and knocked to the ground.

"So, here's what you do." Henry put an arm around his brother's shoulders. "Remember what Grandpa John told you, back when we were in the cave in Oklahoma?"

"He said I was the Jeddak of Jeddaks," John Carter said.

"He said I was the son of a mighty wizard, and the Earth couldn't hold me when it was time for me to go. He said I'd travel far in my life, which would be long."

"You do remember," Henry said.

"So, how do I make my powers work?" John Carter's dark brows knitted beneath the flop of hair that blew across his face.

Henry shrugged as he started to walk away, turning back to his brother, still moving. "You just do." Henry's clothing billowed around him, morphing into dark wings as he took to the sky.

"Okay, Superman," John Carter muttered under his breath. "Let's do this." He closed his eyes and tried to force the spirit to move him. He thought about what he wanted to happen and tried to manifest it. *Trust.* Henry said he needed to trust his powers. He trusted his brother. But the conflict surging around him made him anxious. He wasn't a great and powerful wizard like his mother, his grandfather, or even his brother. He was just a teenage kid with zits and a cool guitar. He didn't even have a car yet.

"Calm your heart," Henry's voice came to him. "Take a deep breath and 'use the Force.'"

"Nerd," John Carter scoffed, but he tried to do as his brother instructed. He took a deep breath and centered himself as he'd done in the karate lessons he'd taken at Boy Scout camp. He wished his brother had given him this information before. It would have been helpful to practice before his mother's soul was on the line.

"Focus!" John Carter ordered himself. He gathered his strength and leaped from the ground, landing on his feet. *Sheesh. Try again. Center yourself. Calm thoughts. Be still.*

Something happened at that moment. He felt a moment of weightlessness, and when he opened his eyes, he was six feet off the ground, a fiery red glow beneath his feet.

"That's it!" Henry cawed. "Now get in here and help me!"

Henry had been right. He didn't need to know how it worked, he just needed to let it happen. He had to trust the magic to work. The sense of flying and floating was both exhilarating and terrifying, knowing he could fall at any minute. Wraiths attacked the soldiers on the ground while the other demons of the sky went after the archers in the yards, circling the round pavement. For a second the ground came rushing toward him, but he reconnected to his focus and lifted before he hit the ground.

"Fear will take you down faster than anything." Henry met up with him in the air. "We need to get behind Enlil. Catch him off guard. It'll have to be a *Kamikaze*-style attack."

"Uh, are you sure about that?" John Carter gulped, his hair swirling above his head in spinning locks. "*Kamikazes* had a death wish."

"Maybe that's the wrong term," Henry acquiesced. "The point is, we need to get behind him and attack quickly, get the orb with Mom's soul in it, and get out. I'll go right. You go left. I'll draw his attention. You get the orb and then get out of there."

"Where do I go?"

"Go back to Nanhi," he said. "I'll try to circle back around and meet you there. Then I'll get the orb to Mom."

John Carter nodded and moved higher, amazed at the beauty of his neighborhood in the fall, even with the wind raking through the trees, ripping the golden aspen and flame-red maple leaves from their branches. He took a wide arc, making sure the Dark One didn't notice him. He tried to imagine himself a bat or a bird, something the Dark Lord wouldn't recognize as an enemy. Henry at least had that advantage.

From high above, he could see the full conflict laid bare before him. Enlil's army of demons was driven back by Saladin's soldiers, who followed his father's command. The battle seemed to rage first one way, then the other, each side cycling through attack and retreat. The undead couldn't die, and while many soldiers fell, they eventually arose again. It reminded him of Sam's soccer games. No one ever seemed to score. Players just chased the ball back and forth down the field. Then it occurred to him that his mother *was* the ball.

"Now!" Henry's voice found him on the wind.

John Carter allowed himself to fall. The laws of physics no longer seemed to apply but down was easier than up. He slowed as he neared the demon, waiting for Henry to swoop in front of him. He did, and the raven form drew his attention for the slightest fraction of a second that John Carter needed.

He swooped down from behind, dodging the horns that rose from the demon's head like a wicked crown. The monster's black wings hovered partially closed, and it hadn't occurred until that moment that the demon might come after him. The stench of demonic flesh wafted up, striking him in the face, as the Dark One's tail whipped up and struck him just as he reached for the cord holding the orb.

He was tossed like a sack of grain to the ground, landing hard, striking his head with such force that it sounded like a pumpkin hitting the pavement. Lightning flashed behind his eyes. "John Carter!" He heard his mother's voice call out to him as the world flickered and flashed, fading into nothing, then rushing up towards him. One minute he was down, the next he was on his feet. A second later, he was back up in the sky. He'd lost the element of surprise, but gained a ball of anger that built in his core and burst from his hands. The demon stumbled and fell back, roiling and struggling for his feet. John Carter looked for an opening but froze when the demon froze. A small child stood in front of him. John Carter recognized his sister immediately. She was his own mirror image in female form. A copy of her mother. "Sarah! Get out of there!"

"You are a bad, bad monster!" She shook her finger at Enlil, who scooted back into a sitting posture.

"And you have the Curse of Cassandra," The demon laughed. "That was my gift to you at the hour of your birth."

"I knew it was you!" Sarah spat the words. "I don't like you! You're ugly!"

The demon laughed and shrugged as if he cared little for what the child thought of him.

"Get her out of there!" Henry crowed.

John Carter snapped out of his stupor and made a beeline for his sister. He didn't slow down as he approached the ground and grabbed her into his arms. He watched as she reached out and grabbed the glowing orb from Enlil's neck as he swept her up.

The cord snapped and the orb shattered in her small hands. She screamed. "Mommy!"

John Carter had planned to take her to Nanhi but realized the fragments of the orb were smoking and swirling between her bleeding fingers. "Take me to my Mommy!" she cried, holding onto her brother's shirt for dear life with the other hand.

John Carter moved in. Henry dropped down at the same time, sending a wave of energy into a circle around their mother, forcing back the demons who clawed to get to her. Lauren paused the fight, her sword falling to the ground as her muscles protested, and she dropped to her knees. Sweat coated her face, and she sucked in gasps of air as Sarah fell toward her and wrapped her arms around her mother. "Mommy, your ball broke."

Lauren let go of her to see what she was talking about. A burst of light broke from between Sarah's fingers as her hand opened. The fragments of her broken soul glistened in the moonlight, throbbing at a tempo that matched Lauren's racing heart.

The Dark One howled in fury as he realized he'd lost the battle. Her soul, set free, returned to her, the burning embers of it circling her like glitter on a windy day. The tone of the battle around her changed. One by one, the demons disappeared in clouds of thick black smoke, leaving behind piles of ash where they once stood. Saladin's army seemed stunned by this sudden change. They chased after the dissipating horde, most of which immolated or imploded before the soldiers reached them.

Rowan raced over to Lauren, catching her as she fell back, convulsing as the fragments of her soul found their way into her. Diana rushed to her side and caught her hand. "Lauren," she gasped. If she'd had time to prepare, she might have had a ceremony to aid the rejoining of her daughter's soul, but there wasn't time. Instead, she intoned a song in her native language encouraging the spirit to reunite with the flesh. It wasn't a spell or a healing ritual so much as it was simply a song of encouragement. Her soul and body would do what needed to be done, but knowing her daughter, she knew it would not be easy for the pieces to come back together, no matter how much the two needed to become joined.

Lauren coughed, and her eyelids fluttered. Her body went limp as she came to. "Sarah," she gasped, weakly reaching for her baby. The little girl came over and curled up beside her, pulling her mother's arm around her, resting her chin on her shoulder.

"Mommy," she said, "Enlil is gone."

"What were you thinking?" Lauren's words came out in a mix of frustration and weak laughter. "You could have been killed."

"No," Sarah sat up. "John Carter saved me. If he hadn't, Henry would have. You're not the only one who gets a protector."

The children all gathered around her now, but her eye found John Carter. "You found your magic." The glint of a proud mother shone in her eyes. "What took you so long?"

"I just had to wait for Henry to tell me his secret."

"And what's that?"

"Use the force," John Carter said, grinning.

"I knew we should have named you Luke." Lauren smirked, reaching for a hand. "Help me up."

IN THE DISTANCE, sirens began to blare, growing closer. Neighbors began to filter from the houses and bushes, stunned at the devastation. Even people who didn't live in the cul-de-sac had taken refuge with their neighbors here, and the crowd swelled as the family gathered in a group hug.

It was finished. The battle had been won. Enlil had lost. The demon had escaped with his henchman.

Rowan took the ring from his finger, dismissing Saladin's Army with a bow. He tucked it back into his pocket. It would have been a different outcome without it. He was grateful for the aid, but he suspected none of this would have happened had it not been for his actions. He'd gone behind Lauren's back, violated her trust, and put her life—and the life of his family—at risk. Enlil was out there waiting, but Rowan had allowed him to attack. He'd left them vulnerable. He blamed himself, even as he limped to the yard and found one of the lawn chairs that had been tossed aside in the conflict. He collapsed into it, too exhausted to go any further.

The neighbors gathered. He recognized the stunned expressions on their faces. He'd seen innocent bystanders come out to inspect the damage after a battle when he was in Afghanistan and Iraq. They wore the mask of shock and fear that would not be easily washed away.

He noticed Lauren move to meet the neighbors. She seemed to be trying to formulate an explanation for what just happened. Then, someone began to applaud. The single pair of hands clapped four times before Dr. MacIntosh added, "Good show!"

"Leave it to the Pierce Family and their Hollywood

magic," his wife tossed out, joining her husband in the applause. "Best Halloween Party finale ever!"

The rest of the crowd joined in, even as fire trucks and police cars pulled into the neighborhood and entered the cul-de-sac. The applause exceeded the sounds of sirens. Rowan met her eye as she turned. The glare she gave him made his heart hurt. She was angry, and she had every right to be.

"Show's over, folks! Let's get this mess cleaned up and get our kids to bed. It's been an exciting evening for everyone."

It took a while longer for Rowan to try and explain it to the police and fire department. One of the medics looked him over, examining his shoulder while he talked down the cops who were ready to bust somebody for something—anything.

"What happened?"

"I tripped over my tabard," Rowan lied as the examination commenced. "Landed hard and wrenched my—" He sucked in air between his teeth as the medic moved his arm and his shoulder twinged.

"Yeah, you need to see an orthopedist," the medic said. "I'll bet money that the rotator cuff is shredded. It could be bursitis, but it's hard to know without an MRI."

"I'll call Monday morning and make an appointment," Rowan said.

"You know a guy? I can recommend a good ortho if you need one," the medic offered.

Rowan forced a smile, shaking his head. "No," he laughed. "I got a guy. I knew this was coming."

"Well, get some ice on that, take some anti-inflammatories."

"I will," Rowan said.

"And, dude,"—the medic's jovial demeanor caught him off guard—"your wife is hot. If you don't mind me saying."

Rowan glared at him for a moment. "I do mind your saying," he said. "But I'll be damned if I can get out of this chair to come over there and do something about it."

Jean-René came over to check on him. "You okay?"

"Yeah." Rowan groaned, trying to get up from the low chair, not having much luck. "You?"

"Your mother-in-law stitched me up," he said. "I'll be fine. Bahati's okay too." He offered Rowan a hand, waving Dr. McIntosh to come over and help him. Rowan bit down hard, biting back a cry as they lifted him to his feet.

"Can't wait to see what you come up with next year, Rowan," Dr. McIntosh said.

"We're going to Mexico next year," Rowan said. "This is going to end up being an expensive show."

"I've got some plywood in my garage. We can board up your window. I'll call my brother, Gary. He does windows. He can fix you up in no time."

"Thanks," Rowan said, scanning for Lauren, who was busy picking up busted pieces of pumpkins and paper table coverings. "Can he get me out of trouble with the Missus?"

Dr. MacIntosh paused, watching Lauren give directions to the children. "That's all you, buddy."

"Great."

WELL AFTER MIDNIGHT, they had the cul-de-sac put back into order, and the rest of the neighborhood had gone to bed. Rowan sat on the front porch with a cup of coffee Diana had brought him. He was still processing the night's events, trying to make sense of everything that'd happened in the past few weeks.

"And here's an ice pack," she said, handing him the cool gel pack. She used an ace bandage to wrap the ice pack to his shoulder, so he didn't have to worry about holding it in place. He sipped the coffee and let out a shaky sigh as Diana sat beside him.

"Everyone in bed?" he asked, sipping again.

"They're in bed, but it'll probably take a while for everyone to sleep," she said, drinking from her own cup. "When Lauren told me about fighting Enlil before, I thought it was some kind of metaphor or something."

"An allegory maybe." Rowan hung his head. "But if that battle in Slovenia was as bad as tonight, it's a miracle she lived to fight another day."

"She's lucky you were here," Diana said. "One of these days, you will have to tell me more about that ring and how you came to command Saladin's legions."

"What's to tell?" He shrugged, regretting it immediately. "Just a magic ring from a Cracker Jack box."

"Uh-huh," Diana huffed over her coffee. "And my daughter is just a woman."

"I've said it before, Mom. She's a beautiful mystery wrapped in an enigma. At her very core, she is a woman of unrelenting passion for the truth. And I'm just a man . . . with a woman I can't handle."

"At least you know your place." She patted him gingerly. "Go to bed. You need to rest, too."

"I call dibs on the recliner."

Diana nodded, wrapping her hands around her cup and gazing up at the sky. "John Carter ate five grilled cheese sandwiches and half a bag of Fritos. He'll probably sleep all day tomorrow. That's what John was like when he had to work his magic when we were young."

"That's something I don't understand," Rowan said before he thought if he should have said anything at all. "Where were Lauren's allies when she needed them? Where was John? Where was Michael?"

Diana drew in a deep breath and let it out slowly before answering. "I don't have all the answers, son. I wish I did. But I can tell you this. In my experience, the gods don't always give us everything we want. They give us what they need, when we need it. Lauren had everything she needed tonight.

She had the kids and your friends. She had her sword. She had you and that magic ring. She didn't need Michael or her father. If she had, they would have been here."

Rowan shook his head, gazing down the street. Processing. "Seems like we could have won it faster."

"The point is, we won it."

"Yeah, this time," Rowan said. "What happens when Enlil comes back? What happens when her soul isn't enough for him? What then?"

"Well," Diana said. "That's a question we'll have to ask another time. Come inside. Get some sleep."

Rowan handed her back the coffee cup, which he'd managed to drain without realizing it. With some effort, he got to his feet, groaning. "I should have asked for some of your magic tea."

"It's not too late for that," she said. "But you might do better with a muscle relaxer and a pain pill."

"That does sound better." He groaned. "I'm getting too old for this."

EPILOGUE

Lauren sat back, carefully considering the offer on the table in front of them. Rowan, his arm in a sling, took his reading glasses from his shirt pocket. He put them on before picking up the copy in front of him. Lauren watched the woman across the table from her, still trying to evaluate her. Vega Sanchez smiled convivially.

"We still have a family to consider," Lauren said.

"The network understands that," Vega said. "*I* understand that. We're more than willing to make any accommodations you deem necessary."

Rowan glanced up from the contract. "This won't work."

Vega's brow lifted. "Oh? Is something wrong?"

"The Toussaints have been with us since the beginning," Rowan began.

"Even before Rowan joined the show," Lauren corrected.

"Yes, and I think at this point, they've earned more than just the titles Director of Photography and Lead Field Researcher."

"What did you have in mind?" Vega leaned in.

"Executive Producers," Lauren said. "The four of us are a team. We should all have equal pay and equal titles."

Vega didn't flinch. "Okay."

"Okay?" This time it was Lauren's brow that lifted.

"The Exploration Channel is under new management, Dr. Pierce. The days of the old boys club is over. I take care of those who take care of our audience."

Lauren picked up her copy of the contract and reached in her purse for a pen. She went to work editing the contract to add the changes she wanted. Over the next hour, the negotiations continued, and the Pierces got everything they asked for. Most importantly, they didn't have to move back to California.

"And you want us to find the stolen artifacts from the museum in Khartoum?" Lauren looked up from her work.

"It seemed important to Rowan," Vega said. "If there's anything specific you want to investigate, the Network will certainly follow your lead."

"The wolf population in Yellowstone is in jeopardy—again," Lauren said. "But there's nothing paranormal about that."

"I'm not opposed to crossover shows with the Wilderness Channel, or any other channels in our network."

Lauren nodded and continued to read. She finally pushed the contract across the table to the executive. "With these changes, I think we can make it work."

Vega stuck out her hand to Lauren. "I look forward to working with you."

———

AFTER THE DINNER dishes were cleared from the table, the family settled back at the table for a team meeting. Diana served apple cobbler and ice cream for dessert and refilled everyone's coffee cup before she sat down. She'd waited all day to hear the results of Lauren and Rowan's meeting with the network.

"So, it looks like we're going back to work this spring,"

Rowan said. "The Veritas Codex is going to be the anchor program for Wednesday night television on The Exploration Channel."

Cheers rose around the table from everyone except Sarah. "Does that mean you're both going to be leaving us?" the littlest Pierce asked.

"No," Lauren said. "We will be making arrangements to limit our travel so that we aren't both gone during the school year. In the summers, we can take you with us to most of the places we're going."

"In that case, I'm staying," Diana announced. She'd already decided on her plans weeks ago, though she hadn't discussed it with Lauren and Rowan yet. "If you'll have me, of course."

"We were counting on that," Rowan beamed. "We're going to need you."

"Does Sarah even have a passport?" Jamie asked.

"Yes," Lauren said. "A few of us will need to renew our travel papers, so we'll all have passports."

"Do we get to go with you to Cozumel?" Sarah asked.

Rowan met Lauren's gaze.

"I didn't tell her," Lauren said.

"How did you know Mom and I are going to Cozumel?"

Sarah's face flamed red, and she shrugged.

"Have you been eavesdropping again?" Rowan asked.

"Not on purpose," she insisted. "But we're not going. Are we?"

"No," Rowan said. "I promised your mother I'd take her to Mexico for our anniversary, and I always keep my promises."

"You promise I can go to Mexico some day?" Sarah asked. "I want to see the Temple of the Rain God and swim in a cenote."

"If everyone wants to make a wish list of the places they

want to go, we'll see if we can make it happen," Lauren suggested. "I still have a few places I haven't gotten to go."

"Like where?"

"I haven't seen the Amazon river," Lauren said. "Or the Australian outback."

"I wanna go to Scotland and find the Loch Ness Monster," Jamie said.

"That's a good one," Rowan said.

"I want to go to Romania and look for strigoi." Kate smirked.

"Of course you do."

"But you promise I can go to Mexico and see the temples and swim in a cenote?" Sarah insisted, climbing up on her knees in her chair, taking her father's face between her small hands. "Promise?"

"I promise. I told the neighbors we'd be in Mexico next Halloween. We'll see if that actually happens."

"You always keep your promises." Sarah kissed him, then sat back down in her chair. "What about Nanhi? Where do you want to go?"

"I don't need to go anywhere," she said. "I'm just happy being here with you."

PREIVEW OF THE EMPTY GRAVE

Mia Flückiger stopped in the middle of Chicago's O'Hare airport terminal—gobsmacked. Right there on the CNN Newsstand was the face of that so-called *scientist* on the cover of almost every magazine. It made her sick. That woman received awards and accolades from the US Government for her latest so-called *amazing discovery*. She may have found the lost Mayan calendar and a lost library in Libya, but she was still a false prophet. Bigfoot, ghosts, and aliens weren't real. Everyone knew it—at least everyone in the real world. "How dare she call herself a scientist?" Mia muttered as the crowds had to work their way around her since she blocked the narrow aisle in front of the newsstand.

That woman somehow single-handedly found a missing pirate ghost ship in the so-called Bermuda Triangle and then sailed it right into the harbor in St. George. The video someone had taken from land had shown her waving like a beauty queen in the Rose Bowl Parade, as if she were riding a float for the enjoyment of the audience. That same video had gone viral on every social media platform, including TikTok.

How long had she hidden in the shadows? Four or five years? And suddenly she was back with a new television show.

And just to gild the lily, she'd found a sunken Mayan Temple in the Gulf of Mexico not far from New Orleans. Why did it have to be *her*? Of all the people in the world, why did it have to be that horrible woman? Dr. Lauren Grayson was a no-good attention-monger who'd gotten incredibly lucky. But everyone was going crazy about a year-old discovery of a crumbling ruin at the bottom of the Gulf.

The world was going to hell in the proverbial handbasket, and this was the drivel that made the cover of *Time Magazine*? Mia's studies—*real* scientific studies—showed that since the year 1880, the average temperature of the Earth has risen by over 0.98° Celsius. What troubled her most was that the previous December was the fifth month in history to ever reach 3° Fahrenheit above normal average for the planet. Climate change was primarily the result of too much carbon dioxide (CO_2) being generated and trapped in the atmosphere. CO_2 acted as a blanket, trapping heat and warming the planet. As the industry burned fossil fuels like coal, oil, and natural gas for energy or cut down and burned forests to create pastures and plantations, carbon accumulation was quickly overloading the atmosphere. *That woman only found the sunken pyramid because of global warming.*

Of course, there were ways to slow it—climate change—if not stop it altogether. For the past twenty years, Mia had become a champion of certain waste management and agricultural practices that had the potential to minimize the problem by preventing other potent global warming gases, such as methane and nitrous oxide from accumulating. Unfortunately, world governments hadn't done much to require or enforce such practices. Her efforts were proving futile. People needed to be listening to her not that stupid Bigfoot woman!

Mia had served as the head of the private sector committee working with regulators to implement such regulations. But after the collapse of The Great Accord, the war in Sudan, and the United States' withdrawal from the Paris

Agreement, her efforts seemed futile. The United States alone was accountable for over 13.9% of the world's greenhouse gas emissions—the second-largest emitter globally after China. China's output of greenhouse gasses was almost twice that of the United States. But the United States was accountable for most of the world's CO_2 emissions. But these stupid Americans would rather praise a sham television *scientist* than ensure their government provided funds for real scientific research like her own.

She tossed the magazine back onto the rack and cursed Lauren Grayson under her breath as she hurried to catch her flight to Los Angeles. At least she'd found someone to pay for her research—a private company interested in developing and promoting *alternative* methods of reducing and preventing climate change.

As the flight attendant brought her a glass of chardonnay, she sat thinking about the first time she'd met the Bigfoot woman. That insufferable woman beat her out of an honor that should have been hers. Mia should have been named *Society of Modern Science's Scientist of the Year.* She—a mere child —had made more contributions to science than either that woman or her husband. Mia's contributions were more than worthy of such an award. That honor was stolen from her. *Yes, stolen.* She'd become the laughingstock of the scientific community. She lost a prestigious accolade to a woman who dedicated her life to pseudoscience and sold her soul to the Exploration Channel rather than go out and find research grants like a legitimate scientist. It made Mia angry to her core. *Damn her eyes! Damn you, Lauren Grayson!*

"Welcome to Geste Laboratories, Dr. Flückiger." A man in a black suit met her in the lobby. "I'm Dr. Revon, but call me Damien. How was your flight?"

"Miserable. I hope this isn't a waste of my time," she snapped. Weather had diverted her flight from LAX to Seattle, where she'd waited two hours for repairs, then spent another hour and a half waiting for a new plane and crew. After hours in customs, she was now late for the meeting that had brought her to the US in the first place.

"We have no intentions of wasting your time, Dr. Flückiger." He smiled. "Come, let me show you the facility and tell you about our work. Then we can sit down and talk about the kinds of research you can expect to do here at Geste Laboratories."

"I read your mission statement on your website," Mia said, tucking her iPad under her arm, and falling in behind him. "*To inspire and support world-class research, commercialization, and economic growth that will change the world; past, present, and future.* Sounds pretty generic."

"We consider it quite specific," Damien said, smiling over his shoulder as he stopped to swipe his security card at the first door. "We want the research being done here to be revolutionary. Our Board of Directors is concerned with the direction our world governments have taken. We don't just *feel* like the climate change we're experiencing might lead to our inevitable doom. We are *certain* of it. We are committed to doing whatever we can to change the course of climate change. *Whatever.*"

"Whatever?" Mia sniffed. "Like there's anything we can do."

"You'd be surprised." He smiled, opening the door. "Come, let me show you the control room for the new superconducting mega collider."

Mia froze, her eyes locking on his. "Superconducting mega collider? Like the supercollider at CERN?"

"If you thought the supercollider at CERN was big, wait till you see SMAC." He seemed exceptionally proud of the double entendre in the acronym. "You'll want to meet Dr. Khasan, too."

"Dr. Ahmed Khasan?" She all but stuttered the name. "Nobel Prize-winning physicist Ahmed Khasan?"

"He's just been nominated again for his previous project," Damien said with a charming smile. "This whole team could win a Nobel Prize if this research bears fruit. You can be a part of that team."

"A Nobel?" Mia thought for a moment. The idea was provocative. If she played her hand right, she could beat out that awful woman for a more prestigious award. A Nobel Prize. "What kind of research is he working on?"

"Time travel."

ABOUT THE AUTHOR

Betsey Kulakowski is the award-winning, bestselling author of The Veritas Codex paranormal thriller series. As a retired safety professional with a degree in emergency management, she is a federally trained investigator and served on disaster response teams at the Alfred P. Murrah Building Bombing, the World Trade Center, and Hurricane Katrina, among others.

She's won numerous awards for her books, including multiple first-place awards from The Bookfest Awards. *The King's Ransom* (Book 7 of the Veritas Codex Series) won first place for Best Published Fiction at WriterCon in 2024.

When she's not writing, she can be found wandering the woods of Central Arkansas looking for Bigfoot or kayaking on the many lakes and rivers. Betsey is also the co-host of The Unfreakingbelievable Podcast, available on most podcasting platforms.

You can follow Betsey on Instagram, X and TikTok @authorbetseyk and sign up for her newsletter on her website at www.authorbetseykulakowski.com.

ALSO BY BETSEY KULAKOWSKI

The Veritas Codex series:

The Veritas Codex (Book 1 of The Veritas Codex Series)

The Jaguar Queen (Book 2 of The Veritas Codex Series)

The Alien Accord (Book 3 of The Veritas Codex Series)

The Monk's Grimoire (Book 4 of The Veritas Codex Series)

The Lost Templar (Book 5 of The Veritas Codex Series)

The Pirate's Curse (Book 6 of The Veritas Codex Series)

The King's Ransom (Book 7 of The Veritas Codex Series)

The Manifest Destiny Series:

The Veil of Secrets

The Night Doctor's Blade

Novellas from Autumn Tales:

No Boys Allowed

City of the Dead

Karen's in the Woods